Goatsucker Harvest

JOYCE BARRASS

ISBN-10: 1507645929
ISBN-13: 978-1507645925

DEDICATION

For my mum, Margaret,
another widdershins weaver of rainbows,
who inspires me with her love, faith and
thankfulness to rejoice in the breathtaking
beauty of creation;
and for Charlotte, Hannah and Nancy, my
precious Yorkshire fore-mothers,
may the many moons between us
shine over your sails forever.

Contents

1 'THISTLE'..1
2. WINDMILL BY THE WATER..........................11
3. LANDLOCKED......................................21
4. OFFERS AND OPPORTUNITIES....................30
5. CARRDYKE..41
6. SHADOW ON THE FEN.............................51
7. WIDDERSHINS.....................................63
8. IN THE DARK......................................71
9. HOMECOMING......................................80
10. FRESH HORIZONS................................89
11. MENDINGS AND MARRINGS.......................100
12. THIS SUFFOCATING PEPPER-POT................111
13. DANGEROUS GAMES..............................120
14. TILL MAY BE OUT...............................130
15. ECHOES FROM THE EDGE.........................143
16. MISSING FRAGMENTS............................155
17. UNDER THE MILK MOON..........................163
18. COASTAL CAPERS...............................172
19. HULL, HELL AND BACK AGAIN...................183
20. DEADLY DELIVERIES............................193
21. WHEN ONE DOOR CLOSES.........................202
22. RAVAGE AND RUIN..............................213
23. MOB RULE ON THE MARSH.......................224
24. FEN-LIGHTS AND RAINBOWS.....................233
25. GRINDSTONES AND GOATSUCKERS.................246
26. I AM THE GOATSUCKER..........................259
27. LOCKED ON TARGET.............................268
28. FAIR WARNING.................................277
29. BEWARE THE GOATSUCKER HARVEST...............286
30. SAILING HOME.................................301
About the author................................309

1 'THISTLE'

"Rise your tack!"

Thirza clung onto the tiller kicking against her, the neck of a huge oaken sea-monster butting her in the ribs. The calls of keelmen and women, wharfingers, the cough of wind in sailcloth, had been her lullaby since before she was born. Voices of salt and shimmering rainbows of sound whispered all around her. She'd heard it all from the snug shelter of her mother Dinah's womb. Back then she couldn't tell the womb's throbbing walls from the sea swell beyond. But she knew they were both her home.

Her brothers played, yelling past her, haring towards the bow of the rocking keel, under the sail without stopping to duck. Thirza joined in whenever they brushed past her skirts in the stern.

"Hand me that stower! The long pole thing, silly, and stand back!"

"Shhh, Thirzie! We're being the Charge of the noble Light Brigade!" shouted Sam, poking Judd, his elder by eighteen months, in the chest with the end of the barge-pole. "Half a league, half a league! You say it, our Judd!" Sam was pink in the face with excitement.

"Into the valley of death rode the six hundred!"

Sam thrust his lance at the Cossack. Judd dodged to

safety along the starboard gangway and cannoned into his father coming the other way.

"Steady, lads! You'll be tripping over the gunwale! Don't want you going stern over stem into the cut!" Jack Holberry, master mariner and captain of the Humber Keel 'Thistle', loved to see his children happy. Since Dinah died, their giddy tomfoolery had kept him sane.

The canal here above Keadby Lock was straighter and stiller than the estuary at the mouth of the river Hull where they'd moored overnight. Thirza could take her mind off steering for a while. She unfolded the newspaper and closed her eyes, breathing in the inky, indoor smell of offices and print shops. Cow parsley brushed the sides of the boat and washed over her senses with a crush of sappy fragrance.

"Read us the news, then, dreamy lass!"

Thirza knew exactly which news her father meant. She turned to the columns where a reporter shared the latest from the Crimean battlefields.

"Does it mention Uncle Jem? Does it, Thirza? Does it say he's killed a thousand Cossacks? Has he got a medal from the Queen?" Sam was acting it out, a sword thrust here, a gallop there, snorting for the charger, puffing out his cheeks and yelling "kaboom!" for the cannon, whistling for the shells and twirling a pretend moustache for Lord Cardigan.

Judd sat down by his sister on the hatch boards above the hold to catch his breath. Sam was off again, galloping the length of the deck, slapping his thigh, whinnying for the charger, harrumphing for the cavalryman. Thirza, now what the law deemed 'of full age', thought Sam sometimes acted more like a child half his years.

Thirza read the headlines in her clearest, calmest voice, while icy fingers of winter wind from the east off the North Sea flapped the mainsail her great granduncle had made in his loft on the canal bank. When she came to details she knew might frighten her brothers, especially impressionable Sam, Thirza was careful to use a bright, reassuring voice, skipping over the worst parts that made her own heart miss a beat. As she told them about the brave soldiers of the British, French and Turkish troops, she pictured what it must be like in the thirsty heat of day and now in the withering grip of winter on the heights above Balaclava and Sevastopol.

"Where does it say about Uncle Jem? Does it say he'll be home soon? Show me his name, Thirzie," Judd jabbed his fingernail at the sketch of a cavalry officer.

"That isn't Uncle Jem! That's Lord Lucan, silly," Thirza moved the page to avoid covering it with Judd's coal-dust fingerprints. "See his name spelled out underneath? L – U – C..."

"Lord Look-on, Look-on, Look-out! Look out, Sam!" Judd quickly lost interest in the wordy bits and skittered away to skirmish with Sam on an imaginary redoute with fifty Russian guns pointing straight at them. The paper often turned into an excuse for Thirza to play at being their schoolmarm. She was the only reader and writer in the family. Dinah had made learning seem like a game to her eldest child. Together mother and daughter read the names of boats painted in rainbow letters on their prows, the names of shops lining the Market Square, the details of goods for sale when they were ashore for a few days on their round trips from Sheffield and Doncaster to Gainsborough, Beverley and Hull. Words were adventures with their fancy curlicues and colourful shapes. Words were gateways into stories, magical and funny, hypnotic and mysterious. Words were keys to kingdoms into which Thirza could escape.

Thirza's brothers, like their father, had no hunger for learning. Jack could sign his initials on a bill of lading or make a cross where a clerk printed out the shape he knew belonged to his name, but he never needed to go further than that. What was the point? None of his friends or forebears, mariners all, had ever been found in a schoolroom.

Thirza was different. Before Dinah's laughing spirit danced away from them thirteen Christmas Eves ago, widowing Jack before his thirtieth birthday with three lively children to raise alone, she'd coaxed out Thirza's aptitude for words, just as Dinah herself learned to spell at her mother

Kezia's knee.

Thirza read out the rest of the article to her father. Jack took in each new fact, asking a question here and there to show her he was still listening, while he adjusted the sails to 'spill the wind' when the stiff breeze off the marshes started to buffet the little craft. Thirza felt 'Thistle' straining and yearning to race along inland. She jumped up to help Jack loosen and haul until the sail heaved like a huge puckered skirt, tucked in at the edges so their quickening pace dropped and the boat steadied.

"I wish spring would hurry up!"

Thirza knew Candlemas heralded the slow thaw of frosts and snow flurries that beckoned even the hardiest canal dwellers to hibernate below deck, huddled round the cabin stove from winter solstice to spring equinox. She snuggled back into the curves of the tiller, worn shiny by the nudging hips of generations of her ancestors. She smiled to herself. She was the luckiest lass alive just to be here on the keel. Some poor souls had to live landlocked every day of their lives! Thirza couldn't begin to imagine how soul-crushing that would be. For her, it was like trying to guess how many stars were in the Milky Way, to imagine what it'd be like to see the same sights day after day, feeling the solid earth sucking you to a standstill. She counted her blessings with a shudder of relief.

Shivering skin and chattering teeth would soon be forgotten for another season. They'd be able to save the money now spent on the fuel they'd to burn every night in the cabin's grate. Thirza loved the way the brass fittings winked at her in the firelight, the buttery toast, potatoes baked on coals under the kettle and Yorkshire puddings wafting blue smoke from the pan. Wintertime on 'Thistle' was cosy and tasty.

What had it been like for her uncle Jem, lying under the bone-white stars all winter with nothing to protect him but his army tent? Thirza at least felt snug curled up in the tiny aft cabin. Her brothers shared a few feet of space in the fo'c'sle with their father. Sometimes this cramped space also served as quarters for a hired mate or purchase man or even the horse marine hired to give them a tow. She knew 'Thistle' was a luxurious palace compared to what the soldiers had for a camp over on the Crimean Peninsula.

Thirza hadn't even known where Turkey was until this war began. She thought of the turkeys on her grandfather Thomas's farm behind the windmill. Had they flown all the way from Turkey? They couldn't even fly, though, could they? They gobbled and shook their wattles of scarlet chin-flap like angry colonels at the head of a brigade. If she closed her eyes, she could hear the jingle of the horses' bridles, the stomp of the cavalry's well-shod hooves thumping through the sands of the Alma.

Thirza opened her eyes lazily, just enough to focus on the wooden bridge ahead of them. Jack had gone below to check on the sacks of grain he'd set apart from the section of the hold where he'd stack the coal bags on the return journey to Hull. White cereal dust and black diamonds didn't mix!

The bridge arched over the canal just ahead, called by Thirza's people of the waterways 'Curlew Trod Bridge'. It was named for the path that ran over the bridge before snaking away through the fen, where the leggy wading birds with their curved bills and mournful cries wandered. This path hid itself from view within a few feet of the bank, even though the land lay flat as a lavendered bed-sheet from the inland port of Doncaster to the coast.

Thirza was watching how the arch of the bridge joined fingertips with its quivering twin in the iron-grey water when a crash made her jump so sharply, the tiller bruised her with a wallop that made her cry out with the shock. Something hard and sharp ricocheted off the mast and came to rest at Thirza's feet. The broken glass stopper from a bottle. Then another. Then another, but this time it was a small round stone. The next missile bounced up off the deck and struck Thirza's shin. She heard Sam yell and her father came rushing up the ladder from the hold.

"Water gypsies! Filthy canal rats!" A head appeared above the parapet of the bridge as the foremost edge of their rounded bow began to travel underneath. A group of youths, not much older than Judd, leered down at Thirza from above.

"Wash your hair, wash your neck, gypsies and jack tars on the deck!" someone chanted. The tallest of the youths raised his arm, fingers curled around another stone that looked bigger than the others. Thirza lunged forward under the sail, cradling her brothers' heads under her arms, pulling them out of the line of fire.

"Look at Lady Water Gypsy! Thinks she's queen of this mucky old brig!"

One boy hung over the bridge and gobbed a ball of spittle into Thirza's hair. Another rock fell with a crack behind her as they went under.

"Go below, you two," Thirza whispered to her brothers. Sam's eyes shone in the temporary darkness under the bridge, as if he wanted to cry but felt too grown-up to give in to his terror. Thirza heaved up the door of the companion hatch and helped first Sam, then Judd onto the rungs of the ladder that led down to the aft cabin. Her father jumped the last few feet up the steps from the hold and picked up the stower his lads had been using in their game and which he usually kept at hand to push off the boat from the banks when it got stuck.

As they emerged into the light at the other end, he shook the pole in the direction of the gang.

"Be off with you! Heroes, eh? Bullies and cowards, more like, frightening kids and lasses! Shame on you!"

Thirza was alarmed to see her father risking confrontation, with the screwmatics in his legs that made him limp when he was tired. It was a regular local sport on this stretch of the journey, bunches of landlubbers mouthing off at watermen and women like themselves. She picked up one of the splintered glass stoppers. Looking daggers at the cat-callers, she dropped it theatrically over the side of the boat.

Behind the gang, unseen by them, Thirza made out another figure. Although 'Thistle' was gliding away out of target range, she saw the figure creep up silently behind the ringleader and disarm him, wrestling a small boulder from him and flinging it away harmlessly along the tow-path. The smaller boys looked round and, seeing the figure, hared away squealing and hooting in the opposite direction, forgetting the keel and all the opportunities for mischief it offered.

The shadowy figure on the bridge was taking the big lad, who'd shouted the most abuse and spat on Thirza, by his collar and dragging him along the tow-path as if to catch 'Thistle' up. Jack stood watching uncertainly. Thirza took a step out from behind him to present a more threatening profile to their pursuers.

"Stay behind me, lass," muttered Jack. Thirza's eyes were fixed on the man who'd now drawn level with the boat, taking long strides. The bully, held firmly by his captor, was unable to keep up and stumbled to his knees on the tow-path. The stranger lifted him firmly to his feet, a scarecrow given dignity by his avenger, thought Thirza, as she stared at the strange pair to starboard.

"You think you're a big man. Be a man, then. Apologise to this lady," the stranger waited for a response, but never took his eyes from Thirza. The youth's head lolled with defeated bravado but his lips were sealed. Over the whisper of the sedge and the sail flapping, Thirza heard the stranger's voice, low and reasonable, absolutely sincere.

"Apologise to this lady."

"I'm sorry!" the youth choked out, snivelling and with a final defiant spit into the water.

"Say you're sorry for what you've done."

Like a marionette, held upright by his collar by the stranger as the pair kept pace with the keel, the boy whimpered, "I'm sorry I swore and spat at you."

Thirza couldn't hear what the stranger said as he leaned with his lips close to the youth's ear to prompt him, but she heard the lout's hastily revised response.

"I'm sorry I swore and spat at you...lady!"

The man released his hold on the lad's collar. The youth fell in an ungainly heap at his captor's feet, then scrambled up and ran at full pelt along the canal side, up over the bridge to where his companions were now specks half a mile away across the level landscape.

Thirza called a thank you, but couldn't tell if the stranger had heard. She thought he nodded and saw him lift his broad brimmed hat as they sailed away from him towards their destination. She watched him standing looking after the keel for a long time until they were almost lost to sight. At last he walked slowly away towards the wetland moors of the Humberhead Levels that bordered the canal and stretched for many featureless miles inland and where no houses or farms or humans were.

Through the shifting mist in the middle distance, Thirza tried to make sense of what she thought she was seeing. The figure seemed to rise up, as if on stilts where there was no solid ground. Hovering like a kestrel, focussing down steadily over canal and fenland, he seemed taller than a human being, now. Where stilts might have balanced on the peaty earth, somehow Thirza saw a rainbow arch lapping and rippling, steam around the stranger's feet - were they even feet? - mixing magically with the mist. As the figure diminished with the distance, she couldn't be sure of anything.

"I've no idea where he came from, but I'm thankful he appeared when he did, back there," Jack followed Thirza's gaze and hugged her close to him.

"He came out of nowhere, just out of the marshes, out of the Chase," said Thirza, straining to see if the lonely figure with his leggings, staff and hat brim almost hiding his eyes was still visible. Soon, the incident started to seem less real as she began to get excited at what lay ahead, not behind. They were nearly at the spot where they occasionally docked to visit her mother's ageing parents at their windmill on Turbary Nab.

#

"There's two alive over here!"

"Mind his leg. His steed's had it, I'm afraid."

"A hundred dead, though. A hundred?"

"Two hundred, more maybe, with those injured. Hell underfoot, the length of the valley."

"What were they thinking? Old Woman Cardigan and Look-on Lucan? What was the aim of such a reckless charge?"

"Here, grab hold. Have you got the other one, lads?"

"Back through the same bloody slaughterhouse! Riding over their own dead fellows-in-arms!"

"Don't harp on it, man! Let's get these two back to camp before they're past saving. That one's out cold. No running, now. Steady! Look you don't go treading on those poor creatures beyond all help!"

The two wounded soldiers being carried from the field had grown up together on the fenlands of the West Riding of Yorkshire. Together they'd joined the rank and file of the Eleventh (Prince Albert's Own) Hussars, taken the Queen's shilling together, sailed for the Crimean Peninsula together. Some assumed they must be brothers as they were inseparable, two noble cavalrymen in Lord Cardigan's proud Cherrybums, his 'Cherry Pickers' with their pristine scarlet pantaloons and dashing busby hats. Together they'd charged with the Light Brigade, betrayed by the same blunder from above. Now together, on stretchers side by side, they were being bundled off half dead to the makeshift wards at Scutari.

The younger of the two, Private Matthew Brunyee, known to his friends as Matty, remained unconscious for many days. In the next bed, his best friend, Lance Corporal Jeremy Kitson, known to his friends as Jem, lay healing physically from the deep gash on his leg.

In feverish darkness, Jem heard them say his wounds were inflicted when his charger was killed under him, galloping down the valley between the Russian guns. Voices in his head were whispering so many different things. You should've objected. You should've asked why, even on pain of death. You should've spurred Samphire faster between the hail of fire.

Jem felt Samphire reach forward and then crumple beneath him, again and again. He heard the starter's pistol crack to start the St. Leger Stakes. Margrave won, a lovely horse, a dark coated chestnut colt with no hint of white, belonged to a famous prizefighter. He looked like Samphire. Not an ugly lop-eared horse like some were saying. Jem saw everything from where he was perched on his daddy's shoulders. Daddy shut the windmill for the whole day to go to the races, leaving its sails crossed over its chest, so Jem pictured it, like the dead crusader in church with his feet on a wildcat. He could see over the heads of everyone in Doncaster. That year, eighteen hundred and thirty two, the winning jockey was called by his name: Jem! Daddy joked the jockey was called Jem too, though his real name was James, just to make little Jemmy smile after the measles! But it made Jemmy cry to see the nice poppo whipped so!

"Jemmy! Jemmy!"

Susan, his sweetheart, calling out his name, handkerchief waving, her long hair streaming under her bonnet, face lit with love for him. He heard the screams of other horses in the ship as he tried to keep Samphire's halter up high to keep his hooves from slipping as the ship bucked and rolled.

"Corporal Kitson! What? Lying idle? You have missed the roll call!"

Jem felt sweat break out on his forehead. Some wounds ran deeper. Some wounds couldn't be dressed by Florence Nightingale's nurses. Even with eyes closed, Jem could hear them walking up and down the ward, ghosts in purgatory in their crisp uniforms. In filth and candlelight, between the crowded beds, they went changing dressings. Yet still wounds oozed and seeped through those bandages while unseen disfigurements pinned the brave and broken to their pillows and made the hospital a seething pit of torment beneath an orderly counterpane of calm.

2. WINDMILL BY THE WATER

Thirza could see Turbary Nab in the distance, a raised embankment stretching from the canal away beyond the little moor-end village that bore its name. She'd enjoyed her visits here since she was a little girl, the place where her mother was born. Glad to visit once in a while, but as she got older, much gladder to sail away again.

Judd and Sam clambered up on deck when she called them. They quickly forgot the bullies who'd scared them so badly. As soon as they realised where they were mooring, they were chattering and tussling again, eager to see if Uncle Jem had beaten them back to his home at Kitson's Mill.

As 'Thistle' rounded the bend in the canal near the Nab, the sails of the old windmill made the only movement on land in the frosty air. Thirza jumped ashore when they were still a few feet from the bank. She grabbed the mooring rope her father was unravelling. Later, the sails would be stowed and the leeboards, that helped the boat steer in deeper, faster waters, would be left on the shore for safe keeping till the return trip. Thirza wondered which of the horse marines Jack would hire to tow them onwards.

Like her mother before her, Thirza preferred to help Jack do the towing herself, strapping on the haulage gear, singing the old shanties as they pulled the keel along, light when unladen and sluggish with a heavy load of coal, wheat or gravel. Thirza never shirked any duty she could do on board. If anybody doubted she could manage, she was all the more determined to prove them wrong and make her father proud.

Jack crouched over the windlass, Thirza wrapped the hemp hawser rope round the metal cleat on the jetty and knotted it securely. These February winds could be as fierce as March in this flat country. She wanted her home to be waiting patiently for her when she emerged from the mill after their visit, not floating on to Doncaster like a ghost ship with nobody aboard!

"Take all your things with you, love," Jack called to her from the boat.

"But we won't be staying long! I'll leave everything in my bunk!" Thirza wondered why her father looked so serious all of a sudden.

"Take it with you, anyway," Jack spoke so gravely, it made Thirza giggle.

"Father, are you bothered those gormless lads might come and steal our things? We've nothing worth taking! They'll be miles away by now. Anyway, they'll soon find someone on the next keel along to torment."

"Take your things inside, I say," Jack disappeared down into the cabin. He re-emerged with Thirza's possessions in a bag that had been Dinah's. Thirza wouldn't want to lose that link with her mother just because she was too lazy to carry it to the windmill and back again. She felt inside the bag to check her precious box was there. Her fingertips tingled along its cool angular edges and textured surfaces. It made her spirit sing. She felt safe again. When Jack climbed onto the tow-path, Judd and Sam bouncing at his heels, he wouldn't let her carry it after all.

"You go on ahead, lass," Jack said, not meeting her eye. Thirza wondered if his legs were hurting or if the nonsense on the bridge had rattled him more than usual. She'd be sure to cheer him up when they returned to 'Thistle' before nightfall. She'd make everything alright again. She'd encourage the boys to start pulling their weight more around the boat. Whatever her father's concerns, she'd wipe that worried look off the captain's face. She kissed him and started up the path to the village.

The boys ran ahead along the Nab, jumping in and out of puddles that gathered where the soft earth of the fen sank below sea level. To this day, nobody could entirely free the countryside here from the encroaching marsh. The Levels and warping drains, dykes and ditches criss-crossed the landscape where Cornelius Vermuyden's Dutch drainage engineers had given it their best shot in the days of King Charles. The peatlands enclosed an eerie, alien universe. Isolated communities toiled for a living against the seeping damp that lurked beneath.

Before they reached Mill Cottage where Thomas and Kezia Kitson lived, Judd managed to push Sam into a waterlogged cart track along the edge of the mill field where their grandfather's small herd of cattle was grazing. As Thirza pulled him to his feet and made him wipe off the worst of the mud on the grass, she saw the sails of Kitson's Mill lapping up and over, a gap-toothed wheel, reflected under her feet like the mirrored propeller of a huge ghostly ship spinning its rigging in the sky. It was so beautiful in its fragile, landlocked way, but she was never fully at home on dry land. At least here on Turbary Nab, nothing was reliably dry for long.

Thirza ran with her brothers along the Nab and into the shadow of the mill. They stood in the yard that linked the windmill to the rough cobbled track leading into the village. Jack couldn't keep up but followed at his own pace, his boots growing heavy with mud as he picked a route along the line of frozen track between patches of sodden turf.

With the sails whirring over them and before Thirza could stop him, Sam was drumming, a pint-sized woodpecker, on the door of the windmill itself. Inside the open doorway, Francis Jacques, the miller's apprentice, was lounging asleep on a pile of sacks. Nearby, a ladder led up to the meal floor directly above.

Francis jerked awake at the hammering. He wiped his eyes with the back of his hand, squinting in the glare of the winter sun that silhouetted three figures against the rectangle of light from the frozen yard. He lurched to his feet, tucking in his shirt tails and trying to sound alert, shouting towards the hole at the top of the ladder.

"Visitors, Mester Kitson!"

The muffled hum and clack of the machinery overhead seemed the only sound answering. Then the old miller appeared on the reefing stage above. Thomas Kitson, dusty white from his cap and silver whiskers, his neckerchief and apron stretched over his ample paunch, right down to his floury shoes, was unmistakeably every inch a miller. With his one good eye he saw his grandchildren and son-in-law. Thirza recognised in that eye the roguish twinkle she remembered from childhood. The other empty socket twitched behind a layer of flour as Thomas's face broke into a broad smile.

"My Kezzie won't half be pleased to see you! I didn't see the keel coming. She must've crept up on my blind side!" Thomas laughed at his own joke. A stray grain had worked its way under his right eyelid and rubbed away at his pupil until it robbed him of sight completely a few years ago. Now he found it harder to judge distances and colours, but his miller's thumb, trained over decades to judge the quality and coarseness of the grain, didn't depend on the clarity of his vision. Thirza wondered whether Granddad's blind side let Francis loaf while Thomas toiled.

Thomas disappeared back inside the mill and stopped the sails. He locked the mill office and squinted at Francis.

"When you've stopped yawning, Lolly Laggard, tie up those sacks we filled. When I say 'we' I mean 'I'."

"Is his name Lolly? I thought it was Francis?"

"I speak as I find, Sammy Skip-Puddle!" Thomas chuckled as Thirza pulled Sam away from the door to let her grandfather out. "Have you grown or have I shrunk?"

Luckily he didn't seem to be waiting for an answer.

Thirza couldn't be certain if he was looking at her or the lads.

"Judd's all but a man, now, fifteen next birthday," Jack filled Thomas in. "Man enough to be mate on the keel. Sammy's not far behind and he's sharp. He knows the knots and the different locks, already. He's shaping up champion."

Thirza thought about what her father was saying, then of all the times she'd helped him while her brothers were playing at leap-frog along the bank or catching minnows from the cog boat with a stick and string. She smiled. Perhaps some day they'd be crewmen but for now, to her, they were still her baby brothers.

Mill Cottage was painted white but stained the colour of peat like all the houses on the village street. Whenever the land flooded, the sphagnum moss that had layered itself up over millennia tinted everything with its own palette of dun, ochre and cinnamon. But the brown wash was outside. Inside was a different world, where Kezia, known in the family as Grandma Kezzie, chased away dust and drabness and kept her little house spotless from any hint of coal or flour.

"Kezzie, look what the tide's washed your way!" Thomas kicked off his shoes in the yard, left his cap and apron on a hook by the mill door and ushered Dinah's brood towards Kezzie's cuddling.

Kezzie was in the parlour, delighted to be surrounded by her late daughter's family. She clapped her hands, chucked every cheek, ruffled every topknot and hugged all her kin, but it was on Thirza her gaze rested when they were all seated round the fire. The grandchildren piled onto the oak settle that struggled to keep them snug. Round its wooden wings, the chill came nibbling its way into the fibres of the walls, squeezing itself over the threshold, between the leaves of the ill-fitting Dutch door.

Kezzie let Sam chatter away. She smiled to see Judd box his brother's ears when the younger lad looked saucer-eyed into his grandfather's face.

"Is Uncle Jem home yet, Granddad?" Sam asked. "Judd and me, we were being the Light Brigade. When I'm older, I want to be a hero like Uncle Jem and go for a soldier with the Cavalry!"

"Sammy!" Thirza hissed. She alone seemed to notice her grandmother's smile cloud over. She saw the wrinkles round Kezzie's lips deepen as she swallowed hard, struggling to form a simple answer to Sam's innocent probing.

Thomas was brushing his trousers free from dust, wisely, to inhabit Kezzie's pristine realm. He answered for his wife. Like Thirza he could see the tears welling in Kezzie's eyes, even with his blind eye turned towards her.

"Well, my laddie, your uncle Jem's still with his regiment."

"He used to be writing home all the time!" Kezzie blurted out fears she'd been bottling up for many weeks."His letters were always full of his joking, weren't they, Tom? Just like his dad! Never a serious bone in his body. Tales of his comrades, things the bigwigs said, what so-en-so got up to. But since Balaclava..."

"Not a word. Not a word. Not a word, word, word," sang Thomas, jogging his knee like a horseman at trot and winking at Sam, who was looking from face to face, wondering why everyone else seemed so serious when life had galloping and gallantry in it?

"Half a league! Half a league! Our Thirzie taught us that! It's all about Uncle Jem, isn't it, Thirza?"

Thirza gave her brother a look. Sam shrugged and pouted.

"He'll be home soon," Kezzie whispered, "or he'd have written to say so. He'll be telling us the war's over. He'll be galloping home to the mill where he belongs."

"We'll be trailing red and white bunting from the fantail to the sweeps!" Thomas sounded jovial enough to set Sam grinning again.

Kezzie patted the seat beside her. Thirza padded over the rush matting to sit by her grandmother. Kezzie stroked her hair, like she used to when Thirza visited the mill with Dinah, once in a while when she was little.

"And you, Thirza," she said, "such a young lady now,

and beautiful too. You've our Dinah's eyes."

Thirza glowed inside. It was a treat to be with one of the few people left on earth who knew how closely she resembled her mother. Jack sighed and looked at his feet. His half hunter watch was ticking so loudly in his pocket. The minutes were crowding and jostling him towards that final second when it would be time. He rehearsed again in his head the words he'd so dreaded to say, right from the moment he decided he had to say them.

Over cups of tea, they shared stories of the village folks and things they'd heard from the lock-keepers. They ate the lunch of cold beef on bread from best flour ground at this very windmill, spread with butter from the cows they'd just passed in the field. Thirza guessed Jack must be anxious to get 'Thistle' back underway so they could reach Doncaster by nightfall. Why else did he look so jumpy?

"Well, we'd better get going while we still have the best of the north easterly off the fen." Jack stood up, smoothing imaginary crumbs onto the floor. Kezzie hurried to sweep them up with a very real dustpan and brush.

"It's a bone-chiller, but it bellies your sail and drives my windmill's sweeps. Suits us both, Jack. It's an ill wind that blows nobody any good!" Thomas shook his son-in-law's hand. Kezzie kissed Judd and Sam on the tops of their heads. Sam shook hands with his grandfather, once Jack had shown him which hand was the right one. Kezzie gathered Sam close to her bosom and squeezed him till he squirmed away. He stuck out his chin and challenged his brother.

"Race you back to 'Thistle', Juddy Slowcoach!"

The lads raced out into the mill yard where Francis was mooching as if he'd run out of jobs to do inside and hadn't the gumption to start on a new task without Thomas's guiding eye, blind or sighted.

Thirza kissed her grandmother on the cheek, but the old lady clung on firmly to her hand when she tried to follow her father to the door. Thirza expected her father to reassure Kezzie in his sensible voice before they left for their seamless wandering on the water. Jack cleared his throat as if he was going to speak, picking at threads in his cap, but still stood on the rag rug just inside the door.

"We'll come and visit again, Grandma!" Thirza said. "Don't be sad. Uncle Jem'll be home soon and you'll have such a celebration. The bells ringing, the sails all festooned with the British flag, just like Granddad said!"

Jack turned round. Thirza was astonished to see tears in his eyes.

"Thirza, I want you to be very brave, now."

Thirza's head began to spin. She could hear her own blood beating in the labyrinth of her ears. She could hear the words her father was saying, she could see his face, too serious by far, the clues he'd tried to give her, to prepare her, but nothing in her soul could take it in.

"You're to stay here with your grandma and granddad. I can't see how there's a future for you on the water. The lads are old enough to be my crew now. They have to be. Money's tight. Tighter every year. You know that. No extra mouths to feed. There are opportunities for you here, jobs to keep you busy around the mill. Handsome village lads. Prospects. You're a bright girl. A good girl. A woman." Jack's voice trailed off as he wiped his eyes on his cap. Then he put it firmly back on his head and nodded to Kezzie.

"There's room for you here, lass," she was saying. "Your father asked me if we could take you on now you're grown. We said 'yes' right away, didn't we, Tom?"

"Course we did! 'Yes' with big brass bells on!" Thomas hoped laughter would sweeten what he knew must come as a shock to the lass.

"No!" Thirza had a thousand reasons but the word burst out before she could make the arguments sound persuasive. "No! I can't stay! 'Thistle', she needs me! You need me! The keel's my home! I was born in her!"

Thirza pushed after her father into the yard. She felt her grandmother's hand on her wrist, still clinging to her, frail looking fingers with a grip of steel.

Jack walked away through the shade of the mill tower. The shadows of the sails that Thomas had started turning again, seemed to be sweeping him fussily away from her towards the canal and the mooring cleat where 'Thistle' waited, all the wind sunk out of her sail.

"Father, I won't leave you! I won't!" Thirza's voice sounded like a stranger's to her, broken and lost.

Kezzie pulled her granddaughter firmly back towards the cottage, stroking her hair like she stroked Dinah's when the wanderlust tore at her after she met Jack. When Thirza could catch her breath from sobbing, she swallowed hard and knew she mustn't cry any more. Her father had suffered so much childish crying and grief when her mother died. She'd been so strong for her brothers since then. She'd tried to teach them how to look at things with thankfulness, no matter how upsetting, just like Dinah did.

Then her bravery deserted her. She ran as fast as she could with her skirts gathered round her, down to the spot where she'd landed from her flying jump only hours before. But 'Thistle' had pulled away from her moorings. Judd and Sam looked back at her from the companion hatch. Her father at the tiller wouldn't meet her eyes.

"I'm sorry, love. Sorry I never told you before. How could I, till I was sure? I may not even be able to keep the keel on. You've a home here, now."

"But 'Thistle' is my home!" Thirza felt frantic. She couldn't quieten the little girl inside her, watching her world, all she loved, float out of reach. "Daddy, please don't leave me!"

"'Thistle' was your home till now, but not your future, love. I can't let you waste your life with me and I can't pretend it'll turn out alright. I love you. Be my brave lass, for your mother's sake."

The boys looked shocked for a moment and Thirza thought she heard Sam sobbing, but before they reached the next bend, they were already galloping up and down the deck on their imaginary horses.

Thirza stood on the tow path alone. Not until the keel was out of sight did she turn back to face the windmill. Dinah had escaped it. Now her daughter was cast adrift from her heart's moorings. She felt herself drowning like a stickleback tipped from a jar, choking in the air of this alien place called terra firma.

3. LANDLOCKED

Thirza wandered round the windmill for many days, an anchor looking for the deep. She learned the names of the cows and the pigs with their different patterns and personalities. She felt the weights and textures of the chickens that scratched in the octagonal field behind the mill. The animals that didn't have a name, she gave names to: names of keels far away in the harbour, names of ships she'd seen in the docks. She fed the birds in the hedgerow with barley and semolina from the open mouths of sacks brought to the mill door. She crooned to the Chaffinch, the Robin and the Wren, imitating their songs when nobody was watching her before dawn. She wept silently when nobody saw her weeping. Kezzie and Thomas thought how happily she was settling into her new life ashore.

Each evening when they missed her as they gathered in front of the fire, her grandfather would go searching for her. He'd find the mill cat purring where it never usually ventured. One morning, Kezzie noticed Thirza's bed hadn't been slept in.

Kezzie had never climbed above the ground floor of the mill. She would supervise from below, chivvying Grace to sweep the stone floor, scolding Francis into tidying sacks from the hopper up on the bin floor. She'd flick cobwebs from the old millstone propped up outside the jamb of the entrance, a ton weight that even Thomas couldn't move without help from a stone dresser and two carthorses. Kezzie had a horror of heights.

She'd once tried to climb the ladder to the stone floor. But her head started spinning, seeing the gaps between the rungs and she never dared try again. That was back when she first left the cottage near the church where she was born, the year before the French queen Marie lost her head in that terrible bitter revolution. Could that happen here?

"Surely never but maybe," Kezzie's father had told her when she asked, that one time on the eve of her wedding to Thomas. Her father, one of the farming Poskitts, laboured silently in the fields from before dawn until after dark. He never spoke more than a word to his daughter, when he thought she was being too noisy.

"Kezia!" he'd say. Kezzie waited for more, but he never said it. So she'd asked him on her wedding eve, while she had his attention, as he stood stiffly in his patched greatcoat and the waistcoat he wore on Sundays, his own father's waistcoat with worsted arms sewn in for the winter.

"Could it happen here, Father?"

He'd not asked what she meant, or looked at her standing there, decked in her wedding garland and her dead mother Happy's corset. But he said more to her in reply than he'd ever said before or would say again.

"Surely never but maybe."

Kezzie shuddered and tried not to worry about such terrible things. Thinking meant worrying, for her. Rumours and whispers kept her from sleeping. Wondering about her Jemmy kept her from sleeping. As a young bride, before Dinah and Emma and Jeremy were born, she'd nudge her head into the miller's strong back. She'd try to curl herself up into the warmth of his body like a living bolster, until he grunted awake and turned to hold his young wife tight in the creaking midnight, but worries still stalked her.

Six years married, there'd been news of triumph at

Waterloo and promise of an eternity of peace. Fifty years on, this from the Crimean, but now her hair was grey. She refused to think about it and so to worry. Jeremy, her baby, her only son, her darling Jem would be home soon and the muttering nightmare of rumour and repercussion would become flat as the fen. Normality and peace would resume like they had never taken leave.

Jem had always been a hero to Kezzie. The mill was to be his inheritance. Now she was worried about Susan, young Susie, Jem's sweetheart. She'd disappeared so suddenly. Where had she gone? Why did she leave the village so quickly? How could Kezzie tell Jem when he rode home, the lass he was to marry had gone away with no word?

Kezzie had seen Jem only once in his glorious uniform, all cherry and gold braid, on horseback before he sailed away. She pictured him with his medals and his horse Samphire with tail plumed and plaited, trotting up to Kitson's Mill with the villagers cheering. There'd be special cakes, baked with their own special flour, pricked with Jem's initials and studded with cherries. He'd be the talk of Yorkshire, so many heroic tales told of his exploits, his feats of daring. He'd be promoted from lance corporal, to Lord Cardigan's right-hand man, his aide-de-camp. Was that what they called it? He'd be the army's mascot, famous as Wellington himself, yet he'd never go away again from his mother and his mill.

Kezzie shook all the worry out of her head like a speck of unwelcome soot on her hearth. Thoughts shape-shifted into worries if you weren't careful. Jem would soon be home, and that was that. Surely never but maybe. Kezzie stopped thinking and polished the brass fender, until she could see her own lined face peering back at her, with grey eyes that Thomas once told her were blue as cornflowers.

#

My dear Jemmy,
I am bereft to be obliged to write to you to

tell you news that I know will perhaps break your tender heart. I expect this letter will find you fighting bravely against the Queen's enemies in the cold winter so far from home. I have tried and tried to bear you not being here with me. I have remembered the good times we had planning our wedding and living here at the mill when you come home a hero.

But, Jemmy, my heart now belongs to another and I cannot help it. Don't be too sad and sorry, Jemmy, my beautiful boy, though I must no longer call you mine. The man I love is rich and clever and kind and oh so handsome, I sometimes think my poor heart will burst with joy at his loving me back.

I am leaving tomorrow for marvellous adventures far from here with the man who makes me happy. Please do not fret for me or try to find me on your return.

Thank you, Jemmy, for the time we spent in childish bliss, you and I. You will find another sweetheart one day, I know, so try not to think of me too badly,

goodbye for ever, now,
Susan

Jem stared for the hundredth time at the blank space at the foot of the letter where no kisses were. He'd dreamed of and longed for her kisses from the day he set off from home, when Susie waved him off with her handkerchief, keeping him strong with her promises of love forever.

"Don't torture yourself, so, Jem," said Matt from the next bed, "Susie isn't worthy of you, if she's found herself another sweetheart so sharpish!"

"It isn't like her! She sounds like somebody different! Susie and I were going to be wed, run the mill together. I can't believe this of her. I won't believe it!"

Jem held the letter closer to the candle, as if he hoped

by rereading it yet again, the words would reorganise themselves into the billet-doux he'd hoped for with his whole being, through these days since the charge up the nightmarish valley ended so many cherished certainties and childish hopes.

But he was still too weak to go out of this room unaided, let alone rush back to England to plead his cause with Susie. She'd made her feelings plain enough. His brooding was interrupted by even deeper concern, as he saw Matt's body contort with agony from the onslaught into which they'd both ridden, from shells, cannonballs and bullets.

Jem pulled out the other letter he'd received from England in the last delivery. This one was more welcome than Susan's, but puzzling. He didn't recognise the writing on the envelope. Inside, along with an official-looking note, there was a small paper pouch containing a single tablet the size of a horse pill. Matt writhed and began to ramble beside him. Jem read the accompanying letter, written with a nib that had left blots wherever it scratched. He held the smooth round white pill in his hand. The top of the only sheet had been torn away, somewhere on its journey from England to Turkey, which added to the mystery that surrounded its origins.

-has told me of your plight and the lack of effective physic for your ills available in the battle zone.

I have taken it upon myself in my capacity as a trained apothecary and itinerant doctor to enclose for you the latest 'nostrum remedium' that is to say elixir in solid form for the relief of a multitude of symptoms with which, I hear from a friend of your concerned loved ones, you are currently afflicted. In specificity, this enclosed pill is the latest innovation in England for the alleviation of pain from wounds inflicted on the battlefield.

Young friend, I advise you to avail

yourself of this marvellous panacea, best swallowed in one gulp without pause to chew.
I remain Dr S. S-

Jem unwrapped the pill and thought how sweet it would be to be free of pain, if only for a brief time while the effects of this wonder lozenge lasted. But Matt's moaning distracted him from his own woes. He leaned across and lifted the glass of water from the table between their bunks.

"Matty!" he whispered, "Matty! A well-wisher doctor from home has sent this pill that cures pain. Look at you, man! You need this more than I. Here, you can have it!"

Matt smiled at his oldest friend. Jem tenderly manoeuvred the glass to Matty's cracked lips.

"One gulp and it's down. There! Swallow it whole, that's the ticket!" Jem watched anxiously for signs of improvement.

Matt lay back and closed his eyes with another smile and a sigh that Jem took for relief. Jem himself lay awake for a long time thinking about Susan, watching the shadows impersonating the faces of absent loved ones on the candlelit walls.

#

"Her bed hasn't been slept in again, Tom!" Kezzie took Thomas's frayed shirt-cuff over her knee and shook her workbox until the thimbles and pins rattled.

"Woman, you worry too much!"

"You said she'd settled."

"Water waifs never settle. They're always sniffing the wind. Our Dinah never did and Thirza's her mother's image."

"Find her, Tom. What if she's fallen?"

Thomas sighed an old sigh. Kezzie had been like this since their own children ran around the mill and found mischief there but rarely harm. Kezzie would never let things lie or trust for the best. He patted her arm and she tutted and poked the needle eye up to the light and sagged her face to concentrate on threading the cotton through. White on white never showed the flour.

"I'll go and look again."

Thomas stepped into the mill. No Francis.

"Nothing new there," the miller muttered. He climbed the ladder from the meal floor, where three more sacks were waiting to be hoisted up to the top of the mill. He would do that job later with Francis to help with the weight. That was one job the lumpen lad could manage.

Thomas climbed cautiously, glancing at the governor, spinning its iron balls to regulate the pace of the grindstones above, listening to the hysterical chattering of the damsel as it clattered its shrill tongue against the grain shoe. Above the noise, he called his granddaughter's name. No reply.

On the stone floor, where the millstones kept the family from the workhouse as they ground the grist into silky flour for the villagers and farmers, the miller leant on the upright shaft that was the backbone of the mill. He squinted out of the window over the prostrate Humberhead Levels, his head crooked to the right to survey the scene with his left. He could see the labourers and groups of village women digging and selling, prizing a living from the murmuring reeds and sucking turves under their feet. They were at their winter tasks along the edge of the wilderness of raised peat bog.

Thomas's forefathers had lived here on the old royal hunting grounds of the Chase from the days of old King Charlie and his invading drainage men. To his monocular vision, the scene had no depth, as flat in perspective as it was from left to right. But he knew his fellow villagers were coming and going on the earth and that as sure as his only son would ride up one day, a hero from the far horizon, his granddaughter would turn up, dreamily perceptive and self-contained as her mother had been. He turned from the window and made his way wearily up the next ladder into the narrowing space of the bin floor.

Thomas heard the pattering kiss of movement overhead as, above the dust floor, the wind direction changed and the fantail turned the sails to face into its blowing, out towards the fen. He climbed the final ladder into the cramped loft of the tiny room below the hornbeam brake wheel, meshing softly with the wallower as it converted the capricious breezes into the staff of life itself.

In the dim light, Thomas could see a figure curled asleep on an unused bin, where he stored old grain sacks waiting for repair. As his eye acclimatised to the gloom, lit only by the thin horizontal crack between the brick of the mill walls and the wooden ogee-form cap, he saw the old embroidered bag that Dinah had taken on board the keel when she ran away to marry Jack Holberry, giving up her life here on land forever. Along a beam, he made out shapes of a woman's shoes and a tiny brass compass, a broken watch glass glinting in the shaft of light and a stump of tallow candle with an old jug beside it. That old box of Dinah's, too, that he'd never seen inside, passed down through the maternal line. Kezzie had kept it in a drawer and never bothered with it.

"Thirza?"

The figure huddled on the meal sacks uncurled and Thirza's red-rimmed eyes looked back at him through the cramped gloom.

"Please, please, Granddad, don't make me sleep inside today! I found this place. I love it!" Thirza bit her tongue to stop the tears forcing their way back into her eyes. Her chest felt sore from a night spent sobbing. She felt a fool and so ungrateful.

"You daft lass. I'd never stop you. The mill's a chattering, nattering mother but she's a good one. Your mother used to climb up here as soon as she could do more than crawl. I used to find her curled up here in the cap, just where you are now."

"I knew she did," whispered Thirza. "When I close my eyes, I hear the damsel clattering like the windlass going round. I hear the sacks thump up through the grain hoist traps. They're our leeboards beating with the waves guiding 'Thistle' forward. I hear the sails flapping outside and I can sleep, dreaming I'm..." but her determination couldn't stop the tears from falling now.

"Home, lass, yes. Don't fret. I understand," Thomas began to descend the ladder to resume his work. "Come into the cottage for your breakfast when you've heaved to at the quay. Your grandma's worrying you're lost in a storm."

Thirza listened to the sounds of the mill as her grandfather stumped down to the ground, floor by floor. She could make life here bearable but she could never make it home. She felt the canal and the river and the sea beyond singing in her blood and the song couldn't be stilled by meekness or determination.

Thirza brushed her hair before descending the network of ladders and washed her face and hands at the pump in the yard. Francis, whistling as if he'd all the time in the world, passed her with a curious look but didn't return her smile. When she opened the door of the cottage, she saw they had a visitor.

"Thirza! Come kiss your aunt Emma!" Kezzie was beaming. "She's got exciting news for you! Special news from the Big House. Imagine that! No more time to droop and drag. You're a lucky lass today."

4. OFFERS AND OPPORTUNITIES

Thirza felt wrong-footed. She wasn't a lass to 'droop' let alone 'drag'. She'd kept her most cheerful smile on show. She'd joined in with all the jobs she could find to do around the mill and farm. When her heart felt it would break from homesickness, she'd gone away by herself, up into the cap of the windmill, so her grandparents wouldn't see her tears or think her ungrateful.

"How tall she's grown. Green eyes like our Dinah. Surely you won't let her keep all that hair, Mother? Dinah did, but then, least said. You wouldn't let me and my Darnell so admires long hair in a woman. Mills are dangerous, ferocious places for a girl's hair, you said. Even Father won't wear a beard."

Thirza tried to smile politely while her aunt Emma walked round her, plucking at her hair, her skirts, her fingers, as if she was assessing fruit on a grocer's barrow.

Emma, middle child of the mill, was the one with the least love for it. Her loathing oozed from her scowls when she looked at it and crinkled her nose in disgust when she spoke about it. Thirza had scarcely met her aunt even as a child. When the Holberrys visited, Emma Salkeld was seldom, if ever, at home.

"Important business and none of yours!" Emma

always snapped if asked where she had been.

Some years after coming of age, the mousy, vain, envious young Emma had miraculously made a good marriage to local farm bailiff, independent engineer and self-styled innovator, Darnell Salkeld. His kin had been employed for generations by old Naphtali Charlesworth's family at Foljambe Hall, living in the lodge nearby, Carrdyke House.

Emma had done better, in her own estimation, than her older sister Dinah, who had run away like a slattern with a penniless water gypsy and died of a hacking cough when the sea-frets sank too deep into her lungs. Better, she thought, than her younger brother Jeremy would achieve (his nickname Jem should have been abandoned at the school gates, in her opinion), if ever he galloped home, sporting his medals and flash uniform. Emma doubted any well-born lady would deign to look in his direction. True, he had once had that saucy hussy Susan Turgoose on his arm like a lovesick mooncalf. Darnell had generously suggested Emma give the girl a trial as a maid in the Salkeld household after her intended left for the war. But the girl had mysteriously disappeared after a short spell at Carrdyke House. No apology. No explanation. No notice. No reference. No forwarding address. Emma hoped in her chilly self-centred heart that time would prove her right and she alone would remain the envy of the whole family, village and county for her gentrified connections.

"Sit down, Emma, do, and tell Thirza what a blessing has come her way!" Kezzie plumped up a cushion.

"You make a better door than a window," muttered Thomas, retreating for sanctuary to the windmill again. Kezzie saw her daughter's character, but believed the best of all her children. If she thought about it too much, she'd worry as she did about everything in her life. Emma glanced round her mother's immaculate parlour yet still wore the expression of somebody who has narrowly avoided stepping in some unthinkable substance left in the road by passing cattle on their way to slaughter.

Thirza could see Grace smirking to herself as she

pummelled currant studded dough at the kitchen table. Emma was an exacting visitor, but a source of comedy to the servants, with her shrill air of superiority. Thirza had heard Grace mimicking a voice like Emma's to Francis, the two servants howling at the blistering accuracy of Grace's portrayal. Now she knew who the butt of their hilarity was, she fought back her own chuckles.

"I can't stay, Mother," Emma breezed on, "Darnell will be driving the carriage back from Foljambe Hall, I don't know quite when, but terribly soon. He wouldn't want to keep me standing around here, all at a loose end."

"Tell Thirza what good news you told me!"

"I can tell her properly when she visits us tomorrow. Do make sure she has stout shoes for the walk back, Mother, as I'm not quite certain that Darnell will have time for fetching and carrying all our relatives back and forth and back and forth from goodness knows where at all hours of the day and night."

Thirza tried to feel thrilled by the warmth of the invitation.

"You know how very busy my Darnell is with his business," Emma continued without a pause. "Business in town, business with solicitors, business at Foljambe Hall, business here, business there. Squire Charlesworth and his aunt Lady Laura so depend on my Darnell in his capacity as bailiff for supervising the common labourers. The squire can't trust anybody else, and those tenants! At least, I think that's what Darnell said Squire Charlesworth said, in front of an M.P. friend of his, in Darnell's hearing only last week. Oh, or some week, I don't quite remember. You wouldn't expect me to carry all the little details in my head?"

Thirza was glad Aunt Emma seemed incapable of pausing for breath. It saved her own opinions coming under her aunt's scrutiny and being found hopelessly, dramatically wanting.

"When should I send her over to you?" asked Kezzie, when Emma finally missed a beat.

"Send her? Oh, my goodness, no. Mother, really!

Darnell will have sorted out all those trifling details by then. She must just be ready tomorrow and Darnell will call in the trap and scoot her across to Carrdyke House. Did you ever taste coconut cake, Theresa?"

Thirza winced. How could she start her contribution to Emma's monologue with a truculent "That isn't my name"? Had her aunt forgotten? She looked at Kezzie for guidance, reluctant to offend and even less keen to visit her aunt and the uncle she could scarcely remember meeting, so pressing did his business always seem to be.

"We did carry a coconut on 'Thistle', once," Thirza offered, "It'd fallen from a cargo ship from the Indies and Sam found it by the capstan. Judd bowled it down the deck so it smashed inside the fo'c'sle..."

"Oh dear, oh dear!" Emma fanned her face and rolled her eyes, "I hear a foreign tongue babbling, my head quite swims! We can do better than all that beggarly trash collecting. I should hope so! Coconut is a cake, Theresa, baked by a cook from Switzerland. One that Lady Laura had spare and was gracious enough to recommend to Darnell after an unfortunate incident with our own maid. Coconut Madeleine! It melts on the tongue like a snowflake."

"Thirza will be ready and waiting. I'll see to that," Kezzie saw Thirza's eyes were beginning to glaze and nudged her to indicate Emma was about to bid farewell.

"Listen for the trap, mind. My Darnell is a busy man," Emma leaned down, though she was no taller than Thirza. Thirza re-emerged from her trance to find her aunt was offering her face to be kissed. Emma tapped her cheek impatiently, just by her bonnet ribbon. Thirza planted a genuine kiss there but as her arms opened to embrace her mother's little sister, Emma's shoulders rose and she snapped her spine back into a ramrod of upright propriety. Thirza let her hands fall to her sides and blushed at her own clumsiness in reading these unfamiliar signs of breeding and etiquette. She made herself a mental note that her aunt was very unlike her comical, easy-going sister Dinah and evidently set her own bewildering compendium of social rules. She wondered what the wonderful news was that awaited her at the Salkelds' home, but knew better now than to try and squeeze a word in edgeways.

They watched Emma from Mill Cottage, teetering away along the village street, scarcely dressed for the icy pinch still in the air, carrying a dimply parasol that wouldn't have kept its delicate frame in one piece, had the wind from the marshes given it more than a playful tug. Emma picked her way between the cart ruts with shoes that looked far from the stout ones she'd recommended for her niece's visit the following day.

Kezzie went back inside and Thirza heard her telling Grace pointedly, "Put away the best china, again, Grace, and fetch the shears through to me."

Thirza's curiosity kept her outside a moment longer, to see if her uncle Darnell would drive up to give his wife a ride back home. Just as Emma reached the far end of the lane, where the pinfold stood, Thirza saw a small jet-black pony pulling a shiny trap. It approached the figure with the now inverted parasol at speed. Thirza looked beyond them. How she wished her path tomorrow might lead to exploring somewhere quiet and free of formality and small talk. Her eyes gazed longingly at the fork in the road, where the right-hand branch dwindled to a lonely track leading towards the moors, melting away into the distance to the north and west. The carriage arrived from the direction of the Great North Road, from the wider track that led towards the isolated Foljambe Hall. Carrdyke, Emma and Darnell's grand house, lay close to the main gateway, in sight of the gravelled path that led up to the Hall itself. The Holberry water-dwellers had never before secured an invitation to this hallowed ground of family legend. Thirza wondered what awaited her there among the coconut cakes and Swiss cooks.

The trap halted abruptly where Emma stood twirling and gesticulating. She seemed to be scraping mud from her wide skirts, shaking her parasol to expel water that sprayed over her from under the wheels. The driver, presumably the elusive Darnell, his hat rooted firmly on his head and reins in hand, whipped the pony so the carriage turned round and gave Emma a second shower of puddle sludge. Then, seeming to acknowledge Emma's presence for the first time, he leaned down, grabbed her forearm and pulled her sharply towards the unopened door of the trap with all the weight of his body as he sat down again. Emma was all but dragged off her feet and up into the seat beside him.

Thirza saw something fall to the floor. The trap was driven forwards over it and then backed up a few steps. Emma jumped down again and retrieved her parasol from below the wheels. Thirza was too far away to hear the snap of ivory but even at that distance she could discern that the angle of the parasol, as it was lifted back onto Aunt Emma's knees, was not a jaunty one. The handle seemed a foot shorter. The carriage lurched away as abruptly as it had approached and Thirza watched Emma's body being flung from side to side by the ruts colliding with the wheel rims, still clinging to her bonnet to retain at least a veneer of unflappability and style.

"Sit down, lass. Grace will do the honours," said Kezzie as Thirza came back indoors. She pulled out a dining chair and began to brush Thirza's long chestnut hair vigorously.

"I can manage that, Grandma," Thirza slid her hand round the brush and turned to look into her grandmother's face.

"It's true your mother kept her hair, but then, she'd other plans when she met your father. Like Emma said, a true mill girl can't be going around with tresses like a mermaid. We'll take the weight of it off your neck. Grace can do a plain but pretty style that'll suit."

Thirza jumped up.

"Grandma, I don't want my hair cut! I want to feel the wind blowing through it on deck. You feel so free when the wind lifts up your hair like a cloud of fluff off the bulrushes!"

"Nonsense! That life's behind you now, girl. The sooner you fashion your hair for your new life, the wiser. Long hair's a danger round the wheels and winding ropes."

"But when I go home to the water," Thirza tried to explain, but her grandmother shook her head and Grace only sniggered in her apologetic, withering way.

"Perhaps the shears frighten you a little," Kezzie tried to be more accommodating, seeing Thirza's determination. "Fetch my embroidery scissors, Grace. Perhaps they'll prove less intimidating. Emma screamed at the shears, I remember, as a young lady. She threatened to bite my hand."

Thirza thought only the coarsest of skin could dissuade her aunt from biting any hand she took against, even now. She hoped she wouldn't need such extreme tactics to persuade her grandmother to leave her hair alone, but even biting would tempt her rather than be shorn and branded with landlocked permanence.

"Really, I can put my hair up under my bonnet. I can plait it or wind it up in a bun, keep it tight and not unruly. Just, please, let me keep it."

"Well, I suppose you know your own mind, like all you girls do. All in good time, things will sort themselves out," Kezzie took the scissors from Grace and sent her back to the byre with the shears. Thirza felt less than reassured by Kezzie's change of tone.

"I'll be going back to 'Thistle' one day, so it'd be such a waste, Grandma, to change things in haste that can't so easily be changed back."

"Surely never but maybe," Kezzie sucked her cheeks in and tried to show that she'd won the argument.

Thirza helped her grandmother until Grace returned to the kitchen and then went out to the chickens and gathered the eggs in her apron.

"I could sell these eggs for you, Grandma. Round the houses. Earn my keep. I can help Granddad in the windmill, too. It won't be forever, just till I go back home."

"Help in the windmill? The very idea. A lass like you. Thirza! You have opportunities, but you talk like a ragamuffin tomboy. You'll be thinking of whittling pegs, next! The windmill's a man's domain!"

Kezzie shuddered, struggling to reconcile the figure of

a woman with the meshing cogs and racket of the messy miller's world. For her, the swooning terror of setting one foot above ground level on the narrow rungs of rickety ladders made her unable to entertain the idea of any female relishing such a job.

"It isn't for a girl to do a man's work," she said, as if that statement was an unshakeable pillar holding up creation.

"But I've helped father on the keel since I was shrimp-sized!" Thirza laughed to see her grandmother so fixed in her belief. "I could help Grandfather just as much. I know the windmill seems a little run down. I could help with repairs. I could raise a little money to help, pay my keep. There are holes in two of the sails. I heard Grandfather say he couldn't afford to get the stone-dresser in till Michaelmas this year, yet he's needed sooner. There are mouse droppings and cobwebs up on the dust floor. Grandma, why not let me help you, while I'm here for this holiday?"

"Holiday? Droppings? Money? Stone-dressers?" Kezzie brushed some soot from the fender as if it too was getting above its station by soiling her hearth.

"These things are nothing for you to worry your head about. Wait till your uncle Darnell comes for you in the morning. There'll be better things to occupy your head with, then."

Later, when Thomas came in for a bite of lunch with them, Kezzie seemed to remember the earlier conversation.

"Thirza dear, how on earth do you know there are cobwebs on the dust floor? That's the floor near the very top of the tower, you know."

Thirza met her grandfather's gaze. He wore an expression of amused innocence as he chewed his bread and cheese.

"She'll have seen the old cat come down with its tail all festooned with spider's spinnings, my love. I know I have, many a time, even with this one eye!"

Thirza was grateful. Granddad had kept the secret of her cocooned den under the windmill cap, under his cap, at least for now. She didn't want to upset her grandmother any more today and gave the old man a thankful smile as she sipped her milk.

When she returned from the visit to Carrdyke House, she'd set about finding proper ways to be helpful. She could sell eggs, or teasels for spinning, perhaps, around the place. There was nothing she couldn't do, her father always told her. Nothing, but stay on the water, it seemed. She'd prove she could do that too, one day.

Her father wasn't always right. He'd been wrong when he promised her Dinah would jump out of her bunk, fresh as a daisy after that horrible long night. Thirza had lain awake hearing her mother's cough through the curtain that separated them. He'd been wrong then. Dinah hadn't woken up or brightened their lives with the ripples of her laughter again. Her father loved her, she knew how much, but he was wrong about there being no place for her on the keel. She'd show them how wrong they all were, one day.

That night, curled in her new den, she reached out and set the stub of tallow candle closer, to light up her scant possessions. She picked up her mother's little box and held it tight to the warmth of her body, eyes shut. It was always this way. In her head the pictures started, one memory after the next like stacked cards all painted with tastes and shapes and textures. Her heartbeat came faster as she saw the strange figure of her rescuer in her mind's eye. He was standing on the canal bridge, meeting her eye, holding her heart with his mysterious, unnerving gaze.

She opened her eyes and he vanished. For a moment she could hear in her inner ear the drumming of his stilts, the creak of the leather straps, the scrape of brass on the frosty cobbles by the bridge, the silver and rainbow sparks, struck as from a flint, melting up into the marsh mists.

Thirza was fully awake again and looked down at the box in her hand. She stroked its lid. It felt like feathers but as cool and calm as marble. She knew most of her family dismissed it as a sewing box, passed down through generations from mother to daughter. She never challenged people when they called it 'that old thing', though she sometimes told herself she felt it wince at the words. Not a sewing box or a simple treasure box, but a weird and wittily crafted little box of tricks and nobody, not even Thirza, quite knew what to make of it. It had its own presence and quirky persona.

"It's nigh magical," her mother had said when Thirza saw it once, tucked away in her mother's things in the cabin. Though Thirza knew it was neither airy nor faerie.

She looked at it in the flickering golden candlelight. It always seemed different and surprising, yet so familiar, her mother's box with the strange bird enamelled on the lid. Thirza liked to think it was no ordinary lacquer. The colours were more vivid and changeable, even though they seemed worn and with a bloom of age. Inside, it reminded her of a travelling clock, lined with silken see-through gauze. There were interlocking rings like a puzzle. One of these rings was looser, but not as if it was broken, just meant to be loose. She could wriggle it free, but whenever she did, she felt compelled to replace it, so as not to lose it. The box always seemed to breathe a sigh of relief when all its elements were in place.

It had layers of wood - was it fruit wood? - like a cigar box hiding tiny spaces of different texture and temperature. It was lighter than wood, sometimes. How could it only be sometimes? Thirza lay awake in the dead of the night when her mother first died and she became the box's keeper, turning over these questions like pebbles rolled in the river. But they never grew smoother or clearer. She loved to sit and sniff it. It reminded her of her mother. Different compartments seemed to hold the scent of the sea behind the market, their old cat's fur under its chin, the alder carr, the sweet roasted smell of burning leaves in October.

In the bottom of the box was an old key with tiny flywheels and cogs embedded in it, as though caught there in the act of exploding outwards. It fitted nothing she ever knew. Then, best of all, there was the tiny clockwork bird with the broken wing. She thought as a child it was a cuckoo.

Before she could ask her mother, her mother was gone.

Thirza closed her eyes and slid the box back in the bag and under the mattress. When she thought of her strange stilt-man again, she found herself waking to the thin beams of the morning sun and a new day of trying to dance in the difference.

5. CARRDYKE

Thirza was scrubbing out the joggling screen that was solid with impacted grain. The 'jog-scry', Granddad called it, in his miller-speak learned from generations of his ancestors. Thirza made certain the machine was disconnected before she leaned in to dislodge chaff from its three compartments, keeping her hair out of the way. Driven by a belt from one of the rotating shafts bringing power down from the whirling arms of the mill, the jog-scry was like a lullaby, joggling to separate the different grades of milled grain from each other, humming and vibrating with a low boom that added to the symphony at the old windmill's heart.

The sounds masked the noises coming from the yard. Thirza was lost in her task, still planning her next move, when a shout came up from below.

"Thirza! Come quickly! Whatever are you up to? Your uncle Darnell's here to collect you!"

When Thirza emerged from the mill, she noticed Kezzie looked as though she was lined up for inspection, grey head slightly bent, facing Darnell respectfully, even when their relative positions in the yard shifted, as if he were royalty, not her son-in-law.

Darnell Salkeld held up his hand and spoke to calm the old lady's confusion.

"Not to panic, dear madam," he said, in his smooth, commanding voice, "I have set aside the whole afternoon to meet with the girl."

Thirza walked up to the trap and held out her hand to shake his. Darnell's eyes refocused. He looked right into her eyes as if he already knew everything about her.

"To better acquaint myself, rather, with our charming niece."

Darnell kissed Thirza's outstretched hand, twisting it so his whiskers brushed inside her wrist. She fought an impulse to draw her hand back, a thread of his saliva unwelcome and warm on her skin.

Thirza climbed into the seat beside her uncle and smiled down at her grandmother.

"I'll be back before nightfall, Grandma," she promised.

"Don't fret now, dear madam! You know you tend to and it does no good."

As he turned the pony back towards the village, Darnell fiddled with the covers around Thirza's legs. She rearranged her skirts and assured him she was comfortable, though he continued to fuss with the blanket, knuckles and fingertips somehow brushing her leg before she could settle tight.

"Still no word from that merry soldier boy of yours?" Darnell leaned solicitously to hear Kezzie's whisper.

"Nothing yet, sir."

"The news gets wilder every day," said Darnell, watching the old woman's expression. "They say the cholera has taken more than the sword. The flower of Great Britain's fighting men and boys. Hero and horse-thief together. Still, never fret, dear madam, never fret. Good day!"

Thirza waved to Kezzie until they were trotting along with Turbary Nab behind them and the peatlands stretching ahead. Thirza planned to go for a long walk out there as soon as she could. Darnell reached the fork in the road where Emma had met him yesterday. As they turned the corner away from the moors and on in the direction of Foljambe

Hall and the scattered farms beyond, Thirza saw two stray sheep being herded into the pinfold through the five-barred gate that connected it with the converging lanes.

Darnell cracked his whip over the pony's back as they turned and again across the woolly backs of the sheep at the side of the road.

"Dutchy! Mind your flock! Pinder, I say! Damn you, mind your flyblown charges!"

Thirza got the impression of a figure inside the pinfold guiding the animals in past his body as he held the gate open with a long wooden staff dressed all in colours of the fen, a brown hat with a broad brim that hid its wearer's eyes, a woollen waistcoat under a pale meal-coloured jacket. A dog at the pinder's feet whined as the whiplash sang in its ears. As the trap picked up speed, Thirza caught sight of two tall poles leaned up by the pinfold wall, each with a small crossbeam set into it like a peg, propped at either side of a bundle of whiskery sedge.

"Hang on tight, girl, we can make up time on the homeward journey. Look out for Foljambe Hall on your right as we come closer to that patch of trees."

Thirza saw the beginnings of a stone wall bordering an estate in the direction her uncle was pointing. She thought how differently this part of the land lay, which was raised like Kitson's Mill above the peat bog wilderness on a widened and flattened section of the Nab.

All was still when they arrived at Carrdyke House. After the buffeting Thirza had been treated to in the trap, her ears hissed with the silence. A walnut dining table and writing bureau, glass cabinets with finest bone china and ornaments were all arranged to catch the attention and make the most of the light from a huge window facing back across the fen. The stained glass panels caught Thirza's attention and she smiled in delight at the purple, crimson and golden light sent fanning across the damask tablecloth, turning the glasses and silverware into goblets and chalices from Thirza's dreams. The view to the horizon was only obscured by the trees that surrounded Foljambe Hall. Thirza thought the Hall looked as if it was trying to turn its back in embarrassment at having its privacy so compromised by the proximity of Carrdyke House and the presence there of its worthy bailiff.

The quiet atmosphere was shattered by the entrance of the lady of the house.

"Here you are at last, Theresa! Look at you, hair quite wild with the wind!"

"Wind-blown as a rabbit in the mouth of a blunderbuss," laughed Darnell, with a glance that Thirza felt sure was taking in her every imperfection.

"You ride so hard, my love," scolded Emma with an exaggerated tutting.

Thirza was fussed over and settled into a chair. Emma fluttered here and there adjusting curtains and rearranging plates. Thirza wondered which delicacy among the display of pastries, buns and sweetmeats on the table might be the famous coconut cake about which her aunt had made such extravagant boasts. She was more used to hard biscuits and homely fare than the offerings placed before her on glistening china and lace doilies today. When the silvery tinkle of the French ormolu clock over the fireplace had reminded them several times that quarter hours were passing with little progress to their meeting in between, Thirza interrupted Emma's monologue of trivia.

"This is a beautiful spread, Aunt. Did your new cook make all these lovely things?"

Emma sank into another chair as Darnell came to lean on the mantelpiece. Before Emma could resume her prattle, it was Darnell who spoke.

"The last maid was a pretty little thing. But she was a troubled soul."

"The things she would say!" Emma almost shouted, but Darnell, pulling up a stool and sitting between his wife and niece with his boots stretched onto the hearthrug, finished her sentence for her.

"The things she would say sometimes got her into trouble. So for kindness' sake, we had to let her go."

"Like the one before. So young, so little idea," Emma

gabbled on, shrill as usual but Thirza sensed a desperation in the way she rubbed at Darnell's shoulder and seemed to watch his face for signs of approval.

"Exactly like the one before, my dear," he said. "Inexperienced and rather simple-minded. Unaccustomed to the ways of gentlemen."

"Of gentlemen and ladies," added Emma, looking at Darnell, as if she'd forgotten both the cakes and the pressing news she'd promised Thirza. The cakes lay untasted and the tea was getting thoroughly stewed in the fancy pot. Thirza wondered if her aunt had forgotten she was there solely at their invitation, not a new stick of furniture to be fluttered round.

"Unaccustomed to the ways of the world. She had an unfortunate manner, which experience will correct, God willing," Darnell concluded.

"Where is your plate, Theresa? You must try the coconut cake. The receipt is a closely-guarded secret and the ingredients imported especially, I believe. Neither the hoi, nor, indeed, the polloi have tasted this."

Thirza tried to guess which of the slices now tilted her way, was the famous confection.

"Nobody before you, dear Thirza," said Darnell. He took the plate from Emma's hands and indicated one of the palest slabs of gateau. Thirza took it, thankful to have been spared showing her ignorance of such refinement by helping herself to a more lowly example of the baker's art. She took a bite. Her mouth filled with the prickly texture of straw and horsehair and a sickly sweetness like treacle mixed with sawdust.

"Your new cook's clever to make something..." she coughed, searching for a polite word that would also be true, " ...so different." 'Delicious' would have been cruel flattery. Different it certainly was from anything Thirza had tasted on land or sea.

"It is a little rich for me, of course," Emma was back into her stride, "for the more refined palate has a delicacy of discernment that cannot be taught."

"Neither taught nor corrected," Thirza realised her uncle Darnell murmured these words for her hearing alone. Aunt Emma was opening one of the cabinets, taking out a small ornament to show her new captive audience.

"See this, Theresa?"

Here were no clues, no forewarnings. Thirza was on her own to decide what she was looking at. The lump of greenish stone studded with tiny jewels seemed at first to be a bird. Though the way it was twisted made Thirza think of a fish contorting as it was drawn in on a fisherman's line.

"Really, we don't have time for a full inventory of the crockery and bric-a-brac," Darnell's eyes took on a lively glint of steel that Thirza hadn't seen there before. It made her heart cringe inside her chest to see how Emma recoiled from him, returning the ornament to its place on the shelf with shaking hands.

"To the news and then to the trap."

Thirza looked from her uncle to her aunt.

"What's this wonderful news?" she asked, aware of the tension developing between Darnell and Emma. The pigeon-like fluttering of her aunt was intensifying into a nervous tailspin.

"Lady Laura Grey, I mean Charlesworth..." her aunt stammered.

"...of Foljambe Hall," Darnell's heavy breathing betrayed his impatience though his gaze was impassive.

Emma closed her eyes. She seemed to be trying to avoid   swooning from the strain of keeping the overwhelming excitement of the revelation to herself for so long.

"Lady Laura has been so gracious as to offer to give you a trial. She has a small team of seamstresses and needlewomen who make all her Ladyship's ball-gowns and carry out repairs on the upholstery and drapes at the Hall. She is waiting to see if you are the girl with the talent to join this prestigious clique. Can you imagine? You, Theresa! What do you say?"

Thirza's lips were dry with the shock. Sewing? Visions

of darning her brother's stockings, the lining of her father's pockets, her own modest working clothes danced in front of her eyes. She managed well enough, she could hem a pennant or sew a tear in a sail if required. But the prospect of even setting foot in Foljambe Hall was an ordeal enough to strike all ready replies from her mind.

"Has the cat made off with your tongue? A girl like you! Such a chance! Lady Laura is so elegant and has such correct taste and manners. Why, she has the choice of the best milliners, hosiers, costumiers in the country."

"In the country? In Europe. In all Yorkshire!" Darnell caught Thirza's eye and pulled a face that made her want to laugh to relieve her nervousness at what was being asked of her.

"You are to begin right away," Emma shrilled, "by showing her Ladyship your capabilities."

"Right away?" Thirza tried to sound in control of herself.

"Right away. Her Ladyship sent word by her nephew, Lucas Charlesworth, Darnell's cousin, that she is willing, at great personal inconvenience, to accommodate you into her schedule today."

"Now?" Thirza hated to hear her own will being shrunk down to a powerless echo of her elders.

"Her Ladyship will, no doubt, put you through your paces with the thimble and needle. She is most particular! You must try to do well."

Thirza became aware of the plain stout shoes her aunt had advised for the journey home, the only working shoes she possessed. Emma was staring pointedly at them, too.

"Your feet look the same size as mine, give or take. You must borrow a pair of my slippers to go to Foljambe Hall. Those common clogs will never do on her Ladyship's Persian carpets."

Emma called in the housemaid, a flustered youngster with her cap at an angle as if she had never had time to put it straight.

"Suzette!" bawled Emma, and then behind her hand

to Thirza, "my maid was christened Susanna, unfortunately, but it is so the vogue at the moment to recruit one's household staff from Europe, that I have quite taken a fancy to the name Suzette. So much more a ring of class to it. Bring my old but serviceable slippers, Suzette," she gushed while the girl still stared at Thirza.

"Make sure you bring the ones with no hole in the sole. That will never do. The slippers are to tread and curtsey to Lady Laura Charlesworth herself. Quickly now, don't stare so!"

Thirza counted the seconds ticking past with the chimes of the Salkelds' clock, her time to escape this unexpected ordeal running out before she could think of a plan to extricate herself.

"I really don't think I'm what Lady Laura's looking for. I haven't trained as a seamstress. I want to help at the mill and then go back on the canal."

Emma knelt at Thirza's feet and helped her remove the heavy-soled working shoes that had trodden the deck of the keel without once drawing attention to her.

"Whatever were you thinking, to sport these monstrous crates?"

"But you said..."

Emma raised her hand, "Enough, please, I have a headache from the sheer pressure of preparing you for this unrepeatable moment. Now. Push! Point your toes. Now the heel."

Thirza felt her heels contact the carpet, hanging over the backs of Emma's impractical footwear, a finger's width shorter than her own.

"I can't wear these, Aunt. Perhaps her Ladyship will allow me to go back to the windmill and change into my Sunday shoes? I could visit the Hall tomorrow when I've had time to prepare."

"Prepare?" Now it was Emma's turn to echo. Thirza heard Darnell sigh behind her, whether in impatience or another emotion she had no idea.

"The only preparation you should need is to know her

Ladyship requires you. You are blessed even to be considered for such a post! This is not the quayside, the harbour or the filthy docks. This is the seat of the Charlesworths, huge landowners in these parts, who hold the whole county in their gracious keeping. That Lady Laura would even be willing at short notice and without a reference to consider you worthy of such an opportunity..."

Darnell leaned down and shoved away his wife's hands. He slid his finger down along Thirza's calf to her ankle, relieving the pinching pressure of the shoe, easing her foot back into a more comfortable position. She gave him a grateful smile.

"Let's go across there," he suggested, "while we still have daylight."

Darnell held the door open for Thirza and she stepped out, telling herself the slippers would soon pinch less and that she would've appeared like a vagabond in her clumsy barge shoes. Perhaps she'd misunderstood her aunt yesterday, or Emma, in her excitement at her secret, had made a mistake in advising her.

"Theresa! Let me... " Emma's strident tones were stilled all of a sudden with a gasp. Thirza heard Darnell's voice, very low.

"Thirza. Thirza! Not Theresa, you ridiculous, affected harpy! I shall dine with Lucas. Don't wait up."

Darnell cracked the whip over the pony's head. Thirza looked back at the house. Emma was waving from the front step as if nothing had happened.

"You mustn't mind Emma," confided Darnell. "Handsome as an ornament but trying at times as a companion and shallow as a confidante." Seeing Thirza's expression, he added, "Excuse my sharpness. Harsh, I know. Regrettable. I beg your pardon, Thirza."

"My mother was fond of her," said Thirza, struggling to remember any fond scenes Dinah had mentioned from childhood. She recalled her own impressions of Aunt Emma, looking her and Dinah up and down with despair and distaste. They were beneath Emma's dignity, too outlandishly dressed to suit her delicate tastes, too much outsiders to penetrate the circle of her confidence.

Thirza took a deep breath as the trap entered between the gateposts and growled up the driveway towards the door of Foljambe Hall. A butler emerged and a coachman who took charge of the horse and trap as Darnell took her arm and led her up the wide stone steps to the front door.

"Don't worry, Thirza. I'll call for you when her Ladyship's decided whether you'll do for her."

Thirza turned to ask her uncle what time that might be but she was almost knocked over by someone coming at speed out of the hallway.

"Cousin Darnell, here you are. Good show! I want you to fill me in on developments."

Darnell seemed to swell with importance at the sight of this young man with his pale eyes and strawberry blonde hair falling over the collar of his fashionable suit.

"Squire Charlesworth, my niece, Thirza Holberry. Lady Laura's kind offer has been most enthusiastically embraced. Thirza, this is my cousin, Lucas Charlesworth, the squire and heir of the Foljambe estate"

"Charmed, Miss Holberry," Lucas smiled almost shyly. "I do hope you will do well here. Lady Laura is an exacting employer, by all accounts, but a scrupulously fair one, with all classes of person." Lucas stage-whispered to Thirza, with a wink to Darnell, "Lady Laura being my aunt, she's a positive pussy-cat once you've got around her with the cream!"

"Now, my dear, on you go. Dazzle them!" Darnell added, "I've a little business with Squire Charlesworth, but I expect to hear great things of you."

Thirza followed a maid up the steps, managing not to trip. She could feel her modest reserves of dexterity deserting her with every second that passed.

6. SHADOW ON THE FEN

Ducks bobbed on the star shaped pool under the nets at sunrise. The little teal, its wing shattered by a farmer's gun over a copse in Crowle, had been drawn here by the misty rainbow light arching between the hoops of the old duck decoy. It swam searching along each arm of the decoy for a place to rest. The gun pellet stung and smarted, but here under the nets, between the screens, the sharpness of the world was numbed. The teal was curious. Mallards were gathered to feast on floating seeds at one end of the northernmost arm of the decoy and the teal made its way to where it could hear them quacking. But these ducks were strange. Some pecked with precise nods, whirring with a hypnotic rhythm that made the teal waggle its tail and relax. Around its floating fellows, the seed seemed as plentiful as when it first arrived. The injured teal ate with grateful gulps, aware only of companionship, not competition, from these unfamiliar waterfowl paddling around him, their feet webbed with gossamer, plumage moist with iridescent crystalline flecks. Above its head, the teal heard a cry:

"Yackoop, Piper! Yackoop, boy!"

The wild swimmer felt the air rush back along its primary feathers, tickling its wing coverts as a dog plunged over a wicket of intertwining willow rods and welcomed it further into the heart of the mesh of netting.

Two hands cradled it, wings of flesh surrounding its own wings, smoothing the down on its breast with strong, gentle fingers.

"Relax, little one! You're much too precious to end up in Doncaster Market. Now you're fed, off you go, free and whole! Choose carefully before you plunge into a decoy pool again. There are no others like mine!"

Bram Beharrell threw the little duck into the air and watched it spin away across the marshes, low towards the east where the rising sun was throwing long shadows from the cotton-grass and sedge. The teal was whole again, the injured wing as strong as the other to carry it back home to its nest.

This duck decoy had hidden itself, far from any path or property for two hundred years. Younger villagers didn't even know it existed. Older ones had either forgotten, or gave it a wide berth, avoiding the waterlogged ditches and boggy patches that caught the unwary by surprise with terrible consequences.

Bram's people had passed down to him secrets from the days of the Great Drainage. His father's forefathers, descendants of the Flemish Huguenots, had intermarried and lived alongside the families of the Dutch drainage workers, his great grandmother's Zeldenhuis kin. His people had helped draw the primordial waters of the marshes into dykes, warps and drains. All had been strangers in the fenland wastes, making an honest living in the simple ancient ways. Some still branded his ancestors 'King's Men', with an oath.

The locals no longer came in bands with sticks to smash drainage engines and embankments, or to burn homes where the Yorkshire accent was mixed with words from the Low Countries as they did generations ago. But they remembered and Bram caught an echo of their memory in a glance or a hissed word behind his back. Bram was the last of his line. Now he alone remained from his particular intermingled Dutch and Flemish Huguenot bloodline on this isolated stretch of the Levels.

Bram's heart was the only human one beating for three miles in all directions. When he lost his father and mother as a youngster, he carried on living in the old hut with his grandfather. His grandfather Jan had built this hut by the decoy with his own hands. Decoys like his were originally designed to catch the wildfowl that flew over the peatlands every year, to kill and supply game meat to the local landowners. Bram's people lived by a different law, the principle they called the 'reversal of ravage' the "omkering van schade." The old crafts his grandfather had taught him, before he too died a few years ago, were Bram's livelihood and his deepest, private joys.

He knew every animal and bird, every reptile and plant by its kind. He noticed the way the lapwings rolled through the spring air squealing "pee-wit" over his head. He knew where the adder slept, the 'hetherd' his people called it, how to avoid stepping on it or enraging it to strike with its deadly venom. He knew by heart the calls of every bird, how to echo those strange cries back into the air so the birds would trust him and come to his calling. He saved them and spared them in ways even he only partly grasped.

There were other times when, unlike the exquisitely crafted clockwork decoys he had inherited, nature itself couldn't knit its broken strands back together and death still held its unpredictable dominion. Sometimes Bram would watch a bird as it gasped for life, moved by its plight but accepting his powerlessness to intervene. He knew the crested grebe exhausted on its way to its summer pastures far away in Africa, or the goldfinch left behind by its bounding whistling flock. Bram could mend a simple injury like a broken leg with a tiny stick of reed bound to the bird tenderly with a curl of sheep's wool spun between his fingers. If there was no hope and only then, Bram would let the little traveller end its journey cradled in the earth.

When the old pinder died, a few summers ago, Bram found stray cattle had wandered over the fen where some drowned or came to other harm. Bram had left his little hut and walked the four miles to Foljambe Hall, with his staff and wearing his hat with the wide brim that sheltered him from wind, sun and rain in their seasons, with his leggings that let him wade into the wettest places, and his stilts that made every dyke and ditch like solid ground to him.

He'd spoken to nobody. He'd consulted nobody, for he had nobody left to ask or advise him about what he should make of his life. Bram knew the eels weren't always plentiful, didn't always swarm to be captured. He'd learned from his time as marshman, in years when severe frosts and banks of snow blocked every road and highway, that cutting sedge, repairing warp drains, weaving willow into baskets and basins, might not sustain him for ever.

So Bram had ventured out to Foljambe Hall, secluded from his own isolated life on the Chase and moors. The landowners at Foljambe had always paid his family the retaining fee for the office of marshman down the years. They left the modest wage hidden in a bleak spot that nobody would suspect or stumble on by chance. If Bram could secure the post of pinder also, then one day he might have the means to support others besides himself, though he couldn't think that any lass would take him on. He knew none.

He'd stepped down from his stilts, not wanting to scare the footmen and maids. He'd entered the grounds without looking back, over the wall that adjoined the path from the moor that only Bram knew. He'd listened to the sounds and judged whether the servants were vigilant. If the old squire was at home, the servants would act diligently, in case he learned if they slacked any duty to him and his household. Bram saw the coachman and groom wiping straw over sweaty withers. He saw venison and cuts of beef being delivered to the kitchen which he guessed only the rich man in residence would eat. Most of all he saw purpose and focus in the servants' eyes.

So Bram stood on the steps and asked if he might talk to Naphtali Charlesworth, known as the squire since his marriage to Lady Laura Grey. Since then, on Squire Naphtali's death, the estate had passed to the only heir, the young squire, his nephew Lucas.

At the time of Bram's visit, the butler was recently appointed and did not see any reason to refuse an audience with the quiet young man. Once inside, Bram had stood on the chequered tiles in the hallway. He'd never seen a staircase like the one with the carved bannister that writhed up like a slow-worm from the floor where he stood, to unseen rooms and corridors above. He'd never, outside a hearse, smelled the false smell of flowers that could never have blossomed on the fen, but had been forced in the Hall's glasshouse under the eye of the gardeners. The inhabitants of Foljambe Hall, in their turn, had never felt icy blasts of horizontal hail fizzing through the cracks in their doors.

Bram had shrugged his coat tighter round his shoulders and waited, looking without envy at the ringlets, signet rings, coronets and brocades that adorned the figures who watched him from every last painting that lined the walls of that staircase.

"Squire Charlesworth will see you now."

On the library carpet, standing before the landlord of every smallholding and tenement this side of Doncaster, Bram raised his eyes to the squire's face without fear or swagger.

"Sir, I've come to ask you to consider me for the vacant position of pinder in the village. If you could pay me the going rate, I would ask no other favour nor waste your time."

"You're the Beharrell boy? Man, I should say. How do you do? I rarely see you around these parts, nowadays?"

"People look through me, sir. Some see. Many choose not to."

Squire Charlesworth had laughed, not unkindly. His own ancestors had also come under the vengeful fury of dispossessed villagers in centuries past. The Great Drainage had changed local lives forever. Some hamlets and farmsteads had become more vulnerable to floods as the water found new levels and outlets under the intricate network of drains Cornelius Vermuyden's foreign labourers and engineers had constructed. The King's drainage men had benefited from lands once held in common and the resentment of local families, who had suffered, then and since, from decisions taken by outsiders, still festered not so far beneath the surface.

The squire had forsaken his accustomed formality, which saw him padding round every stranger to size up their abilities and usefulness to him. He stood stock still, as Bram did, as if to move would be to flush out a harrier from its nest.

"The job is yours for seven shillings a quarter."

"I'll take it, sir, and thank you."

The two men shook hands and Bram's stilts left a double track of square prints in the mud all the way back to the moor. With Bram as pinder, cattle never went astray again from the pinfold or came to grief in the quaggy wastes.

Today, after rescuing the injured teal, Bram slid his stilts under the turf edging of his hut. At a moment's notice he could stride away over the countryside to reach roofs that needed sedge or turf for a thatch repair, or where the waters might breach through the banks. With his head above the level of embankments, he could see the lie of the land, the birds as they flocked and the clouds as they clustered.

With his tasks done, as darkness fell over the marshes, he made a supper of eels and minnows, with herbs that grew in the fossilised stumps of trees that only he recognised, the mace, mint and water parsnip, ground together with crushed angelica and meadowsweet. He roasted his meal over a peat fire, the smoke rising in ribbons through the gusty March air, the ashes soon swept clean away so no trace of Bram was left to brand or pit nature's unscorched floor.

He'd learned the lore he lived by from the cradle. Omkering van schade. Reversal of ravage. Its rules insisted, in the voice of his people, no creature should be made to suffer and no being inconvenienced if it was in his power. He believed he should hold his place on the fen as lightly and yet as sacred as the creatures that shared their home openly with him. There were other mysteries, too, among his skills, that he spoke of to no one.

He threw some scraps of cooked fish to Piper who chomped on them gratefully and snuffled for more in his master's palm.

"Enough for today, boy. More tomorrow, when the curlew calls us early."

Piper was a water dog, a Dutch Kooikerhondje spaniel, bred for the life of the marshes, tolling ducks, herding strays and retrieving small bundles from the water. Bram remembered Piper's mother and grandmother, his father and grandfather's companion animals, running across the moors, learning where to tread to avoid a soaking, understanding where to trot, how to weave between their master's stilts. Each had been bred to work the decoy. Bram liked to think his Piper was the best dog in all the unique bloodline for the job, with a mouth so gentle, even the tiniest chicks were safe with him, like pups of his own litter. Piper brought each bird to Bram without a mark or ruffle to show it had been held in canine jaws.

The ducks' interest was piqued by Piper's red-golden fur, like a fox. As they drew closer to investigate, they would move forwards down one of the spiral arms of the nets, where Bram could move unnoticed to rescue them beyond the last hoop. So wildlife was nurtured back to wholeness by man and dog working together as one.

The art of duck decoying was an ancient one, yet Bram felt as if each time he came to the decoy, the ducks, geese and wading birds taught him new truths about the world of nature. He learned to use his eyes to see the moods of each flock and skein as it flew. He used his ears to hear the tone of birds' contact calls that rang out each dawn in chorus. He used his fingers to feel the weight and condition of animals and birds, the fat beneath the feathers, the organs beneath the fur. He learned to understand their journeys and trace their strength and vulnerability. He used his nostrils to smell the release of pollen and musk and the sap rising, so without words and blundering steps, he could pick a path through this fragile world, half wilderness, half submerged ocean, to move to its rhythms without a ripple, amphibious.

Bram clicked his fingers at Piper and gave a low whistle that brought the dog to his heels, panting in anticipation of their next adventure.

"We'll check the curlew nest and the old Morische Drain before nightfall," he whispered to the dog as they moved off through the gloom.

Bram walked a snail-shell spiral path to reach the place where he knew the curlew was nesting. He sensed the spot was very close, even though the darkness was gathering distorted shadows over the face of the fen. Piper followed obediently at his heels without a whimper. When they reached the place where Bram had spotted the tall, wheaten-streaked wader making its scrape, he knelt downwind, motioning the dog close to his body so their mingling scent wouldn't alarm the birds.

He made out the shape of the bird on the nest and saw the swell of its breast as it covered the three eggs in a shawl of snug feathers against the raw moonlight. Bram looked up. The moon was waxing. Tomorrow would be the full Lenten moon, just three days into March this year, the last full moon of winter. Behind him, he could hear the gurgling of the tame mallards in the decoy, who drew the wild ducks into the arms of the hidden hoops, pipes and screens. He'd left their clockwork counterparts strung securely from the roof of his hut.

But the sound was unearthly and unfamiliar tonight. Bubbling alarm calls, as if creatures were chuckling or sobbing deep in their sleep, reached the edge of Bram's hearing. Surely other ducks weren't on the move at this hour? Looking round, he couldn't see anything moving. Some nights a pair of hares would come boxing past when the moon was bright, dancing along the edges of the fields that bordered the fen as they sloped from the higher, more fertile ground of Turbary Nab to the south. Some nights he'd seen a fox on its way to try its luck in a hen coop, or a wildcat trawling the countryside for shrews, or on its moonlit way towards the dovecote behind the church. Tonight the moon shone, disappearing and reappearing between the clouds, but nobody seemed to be here but himself and the dog.

Bram signalled to Piper and moved away from the curlew's scrape. It was very early for the bird to be nesting. April was usually the month when it would begin to breed, but he'd seen one solitary pair of curlews fly in one stormy evening just a few weeks earlier. He'd thought at first that they might be passing through, then saw the female sitting here when he was repairing the Morische Drain. Could they survive before the earthworms, spiders and beetles they depended on, and the caterpillars the young would be fed on, emerged from crevice and chrysalis?

Bram knew better than to second guess the ways of the fen creatures, but still their welfare occupied his mind as he pulled the blankets around him. He tried to block out the cold until sunrise when the pinfold would need to be checked and a search made to restore any stray animals to their rightful owners.

When he woke again it was almost midnight. Bram could tell the hour by the angle of the moonlight coming in over the sill of his one window. From his hut, out here in the innermost wastes of the moors, the swallowed toll of the church bell from Turbary Nab came through broken and fragmented unless all was perfectly still, which was seldom if ever. Bram sometimes heard the chimes, a boom here, a heartbeat of silence there, another faint thud of metal tongue on bell-metal, beyond the senses to grasp, almost beyond hearing. He felt curiously comforted by the story his grandfather Jan used to tell him, how an ancient Saxon carving in the belfry forbade anyone to ring the bells 'wearing scabbard or spurs.' Tonight he missed the twelve peals of midnight and yet woke when he knew they must have sounded moments ago.

Something made him raise his head from his pillow and listen to the sound of the sedge whistling and the tame ducks in the decoy coughing their little alarm calls to each other. Bram slid his feet out of bed and curled his fingers into the fur of Piper's neck. The dog tautened every muscle. He wouldn't fail his master even in the dead of the night.

Bram inched open the door, its covering of turves muffling the sound of it sliding inwards across the rushes on the earth floor. The moon was behind a shred of cirrus cloud. Not letting Piper rush ahead of him, Bram pulled his coat from the nail at the back of the door and stepped out onto the springy surface of the fen. A few steps brought him to the edge of the decoy, its arms pointing out into the gusty dark. Still the nervous click of mallards' beaks under the netting. Bram knew these tame decoy birds would be gathered at the breast-wall near the mouth of the pipe, positioned to take advantage of the wind that blew from the direction of the North Sea, on a night like this. That same wind chilled his right side as he stood gazing out towards the huddle of birch trees at the far end of the decoy.

He felt Piper's hackles rise. The shape of one of the birches, itself a scrubby tree with thready branches not yet in full leaf, seemed more fattened and dense than usual against the opaque canvas of the moors beyond. The figure of a man was leaning against the trunk, looking straight in Bram's direction.

"Can I assist you, sir?" Bram called against the wind that caught at his breath as he waited for a reply. No reply came.

"Sir, are you lost on the fen? We can guide you back to the highway, my dog and I."

The stranger made no move. He held on to the tree's trunk as if it rooted him into the earth, knuckles standing out white where they emerged from a cloak that obscured his features and hid his identity.

"I am lost. But I know my way home."

Bram thought for a second he knew that voice, though the man sounded so weary, his words had an edge of defeat and misery to them. Bram stepped closer, but Piper hung back, whimpering softly.

"Where from, on a cold night through such country as this, sir?" Bram's spartan hut was the only dwelling for miles.

He wondered whether offering to share it as an overnight staging post to this traveller was the right thing to do, or reckless insanity? Omkering van schade. Reversal of ravage. Bram rarely cared whether others thought him strange. He knew they did. But now he wished he knew where he'd heard that voice before to help him decide.

"From the seas."

The stranger gestured in the direction of the coast. Hull harbour lay some thirty miles away, Liverpool eighty miles in the opposite direction. Bram couldn't tell from the shrugging motion of the man's arm under the cloak from which direction he had materialised or where he was heading.

"The highway to Doncaster's that way," Bram said, "though the canal runs more directly there if you prefer to follow its route on the tow-path?"

"Will you walk with me?" the figure stepped away from the tree and Bram saw the rectangular form of a box wrapped in canvas under the cover of the birches.

"I need somewhere to leave my chest until I can collect it in the morning. I've dragged it with me all the way from my ship. Nine days on the road and I can't take it further tonight."

"I can help you carry it, if I can lift it. There it may sink into the marsh, I fear," Bram moved towards the man and his burden. The traveller didn't resist but leaned back onto the flimsy tree trunk. He said nothing as Bram heaved the bundle into his arms. Bram saw through a gap in the canvas bag the object was a solid oak box with a stout brass handle at the top. As the moon emerged from the clouds, he saw the box was painted black and its covering was not a sack but a piece of tattered cloth, faded and torn but with traces of gold braid at one end and a deep red hue.

"If you've far to go, sir, I can keep your belongings in my hut or inside the wall of the pinfold, which is my charge, until you can send for it."

"I know you will," the stranger replied, but made no move to leave the spot where he stood swaying.

"Look, you can break your journey in my small bed tonight. I can sleep with my dog as a pillow, which I often do. The morning will give you a better chance of progress."

The stranger seemed unable or reluctant to say more. Bram saw his hands trembling and the sounds he still heard from his disquieted decoy ducks now mingled with the intermittent catch of sobs in the man's throat. Bram was alarmed but it wasn't his business to pry or interrogate. He had a mattress and a roof in good repair and that was all he needed to know for now. With the chest under one arm, he offered the other to the man to support him to the hut. The man seemed at first not to know what was expected of him, but then leaned heavily on Bram's arm and let himself be guided inside.

"Thank you, sir. You're a good man."

The man didn't speak again from under the blanket he'd pulled over his head as he curled up in the narrow bed. Bram lay on the rushes with Piper pressed against him, shivering. But he didn't sleep.

7. WIDDERSHINS

Thirza followed the maid into a large airy room where three other young women were sitting round a table. She thought the mouthwatering array of expensive sewing equipment spread on the cloth looked far more exotic than Emma's Coconut Madeleine.

"I am Dimberline," said an older woman, materialising from the far corner where her dress had merged with the wallpaper and who, Thirza decided, must have spent the morning sucking lemons. "Housekeeper." No further courtesies. "Now, do you embroider?"

"I can mend, when I need to, for the sails, or a hem or my brother's split seams," Thirza smiled but the housekeeper remained stony faced.

"You'll sew the latest designs for her Ladyship. Have you brought a sampler of your work?"

"This dress I made myself. I've been wearing this for years. See, this pocket I sewed in to hold a handkerchief or small items, as my mother taught me." The housekeeper seemed unimpressed and waved away the stitching Thirza was showing her.

"That may be adequate for everyday, but her Ladyship's requirements are most particular."

The eyes of the three needlewomen, all about her own

age or younger, followed Thirza as if she had a smudge on her cheek. One leaned forward as if to welcome her, but as Thirza took the spare chair beside her, she saw the girl was holding up her needle at her, just under the table where Mrs Dimberline couldn't see it.

"If you mean to take my job, I'll stab you, don't think I won't! I'm Libby. Elizabeth to you."

Thirza could see the view over the fen through the picture window. She wished she was out there, or anywhere but here, under scrutiny from hostile strangers. From the doorway came a gasp of delight.

"Those slippers! Perfect! Exquisite! If you sew like that, then you'll be in demand here. You must be the new girl, Thirza. My nephew Lucas tells me you are his cousin Darnell's niece. Let me see you properly. Show me your nails and fingers!"

Thirza jumped to her feet again, almost tripping over in her ill-fitting footwear. Lady Laura gave her a look of frank appraisal, lifting her chin and inspecting her hands, squinting through the pince-nez attached to her waist by a thin gold chain.

"Let me look closer! Dimberline, lift the slippers to the light!"

The housekeeper pulled the slippers from Thirza's feet and left her standing, barefoot, flustered and shamed at being completely unprepared for this encounter with an aristocratic lady, who seemed to count as a distant relative.

Thirza muttered her thanks, she wasn't sure what for. She was thankful, at least, that Lady Laura seemed pleased to see her, and in raptures over the wretched slippers.

"Exquisite little pantoufles! Do you see this needlework? Rebecca? Kate? Elizabeth? A new standard is being set which I expect you will all be anxious to follow!"

Thirza saw Libby pulling a face behind her mistress's back. She felt manoeuvred into the position of a Cinderella and, much worse, a fraud.

"If you please, your Ladyship, the slippers aren't my own. Nor the needlework on them."

"Not your slippers? Not your work?" Lady Laura rounded on Thirza, snatching the pince-nez off her nose and peering into Thirza's face like a startled pigeon.

"The slippers are my aunt Emma's."

"Such fine work," Lady Laura stroked her finger over the delicate stitching and held them up at the window to enjoy the colours.

"But I don't know if my aunt embroidered them, I'm afraid," Thirza began to hope her Ladyship might decide she wasn't dressmaker material after all and that there might have been a misunderstanding at the highest level. She could escape, then, without any repercussions.

"Anyway," Lady Laura turned to Dimberline, "hand Thirza my old ball-gown. The one Elizabeth worked in that running stitch. It needs a pretty stitching at the hem."

The housekeeper handed Thirza the heavy dress and indicated the huge work-box in the middle of the table. Out of it spilled a rainbow of yarns and threads of every kind. Plain cotton and canvas were more often over Thirza's knees at sewing time.

"Do what you think best with the hemline, my dear, and I will return before luncheon to see how you have fared. I'll leave you with my girls and Mrs Dimberline will be close at hand to see that you have everything you need. I love to wear spring colours at this time of year."

"Primrose and crocus, then," Thirza was adjusting to the prospect of an hour or two relaxing with needle and thread. The dress was in perfect repair, not patched or faded, unlike most of Thirza's own clothes. Only her Sunday best dress shone with this vividness.

As soon as Lady Laura left them to their sewing, the hubbub began from Thirza's companions. She began to sew quickly, so as not to fall behind the more experienced workers.

Rebecca, who acted as if she was senior to the rest, leaned away from the table to whisper behind her hand to Kate, a tall, pale woman with hair like carded wool of a gingery blond shade.

"Never made the slippers!"

Thirza caught the sniggering from Kate and then again from Rebecca, louder this time.

"Were you born in the village, Thirza?"

"No, I was born on the river. On our keel, half way between Doncaster and Stainforth, while my father was sailing to Hull with a cargo of coal."

There was a silence. None of the women seemed inclined to pursue this line of conversation by revealing their own origins.

Thirza knotted the thread so the silk wouldn't pucker or the stitches run.

"Are you village lasses?"

"What if we are? Better village lasses than water gypsies!"

Thirza felt stung. She'd done nothing to invite such contempt. She hadn't asked to come here, or wanted to. She refused to say so, though. She must make the best of it and win the others round when they saw she was no slacker.

Libby suddenly nudged Rebecca.

"Now, now, Becky. That's no way to speak to her Ladyship's nephew's cousin's niece."

"Lapdog!" Thirza heard Kate mutter under her breath. "Lick lick lick!" Kate winked. Winking didn't come easily to her, Thirza noticed. It made her freckled cheeks twitch and her colourless lashes water with the effort.

"I suppose your lardy-dardy connections got you the position here?" snapped Rebecca, biting off the thread with a vicious snarl, "I suppose they thought it'd keep you from other mischief?"

"Tinkering!" Kate doubled up with laughter at this and elbowed Rebecca in the ribs so she began sniggering too. The memory of the gang of boys on the bridge filled Thirza's heart with dread. Her face burned. Could they be in league with her tormentors? How could they know her? Their prejudices seemed to give them the right to judge and mock her.

She tried to concentrate on her sewing. She chose a

shade of apple-green to contrast with the egg-yolk yellow she'd worked into curling lines around the hem.

"I've no idea who wanted me to come here. I didn't want to, you know. I'm needed on the keel. I'm supposed to be helping at the windmill."

"They keep cats to chase away rats, in a windmill. Oh! And here you are!" Rebecca stabbed her needle triumphantly into the silk as the others roared with laughter.

Dimberline reappeared as the noise level rose.

"Giggling and gostering, indeed! Really! The seamstresses aren't accustomed to rowdy ways, Thirza. Please learn to modulate your voice and have a little decorum as young ladies in this household!"

Thirza bit her tongue. She wouldn't plead her case like a mardy child.

"Sorry, Mrs Dimberline. Thirza tells such stories, she has us all in tucks, doesn't she, girls?" Libby spoke slyly, with a sidelong glance at Rebecca. Rebecca elbowed Kate in the ribs and the younger woman let out a shriek. Thirza hoped they were turning on themselves and would soon tire of baiting her.

"Mrs Dimberline! Mrs Dimberline!" squealed Kate, pointing at Thirza.

"Whatever's the matter, Kate?" Dimberline followed the direction of Kate's needle.

"She's sewing widdershins! Oh, look how she sews all the wrong way round! Widdershins, like a witch!"

Kate paused for effect and tried a tentative sob to add to the drama and to convince the housekeeper of her sincere shock. They all knew how superstitious Dimberline was. She wouldn't allow all sorts of things in the house, no pictures of birds, no shoes on the table and a thousand more rules to ward off evil. The women believed some of these themselves, taught from the cradle to cover all bases with the Almighty and the unseen forces that seemed to drive the random follies of the universe.

"My goodness! Why do you hold the dress that way, girl? Your left hand should support the material, so..."

Dimberline took the dress from Thirza's lap and turned it upside down, "...and your right hand, your right hand, mind, should always hold the needle. Like this..."

Thirza found her hands being squeezed this way and that, the needle forced between the fingers of her right hand, where it felt like something alien and clumsy to her.

"She sewed it widdershins, Mrs Dimberline, witching-ways!" Rebecca reminded everyone, as if Mrs Dimberline's demonstration of the correct way risked letting Thirza off the hook.

"Hush, now. She's still learning our ways." Dimberline withdrew her hands, watching Thirza critically. It didn't seem to occur to her that the perceived fault couldn't instantly be corrected at will after twenty one years of life.

Thirza struggled to control the needle. Now the hem seemed to be all at odds with her, bunched up where before it was smooth. The work ran right to left now. Thirza tried to arch her arm to accommodate the bulk of the material as she reinserted the tip of the needle. Made clumsy by the changed angles and directions, Thirza pricked her thumb and a drop of blood spread a scarlet stain across the delicate lemon silk.

"Look what she's doing now, Mrs D! She's bleeding all over her Ladyship's lovely ball-gown!"

"Watch what you're at, for pity's sake!" Dimberline was beside herself. "Gracious me! The other hand! The other way! Not like that! You'll have to unpick all those stitches!"

"Widdershins stitches!" Kate shouted.

"Witch's stitches!" added Rebecca, sitting up straighter to give herself an air of concerned gravity.

Dimberline sat down. She was going nowhere while such nonsense was afoot. Whenever Thirza's tongue poked out from the corner of her mouth as she concentrated hard on mastering the awkward new rule of the right hand, the others snorted with derision. Frequent mistakes and slacker stitches were soon seized on by her assembled critics.

"Please, Mrs Dimberline," Thirza begged, when hours seemed to have passed under this judgemental scrutiny, "if I can sew like before, I know I can learn very well. This doesn't feel right to me. My hands won't do what I tell them!"

"Her Ladyship is most fastidious!" Dimberline clapped her hand to her forehead and rolled her eyes. "She won't have disharmony among her staff. The sewing room must be a place of industry and peace. The work has been quite spoiled today, since your arrival. Elbows clash when such practices are tolerated. Techniques are compromised, standards lowered."

"I trust not!" Lady Laura had slipped in unnoticed and stood watching the little group silhouetted against the light from the window.

Dimberline faced her employer.

"Your Ladyship, there's nothing to trouble you. Thirza is merely learning to adapt to the ways of civilised society. There has been a little awkwardness from her, but nothing with which we cannot deal!"

"Very well," Lady Laura looked at Thirza, sitting uncomfortably to make the needle move in the opposite way from what came naturally to her. Now everyone was staring, trying to make her somebody she decidedly wasn't. The lump in her throat grew harder to swallow, but she kept her head down and struggled on. She wouldn't let them see they'd hurt her.

"Also, an unfortunate incident with your ball-gown, my lady. Thirza has yet to learn dexterity with the thimble."

Lady Laura knew something was wrong, but was reluctant to intervene and upset the worthy Dimberline.

"You may all take a break for half an hour. Everything will resolve itself when eyes are rested and fingers relaxed. Later, I'll inspect all the sewing from today and we will see about your future with us here, Thirza."

Thirza hung back trying to explain to Dimberline that left-handedness was second nature, not defiance or witchcraft.

"It may be second nature to you," Dimberline warned, "but your first, best nature should be obedience and conformity to what is most correct."

This was said in front of the others. Thirza knew they

took these words as a license to torment her for everything that was different about her. Right-handed is right. Right-handed is right. She tried to learn it like a fact, but inside she felt herself growing so indignant at the injustice and ignorance of it, she was afraid to speak further in case she said something she'd live to regret.

When the others were deep in conversation with their backs turned and Dimberline had disappeared, perhaps to harangue the kitchen maids for a little variety, Thirza thought, she hurried out into the hallway. She had to get away before some arrangement was made from which she couldn't escape. She'd let herself be trapped at Kitson's Mill for the sake of her family, but to be trapped here at Foljambe Hall was a sacrifice too far.

Thirza thought she heard Dimberline's footsteps returning. In panic, she grabbed what she thought must be the front door knob and forced her way through the heavy door, slamming it behind her much more loudly than she'd intended.

"What? What? I say! I say!" Lucas Charlesworth spun round as if he'd been caught in the privy with no rags. Thirza was standing not outside, but in a huge circular room with a domed ceiling and a distinct echo. Before she could apologise for bursting in, the lights were extinguished and she could see nothing at all for the hands, acrid with chemicals and smoke, clamped firmly over her mouth and eyes.

8. IN THE DARK

"Gently! Gently!"

The hands slid down over the contours of her corset in the dark, a rough caress pulling her off balance. Thirza found herself being jerked backwards, unable to get a purchase on the shiny tiles with Emma's smooth-soled slippers. Someone lifted her off her feet, snorting with laughter at her predicament.

She stopped herself kicking backwards to escape or punish her captor, aware he sounded suspiciously like Darnell. The acoustics seemed to change as she was hustled into what she guessed was an anteroom to the bigger chamber. Someone struck a match and lit a candle. She looked towards the flame and straight into the pale blue eyes of Lucas Charlesworth. Darnell stood beside him, doubled up with laughter.

"Thirza! Forgive us! You made us jump like two guilty schoolboys, eh, Lucas?"

"Oh, quite!" Lucas wore a bewildered look that Thirza thought was perhaps something of a fixture on his features. The two men stepped away from Thirza like a matched pair of clockwork automata.

"Lord love me! Miss Holberry! You gave us a start!" Thirza half expected Lucas to continue echoing as he had in the reverberating chamber. "Have you had good larks with my aunt Laura?"

Darnell nodded at Lucas and stepped back into the first room, turning up the gaslight and leaving the door between them only just ajar.

"I don't think I'm cut out to be a seamstress, though I did my best," Thirza found herself looking over Lucas's shoulder at the gas-lit room behind him where Darnell was locking cabinets and clearing away rolls of paper. She couldn't see the room fully now, but she'd seen enough, like a photograph developed on the back of her eye.

The floor fell away in a series of concentric wooden steps surfaced with tiles, like a lecture theatre or auditorium. The walls were panelled in alternate boards of oak and some richer looking wood, perhaps rosewood. A huge flame mahogany table stood in the middle. Maps, diagrams and scribbled calculations were everywhere, on squares of yellow paper, on tiny glass screens, etched with what looked to Thirza like coal tar.

Thirza glimpsed, in those initial shocking seconds when she entered, in pools of light thrown by hissing mantles mounted around the walls, jars of liquids glowing amber, lime and pink like the Aurora she'd seen burning along the northern horizon, specimens pinned to cards, diagrams of devices beyond all imagination, even for a dreamer like Thirza. She wasn't sure if she'd imagined some of these.

What she recognised was the scroll Darnell seemed at pains to roll up tight. On the thick paper, furled up inch by inch out of her sight, like Chinese lantern patterns on a shadowy wall, Thirza recalled, for ever after, the ghost-image etched in her brain, of the sweeps of a windmill, with wings like a bird, the cap angled horizontally like a huge golden bullet tipped with a lethal spike.

"It's unconscionably early for you to be stirring your ladylike stumps to leave us," Lucas was saying wistfully to her as Darnell stepped back in to join them.

"All our boring business packed away," Darnell said, rubbing his hands and taking Thirza's hand to lead her back through their den, as she thought it must be, to the hallway.

Lucas smiled his boyish smile and took her other hand so Thirza was obliged to walk between them down and then up the other side of the curious ring of steps. She longed to linger and devour all the information, touch the mysterious glasses full of strange, perhaps delicious possets. The Big House must have some priceless old receipts for conserves and remedies passed down through the generations, she mused. Jack and Dinah had brought her up better than to ask all the questions that crowded her mind at the sight of these clandestine sweetmeats, if such they were.

"You have caught us, dear Thirza, at our diurnal studies," said Darnell. He seemed to be addressing his comments as much to Lucas as to his niece.

"Ah, yes, cousin Darnell, indeed!" Lucas brightened, as if he'd been reminded in the nick of time not to step on a spring-loaded trap.

"I can't stay here any longer, Uncle," Thirza blurted out, "I'm sorry to seem ungrateful, I know I must seem so, but I can't. I'm needed at the mill, now, and later the keel. I haven't the ways of a lady's seamstress. To be cooped up here..."

"Cooped?" Darnell hooted the word like a Tawny Owl hooting to its mate across a barnyard.

"You're 'cooped up' as you call it, by a life of promise and, may I say, privilege, here?" Thirza found it hard to judge his mood.

"I will go back, Uncle, whether you drive me or not!" Thirza wasn't about to let her resolve waver.

The voice of Dimberline in the hallway outside made all three of them spin around.

"Master Lucas, is that you? Begging your pardon, but the keelgirl Mr Salkeld sent here has, begging your indulgence, run off somewhere and hiddied herself!"

A look of mischief crossed both men's faces. Darnell put his finger to his lips and his half-amused gaze made Thirza think twice about announcing their whereabouts.

Lucas did the talking for them all.

"Good Mrs Dimberline, you know I'm never to be disturbed at my important work in here. I know nothing of the girl's plans or pinksquizzery!"

"Begging your obligation, Master Lucas." The sound of Dimberline scuttling away in confusion was audible above Darnell's snigger.

"While you lock up here, Lucas, I find I must drive Miss Thirza home." Darnell's manner was of somebody in charge of what happened next and of how each happening was to be interpreted. Thirza saw Lucas's eyes widen. He obviously hadn't been about to end the meeting at this point, but like a puppet on wires, he moved round the room, turning out the gas and cloaking all the intriguing items Thirza thought she had seen in darkness, a disorienting mass of dark shapes.

Darnell's arm snaked its way round her back, his fingers catching at her waist as he steered her back towards the balcony and steps at the rear of the Hall, so as to avoid bumping into the others again, for which she felt warmly grateful.

As they came round the corner of the house, Thirza was relieved to see Darnell's trap already waiting. Perhaps he'd known she'd try to escape? Perhaps he always had transport waiting to whisk him away from his intriguing business? Darnell climbed up and took the reins without a word.

"Uncle, forgive me. Please give Aunt Emma her slippers back," Thirza removed them and placed them on the footboard. "Tell her it was so kind of her, but I shan't be needing them again."

Darnell cleared his throat, placed his hand on the seat and leaned over to look into Thirza's face with an expression she couldn't interpret, though she found herself shuddering from a sudden inner chill.

"Never mind the slippers. A woman's ankle breathes," he seemed to lean into the word with a dozen meanings, "freed from fancy footwear. Jump up and sit by me."

Thirza shivered. She thought of her bed in the

windmill. Tomorrow she'd work out how to extricate herself from this stupid situation. Once this branch of her family knew her better, perhaps they'd accept her for who she really was and not throw suffocating expectations over her head like a mesh. She had to fight her way out of that net right now and find out what was really going on here.

Darnell was watching her out of the corner of his eye.

"I confess it was I who suggested you come here, from concern for your well-being. I know you're unsettled, that you pine for hours in the windmill's cap. I have plans for the mill, you see. New equipment. Equipment is dangerous. Innovation is needed. You must see that, a bright girl like you?"

When the trap emerged out of the wide gateway at the end of the Hall driveway, Darnell veered to the right.

"This isn't the way to the windmill!"

The trap was picking up speed beyond the turning to Carrdyke. The whole fenland was a smudged miasma of indistinct shapes to Thirza and the horizon seemed as far away as the Land of Prester John. The ground was haring by at breakneck speed in jerks and judders below her.

"I just want to go back!" Why couldn't she make people take her seriously?

Darnell leaned over to stop her, but he was too late. She thought of her fearless jumps from keel to shore and wharf to deck and launched herself out low with a roll and no cry. The whirling wayside crumpled to a halt around her. She lay for a second, two, three, hearing the creak of the trap wheels growing softer and further off. Her knee was skinned with the fall and studded with gravel. Then she was up and running for her life in the opposite direction.

Darnell had driven her up to the front door of Foljambe Hall, decked out in the borrowed finery of her aunt's slippers, obliged to be patronised by rich strangers, judged as a worthless widdershins water gypsy. Now she was leaving in disgrace with every racing step. She could hear Aunt Emma's strident voice in her head already.

"So unladylike, Theresa! What were you thinking?

How could you? Running off like an ungrateful urchin!"

"I'm no lady!" she wanted to shout back over her shoulder. Not if this false life was what it cost to be one. She vaulted over a ditch and found herself on the lawn at the edge of the estate. It felt like a carpet to her bare feet. On and on she ran and out through the trees that guarded the back of the hall from the open moors. She pumped her legs and arms, lifting her skirts clear of the grass, the icy evening dew slippery under her bare feet as she flew along. Her knee was smarting but she couldn't slow her pace as she dodged out of the trees and onto the open fen.

The squelch under her feet reminded her of the slippers she'd given back. She thought of her own stout shoes, clog-like and ideal for life like she loved to live it, safe on ladders, firm on pebbly banks and slippery quay-sides, easily scraped from mud. How she needed them now! The springy turf was gentler on her feet but now she was shuddering with cold and it was getting dark. Her feet were soaked and already her soles were bleeding from the twigs and pebbles sticking into them. There were so few landmarks here. She glanced back. Her uncle was nowhere in sight.

Thirza slowed to a walk. She couldn't go back to the windmill today. She knew the road from Foljambe Hall entered the village at the point where the pinfold stood on the isolated track out to the moors. Had she travelled that far yet? The road should be on her right with the turning into the village, but now there were clouds over the moon and the tussocks of marshy grass under her feet were blown with shadows as she stumbled forward, trying to get her bearings. Sunrise was many hours away.

Thirza tried to picture her grandmother's face if she turned up, barefoot and bedraggled at dawn. Kezzie was used to Thirza disappearing to sleep up on the dust floor most nights, though Granddad Thomas had covered for her so kindly. How had Darnell guessed? Had they told him? They all cared about her and she was acting gracelessly.

Thirza rubbed her feet and licked her hands, smudging away the blood that still seeped from the crusted wound on her knee. She didn't care how she looked, but knew others would. If she could get her own shoes from Carrdyke, she could slip away down to the canal and wait for her father to come along and take her back on board.

Remembering the day he left her ashore suddenly made her stand and sob in the middle of the fen. The wind took the sound of her sobs and brought other sounds to her ears. The energy and drive were suddenly going out of her. I must stay strong, she told herself, scrubbing away her tears. She sank down on the spongy peat turf. It felt softer than a feather mattress to her exhausted limbs.

She didn't intend to do more than rest for a moment, but when she came to herself, she realised she must have slept for hours. She found herself holding the clockwork toy bird inside her pocket for comfort. She needed the darkness to hide her until she could make it to the canal. From there she could see any keels as they came along. What if 'Thistle' wasn't coming this way? She'd seen other keels she recognised but not theirs, on the stretch of canal that passed near the Nab. Only a few times had 'Thistle' sailed into view, her topsail flapping like a proud Viking longship.

What if Uncle Darnell arrives at the windmill before me? Her mind tried to make sense of all she'd seen at the Hall and the things she'd heard, whispered words between Darnell and Lucas. Time might be running out for her to enjoy her favourite hiding place at the windmill.

If I don't tell my own story, she thought, someone else will tell it and tell it all wrong! She'd never felt so alone. Yet the marshy hinterland here neither rushed her away nor reminded her she was now a landlocked castaway.

She lay still again for a moment, hearing her own heart beating against the turf. High above, she heard an unearthly sound that made her hold her breath. A long trilling note rang out through the darkness, a chirring rattle, a ratcheting cry like nothing she recognised. It continued longer than a human could sustain its breath, then changed to a higher note and went on without pausing. Thirza gathered her skirts and began to run again, forgetting the throbbing in her knee, the thumping in her temples and her plans to head for the canal. Which way was the canal anyway? The dark before the dawn was confusing.

Thirza saw the glow of the land to the east, the Belt of Venus shimmering in yellows and pinks where the early spring sun was preparing to break away from the curve of the earth. She saw the line of the cart track converging with her route ahead.

She kept the wall on her right hand side, steadying herself there as she stopped to look back along the road. Nobody was stirring. Sometimes villagers would venture out onto the moors to cut a turf of peat for their winter fires, but now spring was coming, the place seemed deserted.

Thirza changed her plans as she recognised where she was. Ahead lay the pinfold on the easternmost edge of the village. She'd been skirting along the perimeter of the moor, moving east when she imagined she was running north-east towards the open country. Making slower progress than before, tucking her body close to the stone wall so she wouldn't be seen from far off, she saw two shapes ahead and ducked down behind the wall. She heard two men talking in the road. She tried to steady her breath. Heart pounding, she tried to make out whether one of them was Darnell. She couldn't risk being seen so close to the village.

Thirza pulled herself up to the top of the wall at the back of the pinfold and dropped down inside where a stray cow was cropping the long grass and a brace of piglets was snuffling up beech-mast scattered there for their benefit. She slid down the mossy inner wall into a sitting position and waited for the men to move on. As soon as they moved away from the fold, she could come out and make her way down to the water and follow it onwards, to Hull if she had to. Someone there would know where 'Thistle' was working and she could go and persuade her father what a horrible mistake it had been to leave her here.

As she listened to the male voices, she saw a small black trunk just inside the pinfold gate, draped in a red and gold wrapper, like part of a flag or cloak. She crawled closer.

"I think I can walk home from here, friend. I owe you a debt of kindness."

"I'll keep it safe for you, sir. Return for it when you will."

Thirza lifted the flap of cloth from the trunk and gazed down on the scratched black paint. She made out initials painted in gold and scarlet on the broken hasp:

J.T.K.

9. HOMECOMING

Thirza walked her fingers round the lettering. All ideas of escape left her head. One of the figures was no stranger.

"Uncle Jem!"

The two men were walking away towards the village with their backs towards her.

"Uncle Jem! Wait!"

She expected he'd turn and run to her, amazed to see his young niece all grown up. Jem did turn. He looked towards the pinfold. He stared through her as if he didn't see her at all.

"Lance Corporal Jeremy Kitson," he said, then, frowning as if puzzled at his own words, "Yes, I am he."

Thirza moved forward to clamber over the wall but the taller man who stood beside Jem unlatched the gate and started to help her through. She felt the whoosh of his staff across her naked feet. He was blocking her way now, parting the grasses she was about to step through and signalling her with a finger to be quiet.

She was about to tell him he was being both forward and rude when she saw what he'd seen first: the zigzagging diamonds along the body of an adder. It lay curled in the grass, in the shadow of the trunk, not an inch from her bare toes.

"Stand still as a stock," Bram whispered, "but don't be afraid. Stock still!" In a flash of the staff he lifted the adder over the back wall of the pinfold, out towards its home on the moorland. Bram tipped his hat with a murmured apology. He noticed Thirza favouring the leg that had crunched into the gravel during her flight. He was impressed she lost none of her colour when the snake appeared.

"Your knee's hurting. I can bind it for you," he said. He hoped she wouldn't be offended. He couldn't see her knee at all under her skirts. He withdrew to a polite distance, standing quietly with his staff by the side of the road.

"Thank you, sir. You've come to my rescue, I think, for a second time!" This was her stilt-man! But his manner gave nothing away. She looked from him to her uncle. Jem was watching them as if he was looking at a diorama at a fairground. His puzzled expression hovered like a cloud between them. Thirza laughed to break the spell.

"Uncle Jem, don't you know me? I'm Thirza, Dinah's girl!"

"Our Dinah?" Jem's face lit up. He seemed to be searching for the words. "But she's dead. My sister Dinah's dead!"

Thirza saw tears spring into Jem's eyes as she went to hug him. While she was still hanging round his neck in the middle of the lane, she heard hoof beats and the rattle of wheels in the direction from which she'd fled.

"Pinder, I see you've found another stray in your fold. Has she paid you the fee to go free?"

"She set herself free, sir," said Bram. Thirza couldn't meet Darnell's gaze. His manner now seemed jocular. She wondered if she'd dreamed the past day.

The sun inched higher and knots of villagers passed by on their way to work in the fields. Some nodded respectfully to Darnell, others gawped at the half-familiar figure with the haunted, hollow eyes. Jem looked frail and unshaven, cocooned in his cloak. When the wind blew, the cloak rose and parted, revealing flashes of a crimson tunic and brass buttons on a uniform. Whenever this happened,

Jem pulled the cloak back together around him, as if he didn't care for anyone to see his colours. From his altered face, Thirza wondered if she herself would have known him from a distance, without his initials on the army chest to give her a clue.

"I'll walk home, now, I think, from here," Jem patted Thirza's hand like a polite acquaintance and turned away towards the village.

"Your parents hoped to have bunting draped across the sails for your homecoming, dear sir," said Darnell, "We had no news that your regiment was returning."

Thirza saw Darnell looking at his brother-in-law as if he'd seen a revenant, though his greeting sounded warm. But Jem was already walking away. He didn't seem to have heard Darnell's words and didn't turn back. Thirza caught him up.

"Uncle, I'll walk with you. Let me take your arm. We can walk together."

Bram stepped back as Darnell drove the pony forwards, almost knocking him over.

"Wait! Better still," Darnell jumped down in front of Jem and Thirza, "let me offer my pony for the conquering hero's homecoming charge! I can unhitch the trap, if it suits you better to ride?"

Thirza was relieved that seeing Jem had put the fiasco of her short time at Foljambe Hall temporarily out of Darnell's mind. Jem's expression didn't change, though Thirza felt his grasp on her arm tighten.

"Keep your horse, sir. I'll walk back the length of the valley."

"Hardly a valley, but suit yourself. You must do as you please, but at least let our niece ride with me," Darnell smiled at Thirza, indicating the step with a hand to help her up.

"I'll walk with Uncle Jem, if he wishes to walk, thank you, Uncle Darnell."

Thirza saw Darnell's smile fade. She felt awkward and churlish when he was trying to put her ingratitude behind him. But Jem's needs were more important today.

"At least let me ride ahead and tell your dear papa and mama to prepare the way for you. They'll get such a shock to see you, it might strike them dumb!"

Jem stopped in the middle of the road, disoriented, as if the decision to turn left or right was completely beyond him. Exhaustion was overcoming him in visible waves, the little colour he had drained from his cheeks. Thirza helped Darnell encourage him at last up into the trap.

"Not far now, Uncle! Almost home again. You can already see the sails turning!"

At the sight of the sturdy young horse in front of him, Jem seemed to take heart and come back to himself.

"Your belongings, sir," said Bram, lifting the heavy chest out of the pinfold. Darnell took it from Bram's arms, holding it up for Jem to see as he placed it behind him.

"Now you can arrive home all in one piece," Darnell said. "Nothing more to see, here, Dutchy," he called back over his shoulder. Thirza determined to return to thank her stilt-man properly when Jem was settled back at the windmill.

There was not much conversation on the way back. Darnell walked at the pony's head like a carman, occasionally turning to make sure his passengers were comfortable. Jem stared ahead until the trap stopped under the sails. Kezzie could be seen, fussing with a handbill Grace was passing to her, her back turned towards them in the doorway of Mill Cottage.

"Nonsense! Take this back where you found it, Grace. New mill? How can there be a new mill, when the old one isn't broken? Surely never but maybe. Gossip and rumour!"

Grace saw them first, over her mistress's shoulder.

"Look, ma'am!" she shouted, pointing.

"See the conquering hero comes!" Darnell announced as the old lady turned to face the trap.

Thirza watched her grandmother transformed in a moment from tired old lady into whirling pillar of ecstatic joy. Her little screams of incredulous rejoicing brought Thomas, Francis and several villagers running to witness the scene.

Kezzie was so shocked, the little party was unable to make any progress from the trap into the cottage for some time, as embraces and celebrations rooted them to the spot. Thomas and Darnell almost had to carry Kezzie back into the cottage to sit down. She held Jem's face in her hands, looking into his eyes, then up to heaven, then back into his eyes before kissing him in floods of tears. She clung to him as if to lose him again would be the end of her world. Then she ran out into the mill yard again, crying and shaking her apron, before dashing back into the cottage to squeeze her son's cheeks, exclaiming over and over, "My Jem! You've come home! My hero! My boy!"

Jem stood silent, devoid of all excitement. When Thomas encouraged him to sit in the fireside chair, he complied, still mute, except for moments when he seemed to shake himself into life, answering questions from his mother in monosyllables, all colourless and formal, as if he'd been to the bank in Doncaster, not on a military campaign in the Dardanelles.

"When did you disembark?" Kezzie asked, for the thousandth time.

"Recently, I think," Jem assured her.

"Did you travel with your brigade?" she pressed him.

"All alone," he sounded uncertain.

Kezzie beamed round at her family whenever he spoke, sighing and wiping her eyes, before returning to her questions, some the same, some phrased slightly differently.

"Oh, Jem, did you do proudly for Lord Cardigan?"

"Well, I think." Jem watched her lips for a clue as to what answer might please her or quieten her.

"Did they hurt you, my darling boy?"

Thirza saw the look. She knelt down between mother and son and took Kezzie's hands in hers.

"Grandma, shall we let Uncle Jem rest for a while? He's walked all the way from his ship, I suppose. He must be horribly tired."

"Make up the bed for Master Jeremy," Kezzie was

suddenly all action. "Go on, Grace, the best bed."

"Already made up, ma'am. Miss Thirza's bed that she hardly ever sleeps on."

Thirza looked at Grace pleadingly. Not now! There'd be time to explain her own return. Now Jem was here at last, it was his moment.

"Good, good," Kezzie sounded as if Thirza's disappearing acts were the last thing on her mind. For her, Jem's return made everything right again in her simple world, where all things troublesome were polished and folded away with the linen.

"I can sleep in the windmill, Grandma, or in the cock loft. Uncle Jem can sleep in his old bed again."

"How would you manage in the mill, our Thirza?" asked Thomas, his good eye winking with mischief. He was relieved to see his granddaughter home. He alone had thought her departure for Foljambe Hall ill-advised and too hastily arranged, when he learned she'd gone with Darnell with no date of return.

"I'll manage, Granddad," Thirza gave him a conspirator's lob-sided grin.

Jem let himself be cosseted and put to bed without argument. Once he was tucked up, staring at the ceiling, Kezzie came reluctantly back downstairs. Darnell helped her down the last few treads and spoke to her so solicitously, she seemed almost prepared to relax.

"Dear Mama, when Jem's quite recovered, I know my Emma will be eager to see her brother again. Leave it all to me. You've had too much excitement. Let me help. Call on me at any time."

Thomas kissed his wife on the head and slipped away back to his work.

"Did Thirza do well with Lady Laura?" Kezzie asked, enjoying her son-in-law's relaxation of his usual authoritative tone. Darnell watched Thirza's face.

"She's certainly made quite an impression up at the Hall."

Thirza knew her uncle's words were protecting her,

for this moment, from the shame he could have revealed to her anxious grandmother. She couldn't bear the idea of a return to the loathed atmosphere of criticism and ridicule of which her grandparents were unaware.

"That's good of you, Darnell. You and Emma have been so very kind to introduce her into such a good position."

"Without my clever cousin Lucas, I'd have been powerless to help. I think Thirza has made quite an impact on Squire Charlesworth."

Thirza couldn't imagine Darnell powerless in any situation, or how she could have made any positive impression on Lucas, in the awkward moments they'd been in each other's company.

Thirza brooded on the things Darnell was holding back from Kezzie: the fiasco of the slippers, the bloodstained ball gown, her aborted escape, her unwelcome intrusion into that strange laboratory full of steam and clockwork, maps and diagrams, magical and mysterious, not to mention her flying leap from the trap and night on the fen.

She owed Darnell a favour for his discretion today. Had somebody at the Hall, the formidable Dimberline, Libby, Rebecca, Kate or Lady Laura herself, told Darnell the cruel jibes and accusations she'd suffered in the short time she had endured there? What exactly did Darnell know? Would he take her part or use it to buy her silence?

Darnell took his leave of Kezzie and pulled Thirza gently outside with him, where the old woman could not catch his drift.

"I put in a word in your defence with Lady Laura," he explained, "and made everything right. Her Ladyship is willing to give you another chance with the bobbins and thimbles! I quite understand your reluctance, but as I said, we can't have you mooning about the mill with those lovely locks. We have to look to the future now," he ran a strand of Thirza's long hair through his fingers, "Lucas said you were a girl with spirit and I didn't contradict him."

"I won't come back with you," Thirza was amazed at the resolve in her own voice. "With Uncle Jem home and so weak, I'm needed here all the more. Until I return to the keel."

"The keel? That will never be, I fear, sweet lass!" Darnell's tone had mellowed. Thirza hesitated to risk alienating him by her defiance. He'd saved her neck here and at the Hall. He could so easily force her to comply by all he knew of her failures.

"I can't be who I'm not."

Darnell smiled, Thirza thought, with a look of pity.

"Well, we shall see. I hope Lucas and I will not regret taking your part. My dear girl, look to your future and none of this foolishness."

"I'll occupy myself, Uncle. I won't get in your way, or anyone else's," Thirza spoke sincerely and with unshakeable resolve.

In the end, Darnell had no choice but to leave without her, with a last soft word of confidential advice.

"Look after your precious uncle Jeremy. This infernal dusty old mill is an onerous burden on a young man's shoulders, I dare say."

A few days later, Kezzie was supervising Grace in the kitchen while Jem rested in his room, as he had since his arrival. Thirza walked round the farmyard, gathering the eggs from the coop she planned to start selling in the village. Teasels by the hedge, swarming with goldfinches, caught her eye. She gathered them all in a straw punnet, eggs in one side, teasels in the other. Until Jem regained his strength and could play his part at the mill alongside his father, she'd do her level best to earn money for the upkeep of this landlocked keel. Nobody, from Darnell to the Charlesworths themselves, knew better than her what she could achieve and what was needful.

"What are you up to, our Thirza?" Her grandfather had come out to see to the pigs.

"Selling, Granddad. You need new sails, new paint, and I've got a perfect plan to help you."

Thomas chuckled.

"You're so like your mother, my lass. Always so sure

you're right and a blessing to us all while we can keep you here!"

Before she set out for her new venture, Thirza took the tray up to Jem's room that Kezzie had prepared with toast and crab apple jam, honey tea and a pot of calf's foot jelly to tempt the invalid's appetite. When she first opened the door, she couldn't see Jem, just a pile of rumpled bedclothes where he usually lay curled up. She pushed the door closed behind her with her foot and called softly.

"Uncle Jem, are you awake?"

No answer.

"Uncle Jem, I'll leave the tray by the bed, I know you'll enjoy it later on," Thirza moved aside the little case with the Cherry Picker emblem on its lid and set the tray on the nightstand.

"You don't know. You don't know what I've done."

Thirza pulled back the blankets but realised the voice had come from under the bed, not in it. She went down on her knees and peered into the darkness. She lifted the corner of the counterpane hanging between them and was alarmed by the look of sheer terror in her uncle's eyes. Between his fingers, making flickers of light in the gloom as his hands were shaking so violently, was a cut-throat razor.

10. FRESH HORIZONS

Thirza's heart was hammering, keeping time through the hours it seemed to take to reassure Jem it was safe to let her take the blade from him.

"Nobody can hurt you here," Thirza stroked her uncle's hair, "the war's far away, across the sea. You're safe home now."

"They say I must never go back," Jem emerged and showed Thirza a paper from the army medical officer, saying Lance Corporal Kitson was discharged from the Hussars on medical grounds.

"Good," Thirza put the certificate back in its place in the open lid of the army chest. "You can take your time to rest and recover." She covered him up snug again and put the tray across his knees.

"You don't know what I've done. It's all my fault."

Thirza wondered if all soldiers blamed themselves for the terrible things that had happened. Perhaps only time could heal such wounds.

"He died in front of my eyes!" Jem seemed so distressed, "Thirza, it was my fault he died!"

"I'm sure you're wrong. You wouldn't hurt a fly! It's war that's wrong. Generals make mistakes. We read about it in the paper. It was a horrible blunder."

"Not that! Matty! I'm so sorry!" Thirza managed to stop the tray sliding off the bed as Jem curled his body into the foetal position. She couldn't get another word out of him. Leaving the tray on the bedside table and shutting the razor securely back in the chest, Thirza slipped downstairs, leaving the door open, so they could hear any cry for help and Jem could hear the comforting household noises from below.

She didn't tell Kezzie what had happened but waved to her in the yard where she was pegging out clothes, keeping busy, busy. Thirza popped her head in at the windmill and climbed up to the meal floor where Thomas was busy too.

"Granddad, who's Matty?"

"Lots of Mattys. Popular name hereabouts. Which Matty are you after?"

"Uncle Jem mentioned a Matty?

Thomas tightened the rope to reduce the tilt of the grain shoe on the stone floor above and slowed the flow of the wheat.

"That's better. The old damsel up there won't be arguing with us so loudly! Now, Matty, you say? That'd be young Matty Brunny."

Thirza never knew whether her granddad was being serious.

"He always got called that. Matty Brunny. Matthew Brunyee's his Sunday name. One of those old Flemish fen-drainer names, made easier for us to say here in God's shire. Well, Matty was Jem's best friend. Two heads on the same neck, growing up. Joined the same regiment as Jem. I heard last back end, one market day in Donny, his family had news he'd died after Balaclava. Survived the charge, but died in hospital. That's all they told his parents. So Jem's lost his best friend and his best girl, Susie, who went off with never a word while he was away. Tough on our lad. No wonder it's broken him. I never told your grandma. Didn't want her whittling. You've not said anything to her, have you, Thirza?"

Thirza shook her head.

"Please don't, lass. Matty's gone, but our Jem's home and dry. Just got to count our blessings. Look to the future, like Darnell keeps saying. Alright, love?"

Thirza nodded. Jem would need time to mourn. She kissed her granddad and set off down the ladder, hearing the damsel's chatter speeding up again as the sails flew round.

She picked up her basket full of eggs and teasels and set off towards the village. As she passed the old tree by the churchyard, she saw a notice pinned on the bark. It looked just like the one Kezzie had taken from Grace as they arrived home with Jem. Thirza read what her grandmother had been so furiously denying:

'Come one, come all! For harvest this year, a grand new mill for all your needs. Accessible by a solid metalled road of finest construction, excellent patent sails after Mr Cubitt's design. Householders, farmers, smallholders, husbandmen, bring your grain and be not deceived by inferior milling.
Signed 'Friends of the Future'.

Thirza's skin prickled. The picture on the bill illustrated in bold woodcut printing, a huge complex of buildings, turreted storehouses and in the centre, a windmill of grand design, more modern in every way than Kitson's Mill, yet obviously the same building.

Kitson's Mill had been stuck for centuries at the end of a narrow lane that frequently turned into an impassable quagmire so sacks had to be dragged to the door by unwieldy improvised rafts and pallets. Originally sited on the Nab to help with the drainage of the fens, Thirza knew everything in the old windmill was quaint, home-made, rustic and held together with botched repairs. Sustained by the good will and patronage of the locals, coupled with familiarity and the lack of anywhere closer for milling their grain, its charm was what Thirza loved about it. Like a creaky old brig, it made her feel somehow safe. But this bill spoke of a very different future. Is this what Darnell had hinted at? A future where hard-headedness and business dictated the terms.

Her grandparents were set in their ways. Without money, resources or youth to embrace change, how could they compete with the new advances in engineering she often read about in the papers? If this rumour proved true, then the future and progress were about to threaten the Kitsons' livelihood and very existence on Turbary Nab.

Jem's the one, thought Thirza, who's meant to inherit the mill, now he's invalided out of the Army. When he's well again, he can make all the changes needed to keep the villagers loyal to Kitson's Mill. Maybe with Darnell's help as engineer and inventor? Right now, they needed a miracle and Thirza knew those didn't happen just by whistling and wishing.

A few of the cottagers seemed happy to buy Thirza's eggs, in small numbers. A few of the women took the teasel heads to card wool or comb thread for weaving, for a copper or two. One cottage near the church kept its door shut for a long time after Thirza knocked. She tried not to stare through the open casement as she passed by up the path. She could hear voices inside, children and adults. She knocked again, a little louder.

At last, the door opened a fraction and revealed a woman in her middle years with angry eyes narrowed to a slit of mistrust.

"What do you want?" she hissed through her teeth, making Thirza step back a little.

"I'm selling eggs and teasels, if you need them," Thirza smiled and tipped the basket on her arm so the woman could see the wares that remained to be bought.

The woman continued to glare, as if she'd no need of anything and wouldn't want to buy from Thirza whether she did or not. Inside the room, Thirza saw little necks craning to see round their mother's obstructive shoulders. From the window, a voice shouted, "Mam, it's that water gypsy girl from the windmill!"

The woman didn't scold or contradict. She looked Thirza up and down and then slammed the door. As she made her way back along the path, Thirza could hear the gossipy comments following her into the street, getting louder for the benefit of passers-by.

"They say the miller's lad's back from Balaclava. Nobody's seen him yet. Why are they hiding him away? Bet he's a deserter!"

"I heard that girl stole some swanky slippers from her own family. Then she tried to get another maid in trouble for ruining her Ladyship's ball gown up at the Big House. Then she ran away like the dirty thieving witch she is! Our Kate told our Sarah! Never trust a water gypsy!"

The giggling faded away as Thirza hurried out of the gate. She couldn't face walking the length of the village back to the mill for a while. She thought of the children at the end cottage going out to play with their companions and spreading lies and rumours about her and her family, like a sickness from house to house.

Thirza held her head up high as she walked. Why should she apologise for who she was? She'd done nothing wrong but be born on the keel. But what she'd heard that girl say about her uncle made her furious. It was true Jem hadn't been seen since his arrival. He needed rest after a gruelling campaign. The whole country had been buzzing with news about the Crimean War. Some things sounded so thrilling and heroic. Other stories made her wonder how anyone had survived such horrors.

So what if the villagers laughed at her and cat-called her? What if they gobbled up half-truths about her and churned them out as facts? Her family needed her to be strong, now more than ever to keep things afloat, like a well-rigged ship, until these present winds stopped buffeting.

As Thirza wandered, deep in thought, she found herself by the wall of the pinfold. She didn't see anybody else about.

"Good morning," Bram stood up from scattering beech mast at the feet of the one pig that remained in his care. A cow was tethered to a hook speared into the earth inside. Bram stepped out of the fold and latched the gate securely behind him.

"No adders, today? Your dog's lovely!" Thirza saw Piper's brown eyes fixed on Bram's face, reading his master's movements with eagerness and such intelligence and expectation. "I once saw a dog just like yours on a keel. A barge dog, I think it was, a sweet little thing. What's her name?"

Bram smiled. He noticed something about this lady of which she herself seemed unaware. It took his breath away.

"His name's Piper."

"Oh, sorry, boy! Why Piper?" Thirza bent to stroke the dog's soft ears. He seemed completely relaxed with her.

"Piper's just the name we give to all our dogs. Because, well, because of the pipes!" explained Bram. He realised he'd never told anybody before about his dog or his work out on the fen. Nobody had ever asked. He'd never volunteered any information, either. He was too used to the reaction of villagers to his kind. They all thought they knew his business, despised him for it and avoided him. No, they never asked, they only gave an opinion, a look or called names he pretended not to hear.

"We call them Piper for the pipes in the decoy," he added, cautious not to say too much. The lass's curiosity might easily turn to mistrust.

"You've got more dogs than this lovely lad?" Thirza noticed the man seemed to be edging away, as if the fen held him on a hidden secret thread that hauled him urgently and jealously back to itself, just as the sea sang its own siren-song deep inside her. She laughed in spite of herself as he tipped his hat again, so courteous, more diffident than most men she'd met before.

"I only have one dog. Sorry, I mean my family have always kept dogs like him."

He felt her laughter like a slap. Was this lass, too, so quick to mock him? Piper rolled over at her feet.

"Come on, Piper, we've other flocks to fettle," Bram snapped his fingers and Piper rolled onto one shoulder, obedient to the call, but evidently hoping for one last stroke from this maiden's fingers.

"What's this decoy, then?" Thirza was intrigued.

Bram wondered whether telling her would prove the biggest mistake he could make. People generally meant mischief. He'd learned that long ago. No-one came to the decoy unless they wandered near it by accident when they were cutting peat. No-one respected the old ways of the fen now. The miller's son was Bram's only visitor since his grandfather died. Had he spoken to his niece about spending the night on the fen? Had they laughed together about this wild wanderer?

"You know what a decoy is, I suppose?" he asked. Was she trying to trick him?

"No," Thirza admitted, "I don't. But I'd like to."

Did the young man think her stupid? He'd been so gallant at the canal and then so brave and self-assured with the adder the other day. Now he seemed somehow defensive, awkward and shy.

"It doesn't matter," she heard herself saying, "please don't let me keep you."

Bram felt more disappointed than he'd been prepared for. Wasn't she interested after all? Was she just waiting to tell him how little she cared for his droning on about his lonely life?

Piper trotted to his heel but looked back at Thirza again, tongue lolling.

"Goodbye, Piper, and..." Thirza had heard Darnell call him Dutchy, but felt sure that wasn't his name.

"Bram. Bram Beharrell."

"I wanted to thank you, Mr Beharrell, for your kindness to me and my family with those bullies on the canal bridge. With the adder, too, the other day and for helping my uncle Jem. You're a kind man."

Bram saw she was looking straight into his eyes, not past him or through him, as the villagers always seemed to. He made a decision.

"Miss Holberry..."

"Call me Thirza, please do. Would you show me your decoy one day? I don't think I've ever seen such a thing."

"It isn't my decoy," said Bram, "it belongs to the fen and I'm a steward of it for the future of the fen. So my grandfather taught me."

"The future?" the word jarred on Thirza. She thought of the words she'd recently read.

"If you ever chance by that way," Bram wondered how this lass would ever find herself in the middle of the wilderness he called home, "I'll be honoured to show you."

He looked at the basket on her arm and saw there were holes in it.

"I'm cutting reeds, this morning. I could mend your basket for you."

He meant to add, "if you'll leave it with me," but realised he didn't want the basket on its own if the girl wasn't there to talk to as he wove.

"Sir, I need my basket now. I'm going to sell more eggs and teasels. The windmill needs repairs and I believe there are things I can do to earn my keep while I'm here. A mended basket would cost me more than I've made, today, to be truthful."

Bram hesitated. If he took the basket and repaired it for Thirza, it would be cold and rude to make her wait here while he went to fetch his tools from his hut. But if he took her with him, she would see his hut and find out exactly where the decoy was. She would be let in. Bram had never let anyone in until Jem found him.

"I can do it now. If you'll come with me, it'll be done in half an hour."

It was Thirza's turn to hesitate. She looked into Bram's dark, serious eyes and felt her heart step up through a hidden trapdoor into hope. He wasn't laughing. Not at her, not at life, not at need or distress or difference. He was more an outsider than anyone she'd ever encountered. Her inner compass was her intuition. When she thought things through, she found good sense usually ended up leading her in the direction she already knew by a deep conviction. But often by then, it was too late and the opportunity lost. If she'd listened to her instincts the day her father left her at the mill, she'd have acted on what she knew in her heart, that something was afoot she couldn't bear. She wouldn't have stepped off 'Thistle' at all. She wouldn't have arrived here. She stopped hesitating and nodded.

"That's kind of you. I need to carry more eggs, more teasels, more..." She couldn't think what else. Her scheme to raise cash for the old mill seemed so lame when she said it out loud to a stranger.

"Let me carry your basket for you. I can hang it from my staff and you can be free to watch where you're treading, in case you want to go dancing on adders as you did that morning."

Thirza jumped as his voice came from above and behind her. Startled, she looked up to see Bram towering over her from a height, balanced on two stilts like an extension of his own flesh. He walked on them as if he was tramping along with his soles planted firmly on solid ground, with the staff to help.

Bram laughed aloud, seeing Thirza's look of amazement and momentary panic.

"Don't be alarmed, please," he chuckled, then said more soberly, for fear of making her think he'd meant to frighten her on purpose, "I'm no giant, just a fen hopper, a marshman, a dyke-reeve. March was a wet month and April promises us more showers to swell the drains." He stepped down again and showed Thirza the stilts.

"My great great grandfather's grandfather made these."

Thirza admired the skill, the dovetailing that joined the stilt to the footplate and the leather strap to attach them to the wearer's boots. She saw these were no ordinary stilts. There were tiny mechanisms built into the shafts, with pistons, rods, flywheels, valves and gears and a crystal-clear cylinder that looked as if it was full of milky mist.

"Might I have a go?" Thirza even surprised herself. Somehow everything about this man excited and intrigued her.

A voice in Bram's head clearly whispered, "Omkering

van schade, jongen, for you, now, for you!". He felt his ancestors crowding round his heart, urging him on. Instead of a muttered apology and denial, he heard himself say, "Yes!"

Thirza stared down at her feet. They seemed to be circled by a many-coloured seamless flame coming out of the spongy peat turf.

"Don't be frightened!" Bram lifted her tenderly until her insteps were supported on the foot plates. He buckled the leather straps around her calves and decanted a strange substance out of the fen, a flickering unearthly light burning with a cool radiance, into the labyrinth of elements inside the cylinder built into the leg of each stilt.

"Walk forward and try not to look down."

Thirza stepped out and found the stilts felt like an extension of her own legs now. The tiny pistons seemed to lift her and suddenly she realised she was looking down at the top of Bram's head, the hut, the decoy that looked like a landlocked starfish to Thirza. Had they reached as far as this already? She took a few more strides and could see the tops of the masts in Hull docks, or was it Goole?

"Ooh... wobbling... I'm going to wobble off!"

"Stay calm, keep it gentle!"

Thirza put her other foot forward and found herself some distance away. She tried to turn and could see the top of a church tower quite close through the clouds below her.

"Oh, what? That's not even us, that's Doncaster! There's Sheffield!"

"Steady!"

As she looked round and down at Bram again she felt the stilts starting to vibrate and fold downwards towards the flat contours of the fen below. She felt, more than saw, his hands becoming larger, no, not larger, just closer and closer as he reached up his arms from below to catch her.

"I can do it! Wait, let me..."

As the stilts rooted themselves into the fen again, Thirza staggered, lost her balance and toppled over, gathered into Bram's arms for a long suspended moment until they both found themselves on their backs, gazing up at the sky.

For a moment neither of them spoke. Thirza because she couldn't. Bram because he was working out the best way to explain centuries of his family's secrets without betraying his blood, or endangering this amazing lass.

11. MENDINGS AND MARRINGS

"Staggering! Literally. Maybe just a little bit alarming," Thirza tried not to giggle like a two-year-old, "and if you're expecting me to bombard you with compliments on those things, I'm too out-of-breath!"

"Good," Bram said, "I expect questions, actually, and reasons why not, before the answers. But not from you. Not now!" He blushed and managed not to show her, he hoped. Thirza noticed. She did wonder why this man lived out here where paths were as rare as landmarks in the ocean but she felt the answers would run clear in their own good time.

Bram found himself saying things he'd never planned to say, when he was talking to this girl. He'd normally go speeding away on his stilts so nobody could follow him. Now he wanted to keep his feet on the path next to Thirza. He folded up the stilts so they clicked into a streamlined bundle a fraction of their original length.

Bram took Thirza's basket and they carried on along the path across the fen. It ran out after a few feet and Bram steered Thirza through the unmapped wastes with the occasional gesture and word of advice as to where it was safe to place her feet. Sometimes it was her hands that met the ground when she teetered over on the territory Bram knew better than anyone alive.

"It's here you need to watch your steps, more than when you're stilt-walking! Wherever people tread, there are hidden traps and dangers."

Thirza didn't argue. She felt safe with Bram, somehow, in a way she hadn't felt safe since she stepped off the keel. He pointed out birds and plants to her on the way. She was amazed to discover how many wild creatures lived only feet from where she'd so often sailed by without seeing or hearing them at all.

"How's your uncle?" Bram asked at last. Jem's manner had troubled him deeply. Seeing him standing like a statue under the birch trees surrounding the decoy, silent and ghostly in the moonlight, made Bram realise how vulnerable he was, living cut off from human company, out of calling distance of all help. He thought of his great grandfather Gerrit, of another secretive visitor who had spied on his people on the marsh.

What was he doing, letting the girl come out here with him? Letting her stand on his stilts? This was sacred space to him, home and refuge from people. He was secretly amazed at her quietness, the way she lowered her voice so the snipe didn't scuttle into tussocks to hide, the basking lizard didn't flick away into the wayside pool. He'd half expected the things from which he'd always shrunk away, the squeals and stares of the village girls. He thought of their voices, scattering waders and wildfowl, making Piper's ears twitch, making Bram himself withdraw, watchful until he was alone again.

Now here was Thirza, the water girl. She didn't know these fens and marshes. She didn't belong in the village. He knew nothing of her world, yet something in her manner, so full of curiosity and genuine interest in what he showed her, made him bold to believe she wouldn't break the fragile film of the web he'd woven around his world, all these years in chosen solitude.

"Uncle's finding his homecoming painful. Oh, I don't know! He seems bewildered. Acting so strangely. He doesn't talk much and when he does, he seems tormented. He isn't much hurt, so far as you can see from the outside. His leg was hurt, yes, and he's lost so much weight since we last saw him, but he's like a different person. I'm frightened for him." Thirza hadn't said as much to her grandparents, so why was she opening up to this strange man?

"Kitson's Mill's his, when Granddad retires, as only son. He's home for good now. The medical board let him go. But the days are passing and Jem seems weak as a kitten. I'm sorry, I shouldn't be saying all this, I'm sure."

Bram's heart went out to her, but he felt uncertain what to say. He, too, felt Jem's wounded spirits weren't those that could be revived by a sniff of sal volatile. He'd seen the old Chelsea Pensioner sitting outside his cottage, invalided out of the Peninsular War at the time of Napoleon. That veteran had wounds everyone could see at a glance and every glance was pity for the arm and leg he'd left on the fields of Lisbon. Jem had every limb intact. But something in his manner showed he was missing something for which it was much harder to compensate.

"I'm sorry, too," said Bram. "You must all be worried to know what happened out there."

"You know Uncle Jem's army chest, the one he put in your fold, the one with his initials?" Thirza said, finding it hard to hold anything back, for Bram seemed such a good listener. Bram nodded.

"There's a razor in there. A cut-throat with the insignia of his regiment, the 'Cherry Pickers'. I found him with it. Hiding under the bed. He frightens me sometimes. He says he's to blame. Something about his friend." Thirza trailed off, shocked at her own suspicions.

"Who knows the things he must have seen?" Bram was curious, though he hated the very thought of fighting and slaughter. He didn't say so to Thirza. She might think him weak, or that he judged her uncle. How could he judge him? He'd seen Jem's distress that night, frozen and vacant as if the guns still roared in his hearing. How could he judge, when he'd never left the moors or lifted a musket in anger?

Thirza wondered if she was betraying Jem to talk

about his troubles outside the mill and farm. But Bram didn't offer opinions or judgements. She felt soothed to share the burden which was starting to make the atmosphere at the mill more tense every day.

As they drew close to Bram's hut and the decoy, Thirza saw the ground fell away a few feet below the general level of the land.

"Does this part of the fen still flood?" she asked.

"My ancestors placed ditches and drains all around and planted these few trees so the decoy would be perfectly hidden from every eye in Yorkshire. They fought the water with the skill of their hands. But the water has a life of its own. It won't always stay conquered. Sometimes when the moon sucks the tides back from the shores, the sea finds her way back up the dykes and warps and bleeds back into these parts, with marsh gas, and sulphur and fen-lights."

Thirza found his words like music that her heart could learn to dance to, though his world was so far removed from her own, or anybody's.

"So you're here to repair the breaches?" Thirza looked around in admiration at the tools neatly stacked by the cottage wall. Hooks and nets, scythes, hammers and other implements she couldn't recognise or name.

"I do what I can to reverse the ravage, as my ancestors did, as you're trying to do for your family. Did you know Kitson's Mill was once a drainage mill, built by my people to drain these levels?"

"I've seen the old scoop stored out the back of the mill. Granddad was telling me the other day it used to be attached to the windmill's main shaft, driven round by the sails in the days of his own great grandfather. I suppose my people and yours often paddled this way together before they made it into dry land. I'd give everything I own, little as that is, to be done with dry land and go back to my life on the water."

Bram was moved by the urgency and sorrow in Thirza's voice. He felt no more desire to boast about the achievement of his forebears. This girl's pain at their talk of the Great Drainage ran much deeper than the casual racism and ignorant malevolence he'd suffered from locals before. They still resented the intrusion into their parochial lives and loss of common land to innocent exiles. She felt totally lost here. He thought it might be wise to change the subject.

Bram picked out some twists of sedge to mend the frayed basket and began to weave them in and out in such a deft way and with such absorption that conversation seemed unnecessary. Thirza sat watching him work.

"I'm not sure you'd find enough firm teasels in these parts to sell all summer. How many village eggs could you hawk back to the village?" Bram said, thinking aloud.

Thirza hoped he wasn't laughing at her efforts, but his face was all concentration on the task in hand and he spoke so gently, she sensed he wasn't scoffing.

"I've hardly made a halfpenny all day. Not enough to be much help with repairs at the windmill. To be truthful, the village women don't much care to buy from me."

Bram looked at her. He'd seen the windmill growing more dilapidated each time he passed close to it. The paint was peeling but the rot seemed to go much deeper. There were times the sails themselves seemed to bind as they turned into the capricious wind.

"When people abandon stewardship of the land for business and greed," Bram stopped himself in the middle of his musings. Was he dreaming? "Where on earth did you get that from?"

Thirza saw he was looking at the broken toy bird she was fiddling with as he worked.

"This? It was my mother's. She kept it in a box passed down to her. Its wing's broken, here, look."

She gave it to Bram and he turned it over in his hands. Piper came and sniffed at it, wagging his tail.

"Do you know what this is?" Bram flashed her a look from under his hat-brim.

"A bird? No idea what kind, but weird-looking. I think it might be a cuckoo, with whiskers round its beak. Gapes like a frog!"

"It's a goatsucker. A nightjar. A little nighthawk," Bram was stunned. "See? The plumage, patterned like tree bark and leaf shadow, to help it hide in the bracken. Little feet to perch along branches, tucked in so it becomes invisible to hunters. It lays its eggs at full moon."

Thirza crept closer, seeing her beloved bird with new eyes.

"Why goatsucker? Does it suck goats?"

"Of course not!" Bram sounded almost defensive on the little bird's behalf. "But superstitious people, who rarely see it, blame it for sucking the udders of their livestock."

"I've never seen one in real life. Never heard one either."

"I know every nightjar nest from here to Rawcliffe. They're just flying in for the summer. But this one's something else." Bram looked into Thirza's eyes. In for a penny. Omkering van schade. "Go and look inside my hut. Inside the roof."

Thirza opened his door and gazed up at the makeshift rack hung from the ceiling. Tools. A few cobwebs. Beady eyes. Mechanical decoy ducks.

"They're just like my little bird!" Thirza was incredulous. Perhaps she would wake up in a minute?

"My ancestors crafted them. Used them to help real birds, if they were injured or hunted, or off course. Carved from driftwood, with a mechanism inside. Fuelled like my stilts from phlogiston. My ancestors called it that, a mix of marsh gases and alchemical elements that brew themselves here in the fen wastes. Clockwork and steam and fire from untold places, natural as sunrise. Deadly in the hands of mischief makers."

"How did my mother get hers? It's not even a duck, is it, this goatsucker nightjar thing?"

"No. I don't know. Perhaps it was gifted to your family by mine. If one of my people found one of your people as special as I find you."

Bram looked up. Thirza wasn't listening. She was right inside the hut, handling the birds, inspecting their intricacies. She reappeared carrying a widgeon.

"But, why are they like this? Real birds fly," she frowned at Bram, trying to believe the impossible, "Surely you're not going to tell me these fly?"

Bram had finished the basket. He took the widgeon from her and hung it back up with the others.

"Not often, these days." He handed Thirza her basket with the nightjar toy sitting inside it. "Be careful with it. Mischief makers don't care who they hurt. Perhaps, if you're willing, one day I can show you the decoy properly and mend this for you, too."

She tucked the goatsucker back in her pocket.

"Maybe if you come back, I can show you real nightjars, too. They come out at dusk."

"So they don't suck goats, but they do oblige by living up to their night name?"

Bram smiled. Maybe he'd said enough for now. It felt right to share things with Thirza. But getting closer to people wasn't an option Bram had ever considered before.

"I'd better pay you for your trouble mending the basket." Thirza wished she could stay forever, watching in wonder as he made broken things whole in his strong hands, caressing strands of sedge into place, making holes heal up and mysterious, scary things seem safe.

"Thank you so much," Thirza felt in the pocket of her apron for the money from the sale of the produce. Her fingers closed around the couple of coppers she'd raised. She knew they would be spent again immediately in costs like this one.

Bram waved away the coins in protest, shaking his head to indicate she mustn't give him anything. He understood the plight of the mill in uncertain times. He knew how passionately she felt about helping her family and earning her way back to her own world.

Thirza felt pushed away by his gesture. Does he think I'm just a stupid girl? A little voice raged inside her, still raw from the earlier bullying. Does he think I'm just here begging for charity and a free ride on his generosity? Does he pity me? The little ignoramus who doesn't know a nightjar from a cuckoo? Doesn't have a clue about his precious stilts and his stuffed ducks?

"No! Take this!" she snapped, embarrassed to be in his debt. Bram looked so crestfallen, she wished she'd never followed him out here where she was entirely thrown on the charity of a man again. Visions of being driven away to Foljambe Hall without any explanation, visions of being dumped ashore and not consulted first danced in front of her reasoning. She was convinced now Bram must be intent on doing the same.

Her eyes flashed as she pushed the coins roughly into his hands. Now it was all the coins, not just the halfpenny he might have asked. Her face blazed with shame instead of the joy she'd first felt at discovering this beautiful place and this mysterious stranger.

"It's too much, for a few whiskers of sedge!" Bram burst out. Now she was acting high and mighty, out of the blue, offering him charity. Bram felt confused and hurt in his turn. He tried to soften his words to hide the surge of emotion that overwhelmed him.

"Sedge is for thatched roofs or a comfortable bed for the animals, a stuffed mattress, a carpet. Not gold for a lady! Take your basket and be welcome!"

All the snubs, rejections and humiliations she'd met with since coming ashore whirled round in Thirza's head and made her stubborn and touchy. She wouldn't back down.

"I've no gold, sir, and I don't beg any favours! Perhaps I am no lady!" Thirza let the coins spill through Bram's fingers, as he stood too astonished at her outburst to clasp the payment she thrust his way. Snatching up her basket, Thirza turned and ran the way they'd come. Now she could hardly see her way for weeping, but she kept going and refused to look back.

Piper started to scamper after her, but looking for direction at his master, he sank back on his haunches with an almost human sigh.

"You are a lady," Bram whispered and was angry to

find tears on his own cheeks long after she was out of sight.

When she reached human habitation, Thirza forced herself to slow to a walk. She rubbed her face and ignored the beating pain in her temples that the sobbing had left behind. Already she was regretting her reaction, but now, she thought, it's too late. He'll think me a madwoman, or, worse, a vain and foolish girl.

Thirza became aware of someone following her. Grace Canner had come out of one of the cottages where a woman had kindly bought half a dozen of the eggs from her earlier in the day.

"All sold?" Grace enquired.

"Nearly," Thirza hoped Grace wasn't leading up to some new cruelty she'd picked up from the lasses who knew what had happened at the Hall. There was nowhere to hide in this village but the top of the mill. Even there she knew her family thought her a little strange and even Uncle Darnell had hinted she'd be in his way when he needed to work up there.

"Don't reckon you'll be selling any tomorrow," Grace looked slyly at Thirza, "but then, you haven't been home to the windmill since this morning, so you won't have heard."

"Heard what?"

"No chickens. No eggs. Simple as that, isn't it? Those teasels aren't much use either. Not like the ones my sister had from down south. The bristles are weak."

"I shan't be selling any more," Thirza walked on, as fast as she could, but Grace kept up with her.

"Goatsucker's been our way, by the looks of it," Grace said lugubriously. "When those goatsuckers fly back, they go for the teats. Not just goats either, they'll suck you dry in your bed, my mam says, if you don't keep tucked up tight."

Thirza tried to ignore Grace's prattling. How could Grace possibly know she and Bram had talked about this myth? Grace was always full of old wives' tales. Thirza thought it was best not to ask. The perfectly repaired basket bumped on her hip to remind her what a useless day she'd spent trying to do her part and be sensible. When she arrived in front of the windmill, her grandfather was in the yard.

"Granddad, has something happened? How's Uncle Jem?"

Thomas started as if he hadn't seen her approaching.

"Jem's up and about, he's had to stir himself today. He's clearing up for me in the yard. It's a mess, girl, with the feathers. Don't go out there, just now."

"What mess, Granddad?"

"The damn fox must have got into the hen coop last night. Only one of them dead, praise be. Myrtle and Cobalt and Lucinda and Peckity are still clucking. He just took Tickle, Kezzie's little favourite. I shouted Jem to make himself handy, keep his mother out of the way."

"But they were clucking and scratching when I went for the eggs this morning. A fox hadn't touched any of them, then."

"Well, lass, you're new here. I suppose you didn't notice like a farm girl might. Tickle hangs back in the coop. Not to worry, these things happen. I cast my eye over her and I'd swear it's the fox."

"But Granddad, I'm sure she was alive when I left," but Thirza couldn't be certain.

"Tickle isn't alive now," Jem came into the yard from the field with a dead hen in his hands, followed by Francis. The lad looked as if this was splendid sport instead of working the mill.

Thirza thought Jem looked pleased to be up and about in the fresh air, dressed in miller's whites as if he'd always been here.

"Mother's indoors, busy with Darnell and the squire. She's none the wiser about her little pet. See the neck, Father?"

Thomas peered at the feathery corpse until his nose was almost touching it.

"Steady, do you see? Can that be a fox?" Jem stroked the bird.

Thomas shrugged.

"Lad, what else can it be?" He prodded Francis in the

back as he stood staring from the entry. "Let's get on. Foxes have fine sport any time of year. They find a feast and don't stop when they're full. They go on tearing those pretty ones till they're history. I marvel it's just the one."

"I'll finish off in the field, Father."

Jem watched till Thomas and Francis were climbing the ladders, then turned to Thirza.

"I don't think my father can see right at all any more," Jem spoke quietly, so he couldn't be heard above the creaks and wallops from inside.

"Why?" Thirza was at a loss as to how she'd missed the fox's work when she felt in the hen house.

"Because he hasn't noticed this can't be a fox's ravaging, even with his nose at the bird's throat."

"Show me," Thirza shuddered in disbelief as Jem held the dead bird for her to see.

"This isn't the work of any fox I ever saw."

Not a drop of blood was visible on the feathers. A nick, like a cut from a blade, not a fox's fang, was visible at the front of its throat. The bird's eyes stared from sunken sockets and its talons hung, the skin of its feet puckered as if no veins ran through its body.

It had been sucked dry.

12. THIS SUFFOCATING PEPPER-POT

Inside Mill Cottage, Thirza found Darnell enthroned at one side of the fireplace with his cousin Lucas perched opposite him, reading a newspaper. She could hear the squire's precise, animated tones reading out an article about the famous engineer Thomas Telford as she put her bonnet on the back of the chair.

"Telford is a genius," Lucas was saying, "and then there's our own local man Metcalf. Turnpikes are like quagmires in places, though, for all his industry."

"My horse went lame cantering down the lane," Darnell was confiding, "Emma was all but unseated."

"A Telford for the backwaters, that's what's required," Lucas went on. Thirza thought that for all his sophistication, he had the enthusiasm of an excited child. At that moment, Emma came in from the back room with Kezzie. Thirza thought her grandmother looked too happy to have heard about Tickle's demise.

Lucas smiled up at her as he continued to read. He didn't seem about to mention her appalling rejection of the opportunity he'd arranged. Emma, however, when they were all seated and Kezzie was pouring the tea, couldn't resist a dig.

"Thirza, dear," she gushed, "we don't want you to be

in the least discouraged by the little incident at the Hall." Emma looked at Darnell who sat with his fingertips touching in a constant tapping motion as if he was playing an imaginary penny whistle and approved of all his wife was saying. Thirza was thankful for the small blessing that Emma was using her real name for a change.

"Squire Charlesworth, that is, Lucas," Emma fluttered him a beaming smile, "is prepared to overlook what happened. Her Ladyship has graciously pardoned your peculiar unpleasantness with the other seamstresses."

Thirza imagined Emma thought all the world rotated around the axis of these influential people. The ordeal her niece had gone through was the last consideration on Emma's butterfly mind. Kezzie made her feelings known through a sterling silver pudding spoon which crashed onto the iron trivet several times with conversation-stopping volume.

Lucas folded the paper and gave Thirza his full attention.

"Aunt Laura would be happy to give you a second chance, Thirza. She found you quite charming. Who would not?" Thirza saw him look at Darnell, who continued to smile his inscrutable smile, as if he was completely satisfied she would feel the same, in spite of what she'd tried to explain to him more than once.

"I have washed those exquisite little slippers," Emma broke in, "so they aren't spoiled. I suppose you were stricken with a fit of the vapours to think you might have stretched them. But now I'm not even vexed."

"We were never vexed," Lucas corrected her, "Lady Laura is sorry to lose such a treasure. She thinks your work would do nicely. She spoke to Dimberline about teaching you the correct way to go on, in spite of the young ladies' alarm."

They all seemed at pains to reassure her that there would be no consequences, but Thirza thought the consequences of returning were too costly a price to pay, whatever they'd all decided on her behalf.

"I won't be going back, as I told Uncle Darnell before,

but thank you, Squire Charlesworth, for the opportunity you gave me. Please tell Lady Laura she was so kind to see me. It's helped me make up my mind."

"Your mind?" Lucas sounded as if he'd never thought of a woman possessing such a thing, then looked delighted. "A mind as well as flying fingers! You spoil us with such an embarrassment of graces wrapped in one pretty person."

Thirza wondered how Lucas had time to pore over works of science and mechanics. His phrases seemed, to her, fresh from the pages of florid romantic fiction.

"I'll earn my keep. Now Uncle Jem's back working with Granddad, it won't be long before I won't be needed here. Then I'll be back to the keel."

Lucas set down his newspaper. His eyes lit up.

"What a splendid girl you are, Thirza. Darnell told me you had a mind of your own. Now I see he was more than correct. You are tremendous!"

Thirza laughed, pleased he seemed so impressed, but convinced he might be less so if he knew her better.

Darnell was swigging the dregs from his teacup. Kezzie kept filling his cup each time it came even close to being empty. Thirza wondered why the old lady always seemed all fingers and thumbs around Darnell, in a dithering gavotte of half-curtseys.

"I must have a word with my dear brother-in-law before we leave. Where have you been hiding him, dear lady?" he asked.

"He's well now, after all his brave exploits," cooed Kezzie.

"He's in the mill, ma'am," added Grace. Thirza thought she ought to jump in to stop Grace beginning to chatter, in front of the guests, about chickens and goatsuckers, whatever nonsense that was.

"I heard the most extraordinary thing as I came back from market the other day," Lucas broke in, before Thirza could speak, "Old Crackles, my tenant and his friend Armitage from Worksop, said they'd heard rumours of a new mill to be built hereabouts. Had you heard of it, Cousin?"

"I have, Cousin. Idle rumours travel fast in these parts. I wouldn't want my father-in-law troubled by such a threat. This old mill's been adequate for the needs of the neighbouring farmsteads, if slightly behind the times. Still, we must look to the future, see that we don't fall behind the pace of progress."

As the visitors unhitched their horses, Emma seemed to enjoy the helping hand Lucas gave her onto the mounting block by the mill door. Darnell ducked the sails as they swept past him, like an old hand.

"We're going now, sir, " he called to Thomas, "May I speak to Jeremy?"

Thirza saw Darnell ascending the ladder to see Jem above, as her grandfather appeared on the reefing stage.

"I forgot to tell you, Thirzie, your father's stopping by, tomorrow. He's on a round trip from Sheffield up to Goole, so he's calling here on the way. I sent to ask him for some of his old sailcloth to mend my own sweeps."

Thirza nearly burst out cheering with relief, but something made her keep that relief inside. She wouldn't risk anyone knowing. She wouldn't let the keel depart without her this time. That way, nobody could be hurt, and no-one could try to dissuade her.

So she'd be gone tomorrow, leaving the disappointments of this time behind her. Her father would soften in his resolve to spare her the uncertainty of being a lass in a man's domain. When he knew how she'd failed to make the land her home, he'd have no option but to take her back on board. She blessed her uncle Jem for his rallying health, her father for taking on a trip on this stretch of the Navigation, her granddad for needing the sailcloth. Hopelessness and humiliation were about to melt away. She'd spend her last night up in the cap. Now Foljambe Hall could become a funny memory, to be laughed at on chilly nights in the cabin.

And Bram? Thirza regretted her harsh words to him and her throwing his awkward kindnesses back in his face. Maybe one day she'd see him from the keel again, on those incredible stilts, as she saw him first the day she arrived here. Then there'd be no need of any charity and she could tell him everything had turned out the way she planned. She hoped he'd be happy for her.

Darnell reappeared, looking concerned. Jem staggered down after him, wearing the same expression as when he stood with Bram by the pinfold, trying to be pleased to be home at last.

"I'm afraid you're still overwrought from your ordeal overseas, Jeremy," Darnell patted his brother-in-law's shoulder. He mounted his horse and as he rode by Thirza he muttered, "Look after your uncle, Thirza, he's rambling a little, I think. Chickens? I didn't quite follow his drift, but something seems to have disturbed him. Acting guiltily. Something on his conscience. I wouldn't want to think your grandfather was expecting too much of our fine young soldier."

Thirza saw Jem was looking at his hands, wiping at his clothes to get rid of some stain only he could see.

"Farewell, all!" Darnell cantered away, with Emma some way behind him. Lucas tipped his hat to Kezzie and the men, then to Thirza as he rode close by.

"To the next time, Thirza. I think we could talk of many things, you and I. It's April, yet I feel as though May Day has come when I see your spirit."

Someone could see her spirit. Thirza touched her lip, feeling as if he'd brushed her there, so intense was his look of admiration. He saw her, then, and not just a silly wilful water girl. But tomorrow she'd be just a leap from 'Thistle'. Tonight she'd repack her bag with her mother's box and the broken goatsucker and wait for the sunrise to dawn on the day of her release.

#

Before sunrise, Thirza lay awake in the cradle of old sacks at the top of the windmill. She watched the sliver of light forcing its way through the wafer-thin gap between the moveable cap and the mill's body. She'd heard her aunt Emma call this building angry names. Now she was leaving, Thirza was growing fonder of its strange voice, the whispered groan of hornbeam on iron as the wind-shaft turned, the squeak and harrumph of the brake wheel when her granddad applied the lever, the murmuring wallower spinning to a halt. She listened to the judder and shush of the sails outside.

If 'Thistle' came early, she'd soon hear the comforting flap of more familiar sails above her head, like wings and not this pinioned Catherine wheel of canvas. The knock of the keel's own leeboards, slicing through the water, would replace the rapping of the sacks through the grain hoist forever. She thought about Emma's contempt for this place and lay wondering.

"This suffocating pepper-pot!" Emma once screeched. Thirza was startled by the strength of that rage. Emma made a career of skittering about on the surface of her life, a butterfly in a bonnet, so the fury came as a shock to her niece. Thirza hadn't known her when that hatred was born.

The truth was Emma knew the mill's voice too well. As a young woman, she sat with her beau on the meal bins, hearing the ring and rattle of the joggling screen, the 'jog-scry' as her father called it, vibrating to sort the grain. Her hair was still long then, before her mother got out the shears to prepare her for her wedding. She thought it hilarious that Kezzie feared to climb the mill, so she brought Darnell up out of her mother's way when they were courting. The secrecy seemed to make him hungry for her in a way that flattered and frightened her.

"Are you up there, Emma?" Kezzie called to her. Emma and Darnell almost gave themselves away, but then Darnell would put his hand over her mouth to stifle her laughter. Sometimes she thought he'd cut off the air as he struggled against her, silencing her with urgent fingers. One day, over the jog-scry's pumping frenzy, he put his hands roughly up into her hair and pushed her down onto the machine with its galloping motion she could feel through her hips and up into her soul. After her hair was cut and her marriage vows bound her, Darnell never urged Emma up into the secret belly of the windmill again. She'd shrieked for him to stop, that one time. Now, she wished at least he'd look in her direction. She hated that Darnell still climbed the mill, that he still spoke of his love of hair uncut. Emma wondered if he remembered that day when the mill rattled through her bones in a cloud of silken shocks and made her into a woman.

Thirza saw only Emma's strange aversion to being here for more than an hour. She couldn't work out the reason, which troubled her. But today, no troubles here would drag her down ever again.

Thirza waited until the sun's rays crept through the rift in the sails that her father was on his way to help to mend. She climbed down the ladders, through the bin floor to the stone floor where her grandfather was already working.

Thomas had propped up the ledger, where he kept his records of payments and deliveries in his flowing copperplate handwriting, on the sill of the large window. He was squinting at the open page.

"Thirza?"

"Granddad," Thirza kissed Thomas and hugged him as he frowned at the figures. He kept tilting the page this way and that in the flood of sunlight.

"Have you much to grind today?" Thirza asked, breezy with cheerfulness, "I'm going down to see if I can spy 'Thistle' coming round the bend."

"I must've written too many days in April, old fool that I am. Have a look for me, Thirzie. My eye's tired this morning."

Thomas let Thirza take the ledger. She saw the scrawled script spidering its way across the neatly ruled lines. Now the copperplate had degenerated into scribble. Figures were written one on top of the other.

"It's May Day next Tuesday, I know. Look where April turns into May and tell me how many sacks I've written there."

"Granddad," Thirza hardly had the heart to tell him she could see the muddle he'd been trying to hide. "Your good eye, Granddad..."

"I can manage, Thirza. Just read it out for me. The light's got so dim in here, of late." Thomas rubbed his eye and Thirza knew what was wrong.

"Granddad," she put the ledger back on the sill and turned the old man round to face her. The blind eye winked its wink and the other pupil stared at her, all but sightless. Thirza saw with dread the film there had grown thicker. Each blink showed the bloodshot rims were all but welded shut.

"I can manage, Thirza, if Kezzie doesn't know. Jem helps me now, but he doesn't know the ins and outs yet."

"Granddad, your eye. How can Grandma not notice in time? Is it safe, with you seeing less and less?"

"Kezzie sees what she wants to see, for all that she has two good blue eyes. You know her. I manage, as I must. Francis is a lump, but Jem's a good lad. Darnell's helping, bless the man. He comes over high-handed sometimes, but I don't know where we'd be without him. He's got me a smashing eye bath from one of his clever physician friends and it feels a bit better for bathing. Or it will in time, he says, if I stick with it. Not only that, he's after moving some of his phantasmagoric inventions over here to make improvements so no other newfangled mill can take our trade. 'Friends of the Future', my eye! Blind eye, and all!"

"What about the ladders, the sails? How can you be safe any more?"

"My miller's thumb's true as ninepence, always was, always will be. Barley doesn't feel like wheat. Coarse grain slips under my thumb like sand, the fine, like cream, but dry and cool. I know this mill like my own skin, and the ladders, well, they aren't going anywhere!"

"Why didn't you say before?"

"Pride, lass. You get yours from me, I fear. Now Jem's home, the mill's future lies with him."

"Where is he?"

"He goes out. He wanders. His mind's not easy, but

that Kitson pride's in him, too. He won't tell."

"Where is he now, though?" Thirza tried not to think of the keel coming round the bend. So much to sort out before she sailed, so little time left.

"He goes walking, early."

Thirza knew this was true. She'd seen Jem wandering, a look on his face as if he was gazing into another continent she'd never visited. He seemed to be falling in step with comrades only he could see, more and more preoccupied. After Darnell's visit yesterday, he'd scarcely spoken a word.

"I know, Granddad. Don't fret," Thirza looked at the ledger, "There's a 'one' in this first column and a 'five' in the next. Fifteen sacks of wheat for Farmer Hanson, I think, counting along, and another nine for Mr Temperton. That's all the orders I can make out for today."

Thomas felt the sacks that had come up on the hoist. He counted the two dozen sacks of wheat and tipped the first into the grain hopper above the runner stone.

Thirza saw Francis slouching at the foot of the ladder.

"Quick, Frank, come and empty the grain for your master." She climbed down, unable to recapture the joy she'd felt as the day dawned. Her grandfather going blind? How had she missed the signs? She felt ashamed at being so preoccupied by her own longings and setbacks. All the time Thomas had been soldiering on, hiding his problems from Kezzie, from all of them.

Thirza walked towards the canal and scanned the horizon. Her heart jumped into her mouth to see the sail, golden in the morning light, her father making ready to moor 'Thistle' and Sam at the tiller. Thirza ran as fast as she could down to the jetty that served Turbary Nab and shouted before she even reached the bank.

"Father! Look at you, Sammy! Thank goodness you're here at last! " She thought of her bag packed up on the dust floor. Soon she'd kick off these landlocked leg-irons, jump aboard and never leave her waterways again.

13. DANGEROUS GAMES

Jack hugged Thirza then held her at arms length to see how she really was.

"Have you missed me?" Thirza joked.

"You know we have. But I thought by now you'd be up at the Hall, securing the future you deserve."

"Never mind the future, Father. I'm trying to do what's right, here and now."

"Sammy, frame yourself! Catch hold and help me with this bolt of sailcloth for your granddad."

"I can do that," Thirza was already back on deck, heaving at the stained old sail that would soon be spinning in circles to give the windmill more power to grind.

"Leave it, Thirza," Jack pushed her aside as he lifted the nearest end onto his shoulder, "Sam, take the other end! Look lively, shrimp!"

Sam looked older and sulkier than when Thirza had last seen him. Only a matter of months and he seemed to have turned from the child who treated the whole world as a game to be played, into a lanky youth.

"Where's our Judd?" Thirza looked from bow to stern for her brother.

"Stayed in Hull last time we berthed there. Got a job on the docks, labouring. He wants to get a job on a steamer soon as he can. Or the railway. That's all these two can talk about nowadays."

"Why the railway?"

"He wants to be a fireman," grunted Sam, "but that's rubbish. I'm going to be an engine driver!"

"The railway? Sammy, you'll be captain of 'Thistle' one day!"

"I shan't! Blasted old brig! I'm bored of it. Going so slow everywhere like a snail!"

"Hush, Sam, aren't you glad to see your sister?"

"Course I am, what's up with you?" Sam scowled. Thirza had seen him frown like that when she was washing his neck at the pump on a winter's day.

"Jem's home, you know!" Thirza walked between them, holding up the bolt of cloth in the middle, trying to take some of the weight, but the men seemed oblivious of her efforts to help.

"Stand aside, Thirza, let us get on." Jack said, as they drew close to the windmill.

Thirza bridled at the rebuff. She felt like the millstone propped at the door, a spare part that used to be so essential, now just idle decoration, its usefulness outlived. But she wouldn't be laid aside!

"You move aside, Sam. Go find your uncle Jem to help us."

Thirza eased her body under the roll of canvas so Sam was freed from the weight. She saw the cheekiness of childhood flood back into his face at the mention of his hero.

"Has Uncle Jem brought back a captured Cossack sword with him? Can I have a go with it, if he has, Dad?"

"That's enough, Sam. Don't go bothering your poor uncle. Let's get this onto the reefing balcony." Jack saw how determined Thirza was. It didn't surprise him. He wished the lads had half her pluck.

Sam ran off towards the cottage. Thirza heard her grandmother's whoop of delight as he exploded through the Dutch door, banging both halves of it back against the wall, making the whole house rattle as he bear-hugged Kezzie.

"Sammy, you're so grown-up," Thirza heard her crying, "you'll soon be as tall as your father! I'll have to bake double the Yorkshire puddings I was making for dinner!"

"I can eat our Judd's portion, Grandma!"

The voices grew fainter to Thirza, as she and Thomas helped Jack manoeuvre the old sail up the ladder, inch by inch.

"Where have you been?" Thomas said, his face deadpan as always.

"Under way," laughed Jack.

Thirza felt as if everything was right with her world. She helped her father push the waxed thread through the canvas with the crooked needle. Her kin didn't care if she worked with her left hand. Her own accepted her just as she was. This was her world, her future. She felt safe as she leaned out, balancing against the wooden stock to tie the new canvas in place.

She saw Jem looking up at them from the yard. Sam was standing with him, playing with a blade that looked all too familiar.

"Look at this!" Sam was slashing a razor blade backwards and forwards with great gusto, "Uncle Jem's deadly Cherry Picker razor Lord Cardigan gave him, for his heroic service with Prince Albert's Own Hussars!"

"Steady with that, Sam," Jack was alarmed that Jem was letting the lad play with the weapon as if it was a toy.

Thirza saw the razor case in Jem's hand. He smiled weakly, but made no reply.

"Sammy," she warned, "give it back to Uncle Jem to put away safe!"

"You'll be needing your own razor to shave your shaggy face, soon, lad!" teased Thomas. Then he whispered to Thirza and Jack, "I can't make out any whiskers on Sam with my poor old eyes, but his voice sounds as though it'll be breaking any day now."

"He's not quite there yet," Jack slapped the final sail they were working on, "but he's getting headstrong as a donkey."

Thomas nodded, satisfied at a job well done.

"Hear the canvas, Jack? Sounding healthy again, these sweeps, for twenty more years. They'll see me out. Then Jem can fettle them!"

Jem stood still in the yard. He held the razor case and let Sam gallop round him, wielding the razor itself and shouting. Thomas tried the sails, then applied the brake wheel. They came down to go into the house, where Kezzie's Yorkshire puddings, soaked in gravy, awaited the workers.

"Half a league, half a league!" Sam was showing off for his audience, "Into the valley of death, rode the six hundred!"

Jem whirled round like he'd been pole-axed. For a moment he seemed to stare through his nephew as if he could see someone else, someone who filled his mind with dread and rage.

"You be the Cossack, then, Uncle Jem!" Sam was excited to see his uncle's reaction. He loved nothing better than to have someone willing to join him in his fantasy fighting. Uncle Jem, now the Crimean hero, made the best playmate in the world before the war, always ready to join in his nephews' scampering.

"Shut up! Shut up! Shut up!" Jem's face was contorted with an emotion Thirza didn't recognise in him. He sent the razor spinning from Sam's hand with a swiping blow that knocked the lad off his feet and he fell sprawling into the mud and straw.

It took Jack and Thomas all their strength combined to pull Jem off the boy.

"Where did you come from?" Jem screamed into Sam's face. Thirza could see Francis sniggering in the mill doorway, pretending suddenly to be occupied with the sacks. Grace appeared, fresh from plaiting some dough, her eyes wide. Half the village would hear about this before nightfall.

Jack and Thomas pinioned Jem's arms.

"God help us! On both sides now! Let me through! Let me back through!" Jem struggled to free himself from what he saw as his captors. "Dammit, where's the brigade?" Jem was sobbing now. His physical strength, so weakened, made it impossible for him to break free.

"Calm, now, Jem. It's only Sammy's way. You're a hero to the lad. Calm yourself, do." Jack spoke up strongly and wisely, though Thirza could see that he was shaking. Jem slumped between his father and brother-in-law like a doll of straw. Moments later he looked at Sam, still snivelling on the ground, shaken though quite unhurt.

"For God's sake, Sam, forgive me," he begged. "War's no game. Heroes no victors."

"Go inside to your grandma, lad," Thomas helped Sam to his feet. The lad was still shaking, glancing back at his beloved uncle as if he were a stranger.

"No work to do?" Thomas saw Francis and Grace standing together whispering. "I must be paying you two too much."

Thirza was grateful her grandfather could turn anything into a joke of sorts and make the gloomiest atmosphere seem bearable. She picked up the chestnut razor case and fitted the razor back into its moulded velvet indentation. The emblem of Jem's regiment, emblazoned on the ivory handle in gold and crimson, made it a thing of great value and beauty. Thirza was horrified such a beautiful thing could bring the shadow of suffering to threaten her family. She'd so been looking forward to this day.

As she closed the razor case, she was relieved to see Darnell riding up, alone. How Emma would have clucked and swooned at such a public outburst in the open street.

"What's happening here? I could hear shouting as I rode," Darnell threw the reins over his horse's head and looked at the pale, drawn faces of his family. Thomas was already inside, calming Sam and Kezzie, having taken Jem with him to get him out of the unwelcome gaze of the servants and some villagers close enough to witness their private spectacle.

"It's nothing," Jack motioned Thirza to hand him Jem's razor case.

"Let me see that," Darnell took the case and examined it. He shook his head, sadly.

"I know this. Jem had it with him when I met him the other night wandering about in the fields back there. I was riding out to check on a tenant's wife and child who were very sick. Jem was there with," he opened the case and nodded, "yes, I believe it was this lethal but lovely blade."

"You saw him with the razor?" Jack looked at Thirza and wondered whether it was right for her to witness this.

"I saw him with the case, at first. He seemed distant, distracted, somehow. Not quite himself. You remember how blithe he used to be before all this business abroad?"

"Go in, Thirza," Jack had little hope she'd obey.

"Father! I'm not a child! You don't need to coddle me! I know something horrible is happening to Jem."

"Dear niece, I wish I could say differently. I persuaded him that night to take the blade home and put it back in his army chest where he told me he keeps it close. But then, at some ungodly hour," Darnell went on, his voice full of regret, "I saw him walking with this very blade. I spoke to him, but he said nothing back. I confess I was worried about his sanity. Then he came to himself and I let him go. Now I feel, if any harm had befallen you here, Thirza!" he trailed off, biting his lip.

"It was my brother who enraged him with his pestering about the Light Brigade. Mr Tennyson little dreamed how his clever rhymes would stir Jem up to such a display as this!" Thirza found Darnell's presence reassuring. He would look out for Jem when she left with her father. When they returned, Jem's health and spirits might have improved, with care and understanding.

"This is my fault," Darnell said, "for not bringing him home immediately. He's tired and overwrought. Now this."

Inside, they found Kezzie had put Jem to bed, feverish and distressed at his outburst, quite unable to eat the dinner his mother had prepared for them all.

"Well, you eat. I'll take the case up to him and make sure he's settled," offered Darnell. "That's the least I can do."

They heard quiet words overhead, so soft that Thirza couldn't make out what was being said. She was just thankful

Jem was no longer shouting or upset. Darnell came downstairs after a few minutes.

"He's sleeping like a baby. I've put the razor case safely away, where this lad can't get at it." Darnell ruffled Sam's hair, looking at Thirza. "I'm sorry, as ever, affairs call me away, but it's good to see you, Jack. I know Thirza has missed you all. She's made a good start here."

Thirza couldn't believe her good fortune. Darnell was gracious not to tell her father what had happened at the Hall. When Darnell had ridden away, the meal continued in silence, broken from time to time by appreciative remarks about Kezzie's cooking. By the time slices of home baked cake were passed along the table, Sam had recovered his appetite.

"Grandma, do you think I could have Judd's slice, so it won't be wasted? I think I could maybe manage Uncle Jem's, too. It's very good cake!"

The laughter was easier now. Thirza decided when her father and Sam made a move to get underway, she'd go and fetch her things. She'd no need to worry about Jem, if Darnell was looking out for him. She'd visit as often as she could. With Judd working in Hull and Sam's head full of steam engines and speed, her father would soon be so glad to have her back aboard that this time of uncertainty on the Nab would be behind her. She could say her goodbyes from the deck, leaving just as irrevocably as she'd arrived.

#

Coming in for breakfast the following morning, Thirza was relieved to see Jem already sitting by the fire with Sam, making a railway engine out of tiny sticks and bobbins.

"The wind's getting up. Sam and me, we'd better be getting back, though I'm full enough to bust from sampling the dainties piled on your groaning board yesterday," Jack told Kezzie, who laughed her most girlish chuckle and told Grace to put another rasher of home-cured bacon on the griddle.

"Wind getting up?" Thomas was concerned about his own set of sails. "If it's coming off the fen lively, I'll need to set the new sails at dagger reef."

"I can do that, Father, you stay by the fire." Jem had woken with his own resolve this morning. He'd a lot to prove to show all was well again, after the distress he'd caused yesterday. At all costs, he must pull himself together. He had to begin coping with the demands of becoming a miller again. He went out, looking more cheerful than Thirza had seen him yet, though she wondered if his smile was fixed or genuine.

Soon her moment would come. She'd feel the rise and rock of the river beneath her heels and the kick of the tiller as they went from lock to lock under the salt fret that hung over the marshes. She thought of Bram, but resolved she wouldn't spoil today with regrets for things she couldn't alter.

Sam brought the engine his uncle Jem had helped him make to Thirza at the kitchen table. She sat with him on the floor, among make-believe sheds and sidings, as Thomas and Jack were talking above their heads.

"Good to see Jem more like himself this morning," Jack said in a low tone so Kezzie wouldn't hear him from the kitchen.

"He'll get over this," Thomas said, "for he's a deep lad but he won't easily give in to this melancholy. I hope that was the crisis, like a fever breaking."

"From here forward, 'Calm Sea and Prosperous Voyage'," mused Jack, mindful he'd heard those words once in a tavern, when a fiddler was playing popular melodies to the sailors. He'd thought then, those words described all he'd hoped for in his life's voyage, yet so often been denied since Dinah's death.

"Calm apart from choppy rumours," Thomas grumbled. "People love to gossip in a village. This whisper about some infernal new mill."

"A wharfinger in Mexborough over in the valley of the Dearne was talking some such piffle the other day," said Jack. "He also said he heard some landowner had found minerals under his land near Rotherham. Gold in the coal seam. I ask you! Gold! Black diamonds! We should be rich!"

The men laughed together.

Kezzie came through from the kitchen with a tray full of bacon and eggs which she set before them. Jack began to protest but she tutted and added another rasher to his plate.

"To sustain you on your voyage, lad. I saw that handbill about the mill. Some folk have more money than sense."

"They say it'll have turrets and battlements and a top to the windmill like Hoober Stand or Hoyland Lowe," Grace joined in, "and just as the goatsucker portends death, there's rumours you'd be mad to ignore."

"Hush, girl, your head's full of fancy! Goatsuckers! I shudder to hear you!" Kezzie brushed the notion under the carpet in her mind before it could wipe its feet.

Thirza crawled from under the table. She was getting cramp and Sam had lost interest in his model train and was looking for other diversions.

"Sailors have superstitions too, don't they, Father?" Thirza teased. "Mariner's lore. Don't sail if you see a cross-eyed person, or a priest, or a person with flat feet or red hair."

Jack roared with laughter.

"I knew a master mariner at Althorpe had red hair. I dare say, if half these things were worth our credence, he couldn't look in the mirror to shave his beard, for fear of sinking the next time he set sail!"

"The good Lord made the sea before the dry land, you and Mother used to tell me!" Thirza thought her heart would burst. She'd soon be afloat and home.

"He did that, out of the chaos." Thirza saw Jack's face turn suddenly wistful. "You know, lass, times are hard."

"Hard times, hard measures," Thomas carried on with his own thread of doom as he tucked into the salty bacon.

"I meant to tell you, Thirzie, but I confess, I turned coward and put it off."

Thirza's throat was dry. She felt the bombshell falling

and knew this time she wouldn't be able to dodge its impact.

"You see, it's like this. I'm getting older and my legs aren't what they were for climbing and gallivanting. This last winter's made my mind up. Seeing you settled here's made me proud of you, being so brave and adaptable. Your mother would have been so proud, too, if she were here."

Jack struggled to master his emotions. Thirza felt his words as much as heard them.

"You know, as I say, times are tough on the cut. The railways are spreading like a great steaming octopus and there's talk in future they'll suck up our trade altogether. You should hark at your brothers. They know where their future lies and it isn't on 'Thistle', good old girl as she is," Jack hesitated again, blinking, "anyway, even now, the rheumatics are biting. I've resolved to sell her, when I can tie up my affairs and retire ashore. I can haul as a horse marine or go as a purchase man for my snap and my keep. That's the size of it."

Jack finished in a rush and looked at Thirza. He knew how she'd feel. He felt the same right to his soul.

"What do you say, lass?"

Thirza shook her head till the tears spilled, but she couldn't trust herself to speak.

"Can we go, now?" Sam was growing restless, keen on finding better fun. Adult seriousness made him itch to be elsewhere, even back on the draughty ship.

"Yes, lad, we'd best get off. We'll be spilling the wind all the way to Keadby if its blowing like this," Jack hugged Thirza as he rose to leave. She saw his leg was dragging, after his efforts with the mill sails yesterday. She couldn't just think of herself any more. She could hardly think of anything. She saw her future hopes ebbing out of reach, like the wall of the harbour where the ocean runs out.

14. TILL MAY BE OUT

May Day dawned through the crack in the windmill wall and shone into Thirza's eyes to wake her. For the past week, since 'Thistle' sailed away, she'd been going through the motions of life. As always, she drank life in through her senses, but her head was far away. She heard the sugary hiss of the flowing grain, the buzz of the fantail turning the sails into the wind, the damsel chattering, the tinkling whenever the level of the grain hopper got too low, the bell on its leather strap dragged against the spinning quant. This happened whenever Jem was left to mind the mill. He'd be left in charge when Thomas went below to bathe his eye with Darnell's special eye bath somewhere Kezzie wouldn't spot him and worry.

Yesterday Kezzie doused the fire so it could be lit afresh from the Beltane fires some villagers still kindled around the borders of the peatlands to welcome the spring.

"Old wives' tales again, old wife?" Thomas pushed his luck. Kezzie smacked him tenderly round the ear with the dishcloth.

Jem had grown stronger since he first came back from the Crimea, but he was still preoccupied and distant at times. Sometimes, he was miller for the whole day when Thomas was at market or delivering flour with Francis on the cart.

Some days Thirza heard Jem singing to the rhythms of the cogs and wheels. Other days he'd get a hunted look in his eyes. Thirza had come to know that look and knew then his heart was hurting.

"Vicious damned machine," she heard him muttering to himself as he struggled to keep the mill fed. Like a petulant tell-tale, it would open its throat to scream, with its tyrannical little warning bell, whenever Jem failed to keep the grain topped up.

But this May Day morning, Thirza had other things on her mind. Today, she'd intended to be back on the canal. Now that door was closed, unless a miracle happened and her father didn't sell 'Thistle' or retire to a permanent berth.

"Look what Missus found for you on the doorstep!" Grace was dressed in a white frock and her mousy hair's golden tints were emphasised by buttercups wound through her locks. "May Day? Didn't you celebrate on your boat?" Grace looked at Thirza as if she were an idiot, come down from the moon.

Thirza picked up the little posy of flowers from the table. It was beautiful. Tiny forget-me-nots, blue stars with a tiny coronet of gold in the middle, hawthorn and orange blossom in creams and dazzling white, all tied with a lemon coloured bow. On the bow, written in ink, her name spelled out.

"Where did this come from?" Thirza was a little more frightened than flattered.

"A sweetheart, of course. I got mine from my sweetheart," Grace fetched her flowers from the kitchen, a bunch of Lily of the Valley. Thirza was transported by the heady fragrance of the flowers.

"I haven't got a sweetheart," she said, immediately wishing she hadn't said it. Grace rolled her eyes in disbelief.

"I'd a sweetheart when I was sixteen!"

Thirza went back outside. Kezzie waved from the field at the back.

"Did Grace show you your posy? Well, my lass, you're a dark horse. A gentleman's taken a shine to you, by the look of it. I think the squire writing's not unlike that!"

Thirza blushed. Lucas hardly knew her. What he knew her for best was the ungrateful young woman who'd snubbed his family's generosity up at Foljambe Hall, the beggarly waif who burst in on him and Darnell at their secretive tryst in the big round chamber, stumbling about in borrowed slippers. This was no fairytale!

Kezzie sniffed the posy as she came past Thirza into the house with the slop pail emptied.

"You always remember your first sweetheart!"

"Is Miss Thirza coming to the May Day dancing, ma'am?" Grace asked, as if Thirza were not still in earshot of the open door. "Perhaps they don't have May, where she comes from."

Thirza set off in the direction of the moorland. She tucked the posy into her bodice, then felt conspicuous and put it in her pocket with the clockwork nightjar, taking care not to crush the blooms.

She'd no desire for dancing, but she knew if she was to make her way forward and not keep looking over her shoulder to the past, there was someone she had to talk to. She reached the pinfold, but it was deserted. She'd hoped Bram would be there. As she looked over the wall, she saw something that made her stomach contract. A dead goat, pale tongue protruding and glassy-eyed, lay in the long grass. She'd been less shocked by the adder.

Somebody gave a squeal behind her. Thirza jumped, thinking she might have been set up for a joke, a May Day village prank or custom she hadn't heard of. There were so many of those.

"Goatsucker! Goatsucker!" One of the girls she'd seen in the village was running back towards the nearest cottage, dressed in white, like everyone Thirza had seen today. Perhaps it was all a ritual or a stupid joke after all. Thirza shuddered. On the moors, where few people ever seemed to venture, she'd be free of all this madness, if only for an hour or two. She'd go where maypoles and forced merriment would be far away. Dead goats, too.

She strode out onto the fen in the direction of Bram's hut and the decoy. As she traced her fingertips idly round the ribbon of the posy in her pocket, she felt a raised ridge underneath it. She pulled out the tiny garland and looked at it more closely. She pulled the ribbon aside and saw the blooms were held together with a tight band. It was a thin strip of sedge, circling the stems and holding the nosegay together.

Her heart almost stopped. Was this Lucas's work, or Bram's? She wondered if she should go back the way she'd come. Would she seem forward to seek out the man who'd sent this? That hadn't been her intention. As before, she felt ignorant about the etiquette by which these landlubbers lived. She didn't count herself among their number. Being an alien in this foreign country locked her constantly into this feeling of being cast adrift.

"Turn back, coward, or stride out and face him!" Thirza had a stern word with herself while nobody else could hear her.

At last, as the sun climbed through the soft blue air, she saw Bram in the distance. He was broddling in a ditch, clearing away weeds and bracken litter. He must've seen her but for some minutes he made no sign. Thirza strode on until she was just a few yards away. She stopped and he lay down his tools and wiped his brow with the back of his gauntlet.

"I thought you must've gone away," he said. "I kept seeing keels going along the canal. I felt sure you'd be back afloat by now. I imagined you there as I first saw you that day by the bridge." He took off his gloves. "I'd seen you before that, though you never seemed to notice me."

Thirza pushed the posy deeper into her pocket. Then she decided she had to know for sure. No games. No mysteries. She pulled out the flowers again and held them out to Bram.

"Did you send these?"

"No." said Bram, wishing he had.

Thirza had no idea whether or not she should believe him.

"Look, I'd love you to show me everything you talked about before. I want to see a real goatsucker. I want to know how you live and work. I want to know how you live like you do, on the edge of the planet. I want to understand how you do all that with this...floggy...gisty thing, whatever it is! "

"Phlogiston," the corners of Bram's mouth twitched into a smile at her angry earnestness.

"Phlogiston, then!" Thirza wanted to shake him. "I want you to show me how to work with you, be with you." She felt something warm tickling her hand.

"Stop that, Piper!"

The dog wagged his tail enthusiastically.

"I'll never be crowned May Queen, I'm afraid," Thirza chortled. "Piper knows it! I'm never going to be ladylike enough to prance about in a white frock with flowers in my hair. Show me some more of your fenny phlogiston ways, do, Bram, so I can at least earn my keep in this weird world of yours!"

Thirza saw some leather leggings lying in the grass and began to pull them on. Bram was helpless with laughter.

"Show me, then!" she pulled the leggings over her shoes and stockings and fell over.

Bram offered her his arm and she pulled herself up, pretending to be cross.

"You're supposed to take your shoes off, first," he suggested, trying to sound serious.

"You might have said," she blustered, then wondered if she'd gone quite mad to come here. He seemed the only person on earth who really understood her, but the way they'd parted, she questioned how it could be she felt so certain.

"I want you to show me how the decoy works, what Phlogiston does, where goatsuckers live, how you go broddling out ditches with that thing..."

"My scuppit," muttered Bram, not missing a beat.

"Scuppit, whatever that is and the funny ducks and whatever you do all day, every day, out in this wilderness!"

They were both laughing, now. Neither really cared

why any more. Thirza, in that moment, felt at one with creation, suspended in time, their laughter blowing back beyond the ordinary, through the whispering sedge and alder. She'd forgotten she could be happy, away from the keel, but here she was and here was Bram.

"That doesn't look quite right," Bram watched Thirza adjusting the leggings under her flounced skirts.

"Our skirts are getting wider and our options fewer," Thirza grumbled, lacing up her shoes again. "But I can make myself useful. You were just beginning to see I could, when I so foolishly threw your kindness and patience back in your face."

"Forgotten," said Bram. "It's funny, but I don't remember that at all."

Thirza raised her eyebrows.

"I thought you considered me a case for charity."

"Never."

"I'm truly sorry I was so rude and hasty."

Piper cavorted round Thirza, showing he'd never come across such a spectacle as a lady in leggings before.

"What next, eh, Piper? Breeches and a pipe?" laughed Bram.

Piper cocked his ear.

"Don't listen to your master, Piper. He's teasing you, and me," said Thirza, tucking the hem of her cumbersome skirts and petticoats as best she could into the top of the leggings.

"Most decorous, madam," said Bram.

"So where do I start?" Thirza looked round. If she could handle a barge in a headstrong wind, or the jobs at the windmill and farm when required, it didn't enter her head that working alongside Bram for a few hours would pose any challenge she couldn't meet. She felt she could learn anything, under these open skies with Bram's gentle guidance to help her. She said so to him.

"I know you could. My people have worked this way from cradle to grave since Vermuyden drained the fens. I never yet had to teach the crafts to anybody. But my father and grandfather were wise teachers to me. They didn't use many words, but I see you've two good eyes, two excellent ears."

"And a mouth, you'll discover," laughed Thirza.

"Yes, I noticed. One mouth to every pair of ears and eyes. The healthy balance for a quiet life. All the better for learning the ways of the marshes from the creatures all around us," Bram sounded mischievous, yet perfectly sincere.

"Next time, I'm leaving my stiffeners out," muttered Thirza, still having difficulty making her clothes adjust to her activities.

Bram looked genuinely alarmed.

"They say the next thing will be steel hoops! All these layers of ruffles and flounces, then horsehair braids, that's how we lasses manage to take the paint off both sides of a doorway, sweeping into a room," Thirza demonstrated.

"Well, the only hoops you'll need here at the decoy are the kind that Piper, the ducks and I will show you. Step this way, if you're ready."

"I'm more than ready!" Thirza felt that for every challenge now, she truly was. "Where do we start?"

Thirza followed Bram to the mouth of the decoy without a word. He pointed to the tame ducks and gave her a small bag of hempseed. He indicated she should scatter them in the water in the centre of the decoy, just where the mallards were gathered quacking.

"The wind's coming from the northeast today," he whispered, his lips close to her neck as he lit a taper of peat turf.

"Won't the smoke frighten the birds away?" Thirza coughed and fanned the pungent fumes with the rich tang of roasted earth. Bram quenched the smouldering torch and put it quietly down by the pool.

"That's to disguise the scent of our bodies. We don't want the wild birds to know we're here. No problem with my clockwork, phlogiston powered ones, but I'm showing you the more traditional way. When live wildfowl come at night and any are injured or sick, I heal them. Can you be here next full moon in the evening, so I can show you properly? I'll light the turf so you can see where I am. Then approach me softly in the twilight and Piper and the fowl will show us which of them may need help. Or at least I can show you the way we do it, even if no birds seem to need us. Most marshmen take birds to sell for game meat, but my people taught me a different way. So I gather in the wounded birds, the sick creatures that can't fend for themselves."

"To end their misery?"

"To end their misery." Bram wondered if she really understood his meaning. His heart was beating so fast he felt unsteady on his feet, as though the marsh under them was drifting into another universe, off kilter and on fire.

Thirza was disappointed. She'd hoped to be able to go straight to work, learning Bram's ways.

"But where will they be, if this pond decoys them?" She was still puzzled by the whole idea. Bram didn't laugh at her or mock her for her ignorance. He'd never dreamed anyone would come over his horizon with a real thirst for nature, who cared about its sights and sounds and scents even a fraction as much as he did himself.

"Decoy doesn't mean ensnare. Decoy's the English way of saying 'eendenkooi'."

Thirza curled her tongue around the exotic sounding syllables.

"Eendenkooi."

"It's the Dutch tongue. It just means "duck cage". That's where the decoy came from. The Low Countries are filled with water, canals, boats and windmills."

"Sounds like my kind of place," Thirza smiled.

"I've never been there myself, but my ancestors recreated a pocket of Holland right here on the low country of the fens."

"So you don't decoy ducks away from anything, after all?" Thirza persisted, secretly reluctant to leave Bram here so soon. Next full moon sounded so far away!

"In fact, I tempt them close, away from harm." Bram

came closer to Thirza as he spoke. "They're so curious about the dog and the other ducks, the tame ones and even the special ones you saw, like your little nightjar toy, it gives me chance to tempt them up the pipes. There are your hoops arching over like hidden rainbows, holding up the nets. The screens are meant to hide us from their sight. Then I encourage them into the net, with Piper's help, at the end of the pipe. I keep them sheltered there. Any who need my care I protect and heal with the soothing light and vibrations from the fen, that my people learned to harness. Wildfowl on these wetlands aren't destined for the tables of the rich for their greed. The precious innocent creatures are free to go their ways in peace."

Thirza enjoyed the simple way Bram painted pictures of his craft with his words. He limned each image in her mind's eye with the gestures he made, drawing the stages of the process in the air, or with the tip of his boot on the ground.

"I'd better give you these back for now, then," Thirza started to pull off the leggings.

"Stay a while, if you like. I'm cleaning out this ditch next. To 'fie' it, as we say. You've seen my special tools, this scuppit, for flinging out muddy water overhead without it landing back on top of me, hence this leather cowl. Then the meg here with my old scythe blade on the end. The dydle, with the mesh at the end of the pole to scoop out weeds just cut with the meg. Heavy, awkward work, but it seems to me you don't stay away when things get challenging."

"Great names for keels, those, the Meg, the Scuppit and the Dydle!" Thirza was still struggling to kick off the leggings.

Bram's heart felt shocked by tingles of crystalline power as he looked at her. He hardly knew where he'd found this boldness to talk to her so freely, let alone dare to suggest another meeting.

He averted his eyes as he found himself longing to watch her slender ankle sliding out of its leather sheath. That was too much. He didn't ever want to lose sight of the fact he was her only protector here. She'd placed her safety and her life, for these moments they were together, completely in his hands. He felt his blood stirring in ways he'd never dreamed of before and wondered how such a wonderful, unlooked-for joy had come his way. He thought of the posy in her pocket and sighed.

"I won't try to steal your gauntlets as I did the leggings, or you may get tired of me too soon!" Thirza teased.

"They wouldn't fit tight on hands so dainty, if you're fishing for a compliment," Bram joked, putting the gauntlets back on. She watched him working his way along the drainage ditch and tried the tools for herself between the slats that held back the flow on either side of where they were working.

"Dammin boards," he explained the name of them.

"No need to curse, Mr Dutchy, sir," Thirza loved to make Bram's laugh ring out so heartily it made her own heart sing.

Thirza felt so proud to work side by side with him. She soon found her rhythm and was lulled by the birds calling all around her. She knew the wildlife of the hedgerows and the sea birds that thronged the harbours, but some of the plaintive voices heard when the two of them fell into a comfortable silence were new to her. The hours slipped by until they were standing on their own tall shadows in the late afternoon.

Bram stopped from time to time to tell her the names of the birds they heard, each one a strange echo of its song in Yorkshire dialect. Thirza laughed in delight at the odd names.

"I'll know when I hear a butter bump, a flock of spuggies or a passing ullat hunting over the marshes, but what in earth or heaven's the call I heard when I escaped from the Hall, the night Jem came home?"

Bram tried to imagine which creature Thirza was trying so hard to imitate. She constricted her throat to reproduce the weird rasping cry, scraping and grinding on two clear notes through the misty air, that had chilled the blood in her veins that night.

The effect wasn't quite what she'd hoped for. Bram was hooting with laughter before she could complete the chirring impression of the unknown beast of the twilight.

"Again! That was very convincing. Your face's a picture! I felt the moon gliding up through the dusk and the sun setting over the sedge!"

"You're mocking me!" Thirza scolded as she tried again to recreate the call. It took all her lung power to sustain the notes.

"Sounds to me as though you've already met the bird you carry in your pocket. You've heard the uncanny minstrel, the gabble-ratchet, the nightjar as he's often called, for his jarring song, the churn owl, the puckeridge, country folks call him..."

"The goatsucker!" Thirza took her mother's clockwork bird out and held it up, amazed, "So that was you, goatsucker? But why do folk tell such blood-curdling stories about you? They say you attack cattle, goats and sheep, suck them dry of milk. Grace Canner swore it was the goatsucker killed my grandmother's pet hen! Not sucking milk, but blood! Passing the pinfold, I saw a dead goat and somebody screamed about it being the work of the goatsucker. It's all just a silly tale, right, Bram?"

Bram took in the new information with alarm.

"I left no goat in the pinfold. No stray goats when I checked the tally there this morning."

"One lay dead there when I passed," said Thirza, "I forgot to tell you. I'm sorry."

"I should go back and investigate, as soon as we're finished here," Bram wiped the tools and put them to dry on the roof of his hut.

"How can it be a story, if I heard its call?" Thirza hurried to keep up with Bram as they set off back towards the village.

"The goatsucker is just a bird. You'll hear him at night if you come next full moon. The nightjar's a beautiful, shy creature, but human ignorance persists. We both know about name-calling!"

"But what's all this about blood?"

"The nightjar comes out at night, sometimes lying still for hours, rocking from foot to foot, looking calmly ahead with its huge, wise eyes shining, so it gathers these false notions around it with no reason. It couldn't suck blood or milk, nor harm human or beast. Its song's reserved for wild places. Your mumming of it was amazing!" Bram thought of Thirza's enthusiasm as she tried to mimic the bird she'd never seen and how stunning she was in her abandon. He wished they could spend the whole day out on the moors together. But he wouldn't neglect his duty, or put her in danger. He held the picture in his heart of Thirza coming out to him at dusk under the full Milk Moon. Nothing could steal or spoil that. To share these ancient ways with Thirza, was to share a part of his heart that he'd shared with no other human being. He'd nobody else on earth to whom he could pass his knowledge. She seemed so eager to learn. The days were passing away, he felt in his pulse, when these things would be known without explanation and done without reflection.

They bantered back and forth until the pinfold was in sight and they heard the sound of the musicians playing for the maypole dancing. Thirza stayed as close to Bram as she could without treading on his heels as he unlatched the gate and entered to check his wooden tally stick against the number of stray animals kept there. She looked down into the grass where the dead goat lay. There was nothing to be seen.

Bram glanced at her face. Had she really seen any such thing? Village superstition could sweep people up in a web of vicious rumour and panic. He'd seen it before. He feared one day he would see it again. Superstition comforted those who believed nothing wholesome and compassionate about the world, lulling, trapping and enslaving them in its nets, just like wild ducks in a decoy in former days.

"I did see it! That girl screamed. She must've seen it too."

"Well, never mind," Bram felt in the long grass but there was nothing in the pinfold now but cow-parsley, dandelions and a couple of cow-pats.

"I didn't imagine it," but Thirza was beginning to doubt. Here in the village, her troubles hung around her shoulders as before. The keel about to be sold forever. Her grandfather going completely blind. Jem, so troubled and unpredictable. The villagers' mockery of her water gypsy ways. The rest of the nonsense she escaped whenever she was with Bram.

They stood together, listening to the old melodies floating from the village green where dancing was giving way to drinking as children were coaxed home to their beds after a long day's merriment.

"Will you dance with me, pinder?" Thirza heard herself saying. Bram snorted with laughter at the very idea of his cavorting around in the middle of a crowd all jeering at his clumsiness.

"I must get back, now you're safely back on the beaten path and the fold's tranquil."

Thirza nodded. She wished she'd never shown him the garland in her pocket.

"Till the next full moon, then?" She hoped she'd not dreamed that invitation, too.

"Just at dusk," Bram nodded and tipped his hat, walking back onto the turf that rose imperceptibly towards the moors. Without his stilts, he looked smaller than his own shadow. Thirza stood looking after him.

"Will you dance with me, Miss Holberry?"

She turned to see Lucas Charlesworth standing offering her his arm. She hesitated for a moment, then linked her arm in his.

15. ECHOES FROM THE EDGE

"I don't really dance, Lord Charlesworth. Only reels and hornpipes to make my brothers laugh."

"I don't laugh enough, Darnell always tells me," Lucas led Thirza up to the deserted maypole and bowed to her as if they'd joined a formal ball. She curtseyed, her petticoat layers uncomfortably twisted round where she'd tucked the edges of her skirt into Bram's leggings.

"What must I look like to him?" Thirza wondered. After a few turns, Lucas seemed to lose interest in the dancing, but continued to watch Thirza's movements with approval. He clapped to encourage her, rather out of time with the fiddler's music coming from the beer house. Her nostrils told her he'd partaken of a few jars there already.

Thirza's shoulders and neck ached from 'croming, slubbing and bottomfying' the ditch, in Bram's words. She found herself jigging alone in circles, while Lucas stood in the centre, appraising the angles her lone streamer made as it wrapped itself widdershins round the pole, until she saw him stifling a yawn, so she dropped the ribbon to rejoin its fellows hanging aimlessly.

"Thank you, Miss Holberry, a very study in locomotion. Will you walk back to the windmill with me?" Again Lucas offered his arm without looking at her. "I paid a call on your family with Darnell on business earlier. He's there now, helping with the accounts, as I believe," he examined his nails, "there has been a difficulty."

Thirza thought Lucas's nails were so pink and perfect they'd never seen a day's hard work such as she and Bram had done, or like his own tenants had performed for their supper.

"What difficulty? Is it my uncle Jem?"

"The affairs of men, Miss Holberry. Too troubling for you, I'm sure. On a prettier topic, have you heard of Miss Florence Nightingale?"

Thirza was so taken aback by the implication she was too woolly-headed to understand life, she bit her tongue only just in time to stop herself making a sharp reply.

"Of course, we've all heard how she helps the wounded soldiers in the Crimea. We wish Uncle Jem..."

"Miss Nightingale has done well, in the headstrong, well-meaning way of a woman. Do you read, Miss Holberry?"

Thirza was cut off mid-sentence as Lucas went on eagerly, "I've been reading in the papers about the new portable hospital planned by Mr Brunel, a true hero of our times. Do you know Mr Brunel, Miss Holberry?"

Thirza couldn't resist retorting, "Not personally, I confess, but yes, I know he's a great engineer."

Lucas didn't laugh at her joke, or alter his earnest tone of instruction.

"Mr Brunel plans to ship out this temporary hospital to a place called Renkioi in the Dardanelles. Do you know the Dardanelles, Miss Holberry?"

Thirza didn't trouble herself to answer this time. As expected, Lucas went on at once, uninterrupted by any need for his companion's contribution to his monologue.

"It will be better in every way, in comparison to the facilities Miss Nightingale has already. Better sanitation, better rehabilitation. I was telling Jem about it, this morning."

"Jem hardly speaks about Miss Nightingale," Thirza jumped in, "He never talks, you see, about the days he spent recuperating in hospital, before the Medical Board discharged him. Jem's best friend died in the hospital, Granddad says."

"He grew a little..." Lucas wrinkled his eyebrows, searching for the words, "agitated, shall we say? Darnell assured me Jeremy would be most flattered by my interest in the matter. But then, one can only try one's best to help a lost cause, as Darnell often observes."

Thirza felt a sense of alarm as they walked up to the mill.

"Was Jem upset?"

"I came away to watch the dancing while Darnell was calming him. I didn't want to intrude on your family for too long on their holiday. I'd hoped to spend some time in your company, you see. I fear your uncle Jeremy will prove too much for your grandparents, if he continues so, but you mustn't trouble your pretty head about it. Leave the affairs of the mill to Darnell. He has everybody's best interests at heart."

Thirza knew this was true enough. She also knew how agitated Jem often grew when the Crimea was mentioned, or questions asked. As they drew near, apart from the visitors' horses tethered in the mill yard, the place seemed deserted and the windmill sails left in the position of the St Andrew's cross. This was a kind of code to those outside, that the miller was taking a break and would shortly return to grinding.

As Thirza let go of Lucas's arm, he bowed and she felt the posy, now a little less fresh for its day in her pocket.

"Lucas," Thirza drew out the wilting bunch, "I received a posy today."

He looked down at the floppy flowers.

"Miss Holberry! I thought my gift had miscarried."

"You're very kind," Thirza knew she should be glad of the attentions of such an influential person, but her day on the fen prevented her feeling wholly overjoyed at his admission. She might have known Bram wouldn't have said he hadn't sent it if he had.

"My housekeeper made it up specially."

Thirza hadn't envisaged another party being involved in the preparation of the intimate gesture.

"Darnell wrote your name there for me when he came to call. His penmanship is splendid, don't you agree? He suggested such a trinket might please you. He thought you needed cheering, I believe. He told me in confidence he was sure you have no sweetheart. A sorry position for a lady to find herself in, on a day when the whole world seems intent on such fripperies."

Lucas's speech left a lot to be desired as a lover's, Thirza decided. She didn't know if she felt relieved or disappointed, but she thanked him warmly and he beamed back at her as if she'd made his holiday complete.

"All very satisfactory, Miss Holberry. We must walk out again on such an evening and talk again."

"Thank you kindly," Thirza didn't recall doing much of the talking.

Inside Mill Cottage, Darnell was standing, as usual, at the fireplace, while Kezzie and Grace were in the kitchen and Thomas on the settle.

"Thirza and her special friend are returned, at last, from the dancing," said Darnell, mischievously winking at Thomas, who was in no position to wink more than usual, but looked pleased, just the same.

"Young lads and lasses will sport themselves from dawn till dusk to bring in the May," said the miller. "Thirza, were you Queen of the May? Kezzie said she didn't see you there."

"I found her Queen of the May, or indeed, of any month," Lucas blurted out, as if he'd rehearsed it. Thirza saw Darnell nodding in satisfaction at his cousin's statement.

"Meanwhile, here," he purred, "I'm sure all will be sorted out, God willing, with a little help from us and the indulgent custom of your neighbours."

Darnell put his hat on and nodded again to Lucas. Thirza was glad he could be so sensitive. He never outstayed his welcome, or prolonged a delicate situation. Unlike

Emma, he never made Thirza feel he couldn't wait to be elsewhere, even when his business was pressing.

"I've checked Jem's room," Darnell went on, "and there's no immediate cause for alarm. He must have misplaced the item, that's all. He panics so, which is understandable, after all he's gone through. Try not to be too hard on him, dear Father. Give him more responsibility and I've no doubt he will rise to it."

Thirza wasn't sure what Darnell meant but suspected May Day at Kitson's Windmill hadn't been as tranquil as she'd hoped when she left for the day's holiday. She almost wished she'd stayed here after all.

Outside, after Lucas had paid his gauche court to Thirza, Darnell leaned down from the saddle.

"My cousin has high hopes of you, dear Thirza. I know you won't disappoint him. I always speak in your favour. Look to Jem, though. There was some talk of an incident with a razor again, in the village. I could get no sense from him, but I managed to sort it all out, before the revelries began. I hope I've saved him from any shameful accusations."

"What's happened?" Thirza remembered the goat. Darnell studied her puzzled expression.

"There were reports, idle gossip, of course, that a goat was seen with terrible wounds in the pinfold and that a razor, like we've all now seen in Jem's possession...well, no more. I hope to have sorted it all out, to save further scandal."

He spurred his horse on. Thirza went into the windmill. All was silent.

"Jem?"

No answer.

Thirza climbed the ladders, floor by floor, until she found Jem sitting on the bins, staring vacantly.

"Uncle Jem?" Thirza approached him quietly. "Is all the grinding done for the day?"

"I didn't leave the mill!"

"I know," Thirza kept all the worry out of her voice, as far as she was able. She wished she could get Jem to confide in her, as Darnell seemed able.

"You need to come in and rest yourself, Uncle."

"A farmer came. Roaring about finding blood in his flour. Something about a goat, too. Said his friends had seen the same. They say Francis saw my razor."

"Where?" Thirza sounded more sharp than she intended.

"Francis says so too. He said everything just as Darnell told me he would. I knew I'd lost it. But I don't know where."

"Where did Francis see your razor?" Thirza felt confused.

"In the pinfold. Darnell keeps saying he made it alright. Says he told them it was all confounded nonsense and gave them their money back. Says he helped father with the books. Says he's made them all go away. Says it's so I can be quiet. But I know I'm to blame. He says forget, but then he reminds me, but he wasn't even there! I handed it to Matty and Matty died! Darnell keeps talking and talking, talking till I can't remember my own name. Thirza, I don't know what's happening to me!"

Thirza didn't think it was the right moment to ask questions. She sat in silence with Jem like she had with Bram when he mended her basket. Perhaps Bram's "reversal of ravage" was never more needed than in Jem's shattered life. The minutes passed. Maybe it was working. At least Jem seemed calmer. Calmer or just quieter?

Thirza thought of what she'd seen herself in the pinfold, a goat but no razor! That had to be a misunderstanding. Then razor and goat had disappeared! Had Darnell seen Jem's razor there and hidden it so no-one could accuse Jem? Was it safe to cover for him, if he was capable of harm?

Thirza heard Thomas shout up from below, not sounding his usual sunny self.

"Jem? Jeremy! What are you up to now, lad? Have you finished up there? Speak up!"

It wasn't the first time in recent weeks Thirza had

heard them rowing.

"I'm up here with Jem, Granddad."

"Oh, Thirza, I wondered where you'd gone. Dammit, Jem, what a vexation. Farmer Hanson! Been one of our best customers all these years. I can't understand what happened to upset him, to be sure, but your brother-in-law's smoothed everything over again. Can I trust you to finish up there? The light's going, I can't see to spit!"

Thirza could hear from his voice the old man had had enough for one day.

"I'll stay with Jem till he's finished, Granddad. You go and keep Grandma company. Save some May treats for us."

Thirza picked up the broom and swept some husks and grains from round Jem's feet. She wondered how long he'd been sitting there. The cat was curled up in his lap as if puss didn't expect him to disturb her again for a while yet. Thirza clambered up to the dust floor for a moment to adjust her dress with its twisted layers of ruffles and horsehair. She noticed the sacking, where she slept when she needed to withdraw to her snug little sanctuary, was missing. Instead, there were curious pieces of equipment, papers and phials neatly arranged around the curved walls. They looked much like the mesmerising array of scientific apparatus she'd seen in the secret chamber at Foljambe Hall. No wonder Darnell was worried about her coming up here, getting in the way of his contrivances.

Then she noticed something on the floor near the wall, under the ladder up into the cap itself. She picked it up. The Cherry Picker razor case! Inside, nestled on the velvet lining in its place, Jem's cut-throat razor.

Thirza closed the case again, making as little noise as possible, though her own heart was thumping to the point of being deafening in her ears. What did this mean? Why was it up here? Not certain what to do for the best, she replaced the case on the floor and covered it with a spare sack. I can't ask Jem if he put this here, she thought, stopping herself calling out to him as he sat floors below, in a stupor she couldn't penetrate.

Darnell must have thought this was the safest place to leave the case and its dangerous contents. Was that what he'd been trying to tell her as he left with Lucas? Up here, Kezzie was too terrified to climb and Thomas wouldn't see it in the dimness with his failing sight. Francis never bothered to go anywhere in the windmill unless somebody was telling him what to do and when to do it. Grace let Thirza see to any cleaning up here, since she'd made it her own special den. Nobody would find it.

Thirza rejoined Jem below. She smiled her most cheerful smile and tried to be as calm and still as Bram. It was a sunny evening, but when she reached him, Jem was shivering in his shirt sleeves. He looked upwards towards the ladder, as if he expected somebody might be behind her.

"Thirza, do you remember Samphire? Darnell kept mentioning him to me. I don't remember why. He asked about Matty. Then about Samphire."

"Such a beautiful horse." Thirza thought of the dark stallion. She used to think how spirited Jem's horse looked compared to the shaggy horses that gave some keels a tow. Jem groomed Samphire to a gloss and kept him trim and handsome, long before he enlisted with the Cavalry. No wonder he'd signed up for the Light Brigade. Now Samphire's place in the field behind the windmill was occupied by Nero, a bow-legged old cart horse. Jem would stroke Nero as if he could feel Samphire, his noble charger, somehow disguised under the older horse's scabby coat, waiting to ride him away.

"When I was in the hospital in Scutari, I asked them where he was. No-one knew. I stood at his head, noble lad, holding his bridle, on the ship as we sailed away. So many horses in the hold. When the waves rose, all the horses were dashed together. We stood on watch all night at our own horse's head, holding the bridle up, up, so they wouldn't take fright. Samphire's a fine boy, so brave as we sailed in to Sevastopol Bay."

"Uncle, you don't have to tell me," Thirza was suddenly afraid. It had seemed a good idea that he should talk, but now, as he began to open up his deep hidden wounds, she wasn't so sure of anything any more. The mill creaked, as if it, too, had hidden stories it was aching to tell. She sensed it around them, denied the power to drain the fen, itchy in its cladding of bricks and flour dust.

"You'd have loved the sea voyage more than I did," Jem told her. "It took just over a week for the officers who went on the steam ships, but my battalion travelled on a sailing ship. It took us nearly seventy days after we left England. Seemed more like six months to me!"

"The horses on the ship all that time?" Thirza tried to imagine their suffering and had to stop herself.

"Some horses snorted and bucked whenever the wind got up. Samphire only changed his position to lean against me and kept his head down. I bound his eyes so he couldn't see the others when they fell."

Thirza wondered if she should stop him, but Jem seemed to want to go on. In fact, he wouldn't be quietened. He plucked the scenes that ran through his head and poured them out to Thirza like bottled-up poison, slowly killing him from the inside.

"Some men were so sick with the cholera they could barely stand, but Samphire held me up through the worst of it, proud as a palfrey at King Arthur's court."

"Did the horses calm down once you got them ashore?" Thirza asked, hoping the story would soon turn out happier, though deep down she guessed it wouldn't.

"The sailors tried to help us, but the horses were quite maddened by terror. There was this insufferable stench and heat as we came to shore. I could see some of my friends waving, waving at me from the shallows as I came out of the sea with Samphire. I was so thankful to be landing," Jem's eyes glistened in the darkness, "I waded on through them and never stopped."

"They must have been thankful, too, Uncle, to see you all coming towards them, safely off the ship at last!"

"Oh, Thirzie. They were all floating dead! They'd died of the cholera and our officers..."

Thirza ran all the heroic stories she'd read through her mind like a spinning reel of images, but couldn't pick out one where such horrors were told.

"The officers decided too many of us had died of the flux, too many to be buried with military honours in the hard sandy soil. So they threw them all, feet weighted down, into the shallows off the shore. But the weights tied to their feet were too light, Thirzie!"

Jem paused again. The pictures inside his head wouldn't wait for his words to catch up.

"As we passed through the breakers, our dead friends rose up and waved to us, bobbing in the water as they rotted, our friends, our own! They floated up to greet us, heads and shoulders above the waves, smiling to welcome us ashore."

Thirza sat closer to Jem. He sat wringing his hands and shivering. She wondered how he'd borne such sights at all, or survived such horrors as he'd endured.

"They ordered us to leave some of the horses behind until they were needed. But nobody thought to water or feed them. Many more perished. Some had to leave their chargers behind, even officers, with no forage under that blazing sun. Never saw them alive again. But Samphire survived it all. He was with me till we made the charge into the north valley. I had dysentery that made me stagger, a burning thirst with no mouthful of clean water to moisten my tongue, but at least I still had Samphire under me. They promised they'd send him home to me. They promised, when it's all over. The doctors couldn't say where he was stabled when I was shipped back to England. They promised when he was found they'd send him back to me here, somehow. They promised!"

Thirza knew Jem never seemed to hear from anybody, communicate with anybody outside his family since his return to Yorkshire.

"He went down under me as we charged up the valley. I was dragged clear. I woke up on the stretcher, on the ship half way to Scutari. With Matty. Matty! Why did he die when I was trying to make him better? That pill was supposed to kill pain! Not kill! Darnell's made me remember everything!"

Thirza remembered how she'd tried to skip over the frightening things when she read out the newspapers to her brothers. They'd been thirsty for tales of glory, almost beside themselves to know how their glamorous absent uncle might be dressed in his fabulous uniform, charging through enemy ranks. She'd known even then there must be a huge chasm between the stories and the reality. Now she could see it all in Jem's eyes.

When they were both children, Jem made it fun to play around the mill. Now he crept around the place as if he didn't quite know where things fitted, or how the windmill worked. They'd been treading on egg-shells around him all these months. Thirza often felt she was holding his hand in some profound darkness. Now she had no candle to offer him to dispel the impenetrable gloom. She could listen with compassion, but offer no word of experience to match his sorrow. Was his conviction about Samphire false hope? How likely could it be, after all these months, his beautiful charger was still alive?

"Until he comes home, at least I have old Nero," Jem smiled to think of the old cart horse being any sort of a match for his tall war horse. But Nero was here, and until Samphire came trotting into the mill yard, he was all Jem had.

Now, Jem could hardly bear to feel any horse's sensitive back rippling between his calves. Samphire could interpret his every mood, his every command, before he flexed a muscle. Samphire had carried him some way up the valley after he had been knocked unconscious by a shell from the heights. He started to hear the screams and smell the gunpowder and then let the curtain come down on those visions once more. He had to keep it down, or life was too unbearable to go on another second. This much he couldn't say to Thirza, to anybody. Thirza felt the abyss behind the things Jem was saying. It frightened her more than she'd ever feared anything unseen.

"From Samphire the hero to clopping old Nero," she said softly, hoping her clumsy rhyming might coax the carefree, jokey Jem back from where he'd been cowering. For the briefest flicker of a moment, she saw humour reach his eyes, like in the old days before he rode away.

Thirza remembered the razor case up in the cap. Asking about it might ruin what Darnell was so wisely trying to do for his brother-in-law. She kept her counsel and descended the ladder, inviting Jem to follow her.

"I know I should come in, for Mother will fret if I stay here," he said, without moving.

"We all worry, Uncle," Thirza said, wanting to show him how much they all loved him.

"I worry myself, some days," Jem whispered, rising at last to follow Thirza to the cottage. "Where did you disappear to, today?" Jem snecked the door of the mill behind them.

"Just wandering on the fen. I met Mr Beharrell, the pinder," Thirza was cautious. To speak about Bram to anybody seemed to take a sacred moment from her life and cast it down to be trampled.

"He's a good man, that Dutchy," said Jem, with a warmth that surprised and secretly delighted Thirza.

"I believe he is, Uncle," she said.

16. MISSING FRAGMENTS

May tiptoed towards June in a bridal burst of hawthorn and horse chestnut. Virtually blind, Thirza's grandfather struggled to cope with many daily tasks, tasks he delegated to Jem who, in his turn, seemed glad to be relieved of them by Darnell. Darnell spent more and more time ensconced in the windmill and its outbuildings. He added new padlocks to the doors, in order to, he told the family privately, ensure better security within and without. Giving up her bolt-hole for Jem's well-being seemed to Thirza a small price to pay.

Thirza caught Francis giving saucy replies to Jem that he'd never have dared to in Thomas's presence. She confided this to Darnell, who advised discretion.

"Your grandparents shouldn't have to endure more irksomeness. Leave it all to me, niece."

The longer days seemed to give Francis increasing opportunities for finding pursuits of his own that didn't tie him to the mill's more exacting timetable. He also spent much energy on private errands for Darnell, which rarely appeared to contribute to the smooth running of Kitson's Mill. Thirza was feeding the pigs their swill one morning, when she heard Francis come along with some of his friends from the village. They didn't see her as the sty was behind the mill, but she could hear them talking and laughing in the yard.

"Look at it, though!" Francis was saying.

"Let me have it, Frank," said another voice.

"Give it here, Jim, tha'll get blood on thee and we shall all cop it, if Mester Kitson catches us!" Francis' broadest Yorkshire dialect emerged as he struggled with his mate for possession of the bone of contention.

When Thirza appeared from the far side of the windmill, the group of boys reformed guiltily, whatever they'd been fighting over already tucked out of sight, behind a back, down a sock or in a pocket.

Thirza had no wish to act as a kill-joy schoolmarm. She'd fulfilled that role after her mother's death many times with Judd and Sam. She wished she wasn't always the one obliged to stand at the front of the class. She secretly wished she could be the ringleader of all the fun, as the boys seemed free to be. So she walked through the knot of giggling without comment. As she walked away, she heard the whispering recommence behind her.

"Lady Muck!"

"She's right enough."

"Water gypsy!"

"Leave her be."

"I'm going to see if there's owt else where we found this."

"Not if you haven't stuck it there to start with!"

I can't win, thought Thirza. The voice defending her hadn't belonged to Francis. She was annoyed she'd spared him a lecture.

Thirza had been counting the days to this last day of May, watching the moon waxing, growing fatter over the fens till tonight's full moon. The farmers who had their grain ground at the mill, called this May moon the 'Corn-Planting Moon'. Kezzie rolled her eyes when Thirza mentioned it to her, tittering like a young girl as she elbowed Thomas awake from his afternoon nap.

"We went a-courting under the 'Flower Moon', didn't we, Tom? Do you remember, you old romancer?"

"Romancer? You're remembering another of your myriad sweethearts, Kezzie, my dove," he said, tongue firmly in his cheek, squinting into the brightness where he knew the window was letting in spring sunlight.

"Oh, you!" Kezzie cooed, as if she was ready to step out again under the fragrant arches of blossom along the churchyard path.

Bram called it the 'Milk Moon'. He'd leaned close to ask Thirza if she understood why it was called by that name. She didn't, but hadn't let him know. It was one more thing to ask him tonight when she went out to meet him at the decoy. She wanted to listen to the calm, tender inflection of his voice, talking about so many things he seemed to know by heart and instinct. Her day would drag until then.

Kezzie was supervising Grace and grating cheese at the kitchen table, when Jem came to the door.

"Goody's ordered three small bags of flour meal for today. I've poured them into these twists of sacking she's sent. They look a bit grubby!"

"Always sends those same bags. Been in Goody's scullery since God was a lad!" Thomas observed.

"I can take them," Thirza said, glad to be out in the sunshine, already longing for evening moonrise. If she kept busy, the day might fly, like all things did when you tried to hold them too tightly.

Goody Chester was the oldest woman in Turbary Nab. Goody, as everyone called her, having long forgotten her given name, was the one villagers always called on for the ceremonies in which life forced them to participate, some sad, some joyful. Goody delivered their babies and advised on their bringing up. Everyone on the Nab trusted her to know the answers, or at least to remember the ones who had asked the questions before them. Goody knew which flowers meant what in a bride's bouquet. Goody knew how to heal with herbs. At least, she knew which herbs to grind in her great-grandmother's mortar with the mismatched pestle, so people knew they'd done everything possible, to stave off the crump and crunch of the sexton's spade for another season.

Goody was the one who arrived unbidden on the doorstep with pennies to close dead eyes before the rigor mortis turned blushes into wax.

"Before you even know you're dead yourself!" as Thomas said.

Thirza stood in front of Goody's cottage door and heard the old woman call "In you come!" before she'd raised her hand to knock.

"Put the flour in the bin, Thirza Holberry, daughter of Dinah Kitson, granddaughter of Kezia Poskitt, great granddaughter of Kerenhappuch Wraith."

Thirza stifled a chuckle. Goody wore her role as village family historian on her sleeve. Surely, she must be joking with these genealogies she recited? She did the same for each villager she saw. Thirza hadn't once heard the old lady hesitate. She'd no idea if the names and generations Goody gabbled off were correct, but those who might have known better, never corrected or contradicted her. For men, she'd recite their fathers and grandfathers. Thirza heard her mother's line and the maiden names of her foremothers. She savoured the sounds and flavours the names woke in her memory and imagination: round, pillowy sounds with eider-soft curves, the taste of salt and barley dough, the smell of herring and above it all, the scuffing of the ropes up the masthead and the wheeze of canvas in sails and sweeps.

"You're a dreamer, Thirza. That's your nature. But that doesn't mean you don't see things. You see more."

Thirza tipped the flour bags into the bin in the scullery and came back to where Goody was knitting. She sat in a Windsor chair, hunched over her work, swathed in a shawl even on this hot day at the end of May.

"What are you making, Goody?"

Thirza thought it was probably better not to challenge or agree with the statements Goody had made about her. Goody said things like this to everybody and just like her home-made remedies and rituals at the rites of passage, nobody thought to question her wisdom. Even if they did, they had too much respect for Goody's old bones than to contradict what she pronounced like a self-appointed oracle.

"Knitting. Can't you see?"

Goody held the odd-looking garment out for Thirza to feel and admire. Thirza wasn't sure what it was meant to be.

"Is it for a baby?"

Thirza put her fingers into what seemed to be little holes for tiny arms or legs. The rest of the grey woollen thing looked too short in the body - if it was the body - for anything but a newborn.

"A baby? You're a dreamer, Thirza Holberry! A dreamer like your mother! How can a little bairn pick up a sword and go fighting over the seven seas? It's a special woollen cap, a warm helmet for our boys in Balaclava!"

Thirza adapted her view of the rounded top to try to see it as something else. Jem had described searing heat at Balaclava and she'd read about the bitter conditions there last winter, when warm clothing failed to arrive to protect the soldiers from the icy blasts. The grey wool was worn to a dingy brown in Goody's fingers and by its frequent falls onto the dirty floor of reed matting.

"It's for a soldier's head, a cap to keep him warm. Holes for eyes, a scarf knitted into it, here. I heard about it when I went to Doncaster market six months ago. People are knitting these all over England. Our boys won't be tortured by the Crimean winds next winter, all swaddled up in these."

Thirza wasn't so sure.

"Mightn't they suffocate?" she asked, wondering where there was a place to breathe through.

"Thirza Holberry! If you put your shawl over your head, to keep out the wind blowing off the canal, do you suffocate?"

Thirza still thought the helmet looked uncomfortable and tight, particularly the way Goody had made it. It looked no bigger than a baby's bonnet.

"I thought we were given to hope the war would be over before next winter?" said Thirza. Jem would never be fit to return there. How good it'd be if his comrades and the horses could come back home as well, injured and uninjured alike, without need for these textile oddities!

"It is written all over the face of your uncle, Jeremy Kitson, son of Thomas Kitson, grandson of William Kitson, great grandson of Jedediah Kitson of Kitson's Mill, that he has endured more than we can guess. I think you've guessed it. Guessed his pain and misplaced guilt from his survival. I delivered your uncle from Kezia's womb and your aunt Emma and your mother Dinah before them."

Thirza was thankful Goody didn't launch into more lengthy genealogies for each person mentioned. She'd better make her excuses and leave before that became a possibility. She didn't want to be drawn into knitting in front of Goody. She recoiled from the idea of exposing her left-handedness to the scrutiny of the village wise-woman.

"You knit widdershins, don't you?"

Thirza's heart sank. Goody must've heard it from the village lasses who gossiped about her unfortunate trial with Lady Laura. But Goody's smile was benign, in spite of the hawk-like stare that seemed to see right through her.

"You knit and point and write widdershins, against the common grain, just as your mother did. You put the flour in my bin all widdershins-wise. Take no notice of the envious and cruel, lass. Be yourself. Be true to who you are, not what others would make you in this right-handed world. But you've resolved to plough your own furrow through the deeps, anyway, haven't you? There will come days when that quality of yours will be called on and tested like gold in the refiner's fire. Beware the goatsucker harvest, lass."

Thirza came to herself as if out of a long dream. Goody was looking deep into her. Not just into her eyes but through into her soul. She knew in her solar plexus what the wise-woman meant, with the thrill of a homecoming. Goody did not explain, or need to.

"There are those who would suck the yolk out of the egg of this earth to hold its secrets in their hand. There are those that trace it and tremble at its power. Your mother knew, dark Dinah, and passed it down with love from her mother's mother's mother's mother."

"To me." Thirza's words were no question.

"Widdershins weaver of rainbows, to you. Don't let them cozen it from your keeping. Don't fear to follow what it shows your inner eye, or whispers to your inner ear. Love is the unlocking. He has your missing fragment. He is your missing fragment."

Thirza struggled to be sure whether these last two statements were identical or different.

He has, he is. He is, he has.

As she rolled the words around like stones in surf, she found herself falling away from the moment when she dared to ask who the old woman meant. She knew she'd know in time. When she came to herself again, she found her hand was on the outer latch of the closed cottage door. Goody was singing inside at her knitting, keening and crooning strange words that Thirza had never heard, but understood.

As Thirza left the widow's cottage, she felt thankful to be affirmed for who she was, without reserve or censure, a rare blessing since she'd arrived on the Nab. Thankful, too, for what her heart was learning. Love is the unlocking. Ravage can't be reversed without it.

#

The evening came on, the change of light imperceptible at first, then all at once, half an hour before the church clock struck nine, the sunset bled across the marshes and stars and planets materialised into view in the twilight sky. Thirza quickened her pace out towards the decoy. Her ears rang with the sound of birds singing their final songs of the day, before gathering silence around themselves in their nests, one by one.

By nine o'clock, she could see Venus following the track of the sun, sloping down into the south-west as darkness deepened. She took care where she placed her feet, seeing the cotton-grass springing back under her tread, aware of the curve of the earth beyond the horizons that beckoned her towards the North Sea. She stopped for a second, wondering if she'd missed her way. Even in the darkness creeping over the face of the Levels, the still May air felt balmy and mild to her arms, bare under her linen shift.

"You came!"

Thirza made out Bram's tall, slender figure ahead of her, at the side of the path she was taking, as if he'd put himself there as a signpost, marking her way into the unknown.

17. UNDER THE MILK MOON

"Am I on time?" Thirza cradled Piper's face between her hands as he rolled over at her feet among the sphagnum and sundews.

"See Venus sinking to bed, trailing Mercury?" Bram pointed to where the planets were capsizing through the sunset's orange and vermilion waves.

"I didn't tell anyone where I was heading at such an hour," Thirza said. It gave her a frisson of excitement stepping away from the ordinary, to go wandering about like a true land gypsy onto the moorish wilderness with its hidden adders and startling voices. Only this man was close by as her protector and her guide. Perhaps a lady should be more cautious here in the gathering gloaming? Thirza couldn't convince her heart to quaver at the prospect of being here with Bram. She'd been more afraid of being challenged and forbidden by those who might view her nocturnal outing as a disgraceful breach of common sense and decency.

In fact, nobody seemed to notice her slip away. She said goodnight to her grandparents after supper, without a soul commenting on the direction she'd taken. Jem had been wrapped up in his own personal nightmares. Darnell was busy in his newly commandeered workshop with the door locked.

"Are you well?" Bram noticed her distant look. "I was looking out for you, in case you missed your way or decided to go adder-baiting again by the pinfold."

"You were watching me all that time?" Thirza was incredulous. It seemed too dim between sundown and moonrise, for him to have seen her from afar.

"I'm accustomed to noticing whatever moves on the fenlands. Something, someone I've waited for so long, I'd no intention of missing!"

The two of them walked on in silence, until the shape of Bram's hut and the curved bank of alder and birch scrub that shielded the decoy from detection, crept into view.

"The Milk Moon's rising," whispered Bram, as if just to raise his voice might frighten the perfect disc of pearl back trembling below the south-eastern horizon. There, just after ten, it was breaking free of the line of sedge.

"Why 'Milk'?" Thirza whispered.

"Every baby creature born in spring will be suckling, new and needy, lambs and leverets. Chicks, nestlings, fledglings."

"Birds don't drink milk! Not even goatsuckers!"

"You're learning, lass! She's a Blue Moon, too, the second full moon this May!"

Bram smiled and lit the peat turf on the end of a twig, as he'd shown her before, to disguise all human and canine scent from the wildfowl. Could it be a month ago? Thirza felt as comfortable with this quiet soul as if she'd known him all her days on earth.

The full moon's rays began to make the shapes of things more clear to her, but far from more familiar. She kept close to Bram and Piper as they approached the decoy and Bram snuffed out the smouldering peat which fragranced the air with its timeless, earthy scent.

Bram took Thirza's index finger gently in his hand and laid it on her lips to indicate the need to become absolutely mute and helped her into place behind the head-show, the tallest of the screens. Piper needed no such guidance from his master and melted into the shadows under the low wicket.

"That's the 'Yackoop' Piper springs over," murmured Bram into Thirza's ear.

"He'll 'yackoop and over'" Thirza whispered back, mimicking Bram's distinct vowels.

"Yes, canny lass," Bram's eyes twinkled, "he'll drive the ducks further up the pipes into the holding space of the tunnel net at the end of the line of hoops."

Thirza made out a little group of birds in the mouth of the pipe, mallard, teal, gadwall and shoveller with widgeon and pintail, feeding on seed scattered on the surface of the water for them to find. Looking closely Thirza saw some were live tame ducks while among them paddled the exquisitely crafted feathery automata with their immaculate plumage and lifelike movements.

Bram gave a low whistle to the dog, that sounded every bit as natural as the calls of the upland waders, bleak and wistful. Then Piper sprang over the succession of low dog-jumps. Further along the pipe, he disappeared from sight, backing away, drawing the wildfowl onward up the pipe. They seemed fascinated by the little hound. Beady eyes winked in the moonbeams shining down. Milky light turned everything into a mysterious pageant in which Thirza, to her utter delight and astonishment, found herself taking her place. It felt so natural to her, she hardly realised how Bram was guiding her with his eye. Thirza found she understood the signals that passed between man and dog, even though the meanings behind the strange names and words were lost in the mists of time.

"I normally do this in winter, but I want to show you how I work the decoy, so when winter comes and more birds fly onto the fens, you'll already be an expert!"

"Piper seems to know what to do, even before he sees your signals," Thirza whispered as she followed Bram along the sunken path beside the screens and the low jumps that connected them in a zigzag pattern alongside the netted pipe.

"Why do the birds on the pond not fly away when they see their friends swimming off like that?" Thirza tried to keep her voice down as low as Bram did.

"Because of the elbow back there," he explained, "that's the angle of the bend in the pipe. I have it all laid out so the wild birds on the pond don't panic or injure themselves. Once they're exactly the right distance up the pipe, beyond the head-show, as we call it, there's no way back to danger or damage."

Bram knew he could trust Thirza to do her part, so he showed her how to stand behind the head-show, how to show her own head to the ducks further up the pipe, to prevent them scattering past her and back onto the pond again.

Thirza watched him. She could feel her heartbeat flickering in her throat and the hairs on her neck thrilled as if tickled by breath whispering past a warm tongue. Bram seemed to be blowing over the hoops and nets with an expanding globe of sighing that spread from his fingers and radiated out over the fenland in a shimmering, keening rainbow.

Thirza closed her eyes and placed her fingertips on her lids. She opened them again, peeking out at the radiant land. The rainbow was lifting, blossoming, whickering round them. She felt Bram standing behind her, strong palms just circling her without pressure or possession, lifting her back into the warmth of him.

Scarlet, apricot, canary, emerald, ocean blue, cobalt, amethyst, Thirza watched the colours arching through her fingers like gossamer skeins of glory. She found herself weaving them, by instinct, reaching to pluck right over left, widdershins, under and over, into an iridescent hollow of light.

"Bram, look! What is it?" Thirza saw flickering lights just beyond the corner of her vision, fed by tiny fountains of vapour, hovering inches above the turf all around.

"Fen-lights. Will-o'-the-wisps. Phlogiston. Marsh fire my people harnessed here to heal and shelter fragile things. Reversal of ravage. Omkering van schade. Can you listen and not stop me to ask?"

"With you I can do anything."

Thirza put her arms around Bram's shoulders as he helped her onto his stilts again and she let the motion of his feet teach her where to place her own as they explored the silvery terrain in the moonlight. Then she lay down with him on the soft turf, watching the fen-lights and listening to his breathing. From one birch tree near at hand to an alder in the distance, a dark shape fluttered, uttering a familiar rasping cry. Then there was silence. Bram stood up and walked around behind her. He took her hands tenderly in his and clapped her palms together in the air above her head. The bird returned, clapping its own wings in answer, its bubbling notes rising and falling through the dusky air in time with the quavering bursts of phosphorescence all around.

Thirza watched the moon pulling strands of chiffon over its face and wondered how near to it she'd just been, or if she was dreaming.

"Goatsuckers..."

"Mating and laying their eggs in the full moonlight."

"That stuff I saw."

"The rainbow stuff, our special phlogiston. Diaphanous lightning that makes things burn and melt away at the same time. My great grandfather learned the rhythms of the fen, dwelt with its riches and responsibilities, the complex web of nature. He learned by lading and teaming these phenomena back and forth, exactly the proportions that made it malleable. Navigating by compassion for all creatures, respect and love. Mixed the marsh gas, with a skerrick of peat, to free this phlogiston, this elusive fuel that does all you've seen, and more."

Thirza jumped up.

"What's up?" Bram looked up at her, full moon haloing her hair.

"Thought I heard something."

"Piper didn't, and he's trained to hear everything and warn me."

Thirza lay back down, closer to Bram this time, close

enough to feel his pulse with her eardrum next to his body, hearing the sigh of the land for miles around.

"My great grandfather Gerrit passed that down to my granddad Jan and he to me, when my father Isaac died. How can I explain it? My granddad told me we're just stewards of it, to make sure it's only used for fair, not foul."

"That's what powers your stilts. That's what makes the wildfowl well."

Thirza took the clockwork goatsucker out of her pocket and held it up in the moonlight, seeing its broken wing perfectly whole, whirring with its white-tipped tail and fluttering like a moth navigating round a tallow candle.

"It's even gone and mended my clockwork bird!"

Bram kept quiet. Piper came up and licked his hand, then Thirza's. Then he whimpered and sniffed the air to windward.

"That noise again! You shouldn't be living out here all on your own. It's dangerous!"

"I have to!" Bram almost shouted the words. They sat, half-raised on their elbows staring at each other.

"You don't have to!" Thirza took Bram's face in her hands and rolled him over into a passionate kiss and an embrace that seemed to have no edges or endings. The urgency of long waiting overcame both of them in the same moment.

Piper whimpered again and Bram sat up, cradling Thirza's head into his chest as he strained his ears. Piper barked, once, twice.

Bram reached out his hand and his fingers closed round the left stilt that lay nearest. He looked over towards the hut. Thirza peeked over his shoulder.

"Don't move. There's somebody over there watching. Or is it the trees?"

Bram looked over to where she was indicating.

"No trees there. Piper barked twice. That means he saw two people."

There was nobody visible now as far as the horizon.

"Listen, this is important. You have to be careful. Back

in my great grandfather's time, someone else saw him one night out here, working with the decoy, rainbows and fen-lights. Calling down the nightjars. Sharing the healing. Crafting phlogiston out on the fen."

Thirza could feel Bram's meaning in her heart before she heard him say it. Bram looked all around. Piper stood sniffing the wind for unseen intruders.

"The man who saw was my great grandfather's acquaintance, a man called Pagnell Salkeld."

"My uncle Darnell's kin!" Thirza almost sobbed the words.

"Pagnell Salkeld hung around my great grandfather, pretending to be a friend and ally. All the time lurking like a noxious fog, haunting the margins, crouching in dykes to hear echoes of what my ancestor inherited for a blessing."

"What did he want?"

"To use this phlogiston power to wipe the wonder out of this world. To use the fen against itself, to spread death and devastation, my granddad said."

"Did this Pagnell tell your great grandfather what he intended?"

Bram wondered if he had already said too much.

"You think my uncle Darnell was watching us tonight?"

"I don't know. Piper signalled easterly, over towards the coast. Whoever it was, went that way."

"We could follow!"

"You mustn't. I must. It's too dangerous."

"Then we'll follow together!"

"Go home, now, Thirza. I beg you. I'm worried for you."

Thirza wrapped her arms around Bram as he stood up. He pushed her away very gently, folding up the stilts till they were neatly dovetailed into themselves and half their normal length. He strapped them securely onto his back and put his greatcoat on over them so they didn't show.

"They stick out under your coat," she said, without looking. As Bram tried awkwardly to hunch his back and slide them further up out of sight, Thirza hugged him, sliding her hands round his body and nuzzling her face into him, before adjusting the lumpy places where the stilts now looked too obvious to her.

"I'm going with you. Willy or nilly, as my granddad would say. Why don't we go on the stilts, one each?"

"It's not a game, Thirza! Not this!" Bram's uncharacteristic snap of sharpness stung Thirza to her heart.

"Go back to the windmill. This is my people's danger, my business."

"It's our business. Shared. Shared!" Bram saw the determination in Thirza's eyes and the tears a heartbeat behind that steely will. He shook his head and put on his hat.

"I won't use the stilts while someone might be watching the decoy. We should go separately. Why don't you go home and get some sleep? Then maybe later, I'll come and tell you if I find out what's going on."

"Or vice versa!" Thirza hissed.

Bram whistled to Piper to lie low and guard the hut till he came back and set off to walk Thirza back as far as the pinfold. They walked hand in hand, their long shadows licking in front of them over the flat ground.

"Did you hear that?" Thirza meshed her fingers tighter with Bram's and hung back.

"Don't start imagining things."

"The goatsucker. Chirring three times. Isn't that what the villagers say portends death?"

Bram gave her a look. He stopped short of admitting to her, he'd heard nothing. The white noise of the moonlit marshes washed over him with no landmarks.

Thirza shrugged. She couldn't prove she'd heard the strange cry. Flouncing on a few strides ahead of Bram, she stumbled over something in a pocket of dark near the churchyard wall.

"Bram! Look! It's a lamb! But look!" Thirza registered the two pairs of eyes staring blindly in opposite directions and the gaping bloodless gash in the little animal's throat.

Bram pulled her back away from the creature and on

in the direction of the windmill.

"Checking where we were, then leaving this poor ravaged thing for us to find."

"But Bram, it had..."

"...two heads. It happens, Thirza."

"Two heads, four eyes, its two tongues so swollen..." Thirza shook Bram's arm as he strode ahead.

"You could save it. Why is it like that?"

"I'm not God, Thirza. I can't bring back the dead, only heal what lives, and even then. You can see Kitson's Mill from here. Go quickly now before anyone sees us here together. I must get back to Piper. Then, whatever we hear, we'll warn each other."

Bram glanced round him, pulling Thirza closer for a second, surrounding her with his open coat that smelt of wood-smoke and the strange misty drizzle that masked his home from prying eyes. Most of the time.

"Go swift, go safe," and he was gone, back towards the marsh with a tip of his hat and no backward glance. Before he was out of sight, Thirza ran the rest of the way to the mill. The sight of the lamb was stuck in her brain. Who would do that? Who?

Everything was silent. The lights were off in the mill tower and Darnell's workshop. The sun was still hours from rising. By the light of the full moon Thirza saw hoof prints in the mud leading from the lane into the mill yard. She leaned closer and saw the distinctive nick in the horseshoe's shape. She knew it well from seeing these same tracks daily about the place. One horse always left tracks like these. Jem's elderly nag. Old Nero.

18. COASTAL CAPERS

In his dream, a sound like the muffled click of a razor replaced on its stand after a close shave, made Thomas raise his head from the pillow. Kezzie was snoring beside him, the noise the grindstone makes when a fragment of stone goes stuttering along the grooves. The old miller needed to get up to use the chipped chamber pot under the bed. Even with his bladder swollen the size of a marrow at harvest, he held his breath as he fumbled in the darkness, trying not to wake his sleeping wife.

Jem was more and more troubled. That must be him pottering about now before sunrise. Kezzie said little about it, but Thomas, all but sightless, sensed her agitation in the pernickety way the bread loaves were pinched and punched, the way the besom switched the floor with a more intense ferocity than usual.

"That you, Tom?"

"Who did you think it was, woman, tinkling in your own thunder jug?"

"Who's started the sails then?"

They both listened. The unmistakeable sounds of the mill being tweaked and coaxed into action. But something new, too. A brighter, higher whine.

"Darnell's been up in the cap tinkering all month,

making his improvements." Thomas felt grateful for Darnell's interventions of late. Even though he was largely in the dark about details, where the devil was rumoured to hide.

His own pride in the mill had led to some unfortunate mistakes and accidents recently. Some locals had forgiven. None had forgotten the inconveniences nor the rumours beginning to spread like toxic ripples through this becalmed backwater.

"Best never to mind and never to meddle, old lad," he muttered to himself. "Good to see Darnell giving our Jem a hand." he added, more loudly. "Though the new way he's set the sails and rigged up the fantail, it sometimes sounds like a pack of playing cards riffling. That new needle at the top sounds very modish. Not that I can squinny the shape of it now. The way the old girl's patty-caking her sweeps up on top this morning, sounds like gypsy cards with the Tower come out on the top of the stack."

"Thomas!" Kezzie's superstitious mind fluttered like a dovecote full of flustered feathers. "Stop that talk of dark diddlings, will you, at this hour?"

Thomas laughed and blew a raspberry of a kiss in the back of her wrinkled neck.

"This old wizard better get up and see what's doing. While you, my bonny lass, better enjoy your half hour's beauty sleep you fairy princesses need." Thomas dodged the pillow Kezzie aimed at him as he padded down the stairs still chuckling.

#

"I've vital errands in Kingston-upon-Hull, as I like to call it, to prevent infelicities of confuddlement, I think Darnell calls them, or is that my father's phrase?" So Emma had blustered in answer to Kezzie's suggestion her daughter might like to stay for tea one day. "Well, anyhow, I've a frightfully important assignation there, the day after tomorrow, Mother. I can't be in two places, you know.

Darnell's mightily overstretched here with his ameliorations to the mill and things of that nature, minding my poor brother, helping Father with all the blindness and such."

Emma's sketchy details about the timing of her trip were all Bram and Thirza had to go on in planning their own expedition to Hull. Thirza daren't ask how her aunt planned to get to the port, with whom, on what mission or at what hour. Only the day, Wednesday next. It sounded like a trip to complete business already arranged, from what Thirza had overheard. She conveyed this to Bram during their hurried exchanges over the pinfold wall.

"While we're there, I want to see what's happening with 'Thistle', too," she told Bram. "I know whereabouts my father often berths her. I have to see her!"

Bram had given her a brisk assurance they could do that too. He didn't add he hoped her mind would stay clear and focused, if he was to be sure of protecting her from whatever mischief Darnell might now be plotting.

Even in broad daylight, Bram insisted it'd be safer for Thirza if they made their separate ways to Hull, so as not to give Darnell any clue they suspected him of anything less than honesty. Bram wanted to give the man no excuse to threaten Thirza or to guess the threat they might pose to his designs, whatever they proved to be, by their partnership.

So it was, that early on the following Wednesday, Thirza found herself hurrying along the canal bank, keeping a low profile where the towpath seemed too wide and watched. She'd no idea how she'd locate Aunt Emma once she got to Hull, but she remembered the urgency in Bram's voice. She distracted herself as she first set off by the thought of Emma aboard a boat, trying to pass herself off as a keelgirl with her pelerines and furbelows. This picture made Thirza laugh to herself, in spite of her downcast state of mind. There had to be more to this trip than Emma paying a call to offer her brother-in-law Jack coconut cake and a cup of Earl Grey! Perhaps Bram was nearer the truth, that she was on some clandestine business of Darnell's. Clandestine was not a concept her aunt could easily grasp. Who had been near the decoy at Milk Moon?

After trudging for hours, zigzagging between the Levels and the snaking waterway, Thirza saw a bridge ahead. This wasn't a simple arch like Curlew Trod where she first met Bram, but a swing bridge along a curved section of the canal, known to mariners as 'The Rickety Rainbow,' with a lock and weir just beyond. It meant Hull wasn't far away now, journey's end.

Thirza was caught up in her own dreams inside her head, watching a group of mallards with their chicks, in the shelter of the far bank. She mused how Bram would weigh and estimate each bird's body with his steady brown eyes, even from here, knowing where they'd come from and whither they were bound, their health and history and how he might help them. Her mind wandered to her own goatsucker toy, its wing mysteriously mended amid the phlogiston flickers around Bram's decoy that night.

"Where are you buzzing off to like a bee in a boatman's bonnet?"

Having missed seeing a keel, low in the water laden with coal, Thirza was too late to take evasive action. It wasn't her father, standing at the tiller, or anyone she knew well, though the chap acting as mate to the short man steering looked familiar enough. The keel's paintwork was peeling and the name wasn't 'Thistle' but 'Jaunty Anna'. She looked like any attempt at being jaunty was a thing of the past!

"What are you up to, lovely lass?"

"Just walking. Going into Hull. On errands and such."

"You're Jack Holberry's lass, aren't you? Saw Jack boat-hauling on the quay last time around. Down by the Old Harbour, wasn't it, our Albert?"

The man at the tiller grunted but never took his eyes from the middle distance.

"Have you seen our Judd and Sammy?"

"Heard your Judd had gone for a warehouseman down the docks, though I've not set eyes on him of late. Your Sammy was always full of the iron hosses, wasn't he?"

The man at the tiller spat into the water at the

mention of the railway. Thirza noticed a newspaper on deck and asked if she could see it.

"Course you can, flower. It's last week's, mind you."

Thirza thanked them and jumped down onto the deck, scanning the columns of newsprint for any nuggets of news from the Crimea she could pass on to cheer Jem up. She read the latest about Florence Nightingale and how conditions out there were so exacting and sickness so rife. She made out the word 'Renkioi' that Lucas had talked about with such boyish animation. Miss Nightingale was quoted as referring to the hospital design as those 'magnificent huts' Mr Brunel had so cleverly made, though she'd not yet seen them with her own eyes. Thirza thought of lamplight flickering on tents made of sailcloth. What might Miss Nightingale not achieve for those poor struggling soldiers if she had the ancient knowledge of which Bram was a modest custodian? One day they'd bind these deadly plagues with light, splitting rainbows and powered by phlogiston.

She also read that the famous Norfolk engineer, millwright, canal and railway designer, Sir William Cubitt, was due to visit Doncaster Plant Works in October. Darnell would love that! Lucas always said the great man was Darnell's particular hero.

"We were just going to tear that into squares, lass, to hang on the nail behind the door, you know where! All that learning's making you a dull lass."

Thirza glanced up to see the mate wink at the captain and rattle something behind her back. She spun round as he tossed something to the back of the boat where the man at the tiller caught it. Thirza felt in the pocket of her dress.

"That's mine. It was my mother's! Give it me back!"

The master at the tiller laughed raucously and spat again, holding the box above his head. Thirza knew the watermen's ways, joking and teasing. Showing too much pertness in response or chasing after the prize, would only result in worse taunting.

"Handy-dandy, isn't it, your little sewing box here? Got some trinkets and tranklements in, too! Off to sell it down the docks, love?"

The laughter grew louder and echoed across the level fields.

"Hush, Albert. This lass got prettier things to sell with her comely curves!"

Thirza was grabbed from behind by a third man who appeared from nowhere. He must've come up the ladder from the hold, judging by the way he was coated from cap to boot in coal dust. The other two played a clumsy game of piggy-in-the-middle with the box, while the slavering man from below seemed to be enjoying his task of pinning Thirza's arms behind her.

"I knew you when you were just a bairn! Nothing lardy-dardy, eh? Give us a rub here..."

He pulled her hand along the welt of his oily knitted gansey and slowly on down the front of his grubby breeches, leering over her shoulder to watch her reaction. As she drew her elbow back to hit him where it would hurt him most, a cacophony of barking rang out from above them on the bridge.

Thirza watched the eyes of the watermen lift in slow motion up from the deck, taking in every inch of the impossibly tall figure towering over them.

Above Piper's baying, which gradually ceased as he was reassured by his master's voice, the giant addressed himself to the terrified mariners.

"Give this lady her property. Now."

Coal dust man stepped away from Thirza, holding his palms open as if up before a magistrate.

The mate, most loquacious of the three, seemed too tongue-tied to stammer out more than, "S-s-s-sorry your sirship!" amid a frenzy of forelock tugging.

Bram pushed Piper gently out of sight behind the parapet of the bridge with the end of one stilt, as he saw the friendly foxy tail begin to wag a shade prematurely.

The captain himself seemed wholly incapable now of coherent speech or further spitting. As he continued to lean hard with all the weight of his stocky frame on the tiller, his goggle eyes rooted on the avenging angel now visited on his boat, there came an ominous crunch. The 'Jaunty Anna' ploughed into the bank and, turning with the impact, drifted around to scrape along the brickwork of the lock. Thirza jumped ashore before the clinker-built craft sustained another bump, as it met a patch of shallower water and found itself ignominiously holed close to the unopened lock gates.

Bram shifted his weight onto his back foot and lifted the other stilt, with the marsh chemicals hissing and the piston pushing the brass ferrule just inches from the mate's ashen face. Gingerly, as the intricate cogs inside the device ticked round, he let the ferrule tamp menacingly into the man's fleshy shoulder several times.

"That box. You were handing it over to this lady."

The man held out the box, its contents unharmed in spite of Albert's rifling through them, towards Thirza, now standing by Bram's side on the bank.

The end of the stilt, its ferrule superheated by the phlogiston mix, worked its way behind the mate's head, which bent lower and lower in an awkward bow, to avoid the sizzling he expected every minute to scorch his seldom-washed neck. A squittering report of quite another source of gas, was heard to escape him with every lower stage of bending.

"God, Albert, what the hell is it?"

"Apologise to the lady."

"I'm very sorry, lady. Very bloody sorry, indeed! Pardon me!"

While all eyes were cast down, all knees bent in humblest obeisance, Bram gave Thirza a quick grin and gestured to Piper, whose tongue was lolling in a convincing approximation of a canine guffaw. Round the curve of the canal and out of sight of the stranded keel, the three of them picked up their pace and saw in the near distance, not more than a few miles ahead, the port of Hull.

The terrain changed from grass and towpath to cobbles and ropewalks. The noise level rose from rippling

water and sighing sedge to competing costermongers'
shrieking cries, honed like knives to cut through their rivals'
ditties as they hawked often identical wares. Harsh yelps
from gulls wheeling overhead, eyeing up abandoned
fishbones and vomit from last night's hard drinking exploits
of sailors and merchants, had Bram looking up and bumping
into things.

Thirza, meanwhile, was weaving her way with
confidence through the alleyways and yards she'd known all
her life, avoiding cartwheels and mountains of night soil,
using the liquid map of the coastal channels, the familiar
tang on the breeze of ship's chandlers' shops, oilseed mills
and fish oil, as her inner compass.

After a quarter of an hour dashing through the Old
Town towards the place she'd an idea Emma would be,
Thirza realised Bram was no longer behind her. Various dogs
were snuffling round the doors of the abattoir across the
street, but none of them was the sleek little duck tolling
spaniel she was hoping to see, shadowing his master.

Thirza gathered her skirts closely round her and
slipped into a narrow passageway, leading to one of the
teeming back-to-back courtyards near Coelus Street and
Chaffer's Alley. She knew her way from here. The walls ran
with damp and she leaned against a drier patch, furry with
salt bloom, getting her bearings and hoping Bram would
appear as suddenly as she'd lost him. It was a good vantage
point here to see the main street down to the docks. She'd no
way of knowing the time, other than the angle of the sun
which told her it wasn't yet noon.

She slid Dinah's box out of her pocket and, making
sure she was unobserved in the lee of one of the outhouses,
rummaged through the compartments. The tiny compass
needle was stuck, until she tilted the box at exactly the right
angle. Then it spun wildly for a second before pointing
northwards towards the river. The clockwork bird, the
interlocking rings, the lockless key, the skeleton of the fob
watch, maybe one of these would give her an excuse to enter
one of the emporiums where Emma might be trying on the

latest fashions.

Thirza tried to imagine what it would be like for Bram in this whirl of racket, seething activity and stench. She saw in her mind's eye his disoriented eyes looking in wonder and apprehension. She'd been too excited and self-absorbed to notice much. Or, she admitted ruefully to herself, she did notice, but hadn't paid attention enough to supporting him on what must be, for him, a bewildering journey into the bowels of hell itself, to protect her and her family.

She was nearly at the Albert Dock, where she felt sure 'Thistle' would be in dry dock by now, perhaps being caulked by strangers or having a new name painted on her proud old rump.

She should go back and see if Bram had somehow lost his way back near the abattoir. Piper might have been distracted by the lumps of meat and discarded carcasses. Perhaps the little dog had followed some trail of pungent urine from the adjoining tannery? Perhaps Bram had followed him and not seen the turnings she took? All that had been on her mind was 'Thistle'. Now Bram might be in danger, alone in this unfamiliar city where she was the one he'd trusted to guide him. He'd only rejoined her to rescue her from unwelcome attention, after all!

As she was setting off back towards the part of town where she'd last seen man and dog, raised voices caught her attention on the quayside. She made out the figure of a policeman, brandishing his notebook and waggling his truncheon in the face of a tall man and next to them, a woman in a long cloak and a mob cap, a bun pulling back her hair severely from her face.

Thirza crept closer and picked up the conversation, which seemed mostly to be between the police officer and the strange woman.

"This impertinent fellow has been following me, officer! All the way from the quay where my ship docked this morning!"

"Now, madam, from the beginning." The policeman removed his helmet and tucked it under his arm while he solemnly read back what he had written in his notes.

"Let us see. You arrived at ten o'clock this morning on the ship Canada from Chimaera..."

"The HMS Chimaera from Canada!" The woman sounded exasperated. "I returned from visiting my family in Quebec and happened to see a couple on the quayside here with whom I was passing some pleasantries on the way to my hotel, when this impertinent fellow began to hover and stammer in the most disconcerting manner!"

The officer was noting this down, but what he was writing didn't seem to Thirza to be keeping up with the woman's words.

"After you met your friends...

"Acquaintances!" the woman spat out the syllables as if she wished her own tongue could etch the meaning into the policeman's book. "Acquainted for all of a moment or two to pass the time of day!"

"After that, you saw this gentleman?"

"Loitering along!"

"Loitering with intent," the policeman made a great show of writing his chosen phrase in the notebook and consulting his watch. "Who were these acquaintances, madam?"

"I haven't the vaguest notion who they were! Except they had more decorum than this fellow, on whom I have never clapped eyes before in my life. He sidled up bold enough to give me the vapours!"

"...not the vaguest...never clapped eyes...gave me the vapours..."

Thirza was close enough now to see what the officer was scribbling in his meandering, childlike script. She caught Bram's eye, but he looked pleadingly at her and shook his head slightly as if to beg her not to intervene. Her fiery temper could be relied on to make things infinitely worse.

"And you say this fellow was following you? Sidling up and spying on you?"

"Spying! That's the very thing, officer. Spying! He was lurking in a doorway in one of the warehouses, eavesdropping! He only approached me when the nice couple left. He has some kind of a weapon, like a gun, concealed beneath his coat! I could see it hidden there when he approached me!" She fanned her face with her hand, "Poking out!"

"A weapon, you say? Hand it over, then, sir, account for yourself or I'll be forced to call for assistance and have you arrested here and now."

19. HULL, HELL AND BACK AGAIN

Thirza saw Bram turn the colour of sailcloth. She couldn't restrain herself any longer.

"Excuse me, officer, please, I know this man. I can vouch for him! This gentleman's Mr Bram Beharrell, the pinder at Turbary Nab on the Chase near Doncaster. He came here with me to check on my father's boat in the harbour. The weapon this lady saw, well, Mr Beharrell would never use a weapon on anybody! I think what this lady means, might be his stilt, you know, the stilts marshmen use to paddle?"

Thirza looked apologetically at Bram. Paddling didn't somehow seem the right word for what he did with his special stilts. Nor was he anything like a common-or-garden marshman in her estimation!

"Stilts, eh?" the policeman looked unconvinced.

Bram reluctantly pulled his belt and the leather straps he'd made to attach the folded stilts to his back, around to the side. He extracted the left stilt, carefully holding it by wrapping his hand around the ferrule with its mechanism of cogs and pistons, so only the ordinary wooden foot plates and shaft could be seen by his interrogator. The policeman tutted and examined the brass plated elbow of the contraption that allowed it to fold into itself to make it more easy to carry.

"It is, as this young lady has indicated, madam, nothing more sinister than a stilt. Fine craftsmanship, rather unusual in these parts, but a stilt nonetheless, in my appraisal. Not a gun. Did he threaten you with the said implement?"

"He didn't threaten me with the thing, as such," the woman snorted, "but why was he following me at all?"

"Forgive me, madam," Bram tried to think on his feet, "I'm sorry I frightened you, but those people you were with..."

"I told you," she snapped, addressing herself to the policeman again, "I met the gentleman and lady quite by chance. Ships passing on a crowded quay!"

"I thought those people you were talking to were known to me, that's all. My mistake. I beg your pardon."

The woman looked Bram up and down, but seemed not to be about to press charges.

"Well, madam, I see no grounds to arrest this chap, unless he has made an assault on your person. Nevertheless," the policeman took Bram by the arm and marched him a short distance away from the women, "nevertheless, I advise you that loitering after respectable ladies you happen to see on the harbour side, is most unwise when an officer of the law is nearby. Watch your step, sonny boy. Keep your bag of circus tricks," here he winked salaciously at a mystified Bram, "under your coat in future and don't go harassing the ladies on my patch with your twopence ha'penny balder-flummery."

When the officer moved away, making it obvious he still had his eye on the pair of them, Bram hastily tipped his hat to the woman as she headed off to her hotel in the direction of the station, grabbed Thirza's elbow and steered her off towards the dockside.

"What on earth were you up to? And where's Piper?"

"Piper started running ahead of me, following some trail. He couldn't hear my signals, I suppose, with all the banging and squawking!"

"Banging and...?" Thirza herself squawked with laughter at Bram's expression. He looked thoroughly flummoxed at the way people were bawling to be heard over the thunder of heavy machinery, the loading and unloading of cargo from the ocean-going vessels and the distracting sights and smells, so different from Bram's calm, understated existence on the moors and marshes inland. It looked to Thirza like he felt his ears were being boxed by some unseen assailant, bent on assaulting his finely-honed senses.

"I was following Piper closely as I could. I couldn't catch your eye when he galloped off. I lost you somewhere back by the slaughterhouse. You're like a native here, I knew you'd know your way about. Unlike me, it seems. Next thing I know, Piper's brought me here to the dock, but then I couldn't see where he'd gone, all among the feet of people getting off a big boat, all chattering in different languages. German, French, some broad accents I suppose were English, but not from round here, even my ancestral Dutch, but gabbling like Babel all at once!

"Double Dutch!" Thirza chortled, then grabbed Bram's arm and hid behind him to avoid being seen by a couple on the quayside.

"Quick! Look!"

From behind a stack of wooden pallets, they peered out at two figures standing close to the edge of the harbour. The man had a top hat and a cane, the woman, a bonnet and a parasol she was twirling theatrically.

"Aunt Emma! It's Emma and Squire Charlesworth!"

Bram made sure Thirza was hidden from their eye-line in case she spoke too loudly in her astonishment. The pair were deep in conversation. Emma kept touching Lucas intimately on his cheek with the back of her lace gloved hand and shrieking with that edgy, ostentatious snicker that made her own husband grind his teeth.

"I knew it was them with the passenger woman before! I hid myself until they moved away and then went to try and find out something useful."

"You did. Your stilts are scarier than you think!"

"I wanted her to think I thought they might be bothering her, so she'd open up about how she knew them."

Thirza's look asked the question. Bram raised his eyebrows and shrugged apologetically.

"It didn't go down too well, I won't lie!"

"They were just passing the time of day!"

"I didn't see them at first. I was looking for Piper, as I should be now. I spotted them standing a few yards away from me. They didn't see me, I hope. Careful, they're coming this way!"

Bram and Thirza hunkered down at the opposite side of the stack of pallets. They watched as Lucas, with Emma mincing along on his arm, in slippers Thirza recognised with a grimace, approached a man who was beckoning them inside a shop fronting onto the quayside. They disappeared inside.

Bram couldn't hold on to Thirza firmly enough to prevent her darting across to the shop-front to get a better view. He watched as she made a show of dropping a bun penny, so she had the opportunity of crawling along under the window, ostensibly to retrieve her coin. She rejoined Bram behind the pallets.

"It's a glass shop. All sorts of goblets and bottles and glassy things. Notice in the window says new technique that means this glassblower doesn't need to use that pointy thing to hold the finished glassware."

"A punty rod?"

"Yes, that! Trust you to know! Something about a new 'snap case' tool. Says he's a master glassblower, a glassblowing virtuoso. Couldn't see any more."

They watched as Lucas and Emma came out of the shop. Emma had a new pair of glass bead earrings and was flinging her head this way and that in the hope they'd catch the light in a way that would draw compliments from her companion. Lucas however, was shaking the hand of the shopkeeper, before moving back into the crowd holding a large bag. Emma followed and started to prise the mouth of the bag wider. Bram and Thirza strained to hear the gist of what they were saying, until Lucas hushed Emma and hastily closed the bag again.

Thirza moved out from behind the pallets to get a better view as the couple walked towards a carriage Thirza recognised as the one from Foljambe Hall, its livery disguised by some sort of oilcloth.

"What are they up to? Lucas is tying something over his mouth. He's too muffled up for a day like today. Now he's tying something over Emma's mouth too. Darnell would approve of that!"

Bram's face fell.

"I heard Emma saying Darnell's name, didn't you? He's behind this somewhere. But he's sent his minions to do his dirty work so he can't be traced."

"Traced to what? What's he want with some specialist glass thingummy?

Bram sighed.

"Trouble."

Lucas helped Emma into the carriage and shut the door as the coachman drove away.

"That's the coachman from Foljambe Hall," said Thirza, though he too had his face covered with some sort of muffler made with thick thread and gauzy stuff, just like the ones Lucas and Emma were wearing.

"It's like they've got armour on their faces" Thirza went on. "It's like even in June, they're scared of catching a cold."

"Or being recognised."

At the same moment they both stopped dead. The sound of barking was coming from the water. Looking over the edge, they saw Piper sitting in an unladen boat, stripped for repairs. He was wagging his tail and laughing up at them with his tongue lolling.

"I think he's found 'Thistle' for you, Thirza," Bram smiled.

There seemed to be nobody else on board but the dog. Jack was nowhere to be seen and none of the foreign sailors hanging around in the nearby crafts seemed to know where he was, or even if he was still the owner, when Thirza enquired.

"I could just wait here for my dad."

Bram looked up and down the quayside.

"I think perhaps someone was glad you were out of the way today, Thirza. I think you should get back to the mill before it gets dark."

"You're doing a lot of thinking on my behalf, Mr Beharrell," Thirza teased but she saw that Bram was deadly serious. All the wind seemed to have gone out of the sails of his joy at being with her on this adventure.

"It's not safe for you on the canal. I should never have let you go as far as you did all on your own. I've been remiss. It isn't safe on the road, either, if those two are travelling that way. I know you don't like the trains and I'm afraid I haven't the money with me to pay one fare, let alone two."

"You think I'm in danger?"

"I think we may all be in danger."

"If Piper hadn't led you to this spot, we'd never have seen what Lucas and Emma were up to."

"Good boy. I think." Bram knelt down and Piper sprang ashore, licking his master's face and beaming up at Thirza.

"Come on. We must get back before the day clouds over."

Thirza didn't press Bram to say more. When they were out of the main town again, they looked across the Humber and saw the Humberhead Levels stretching before them all the way to Thorne, bathed in that weird between-worlds light that held in it all the tones of rainbow weather. Bram unfolded his stilts, clicking the joints and fitting the pins back into the holes so they stood firm and extended the foot plates so there was room for two pairs of feet inside the shafts. Behind a hedge away from prying eyes, Bram carefully took out a prism and oasis and after a few attempts, managed to spark several bursts of fen-light from the ground.

"No fen-lights at all, then they all flare up at once!"
Bram shepherded the flame into the oasis with a marble-sized lump of peaty soil and pulling it asunder, placed a small piece in either side of the stilt mechanisms.

"That should get us home a little swifter."

"Will we get back before Lucas and Emma?"

"We'll take the straight way across the river and fen. Then somehow we can see what they mean to do, with whatever it is they came all this way to collect for Darnell."

Bram mounted up and when he'd got his balance, held his arms so Thirza could climb up, too. Cuddled into each other, his arms and coat wrapped around her shoulders, they rose with a hiss like distant rain and sped like a hovering crane over the dykes and drains inland towards home.

#

Darnell drummed his fingers on the convex glass cover of the dial he'd attached to the gauge last night. He couldn't suppress a smirk of satisfaction, in the early morning dimness inside the cap of his creation. He scarcely referred to it in his own thought processes as 'the windmill' now, let alone as 'Kitson's Mill'. It was his, or would be very shortly, product of his wit, machine of his mastery, daughter of his ingenuity, doer of his will. They all were.

He polished the opaque tubes of the empty reservoir and wondered how long before Emma and Lucas came back with the vital components. He'd impressed on Lucas how it was imperative Emma didn't run away with her original notion that certain phials were full of perfume, in case she took a sniff. He wished he could have been the one who had the joy of tying the barrier mask over Emma's twittering lips, tighter and tighter and tighter.

Lucas had been easily persuaded there was a deal of toxic wiffle-waffle in the substances. Abroad, there were even more potent toxins awaiting, if this prototype worked. After the try-out, he could stockpile deadlier viruses and poisons for later experiments. Could he trust the discretion of these bunglers? His various contacts had reassured him in letters, now burnt and buried. Pagnell's journals were back under lock and key, facts extracted, memorised, synthesised.

Darnell wiped the oil from his hands on a silk handkerchief. It was starting to run clear, now. The peat was refined down with the nitrous mix, until he himself could hardly have spotted its origins in this god-forsaken barren wilderness of a place.

He glanced at the latest diagram. He'd convinced Lucas this was to construct the crux of the mill, as he referred to it to his curious backer, to make the top section of the new mill better able to turn without friction, thus to increase output and reduce noise.

"Only a white lie," Darnell purred to himself, sniffing like a suspicious ferret at the gasket between the 'Phlogistox' - could he trust Lucas to see to the last stages of patenting that name? - and the swelling head of steam from below. Too combustible? Too inert? Such a fine line.

He heard something moving outside and hastily blew out all potentially unattended flames in case he had to account for himself to outsiders. He looked over the sill but at first couldn't see any intruder. Then he saw the old man feeling his way along the fence towards the field. That wouldn't do. He hadn't quite finished stage-managing the scene out there. It might be interpreted quite wrongly and his efforts in cornering that bow-legged nag in the wee small hours would be completely wasted.

"Father-in-law, dear man, if I've told you once, I've told you a dozen times, there's no need to worry yourself any more about your morning tasks here. I have it all in hand, as I promised."

Thomas looked up in the direction of the mill's uppermost window, though, by now, the blurred shapes that danced behind his eyelids bore no resemblance to the world of vision. The eye bath Darnell had procured for him seemed to be having no effect, even to be making things worse and his eyes dimmer yet.

"Thank you, Darnell, I was just going to check on..."

"Now, now, now," Darnell smiled with an effort. The old fool couldn't see him, he knew, but the rictus set of his facial muscles during such exchanges with the unenlightened, made his voice sound more persuasive and charming, he thought. He knew it did, from years of practice on Emma.

"Very well. Mind your step and let your manners take care of themselves." Thomas listened for an appreciative chuckle from above. None came. He shuffled back into the cottage and shut the door behind him with a sigh.

"Meddlesome old buffer," Darnell turned back to the heart of the machine. The backbone, rather, he corrected his own inner monologue sternly. The backbone, spindle, nose-cone, payload. It had no heart. Lucas on the other hand, had too much of one. Darnell considered his cousin's dithering ways with women. It was time he encouraged, no, time he forced Lucas's hand, to get on with the business with Thirza. She was attractive. Lucas was wealthy and handsome. What was the delay? If only the two of them were as easy to manipulate as the oiled clockwork, cogs and flywheels here. They would have been making babies long ago. Thirza wouldn't still be mooning about unfettered, seeing more than was convenient. It should be child-bed and chattel time by now, he thought, with an inner flicker of impatience.

He was almost there with the old people. They were all but deactivated now. Kezzie, grounded by her neurasthenic anxieties. Darnell rolled the word 'neurasthenia' contemptuously over his tongue, remembering the way he'd exchanged that word with Emma's doctor once when she was out of the room. He fancied himself as a psychiatrist on top of all his other accomplishments. Then there was the old man. Ailing, failing, eyes dimming, dimmer, dimmed, bat blind. Darnell chuckled at his own cunning. Then the boy-man Jeremy. That was going well. Closer to the edge, closer, closer, teetering. Just a last little push now and then it would be over. Just as it should have been after the Charge.

#

Bram set Thirza down carefully on the springy fen turf.

"Don't forget this." He handed the clockwork bird back to her that he'd held for safekeeping as they stilt-strode. Their fingertips touched in the half-light.

"You take care, now. I'll come over as soon as I've had a chance to put the pinfold in order. Don't do anything till I come for you. We can watch what Emma and Lucas do, then plan how to stop Darnell, whatever he's scheming."

Bram wished it would prove as easy as he'd just tried to make it sound to an exhausted Thirza. He saw Piper sniffing a scent and pointing towards the pinfold.

"Don't look now, but I think somebody's already there before me."

"Someone or something." Thirza made out a shape that looked like the head of a figure behind the walled enclosure, where the crepuscular rays of the breaking dawn were wheeling over the ancient stones.

Bram broke into a run. As he drew closer, he thought he saw the figure duck behind the wall, out of sight. But when he arrived, no-one was there, only Piper pointing and straining, his nose almost touching a cut-throat razor with a cherry coloured handle. But no, not only the handle was red. Bram pulled the dog away.

"Please don't go in there, Thirza."

But Thirza had run with him and entered before he could stop her. On the ground lay Jem's razor, scarlet smears from hilt to blade-tip, plain even to eyes quickly averted from the sight, gouts of blood, that had dripped from the razor and been wiped on the grass all around.

20. DEADLY DELIVERIES

Thirza and Bram skirted round the back of Kitson's Mill, approaching from the meadow on its blind north side so as not to be conspicuous to any of its visitors or to bump into any of its occupants. They stopped short behind the hedgerow, out of sight of the mill tower and the back windows of Mill Cottage. In the middle of the paddock, they could make out the shape of an intricate maypole laid out flat on the ground, ribbon streamers pointing in every direction, stretching towards the horizons.

As they crept within yards of the dramatic pattern on the grass, they saw the thing was a convoluted carousel of intertwining ropes of sinew and intestine, leading the eye back to the ghoulish centrepiece, the hideously mutilated head of a horse, meticulously arranged, eyeballs staring as if astonished at its own fate, from where its nostrils once had flared.

Bram barred Thirza's view with his body. He looked around to see if the 'Goatsucker' perpetrator could still be here, much more deadly in prosaic human form than in the whispered rumours of a malicious myth. Thirza pointed, trying to make her voice work, trying to pull free from his arms, to run to the far side of the field, where a crumpled figure was slumped against the fence as if dead. Still Bram clung on to Thirza. Slowly he realised that the long, low sound he had thought must be somebody slaughtering pigs for market, was, in fact, an unnerving, desperate human cry of grief, wailing like an incorporeal being from the direction of the crumpled form.

Thirza broke away at last and ran full tilt towards the far fence. When she reached Jem, nothing she could say, no amount of hugging him close, no end of rocking him like a little child or speaking his pet name could stop that awful sound escaping his lips and echoing across the level land from horizon to horizon.

She watched Bram clearing away what remained of poor Nero. Minutes seemed like hours there in the field behind the mill. In all that time, apart from Thirza's soothing words and reassurances whispered to her uncle, his own disconcerting cry like a wounded animal in a trap, there were no sounds but the birds in the hedges waking to another day as spring warmed into summer.

Bram approached them slowly, hands wiped so as not to alarm Jem further with the sight of blood.

"I'm going up there." No question or apology in Bram's tone. Thirza looked up at him from where she was crouched, her skirts standing out around her like a billowed tent, under the edge of which Jem now lay shuddering and muttering.

"Why don't you take him inside?" Bram said, but saw the pleading look in Thirza's eyes.

"They'll all think he did this. Did it himself with his razor!"

"Not all," Bram looked up at the silent sails, turned away from them, spread in a shrug of denial. This wasn't the right time. So the pair of them returned the way they'd come, through the back lanes, the rarely trodden tracks where travellers ventured only when the fen-lights called them off the beaten paths on lonely nights, travellers fearful they might never be seen again by those who waited for them at their destination.

When they drew close to the decoy, Bram lifted Jem

onto his shoulders and carried him into the hut, laying him down on the cot. Jem lay on his back, face flushed as if with fever, now, teeth chattering. When Thirza held her ear to his lips she could hear what seemed to be words, but which had left their sense and meaning somewhere in a shuttered cell deep in her uncle's troubled mind.

"... make him wake up...promised to bring him home!...please!...Sam!...fire!..."

Thirza held Jem's hands and tried to warm them in hers, even though the air here felt mild to her, the peat holding yesterday's heat in its fibres like woollen sheets in a bed still cosy from the warming pan.

"Fire...Sam...fire...Sam..." the syllables on Jem's lips grew more insistent, more rhythmic.

"Samphire?"

Jem's sudden scream of grief made Thirza topple backwards to sit among the rushes.

"He must've been there to kill my Samphire! He wants to kill all my loved ones! Kill us all with fire and poison! I never, never did it! Murderer! Murderer!"

Thirza shook her head at Bram. This was traumatised madness and rambling.

"I should go back to the windmill, Bram. Can you help Jem?"

"I'll do whatever I can."

Thirza saw something in Bram's hand. It was the Cherry Picker razor. She couldn't formulate the words to ask.

"Do you think...?"

"Thirza, I don't know any more. Any more than you do."

"Give it to me," Thirza held out her hand and Bram placed the beautiful, dangerous thing onto her palm. He called after her as she hurried off in the direction of the village.

"Don't do anything in haste. Keep your suspicions close! Keep your powder dry! Please!"

The mist across the Chase was burning back like an ebb tide under the sun and Thirza's dress was soon a distant flickering flame on this canvas to Bram's tired eyes.

"Please be careful!"

#

Lucas and Emma called in at Carrdyke House so Emma could change her costume after their breakneck ride.

"This dear little muffler is divine! If Darnell wasn't so peculiarly insistent on our keeping our scarves under wraps, I should adore wearing mine to show the ladies in town how jaded their fashion sense has become!" Emma twirled Darnell's improvised barrier mask around her fingers and held the metallic threads up to the light. Darnell had them made by the seamstresses at Foljambe Hall on the pretext of trying out the latest fashions from Paris.

'Dual-function disguise and particle filter' he'd written at the top of the page above his sketch of the mask in his design journal, now locked in a drawer in his workshop at the windmill. His real purpose was, naturally, not communicated to Lady Laura's seamstresses, or to his wife. Just believing that possession of the mysterious accessory, marked her as wearer of the latest de rigueur item of haute couture, much like the exotic élan of the coconut cake, sent Emma into a frisson of ecstasy she found it impossible to contain.

"Better unconstrained vanity than incontinent curiosity in a woman," Darnell had said privately to Lucas. Lucas had laughed uproariously, though wondered why Darnell had sworn him to secrecy too. He was deeply puzzled about their mission to Hull and the phials, flasks and specially commissioned tour de force of the glassblower's art they had been charged with transporting.

Lucas removed the scarf from his own face and looked at it. Darnell had hinted such things would be necessary due to his development of the mill with its ultra-fine, airborne meal.

"For precaution's sake, my dear fellow, all involved must use their utmost discretion and do as they are bidden."

Lucas supposed this was to prevent inhalation of fine particles. Lucas puzzled even more over the calculations he'd come across on Darnell's desk, when he arrived unexpectedly early to a meeting with him one afternoon. He knew genius was close to madness, that one had to speculate to accumulate, as Darnell frequently told him. However, he failed to see what the sums to do with altitude and elevation, the chemistry of volatile substances, common poisons and toxins destructive to nervous tissue, had to do with the fineness of flour or the rate of rotation of sails or gears.

Lucas took a deep breath. Figures on paper, money in the bank, assets, patents, an unimpeachable good name and wealthy connections, in these lay his expertise and useful input to the project. He might be rather losing track of the chemistry and physics behind what Darnell was creating, almost obsessively, up at the mill now, but what of it? Some parts of the contraption sounded very specialised for mere grinding, but when he asked, Darnell had kept him up half the night, blinding him with complicated formulae that began to dance and dazzle once Darnell had plied him with a series of glasses of his own best port. Then he found it hard to follow Darnell's precise train of thought. With his cousin's dark eyes glittering through his goggles as he rearranged sketches on the table and theorised about aerodynamics and 'the finer points', Lucas found himself nodding and "Indeed, cuz"-ing, long after his brain had drawn the curtains for a tipsy snooze.

Lucas drove Emma to the windmill as soon as was practicable. This was as soon as he couldn't devise any more ways of assuring her how young she looked in her new crinoline with extra flounces and as soon as he could assist her in cramming these decorously around her, exposing less than an inch of ankle.

As instructed, in Darnell's jocular but most precise way, Lucas placed the special scarves in a lockable cabinet and carefully laid the apothecary's box of tricks in a trunk with several layers of metal lining it. Darnell had commissioned this, apparently, from some discreet cabinetmaker in Bawtry, was it? Lucas tried to remember, while attempting to make polite rejoinders to Emma's endless chattering, as she kicked her heels to show the 'divine fall' of her skirts.

"Lucas, my dear, I may call you my dear, mayn't I? It's just my way, you mustn't think me forward, I feel as though I know you intimately, after our adventurous little tête-à-tête on the coast! You, Squire Charlesworth, have that, what Darnell always calls 'Jenny Says Craw!'" Emma snorted and giggled in a manner Darnell once referred to as 'girlish'. Lucas smiled at her, watching the hedgerow fly by over her shoulder, dazzled by her new glass earrings, wondering what on earth he could devise as an excuse, should Darnell ever again require him to take her on another such errand.

At the mill, Darnell met the carriage and made a great show of helping Emma down the steps and ushering her into the cottage, where Kezzie was waiting.

"Squire Charlesworth and I have a couple of matters to see to up aloft," Darnell said, "something I can't quite manage on my own without a twanged muscle or two, you know! The damned grindstone, dear father-in-law, is worn down so in places. I shall certainly send to Wickersley for a new one and have it ground just so, just so."

Thomas rubbed his eyes. They seemed to sting and smart worse than ever with the new eye lotion Darnell had sent for, from a physician in York, especially for him. Darnell was his usual affable self and Thomas listened to his son-in-law's purring reassurances, calm compared to his daughter's airs and affectations that seemed to fill the compact rooms with exploding bubbles of loquacity, like acoustic shrapnel ricocheting off the horse brasses and delftware.

"No arguments, sir," Darnell was saying, "I won't hear of you footing the bill. The new stone will be at my expense."

Climbing the mill tower, Darnell said to Lucas, "You can run to that small thing, I trust, Cousin, to satisfy the old man? It will be necessary to make our new mill's efficiency secure. No good spoiling the ship for a ha'porth of tar, eh?"

"She's a saucy ship indeed, with your improvements.

Alma Mill will be the talk of the whole county of York!"

"The county? The country!" Darnell slapped Lucas on the back and let him lead up the ladder. Behind Lucas's back, he allowed himself a smile at his benefactor's naivety and a roll of his eyes at his enthusiasm for the new mill's name, that he himself had suggested during their long nights at the drawing board. Alma Mill. A saucier ship than any Lucas or anyone else could ever imagine!

"You visited the apothecary and the glassblower as we agreed?" Darnell sat astride one of the beams and let Lucas sit on the little bench that curved itself into the circular space perfectly, as if by design.

"Visited, signed, sealed and delivered."

"You made sure?" Darnell raised one eyebrow.

Lucas tapped the side of his nose theatrically, almost missing the tip.

"I made sure your lovely lady wife thought our impedimenta contained, inter alia, noxious matter, but in a harmless way. She wore the mask all the way home with hardly a squeak."

"Were you seen by anybody on the way?"

Lucas shook his head.

"Nobody but staring cows and ignorant watermen. I've stowed the chemic what-me-nots securely at your place."

"And the lodestone, as it were, of your endeavours?" Darnell was all but salivating at the prospect.

Lucas produced a folded kerchief with a flourish from the top pocket of his frock coat and opened the stiff framed top of the bag he'd taken all the way to Hull and back. He shook the kerchief over an object hidden in the recesses of the bag and lifted a heavy sphere out into the light inside the mill. Only the cloth made contact with the curved contours of the orb, leaving no finger-mark or other imperfection on its surface.

"Here, my dear chap, is the other item you ordered. The glassblower said he could scarce make another so perfect. It has no bubbles, flaws or distortions. Whether for light, or refraction, or..." Lucas fished, trying, not for the first time, to induce Darnell to confide the purpose of the object to him. Darnell only peered at it over the top of his magnifying goggles, before lifting his eye wear by their leather straps onto the top of his head so he could eyeball the thing close. He took it from Lucas tenderly, not for fear of breakage, Lucas thought, but almost as though in awe of it. He opened and closed the hinged brass lid in the top several times, listening to the ring of the glass each time it shut. He ran his fingers lovingly down the organic brass twigs that held the shutter in place by embracing the orb in their tendrils.

"This is exquisite. It will do very well. Very well indeed," said Darnell, drawing the kerchief over the hollow glass ball again and lowering it back into the bag. "But I almost forgot. While you were engaged in this important business, another grave affair was unfolding here at the mill. My unfortunate brother-in-law Jeremy has quite lost his wits, I fear. More than we previously thought. I found him blubbering like a lovesick girl over his old horse that his parents insist on letting him keep. I tried to warn them how unstable he had become. Next thing, he attacks the poor crock of offal with his cut-throat razor." Darnell paused and looked to see the effect he was having on Lucas. 'Crock of offal' was perhaps to veer too blatantly away from the hallowed portals of sentiment.

"Indelicate as it is, unbelievable as it may be, while none of us was minding him, he rushed out into the meadow here, did the awful deed, but instead of matter for glue, or horse meat or any useful thing, he..." again Darnell paused for effect, "...disembowelled the poor creature, hacked it into strips and strung them around the field in a tangle of knots like a whore's wiry wig. Then he took the head. I cannot well tell you what he did with the head, for I confess, it quite unmanned me to see it. I think the pinder is involved. The Dutch recluse who hangs around, to the shame of her family, with my blossoming young niece. I saw him from the mill when I was working here at first light. Disporting himself in the entrails. Could it be an affectation of the brain, do you suppose? The womenfolk and servants must be sheltered from him. Saved from him. Protected from him."

"From Dutchy Beharrell?" Lucas was giddy from trying to follow the plot, while keeping his breakfast down.

"From Jeremy Kitson, cousin, from my benighted beggar-crazed brother-in-law!" Darnell pushed his tongue against his teeth and willed himself to leave it there. Enough and just enough. Steady there, let the dog see the rabbit.

"I fear for the lovely, innocent Thirza. Too much in company with that wastrel duck-botherer. Too much in danger from her other uncle until he can be, when I can best arrange it, whisked away for his own best interests and the safety of all hereabouts, to the County Asylum. Wakefield is distant, or should I say, Wakefield is the best place in Yorkshire for the weak of wit. I wish you would make my niece the offer she deserves, Cousin, and that as promptly as might suit you. I fear the devil Dutchman will lead her astray if the day of her betrothal is much delayed."

Lucas seemed unable to speak for some time, in spite of several encouraging nods from Darnell. He began by offering condolences for the horse, which Darnell waved aside, then to express regrets about the state of the returned soldier's mind. Darnell found a half-full jeroboam of wine he'd left cooling on the fantail platform and two chipped glasses, thick with flour. He handed one to Lucas and watched as he necked the alcohol, hoping against hope it might imbue the squire with less hesitancy and more amorous designs.

"When I next see your niece," Lucas finished the glass and held it out hopefully for a refill, "I shall do her the honour. Do myself the honour, that is, to save her from further unpleasantness."

Darnell went for a third refill of Lucas's glass while he had the advantage. Seeing this inebriated dolt down the ladder in one piece was perhaps the most challenging thing still to be accomplished today, he thought, as he emptied the bottle.

21. WHEN ONE DOOR CLOSES

Dear Mr Salkeld,
Thank you for your letter outlining your plans for developing the potential of the bladed windmill mechanism. I am flattered that you are desirous of my advice on the matter of patenting your future inventions.
You write of my innovations in the fields of milling, canals and railways and these indeed are my areas of expertise. What concerns me most about your own ingenious device, as I understand it from the diagrams you enclose (and which I now return to you) is the infinite potential for harm and misuse inherent in its design. I was equally loath to accept that my original design for the treadmill, now used in prison establishments such as the one at York Castle, became a mixed blessing once it had left the drawing board. My treadmill design is now universally employed as a form of drudgery, punishment and torture in the gaols, whereas I had hoped its use would involve meaningful employment for the rehabilitation of criminals for the good of society and the weal of my fellow

citizens.

> *I find myself hard pressed to imagine that your own design for this flying rotor mill, viz 'The Phlogistox Flyer', could not also be used for purposes other than you envisage. I also have grave practical reservations. I doubt your concept of a cell propelled over great distances through the air in precise dirigible flight, is even remotely possible.*
>
> *In light of this, sir, I must decline to involve myself in your project now or in future.*
>
> *I remain, sir, yours in the pursuit of engineering excellence, etc*

Darnell read the signature at the foot of the headed paper for the thousandth time. Every time of reading, he had an impulse to screw up the letter and fling it away, burn or tear it. He only read it when he was sure he was alone. Nobody would ever catch sight, he told himself, of those tears that stung his eyes the first time he perused this knock-back from his greatest hero. It had not been the first time he'd written to the esteemed engineer, Sir William Cubitt, about his design. But the first half dozen carefully-penned proposals had been met with no reply at all. Then, after enclosing a basic design sketch with his last, he couldn't have put into words the thrill of excitement that gripped him when this letter, penned by the great engineer himself, was delivered to Carrdyke House.

He'd waited until Emma was out and the servants occupied about their trivial tasks. Then, standing on the carpet in his study to savour the moment, he'd taken his oriental brass letter opener in the shape of a dragon with its tongue aggressively extended through snarling lips and with meticulous care, slit open the disappointingly plain envelope with its penny black stamp before sliding out the letter, licking his lips in anticipation of his fortune made.

Today he compared his feelings to those he'd

experienced on the day the letter arrived. Then, he'd felt huge envy at the esteem in which Cubitt was held in engineering circles. Sir William, child of a miller, like Darnell's own wife, had distinguished himself over a long and illustrious career. His was the hand behind not only the design of the treadmill, that tortured those who had transgressed against the law of the land, but those windmill sails he'd patented which bore his name to distinguish them.

He was influential also in the world of the canals, designing and building bridges. Not satisfied with these accomplishments alone, the railways too owed him a debt through his unique inventive genius. The Plant Works at Doncaster had been recently opened, to his design and that of his bright and capable son Joseph, making the Great Northern Railway an important highway for this part of the country.

Darnell found he was grinding his teeth. Now his esteem for Cubitt was totally extinguished and supplanted with seething hatred. He shoved the letter back into the envelope and noted with a pang how it was starting to crack a little along the folds where his fingers had played so many times while planning his revenge. He would not be overlooked. He would not be bypassed. He would not be unnoticed. He would make the great engineer sit up and beg him to share his design.

Advice? Pah! He needed no advice now, no forelock-tugging to the senior man or his snivelling offspring and their sycophantic entourage. In fact, Darnell had never met Cubitt, but in his mind, after so many hours of playing out their meeting in his head, he knew exactly what Cubitt would say and do, confronted by the man he had snubbed. So many patents. So many business opportunities.

"But that will all be as dust down a grain chute when I have my day of glory!" Darnell was saying the words aloud when he heard the door click shut behind him.

Emma's hands fluttered against his eyelids.

"Guess who, my clever angel?"

Darnell snatched her hands away and spun round, a

sudden rage making his ears sing.

"Why the hell are you creeping about like that, woman? I thought you were shopping in town?" Darnell tried to master himself. Emma pouted.

"Such a crosspatch, Mr Salkeld! So snappish, when I have brought you this!" She slid the top of a newssheet out of her bag, hiding it quickly again when he showed an interest.

"Quit your schoolyard games, woman!" Darnell snatched at the paper. Why could she not shut up and let him read it in peace? His impatience mounted as her chatter rose to a crescendo to let him know what she had discovered in Doncaster.

"I was looking in the milliner's window in St Sepulchre Gate and I heard two gentlemen talking together. They weren't at the milliner's, of course, they were in front of the tallow chandler's shop."

Darnell bit his tongue and scanned the crowded columns of print for something relevant. It crossed his mind that now they'd removed stamp duty from newspapers, there would be more and more of the infernal things crammed with tittle tattle, telling people what they ought to be thinking! Not that Emma would ever risk thinking in the first place, he thought, with an involuntary wince. He noted the news of the death of Lord Raglan and wondered if this was what had interested the good burghers of Doncaster today. One less mouth to tell what really happened after Balaclava or initiate inquiries into any unexplained deaths among the cannon fodder!

"You'll never guess who's coming to town later this year. Not her Majesty the Queen, not the Prime Minister man, Mister..." Emma's brow furrowed.

"Viscount..."

"Mister Viscount, as you call him."

"Viscount Palmerston!" Darnell tried not to be so withering as to trigger a full-blown sobbing outburst.

"Yes, dear, but it isn't him. The gentlemen were talking about the new railway works on the west side of town, what do they call them, the Flowerpot, is it?"

Darnell wondered sometimes if Emma could actually be in jest, perhaps in drink.

"The Plant Works. The Plant!"

"There, dear! The very place! Well, these gentlemen were talking about a visit later this year by this man..." Emma pointed at the foot of the first column of the local news. Darnell saw the name at once, springing out of the page at him, but Emma was already filling in every last detail in a breathless flurry.

"Sir William Cubitt! Your hero! He's coming to Doncaster to deliver a lecture. There's some inspection of the works. Well, he did build them in the first place, didn't he? So these gentlemen said Sir William's being feted at a civic reception or was there some award? I knew you'd want to know, my love!"

Darnell finished reading. He placed the newspaper on the desk, turning his back on Emma's onslaught of gabbling. He smoothed his hands over his temples. They hurt. They throbbed.

Suddenly, without any warning Emma could read, his fist banged on the table, making the inkwell rattle and the sheaves of stacked papers teeter and slide off onto the floor.

"Oh, my dear, my dear, I thought you would..." Emma reached a trembling hand to touch him, to diffuse this mood she could never predict.

Darnell spun round to face her, glaring down into her eyes.

"Thought I would what? Thought I would be grateful that my mocker will be close enough to crush me in person? Thought I would be glad to hear my rival is to be given yet more adulation and the keys to the kingdom? Thought I would want to spend the rest of the afternoon listening rapt to your ignorant prattle?"

He pushed past Emma and out of the house. He would make the 'Phlogistox Flyer' the talk of every town. With or without wretched Cubitt and his kind. He would outshine them all. He would show them. His practice target had just self-selected itself. The world would never forget

Darnell Salkeld.

#

At Mill Cottage, Kezzie was busy in the dairy. Thomas was snoring in his chair with a damp cloth over his sore and blistered eyes that seemed to get worse by the day. Thirza felt too distracted to hang around for small-talk and politeness. Her heart felt broken. Jem's distress and Bram's quiet concern, the smile that had gone from his eyes when he looked at her, made her soul ache.

She knew she must be quick. She knew at any minute, these days, Darnell could come into the cap. These days she no longer felt safe up there. She felt like an intruder in his important workshop, his personal laboratory, helpful though he always was to all of them.

She ran up the ladders without lifting her head. She could hide the razor somewhere in the mill, like Darnell had that time, so when the opportunity arose, she could put it back in Jem's room in his army chest without anybody seeing her do it. As she reached the stone floor she wondered, was she really so sure who was doing all these dreadful things? What made her so sure it wasn't Jem? The villagers thought so. Jem or the phantom Goatsucker. She knew that was all a crazy tale, didn't she? But then again, Bram had shown her many weird and wonderful things out on the moors, things she'd never dreamed could be. She'd glimpsed rainbows that healed and mended, lights that sprang out of the earth, flickers of lightning that buzzed up out of the marsh, stilts powered by phlogiston that made you feel you were flying, mechanical birds that actually flew, living birds that croaked strange songs overhead in the darkness like ghostly grasshoppers, half cuckoo, half kestrel. So many, many things she felt sure of when Bram was holding her. But how could she trust her heart?

The shock of seeing Lucas made her gasp out loud. He was sitting under the wallower, his gloves in one hand, his top hat on his knees, smiling as if he was expecting her.

"Thirza, at last!" He stood up, pale eyes intense in the half-light of the mill. He ran his fingers through his hair and she noticed, not for the first time, that it was the colour of the wheat ripening in the summer fields outside. She had to accept her family's estimation that he was handsome and rich and personable and that she never gave him the time and attention he deserved.

"I'm sorry, Squire Charlesworth, you startled me!"

"Forgive me. I came up to bring some trifling thing for Mr Salkeld and seeing you there," he went on in a rush, "I hardly know where to start. But I believe an honest word is best said honestly. I have waited for this moment all my life."

He saw her eyes open wider with surprise and he hurried on, so as not to be deflected from the goal Darnell had urged him to accomplish before nightfall. God knew, he wanted the same thing himself, for all that he was so tongue-tied without a drink in his hand to boost his courage.

"I'll not beat about the bounds, Thirza. I love you. There! You haven't slapped me and I've said it! How easy it is to say, though my foolish delay has made the ghost of the words throw a long shadow on these wheaty walls."

He moved forward awkwardly. Thirza couldn't even conjure up one syllable in her head that might do for an answer. She stuck the razor, blade-downwards, into a sack of wheat behind her and prayed she'd be able to retrieve it once she'd dealt with Lucas's odd outburst without hurting his feelings.

"I'm flattered, Squire Charlesworth...Lucas," Thirza touched the tip of the razor hilt again in the flour sack to make sure she could still find it later, "I'm flattered but I fear you don't really know me at all."

Lucas lurched forward, to Thirza's alarm, blushing and spluttering, his long lashes batting at the ceiling as he floundered about for further utterances in which Darnell had coached him.

"Thirza, I have long felt an affinity with you. I love you. Yes, that's the thing. I love you."

Thirza backed away, rocking the razor in the flour till

it was nearly out of her grasp and her cuff was white with dust.

"I would marry you. No, wait! That's come out all clumsy and wrong. Miss Holberry..." Here Lucas went down on one knee with a crunch that made Thirza gasp and the nearby timbers rattle. "Will you do me the honour of becoming my wife?"

Thirza found herself staring open-mouthed at the glittering ring Lucas was wrestling out from his pocket, like a living thing he had no idea how to control. She stepped forward to help him, as he seemed about to topple from where he was now precariously balancing on a three-legged stool with his other knee. Before she could register what was happening, the wretched ring had leaped out of Lucas's trembling fingers and rolled across the boards, before disappearing down through the hole in the floor where the ladder was. It could be heard cannoning from rung to rung before continuing its erratic bowling course across the floor below.

Lucas looked so mortified, Thirza stifled her giggle at this surreal turn of events. Lucas looked from the ladder to Thirza and back at the ladder again, as if he couldn't decide whether the correct course was to wait for her reaction to his proposal or to disappear from view down the ladder to recover his jewelled pledge of passion, fast escaping down through the mill.

"Will you be so kind as to give me your answer? Some solid hope that you will accept my plan? I mean to say my p-p-proposal..." Lucas was stammering now. Darnell's talk of the matter in terms of a foolproof business plan was intruding into his attempt at romance.

"I can't give you my answer right away, please understand. I'd not thought of marriage. But if I did..."

"Oh, think of me, Thirza! Say you'll consider what I've said? Since the day you accepted my posy, you've been my Queen of the May!"

Thirza laughed and shook her head at Lucas's overeager lovesick expression. He put her in mind of Sam or

Judd fighting over who should help open the next lock. Then they both stopped short, straining to listen. A sound came from below like the creak of a boot that had been standing for some time on the same beam and finally shifted its weight.

Then silence.

Lucas put on his top hat and picked up his gloves from where he'd hung them on the wallower. The insistent rhythmic tapping of the joggle-screen, the chatter of the damsel, seemed to become louder between them.

"My cue to be gone, Miss Holberry," Lucas seemed to take the sound as a signal. "But say when? When will you decide?" Lucas put a foot on the ladder and seemed to catch the eye of somebody down below and to nod and smile.

"I'll give you my answer after Harvest Festival," Thirza wasn't certain of the date, but knew it was far enough away to give her time to let him down gradually, at summer's end.

"I follow the festivals these people celebrate and they all remind me of you. You'll be my Ceres, with the corn in your hair," Lucas was talking as though he was running out of rehearsed formality, but still couldn't rid his speech of flowery overblown images that made Thirza want to throw all caution to the wind and laugh till the tears ran down her cheeks. Like she laughed with Bram.

"Till then, I'll not ask again." Lucas leaned forward and kissed her on the cheek, politely, lips chilly as curd on a ladle. Thirza watched him disappear through the hole in the floor. She wondered if she was dreaming. Lucas had paid her court before, in his foppish harmless way, but she'd never imagined for a moment he'd see her as a suitable wife.

She couldn't see in the dim light below who had come in on them, or indeed if anybody had. It might have been her imagination and Lucas had hurried away not wanting to press her for an answer. He was gauche and funny and strange. Thirza almost wished she could be simple and selfish. She thought how easy it would've been to throw her arms round his neck, say "yes" and never want for anything again. But the things Lucas's title and wealth could buy her, were things that meant nothing to her and never could. Perhaps no man alive could give her what she needed, without cramping her in a cabin of his own needs and opinions. Perhaps nobody on earth.

She heard Lucas's horse galloping away from the mill. He must've found the ring. He might need it in future for a more suitable bride. Thirza didn't intend to be cruel by letting him dangle for months, it'd just give him space to withdraw his offer without embarrassment. She already felt sure her answer would be "no", though a kindly "no" of friendship and respect. He'd surely reconsider before harvest and today would be laughed off and forgotten.

She was alone in the mill. A rare moment unobserved. No more time to lose. She climbed up to the very top and found the cap was not as it was when she'd arrived fresh off 'Thistle' all those months ago. Now the simple curve of the room was crammed with new machinery that looked quite foreign to her. Up through the ceiling, a shaft protruded. She poked her head out by the fantail and looked up. There was a tall spike, pointing like a compass off into space.

It was her nose that told her something else had changed. Once there was only the tang of the oil, the meal, the dust that caught in the back of her throat, the damp richness of hornbeam after a rainy night. Now there was something else. What was it? She'd smelled it before, somewhere, but not here. She recognised with a shock the sweet heady stain on the air: phlogiston and peat. The secret fuel of Bram's people, that Darnell's great grandfather had tried to steal while pretending to be an ally of Bram's kinsman.

Thirza's gaze fell on something shiny and stunning, lodged inside the column now partially installed in the shaft of the mill. Inside brass tendrils that held it rigid, a large glass globe with a hinged lid at the top, facing up to the top of the mill. The design of the erect column, the angles it made with the sails whirling by outside, the connection to the fantail and the floor beneath her feet, made her mind's eye open on a swirling scene. There she saw the sketch she'd glimpsed in the chamber at Foljambe Hall, that her uncle had been at such pains to stow away where she couldn't study it. She recognised the scaled-up model of the tiny engines, the minuscule blades, the rotors such fun to spin like a spinning top, on her goatsucker and Bram's mechanical ducks. At first she'd not understood, but now she did. This was the same as Bram's phlogiston engines, but on a grander scale and totally hidden, at one with the heart of the windmill, yet as alien to its purpose as a gunshot to a lullaby.

She stood up to stroke the perfect sphere, standing on a box to reach it. She saw her own face reflected in the glass, her eyes too wide apart, her nose huge and the room receding backwards behind her distorted silhouette. She narrowed her eyes to make out a shape in the room faintly mirrored that wasn't like the image of familiar things or those that should surround her.

"So! Snooping, niece of mine?" Darnell had climbed the mill, letting the joggle-screen's rhythm mask his footfalls until he was standing right behind her. Thirza jumped so violently she almost knocked the glass orb out of its bracket and had to cling onto it to keep her balance on the box.

She felt Darnell's hands round her waist, but instead of immediately helping her down, he seemed to be holding her in place so she couldn't turn to left or right. She could only see him through the distortion of the glass, for to turn her head would have turned her giddy enough to fall.

22. RAVAGE AND RUIN

"Has my cousin popped the question?" Darnell maintained his grip and his even, reasonable tone, as if he were asking her the time of day or to read him the business news from the paper.

"Uncle, you came up like a cat! Yes, Squire Charlesworth was here only a moment ago and yes, he asked me to marry him."

Darnell supported her down from the box and stood smiling as she turned to face him.

"You've done very nicely for yourself. That young man will be the making of you."

"Oh, Uncle, you mistake me. I didn't give him my answer yet."

Darnell frowned as if he was hearing a language from another planet.

"Not...answered him?"

"Not yet! I only need time to consider the wisdom..."

Darnell went and leaned on the sill, looking out, saying nothing. Thirza saw his fingers clenching and unclenching and a muscle in his cheek that tensed taut as a drumhead.

"Wisdom." He thought of Thirza spying up here. He thought of the marshman, always in the background, living proof of his own ancestral rivalry. Why were they always together? He thought of Lucas, bumbling like an inflated balloon, facing here, facing there, as he himself tweaked the rudder with alcohol, or schooled him over and over what to say and do. He thought of Jem, frustratingly slow to be unhinged by his schemes, still too fondly loved and excused by these ignorant villagers and his doting parents who pleaded his case. He thought of Francis, only as reliable as the last groat to bribe him and terribly indiscreet. Then there was Cubitt, hero from Darnell's youth, now his bitterest enemy, thwarting his plans, thief of the fame and fortune which should be his, shortly coming to crow in his face. He would show them all. All!

Darnell felt the pressure of rage threatening to bubble over. He let it build like a head of steam straining to burst the seams and blow the stopper sky high. But the time to let it blow was not yet ripe. Steady, boys, steady. These tiny people were but flies in the ointment, irritants, grit in the grain.

"What's happening, Uncle?" Thirza found her voice, "The top of the mill seems so different. Not like a flour mill at all. It's like the things I saw in your special chamber at the Hall, like a great big whirring engine!" Thirza played for time, determined she could somehow persuade Darnell to leave her alone here again for a moment to go and retrieve Jem's razor from the flour sack. It would be a game like bobbing for apples in a bran tub at the fair.

"Come down with me!" Darnell waltzed Thirza down the ladder to the floor below. "Can't have that lovely hair catching in the mill, can we, eh? How many times have I told you? Why won't you be told?"

"Uncle, I've seen..."

In a stride, Darnell was pushing Thirza up against the jog-scry.

"Seen? What have you seen? To the point, why are you spying on me?"

"Uncle, I don't understand, but you're always up here. I was just curious, wondering why. I think someone's trying to hurt Jem." Thirza suddenly found her courage. Why shouldn't she ask when Darnell seemed to have so many secrets? Jem was suffering from rumours and untruths that Darnell could easily dispel.

"The shop in Hull where you must've bought that beautiful glass up there..."

Dinah had always taught her to ask honest questions, if anything troubled her. Those who really loved you would tell you the truth.

"You?" Darnell's rage exploded and would not be bitten down. But something else stirred in him, seeing her standing there so full of wit and spirit. Lucas would never be man enough to quell that spirit and keep her out of their affairs. He saw Emma, her hair streaming down her back, the red mist rising. The jog-scry's motion with its echoes of past conquests aroused something in him he could not, would not ignore. He unbuttoned and shuddered with anticipation.

Thirza tried to scream for Kezzie. She screamed through his fingers, cried out for her grandmother, even though she knew Kezzie had never once dared to climb higher than her own bedroom, with a firm hold on the bannister.

Darnell pushed her legs apart with his knee over the jog-scry as he had done with Emma before they were married, his fingers running through her long hair, Emma's lovely shining locks, uncut and unmanageable. Thirza squirmed and tried to bite his hand but he pushed her down under him, where the golden husks were shaken from the shining stream of meal. Trying to focus and block out the pain as he rode the mill's motion with a deafening yell of release, she reached back over the sack of meal where the Cherry Picker razor was hidden. As he rearranged his clothes and laughed at her terror, she plunged her hand down into the flour and seized the prize. She turned, like something possessed, someone she did not recognise or want to be, gripping the blade in both hands and holding it up towards him.

"Steady, my pretty niece. That is your mad soldier

uncle's blade, as all the village knows. He kills cattle, goats, chickens, lambs, horses, you know. Would he also kill me? Who will believe him? Who would give credence to a madman? Or a lost canal girl gone wrong?"

Darnell reached into his trousers again, this time producing the ring from his pocket that Lucas had lost down the ladder.

"Do you want to wear this, sparky little maid? Or should I call you madam, now?"

Thirza couldn't stop shivering, but refused to let out the sobs that rose in her throat like a storm.

"Give me the razor."

Darnell held out his hand with an ominous calm that Thirza knew she couldn't match. She folded the blade into the handle and placed it on her uncle's palm, as Bram had placed it on hers what seemed a lifetime ago.

"Nobody will believe you. If they do, they will reject and contemn you. Now, this exquisite ring must find its way back to its owner and you, my dear, will embrace the only man who will have you. Or shall I?"

Thirza recoiled.

"No, enough." Darnell pocketed the razor and ring with a casual shrug and chuckle. The joggle-screen had stopped and the alarm bell sounded warning there was no more grain.

"My seed is all spent," Darnell pulled on the cord, "for now," and went to nudge the mill brake.

"I've confided in your grandparents my very real concerns about the time you spend on the moors with that wastrel pinder. They share my anxiety for your good name. I believe your union with the squire will make their old age contented. The threat of disgrace from carnal fumblings with dirty Dutchy will be a thing of the past. Oh, take your time, by all means. There can only be one answer, as I'm sure you now realise, for all your modern ideas."

Thirza looked at the man she'd only thought she knew till now. She wiped her floury hands on her skirts, but nothing could make her feel clean inside. She could tell no-one about these moments. She should never have come here alone, so sure of finding out secrets, exposing lies. She felt her choices narrowing like the neck of a corroded pipe. Who could she tell? What could she say?

"Oh, and dearest niece, don't go worrying your pretty noddle about mad Jemmy. If there's just one more little incident here, I'll have him committed to the asylum. More disgrace for the family? Oh, no. I don't suppose you'd want to heap horror upon horror, would you? I've already had the unpleasant task of warning the villagers to look to their cattle. Strange indeed how the pinder has such carnage visited on his charges, is it not? The villagers are so afraid of the Goatsucker, they're grateful for any insight into those who'd bring trouble on them with their wild and wandering nature. I am the bearer of such insight. Until next time, dear Thirza."

Thirza staggered out into the yard and washed her hands at the pump. She washed her face, burning hot, though the silent tears had dried on her cheeks. The sobs that had threatened to let Darnell know her weakness, felt like stones made of ice in her chest. She washed her hands and washed them again, until her grandfather came out and asked her what she was at.

"You'll wash yourself away, our Thirzie, scrubbing so, and we'll have to send for a new granddaughter!" Thomas wondered that Thirza didn't laugh at his joke, but he was getting old, maybe some of his jokes had seen one outing too many? He couldn't see her face as she rushed past him into the house. She clung onto Kezzie until the old woman thought she'd hug the breath right out of her if she didn't push her away and ask her where Jem was, and had he taken Nero, as they'd seen neither man nor horse since yesterday?

#

Jem stared up at the ceiling, watching the eyes of the clockwork ducks glinting in the light slanting through the door. He could see Matty's dead face picked out in the shadowy patches, the feather patterns, the texture of the turves above him. In his ears there was a rush of sound, the pulse of blood washing out from under Samphire's hooves as they ploughed back up the Valley of Death. The screams of his brothers-in-arms, the clash of sabres and the shattering of shells all around. He picked out the line of the guns where the French were routing the Russians on the valley side, trying to hold off the rain of shot that was rushing down on him.

From the doorway, Bram made out the line of men with weapons, a thin lateral smudge at the edge of the village. They were still a long way off, on the margins of the marsh, not eager to advance on the uncertain wastes, but he could make out their weapons were spades, hoes and, in the hands of the leader at the forefront of the mob, a scythe.

Bram couldn't see their eyes, any more than they could see him in the camouflaged seclusion around the decoy, but he could sense what was in their hearts. He slipped back inside and knelt by Jem.

"I think it's time, young master."

Bram tried to keep alarm and insistence out of his tone. Jem's eyes were fixed above him.

"I hope you'll keep yourself safe here out of sight while I go and reason with them. I fear the rumour mill of lies and old enmities has been grinding its bitter grain."

"We won't surrender, will we? Back up the valley, but we reached the big guns, didn't we?" Jem turned his head towards Bram, but his eyes were unfocused, filled with fear.

"We won't need to surrender. I promise."

Bram went out and strapped on his stilts, igniting the phlogiston to power and protect his path with a smooth gesture that drew the lambent flame up from the damp ground. He picked up his staff and looked back at the boat upended under the lip of the bank near the decoy. He listened to the wisdom of his heart telling him he should help Jem into it and paddle for all he was worth until the curve of the earth put its protection between them and these superstitious minds and volatile tempers. But he couldn't just go, not yet.

He tucked a couple of heads of cottongrass into his belt in case he needed to fire up the stilts again, or staunch any wounds. Then he strode out, following the firmer track-ways laid by his forefathers with tree trunks and birch branches. The way meandered and at times he could no longer keep his eye on the distant aggressors. Those moments were precious. In those seconds he saw the bog rosemary tossing its salmon pink bells in the breeze and the dragonflies fanning the heath with their rainbow wings. The Reed Bunting kept the beat and the Stonechat, as if chatting together its inner stones that gave it its name, bent the sedge below him with a thrill of encouragement and colour. In those moments he thought of Thirza and how he could best protect her. Precious moments, but every curve in the way across the wastes that brought him in sight of the mistrustful ones, took him closer to confrontation, until he was standing just downwind of the pinfold, with half the village facing him, armed and full of fury.

#

At the other end of Turbary Nab, from Mill Cottage's window, Kezzie noticed a small group of village women pulling their children away from the pump. Kezzie didn't have time to react as one of the youngsters produced a handful of pebbles from his pocket and hurled one up towards the sails, while another ricocheted off the windowpane, mercifully without cracking it, right in front of Kezzie's eyes.

"Good Lord, Missus! What's to do?" Thomas jumped in his chair.

Kezzie opened the top section of the door, calling out more confidently than she felt.

"You cheeky scamps! Be off with you!"

Kezzie held the gaze of the mother. There was no warmth or apology. The woman followed the rest of the group towards the church end of the village, pulling the child who looked back over his shoulder, scowling. Kezzie felt so shaken, she couldn't go after them or call for an explanation.

On the doorstep, Grace pushed a note into her hand.

"This was wrapped round that stone, Missus K!"

Kezzie read the scrawled message.

'I KNOW WHO IS THE GOATSUCKER!'

Kezzie held the scrap of butcher's paper this way and that, willing it to say something different or something less alarming. But the letters blazed back their terrible certainty until Thomas snatched it from her and squinted at it as if he had the slightest hope now of making it out.

"What does it say, woman? What's afoot?"

Darnell suddenly filled the open doorway, having made urgent strides down from the mill tower, judging by his breathlessness. He sat Kezzie down, for she seemed on the point of apoplexy and quite struck dumb.

"Never mind, mother dear, I saw it all. Now, now. It's nothing to fash yourself about unduly. Come, come!" Darnell chafed Kezzie's hands between his with all the tender attentions of a dutiful son-in-law. Then he took the note from Thomas and flung it into the fire, riddling the embers with the poker.

"That's that and there's an end to this nonsense. I didn't like to worry you, but I confess it now, as I should have before it came to this. I've heard mutterings, no more than mutterings, that some villagers, some farmers, are dissatisfied with the way Jeremy is coping here, since his return. A petty local embargo of the mill. Foolish gossip. But you know how rumours spread."

Darnell paused and listened with satisfaction to the nervous rise and fall of Kezzie's breath and the grumpy incredulity of his father-in-law, now slumped on the settle rubbing his eyes.

"I've been covering for Jeremy. God knows, it's the least I can do, dear pater & mater, for that's how I think of you, as if you were my own flesh and blood and not by marriage merely."

Darnell reeled off the sweeteners and saw the old people soothed, at least enough to serve his purpose for now.

"I didn't say much before, but I notice Jeremy has made a cack-handed attempt to make do and mend with the ancient millstones here, until they're quite spoiled. No doubt that's been the cause of botheration for some of the more fastidious farmers."

"I never yet heard a complaint!" Thomas felt himself sidelined and helpless with a frustration he'd never felt till now. For centuries the mill had served the people of the area. Now, somehow, its failure had crept up on him unawares. Why couldn't Jem brace up and do his duty?

"Now, sir," Darnell used his most placatory tone, "I'm your right arm and your eyes and ears. I'm helping Jeremy send to Wickersley quarry, over Rotherham way, for a new runner stone. In fact I'm going out presently to organise matters. Once the mill's back in fine fettle, these disgruntled yokels will be beating a path back to the door."

"Not armed with more missiles, by crikey!" Thomas tried to make light of it. Darnell was so capable where his own son seemed unable to cope with the simplest tasks. Where was he when he was needed, anyway? They listened to the sounds of Darnell riding off at speed. Always busy, always their champion.

#

Jem rolled over and put his fingers into Piper's collar. The hairs on the little dog's neck were standing on end. He'd gone to the door a dozen times whining and longing to follow his master, but Bram had stroked Piper firmly, pointed at Jem, then quickly closed the door behind him. Now Piper was looking right through the wall, straining towards something or someone he seemed to sense without need for sight.

Jem heard it too, the sound of someone moving around outside. Had the Cossacks come for him, even out here? The swish of the reeds was the stir of feathered plume and uniform against the horses' flanks. He wouldn't cry out. He wouldn't give his position away.

Something brushed the door with its turf and leaf-litter camouflage, making the dog lurch forward out of his grasp. Was this Mary Seacole, with her dark eyes and certain step of motherly sense and comfort, bringing biscuits, rum and soft blankets? Was she here to try and revive Matty again? The nurses tried so hard to bring him back alive after Jem slipped that pill in his drink from the doctor in England, sent him as a cure-all after the Charge!

The door swung on its hinges and was shut again in an instant. Piper leaped out in the moment it took Thirza to enter. She stood panting, back to the door in the darkness.

"Mother Seacole. I'm shattering. Shivering in shards like glass."

Thirza crouched close and held her uncle tight. She held him tight so in the darkness of the hut he couldn't see her tears.

"Jem, where's Bram?"

"He's gone. He said not to move. They've taken the redoutes. I hear them at the other side of the valley. Listen!"

Thirza peered out of the tiny gap between two woven slats of marsh grass but could see nothing to account for the noises she could hear, close at hand, where the decoy should be. She heard the tap of one screen against the next, dull thuds and steps stumbling to and fro. Bram never trod like that. He had a soft tread that hardly made a dint in the turf. Someone out there now was knocking clumsily into the hoops. She heard a snap like a gunshot and heard Jem's breath catch in terror.

Why was Piper not barking? She must take her cue from him. Be silent. He'd rushed out as if he knew who was behind her on the path along the track through the peat, skirting the pools. He'd dashed out as if on a mission, as if he knew his master needed him to yackoop, wake up and be ready, obedient little lad.

Thirza huddled on the floor next to where Jem lay on

the bedding, wide-eyed and gasping as if he'd run along the Valley of Death with the enemy at his back and his horse killed under him. As Thirza knew, in his mind, he might have done for the thousandth time. With all her heart she wished Bram would come back through the door. Yet she didn't have the first idea what she could say to him about what had happened with Darnell at the jog-scry. Just picturing the infernal machine in her mind's eye made her ready to retch. She could never tell him.

She had the sensation of being followed all the way from the windmill, even though she'd picked an obscure way over the marsh, using the hidden map of wisdom, listening for clues as Bram had taught her. She wanted to sit and sob, for she felt like such a different person from the childish girl who skipped off 'Thistle' an age ago and met her strange wonderful marshman. He can never be mine, now, she thought, then sternly stopped the thought in its tracks for fear of letting him down and upsetting Jem again. She'd need to keep him calm till Bram got back from wherever he was.

She listened, trying to interpret the sounds she was hearing. Another crack, like bone snapping. A growl bristling like a warning. Or was it a pleading human moan? A dull throbbing thump, a ripping sound and a splashing like the staving in of something brittle. At least Jem was silent now, too silent, Thirza thought, internalising the sounds in his own way, reliving their terrors as the horrors of combat on foreign shores. For Thirza they held terrors enough, right here at home.

23. MOB RULE ON THE MARSH

"You aren't welcome here, Dutchy!"

"Dutchy! Bringer of floods and killer of beasts!"

Bram was determined not to quail. Now he was close enough to read the hostility and fear in their eyes. Those not bold enough to put their thoughts into words hung back and glared at him, while those too bold for their own good thrust themselves forward, self-appointed ringleaders.

"Who's set you on to say such things?" Bram knew, but asked anyway. Perhaps he could help them see how they'd been deceived.

"Where is the goatsucking ripper? The mad miller? They say you're in league to kill us all in our beds!"

"Who is this 'they'? When have we ever hurt you?"

Bram kept his voice calm and audible above the growing tide of muttering and cursing. Those at the back were gaining strength from the spokesmen at the front. One man lifted a bill-hook above his head. Immediately, a small forest of farm implements was raised against him, though nobody quite seemed to know what to do with their makeshift rampart of weapons. Nobody was willing to break ranks.

"I live in peace. I come in peace. I've done you no wrong. The young miller, Mr Kitson, is sick from the wars, that's all."

"Goatsucker! Goatsucker!" This voice was further off, joined by others taking up the chant. Bram saw stragglers, even women and youths and little children, coming out into the summer sunshine to have their sport.

"The flour's tainted! You've tainted it, consorting with madmen and goatsuckers!" This speaker faltered, looking round for reinforcement.

"Tainted it with your otherness! You're not one of us!" a female voice blurted out, giving courage to more of her companions to shout out their grievances.

"Lay down your arms. I come unarmed, in peace!" Bram faced them all down.

"Since you've been pinder, the Goatsucker's struck and struck again!"

"Struck time and again on your watch, Dutchy!"

"Conspiring with that savage mad hussar! Where is he now?"

"His own old horse was cruelly killed," said Bram, "so how would he be the culprit? It's made him weak with grief, recalling Balaclava."

The muttering dropped in volume and Bram could see this was a revelation to the crowd. They'd been set on to revenge by someone who'd chosen a different interpretation.

"You're out with the goatsuckers and creatures of the marsh all day and all night, pinder. The fen-lights that draw us off the beaten path to drowning, they say you rein in and use for your own ends. Things of mystery and danger are in your thrall."

"You're mistaken. I've lived on the wastelands of the Chase all my life. But there's waste here only for those who lay waste what's given as a gift. There's danger only if you don't listen and learn. My forefathers and mothers learned to live lightly on this land, to harness its spirit and seasons for good. These killings are not my doing, or the young miller's!"

"He went as a hero to war. But now we hardly ever see him. We hear tales of his lunacy, under your protection!"

"Better you were gone, Dutchman!"

Bram couldn't tell which figure had shouted this out. He'd learned the hard way that reason against superstition is an uneven struggle. The quiet rhythms of his decoy, the old ways of the marshmen, drawing rainbows and flickering flames out of the earth, natural mysteries, seemed too risky to convey, too sacred, standing here in this half-light world between the mystical marsh and the cultivated Nab.

Bram heard another voice from the back of the group. The speaker must have arrived from the cart track that led all the way to Doncaster past Carrdyke House and Foljambe Hall. The mob, smaller every moment, drew back to reveal Lucas Charlesworth, with Emma Salkeld disengaging herself from his arm.

"What's going on here? Half my tenants with so little to do of a summer's afternoon?" Lucas's smile was strained, though Emma's eyes sparkled with secret amusement to see the squire's tenants put on the spot by the unexpected appearance of their landlord.

Nobody seemed eager to explain. Bram held back, not wanting to accuse or stir, then chose his words carefully.

"Squire Charlesworth. These people are concerned about the mutilations of late. I think they've been deceived that Miller Kitson's son is somehow involved and that I have abetted him."

"Have you, sir?" Lucas's tone, often so laconic, now turned as sharp as a lawyer for the prosecution.

"No, sir. I never harmed a living thing by choice."

"By choice? You're a deep one, Dutchy! So my cousin tells me. I wonder what you do intend, out there on the wild moors day in and day out?"

Bram bowed his head. He let the accusations and assumptions float over him, sticking wherever they chose like cottongrass seeds floating across the reed beds. If not he, then Jem would perhaps be bearer of the brunt of this outcry. He was here with the sole purpose of deflecting them from pursuing Jem until he was recovered. He'd no intention of pleading his own case or excusing himself for eking out an existence beyond the bounds of what the uncivil called civilisation!

"Did I hear lips spitting slanders about the mill as I came up the road?" Lucas looked from face to face. The foremost characters, so recently more than eager to shout the odds, began to fall away, examining their tools as if they wondered how on earth they'd come to be in their hands, or how they'd mistaken them for potential weapons. Someone was whistling tunelessly. One woman stalked away with her poke bonnet cocked up on her head like an indignant chicken already plucked, leading her children by the hands as orderly as if they were on their way to Sabbath School.

"Please, milord, we meant no mischief. Only to make known how grievous is this business of the Goatsucker and the things we've found in the flour."

Lucas knew, mainly from Darnell and Emma, about the killings. He knew Darnell insisted the incidents were down to the increasing sickness of Jem's mind. He determined to encourage Darnell to write, as his cousin had already offered, to the Master of Wakefield Asylum, world renowned and ground-breaking far beyond the confines of Yorkshire. If things went on like this, the Kitsons themselves would see the wisdom in putting the fellow away where he could no longer harm the local livestock or, worse in Lucas's estimation, disgrace his family into which he himself hoped to marry.

"Be patient and we shall say no more about this regrettable unrest and agitation." Somehow, Lucas instantly turned the commoners' protest into a petty crime he, as the local magistrate, could dismiss magnanimously from the bench.

"Patience is a virtue. Only wait for the harvest time, and I promise you, you'll see great changes at the mill to your advantage, to the advantage of your families. No more the wolf at the door. No more the empty pocket and shrunken belly. No more of all that."

Lucas thought of Darnell's finger on his lips and decided he couldn't reveal any more to the gathered tenants. As Darnell advised, the great design must remain a secret until its grand opening at harvest festival. All the better that locals were becoming dissatisfied with the old. This little uprising had doubled the effect of their surreptitious leaflet campaign, by Jove! The new would sweep all away before it, the fields would indeed be ripe for harvest. 'Friends of the Future' would burn a course down those ringing metalled rails into tomorrow, never looking back. Darnell's name and his own would join the illustrious company of those already in the engineering Hall of Fame. They'd be the toast of the next Great Exhibition, stamped by the approval of her majesty Queen Victoria herself. They'd have mill owners and confectioners, yeomen farmers and businessmen everywhere beating a path to their doors. There would be parties with bottomless kegs of alcohol, too!

Lucas came to himself again, out of his reverie, with Emma calling at the top of her voice.

"Cooee! Cooee! Look who's coming over the fen!"

The villagers who hadn't already returned to their own homes or jobs, now scurried away with a final tug of the forelock to Lucas and a muttered word that might have passed for apology to Bram.

From the direction of the decoy, Bram turned to see Thirza and Jem coming towards them. Jem was weaving, wild-eyed, as though he could see a landscape peopled with terrors and landmarks hidden from all eyes but his own. Thirza was guiding him step by step so he didn't lurch off into the treacherous flushes and tricky ponds. Bram could see the stricken look on Thirza's face, but it took a moment for him to realise what it was that she carried in her arms, tenderly cradling the thing made of fur. She placed the fox-gold crushed form of an animal straight into his own arms. He touched the body. It felt as though life was totally extinct. Yet still there was a thready pulse and irregular breath, in spite of the wounds. It was Piper.

Before Thirza could explain, Emma was shrieking.

"Theresa! Where did you get that pathetic, wretched thing? Out there in the filthy waste? Why, it might have the rabies or some dreadful pox! Ugh!"

Emma fanned her face and looked to heaven.

"There's room for you both in the back of the trap. Let's get my brother home, before more village scandal's kindled by his lamentable foe-passers!"

Thirza helped get Jem into the back of the carriage. He seemed only to want to be led. He didn't look at the faces of friend or family. He was focussed on an inner scene of total destruction that took all his energy and wit to keep at bay, to stop it bleeding out into the real light of present day.

Lucas beamed down at Thirza, seeing her in his mind's eye as his intended. How could she answer anything but "yes" when the longed-for day arrived?

"You look so tired, my dear."

"Give me one moment to speak to Mr Beharrell, Lucas, and I'll follow on foot."

Reluctantly, Lucas drove the carriage forward, never taking his eyes from the girl at the side of the road. When they were out of sight and out of earshot, she and Bram walked back along the side of the boggy path out to the marsh.

"You can heal him, can't you?"

Bram held Piper in such a way that none of his many wounds felt any pressure.

"He will live, won't he?" she sobbed for the first time since she'd found Piper scratching at the hut door, too weak to whine.

"He must live! I found him like this, by the hut. He went out when I came looking for you. Where did you go? Why weren't you waiting? Now it's all too late!"

"I thought you weren't coming back, as the time went by. I'm sorry I missed you. I had things to do, too." Bram stroked Piper's head and knew there was no time to lose to steady his breathing and wrap him in love and the decoy's peace.

"What happened to you, Pi? Yackoop, yackoop, boy." Thirza didn't recognise the whispered string of soft Dutch words Bram was breathing in the little dog's ears. Usually so attentive, there was no reaction, no wag of the feathery tail.

"I don't know. I came to find you, but there was only Jem in the hut. When Piper got out I stayed inside because I heard noises. I think I was followed. Someone trailing me. I heard hooves, boots, twigs snap as I came along the edge of the marsh from the windmill. But every time I looked back, there was nobody there."

"Piper was out there on his own? Surely he would have given his signal, his special barks if there'd been trouble, or somebody was hanging about?"

"I don't know!" Thirza suddenly felt the whole of the time trapped with Darnell in the windmill sink down on her like a bane. She wanted to scream and push the racing clock-hands back around and around the face of the days until she was the carefree girl again who laughed with Bram and came alive in his company. Now there were so many things she needed to say which climbed up as far as her tongue and then choked her into miserable silence that must surely look like brooding to Bram. How could she tell him? Now this with Piper. It was her fault! She'd let him out and let this happen. She thought her heart would break. But it was already hopelessly broken.

Bram gathered the little dog up and kissed the top of his skull with adoring tenderness that made Thirza's heart ache to be held so, for always.

Bram glanced up at her. She was so quiet and pale. How had he let this happen to her? Followed from the windmill! Who had meant her harm? He hadn't gone to fetch her when she was late. She seemed so distant with him. How she must hate him now for letting her down. She looked so fragile, standing there, so spent.

"You should go home, Thirza. I'll take care of Piper. He needs to be back at the decoy. I don't like the idea of somebody being out there and you being in danger. Go back to the mill."

Thirza heard the words. Go back to the mill. Bram didn't want her here. She'd let him down and now his companion was at death's door because of her negligence. He didn't want her here, weaving the rainbow widdershins and flushing the secretive skylarks from their nests with her wandering off the way. Go back to the mill.

"I will go." Thirza put all her heart behind the words. He wouldn't see the grief inside where her joy and comfort was ripped and outlawed from her body. He must never see it. Nobody must. Not Lucas or her grandparents. Least of all Bram.

She brushed his arm with her fingers, but he was looking down at Piper, watching the erratic breaths like a husbandman bringing a lamb into the light of day from the womb of a sheep already slipping beyond hope.

"Take care, lass." Bram carried the dog away from her and she watched him go, sure-footed, reading the way beneath his feet by instinct, stilts folded under his light summer coat, hat shading his eyes against the heat of the day. She needed so to run after him, but the world swam in front of her and she turned for home with a sense of doom. It was less her home than ever and there was nobody to tell without endangering her family and bringing disgrace on them all she could never mend.

She met nobody on the way back until she was passing the churchyard gate and she saw Goody Chester standing in the deep shade by the wall. She beckoned Thirza in and stood with her, looking at a spot of disturbed earth, surrounded by tiny blue flowers with a jewel of yellow in the centre of each bloom.

"Forget me nots, Thirza Holberry, daughter of Dinah, daughter of Kezia, daughter of Kerenhappuch." Goody's predictable, comforting word-weaving made Thirza smile, for the first time that day.

As she walked on out of the lych gate, Goody called after her.

"Forget me not, young mother child. There are those that know and will not blame."

Back at the mill, Thirza heard from Kezzie and Thomas the tale of what had happened with the stone-throwing and Darnell's kindness. Jem sat rocking in a chair in the corner. He said nothing of what had happened to them. Neither could Thirza. But she thought of nothing else till nightfall.

Bram approached the dip where the decoy lay, coaxing the landscape around it to lie still, licked by the wispy fen-lights when the sun burned low. He stood before it now, with Piper more dead than alive in his arms. He saw the broken hoops and the screens bent and scattered. He saw the diaphanous nets torn away and trampled in the mud. He saw the young birch trees from the screen snapped and thrust into the head-show. His beautiful eendenkooi, the magical sanctuary of the wonders of love, the reversal of ravage, omkering van schade, where creatures could flourish and no harm could thrive. He saw it and wept.

His hut was whole. Nothing had been taken. Bram placed the dog down on a dry piece of ground near where parts of the end cage were still whole, though knocked flat. Bram lifted the prism out of his pocket and pushed it down till he felt the shift of phlogiston under his sensitive fingertips. The light through his tears already made a rainbow in his sight and the dog lifted his head and licked Bram's hand.

"Yackoop, my brave lad. Yackoop!" Bram whispered and stayed all night with the dog's head resting lightly in his upturned palms. Even when his legs felt cramp and he had to shift his position without waking the dog, there was no sound but the nightjars chirring over their heads in the moonlight. Bram waited for the circling planets to fade into the shifting dawn light.

"Tomorrow will keep. Even then, I will not leave you," he whispered to the slumbering animal. What now? Who meant such harm that they'd threaten all he held precious to rid themselves of him?

24. FEN-LIGHTS AND RAINBOWS

Thirza spent as long as she could gathering eggs, sorting and packing them. She put them in a crate with straw as she always did, but was reluctant to go anywhere near the windmill itself to store them. She left them tucked under the hen coop and prayed no predators would find them to draw attention to her reluctance. She heard voices from the cottage as she went back inside.

"My brother is no raconteur or social butterfly these days," Emma was saying, quite loud enough, in her father's estimation, for travellers on the Great North Road beyond Doncaster to hear, over ten miles to the west.

"Butterfly? Poor lad scarce emerges from his cocoon, these days," said Thomas, while Kezzie pinched Thirza's cheeks and fussed over her to try to overcome the girl's sudden dampened spirits, which frightened her grandmother even more than the general run of circumstances.

Emma filled Mill Cottage with shrill chatter and made a huge drama out of their encounter with sweaty yokels on the road. Lucas exchanged his usual pleasantries with the family and his particular clumsy courtesies to Thirza. She was glad of his uncomplicated gallantry. Her need to be ladylike and gregarious wasn't overtaxed, as Lucas soon excused himself to go up the mill tower to do business with his partner.

"I'll leave you lovely ladies to amuse yourselves," he said.

"Not so much of the lady, Squire," Thomas jested, before Lucas realised his mistake, "but the lovely I'll take as a compliment."

Lucas found Darnell in the mill shed that served as his main workshop. He was comparing a scaled down brass and waxed paper model of what looked like the fantail, with a new set of draughtsman's drawings. Lucas was a little surprised to find changed padlocks on all the doors that he didn't recall. As Darnell pointed to the way the fan blades made an elaborate concertina pattern and lifted them up to let them fall, lighter than air and spinning like a spiral of interlocking sycamore keys, Lucas noticed Darnell's hand was sporting a bandage made from his silk handkerchief.

"A lethal thing, that mainspring," chuckled Darnell with a disarming smile at his cousin.

"Malicious wounding, courtesy of clockwork," added Lucas.

"I'm usually so careful." Darnell tapped what looked to Lucas like a sophisticated escape wheel with teeth of varying lengths and angles. He noted it wasn't exactly like the one Darnell had spent a couple of hours explaining and discussing with him in his laboratory at the Hall the other night.

"The dashed thing snapped. Next thing I knew it caught me out and sliced into my finger. Nipped clean in like a bite with its sharp teeth. But it will heal."

Lucas made sympathetic noises, which Darnell waved aside.

"My own fault. It's a poor engineer who blames his inventions, eh?"

Lucas pored over an unfamiliar model that Darnell had locked inside a glass fronted cabinet against the inner wall of the room. He admired the intricate machinery through the glass. Then he unlocked and slid open the door and was about to run his fingers round the inner mantel, when Darnell launched himself at the astounded squire and knocked him out of the way.

"Don't touch that! I mean, by your leave, best not put any pressure there. Or there. Or there."

Lucas gave up trying to find places to touch on the curious contraption. He looked quizzically at Darnell, who was now pouring out some pale liquid into a glass and handing it over.

"What's the white powdery stuff? Superfine flour? How splendid!"

"Wash your hands, dear chap. We had a visitation from rats. The hazard of doing so much of the work inside the mill itself. Rats have been running amok in here of late, so I invested in some poison to see the curious creatures off."

"That explains that lethal looking thing!" Lucas looked back at the conical tablet sitting in a small dish inside a glass bulb. "But how do the rats get in there?"

He wiped his hands on the rag Darnell was holding out to him, dangling it just far enough away to force him to step away further from the cabinet.

"My dear cousin, those curious rats can get anywhere and everywhere. Believe me, the wiliest cat can't compete. Not without dirty tactics, that is."

Lucas wiped his hands down his waistcoat for luck and downed the whiskey. The room now looked in order and the questions he'd been storing up in his brain, the points of clarification, well, he couldn't now remember what they were.

"You're getting along splendidly, old chap!" he said. Darnell plied Lucas with a few more glasses before taking him up into the windmill tower itself, which Darnell was careful to keep filled with equipment that nobody would question during the familiar everyday running of the place. When they came to the ladder up to the cap, Darnell paused.

"Talking of rats, what do you make of this?"

Lucas saw he was pointing at another film of white powder, this time on the ladder rungs themselves.

"Poison again?" Lucas tried to keep a step ahead so as

not to look a complete buffoon.

Darnell betrayed no impatience.

"Flour. Just common wheat flour. I mean, what do you make of these traces in the flour?"

"Mildew?" Lucas could feel his acuity waning.

"Not mildew. Human prints in the flour."

"Could it be the cat?"

"A pretty cat." Darnell wondered how Lucas got through the day sometimes, with a wit as slow under the influence as his seemed to be.

"Oh!" A dawning light illuminated the fog of Lucas's understanding. "A pretty lady cat! You mean somebody has been up here?"

"Snooping."

"But who would want...?" Lucas finally read Darnell's expectant expression.

"Surely not? Your lovely niece?"

"I fear I've had occasion to reprimand her for snooping where she has no business. She used to spend hours up aloft, sighing and such, before she met you, of course, Cousin. But now we're so close to the launch, we can't have her always here, meddling. She almost broke a vital element up there. She was so upset when I gently set her straight. I beg you, Lucas, to look to her. Keep her occupied, as a future husband should."

Lucas looked blank for a moment, then blushed.

"I will, cousin, I will."

"Keep her out of the way. There is danger here. Rat poison. Hazardous equipment. The new mill even more than the old."

"I take your meaning, Cuz." Lucas hoped he did, at least. He'd always thought of the new mill design as bringing health and safety to the region. They'd talked about 'Friends of the Future' bringing the last word in design into this corner of the empire. He kept wondering now if he was really able to follow and keep his finger on Darnell's ambitious plans. But never fret. To have his family name associated with cutting edge technology, to strengthen this new engineering dynasty by marriage, that was enough for any bright young man, to be sure. He raised his glass to clink it with Darnell's before realising he was drinking alone, and Darnell was watching him with what he could only call an enigmatic smile.

"About the millstone, I've made initial enquiries," Darnell said, "on Jeremy's behalf."

Lucas nodded with enthusiasm. Here was something he could manage with no trouble, the bankrolling of this whole enterprise. He liked to think of the headlines in the future newspapers, name-checking the magnanimous, academical young heir of the Foljambe estate. Lady Laura would be so proud of him.

"I can run over there and fetch it from the quarry in Wickersley," said Lucas, "if it's the one over by the church fields that I know. I've a friend over that way I may call on for a visit to break the journey. My little cart should take the weight of your average runner stone."

"Nothing average, please!" Darnell steered the conversation with his usual dexterity, "Perhaps you can persuade Thirza to ride out there with you? Save her from mooning about here, getting underfoot."

Lucas felt the day could hardly be going better at this point. He made a note of the details while Darnell locked the padlock on the workshop door and slapped his pocket with satisfaction, pulling out his fob watch ostentatiously.

"There's no hurry today, Cousin, but the sooner the sweeter. That trouble you mentioned with the natives?"

"Once Alma Mill is unveiled," said Lucas, "they'll be eating out of our hands. Not so very long now before harvest and then..."

"Then the beginning of the future, dear chap," Darnell gave the words all the weighted significance he could muster to make sure Lucas got his drift.

Back in the cottage, Lucas asked permission to walk out for a turn round the meadow with Thirza, while Darnell and Emma prepared for the drive back to Carrdyke.

"Wait for me, Cousin, I won't be long," Lucas called,

as Kezzie took her chance of offering more cake all round, albeit not the coconut variety.

Thirza was glad of a chance to escape for a while into the cool air, with Lucas's attentions that often struck her more like an elder brother's than a lover's, so diffident was he at times without Darnell urging him on at his elbow. She was even more thankful not to have to make polite conversation with Darnell himself, or risk him brushing against her, as he often contrived to do.

"I've an errand to run, a drive over to Wickersley, to fetch a new runner stone for Alma...for the mill. I wonder if you would make my day by accompanying me, Thirza? There's pretty countryside on the way up to the plateau. High and healthy for you, up there, after languishing here with the marsh air making you so pale. My friend who lives there calls it the Wuthering Heights of Rotherham after our own Miss Brontë's work."

Thirza hadn't read much of any of the Miss Brontës' work. She had an idea it was Emily who'd penned that exciting title, but reading a romantic book like that to her boisterous brothers, would be to depart into the realms of speculative fiction herself. She imagined their yawns and snorts of derision at her reading them that 'girly stuff'!

Lucas drew closer, seeing her amusement. He hoped it was he who amused, in a good way. As his face drew near to hers, walking back across the meadow to the cottage, she caught the whiff of alcohol on his breath.

"I wonder if he has to drink to like me?" Thirza's heart sank. Perhaps all men but Darnell would need to get drunk to endure her looks and company soon. She thought of Goody's words at the churchyard. She thought of their meaning. Then she pushed the thoughts away furiously and screwed down the lid of her heart so tight it made her feel sick and empty. Lucas was so kind and good. She must try to love him, somehow.

"I would love to go to the quarry with you, Lucas. When should I be ready?"

They made the arrangement. Lucas followed Darnell

and Emma in their trap, looking back at Thirza as she stood in the road watching him go. Before that trip, she knew she must try to slip out for a moment to explain to Bram. He knew nothing about Lucas's proposal, nothing about the horror that had followed. She couldn't even give it a name in her head. She must do what was right, even though everything in her world now seemed too wrong for Bram to fix with his fen-lights and rainbows.

#

Piper felt the warmth. He smelled the herbal sweetness of the marsh flowers in the little bowl. He heard his master crooning an old song with words he remembered from when he'd gathered injured plovers and goslings in his mouth and whisked them tenderly out of the nets to lay them in Bram's hand. He tasted the sweet paste of marsh horsetail mixed with the adder's tongue, a plant he loved to sniff along the limestone reach of the old canal tow path. This was pure, pure ferny sweetness, not cloudy with the smell of his own urine from his marking each clump for safe returning.

He panted. Deeper breaths brought him the scent of Lady-fern crushed together with - what was it? - Pod Grass? His master must have fetched this especially for him, risky business, from the undrained reaches of the boggiest corners. His front paws began to paddle slowly in empty air. He felt his master's hand on the crown of his head. All the pain, all the dizziness, all the fatigue was draining away. He'd come home from the dank tunnel where everything seemed empty, without trail or scent, like nowhere he'd ever wandered or wagged his tail. His master was here now. That was all that mattered to Piper.

Behind Bram, Thirza was silently weeping. To see the little dog coming round was overwhelming her fragile emotions. What was the matter with her? Useless! Useless to anyone like this.

"All fixed and fair, little one," Bram spoke into the dog's furry ear as he caressed the whole body with tiny sweeping strokes that seemed to put him back together again and join up the wounded spots to make him whole.

Piper stood up and shook his head without a stagger and smiled up at the man he loved and the special gentle lady. Why was she all salty like the sea-frets? Bram followed Piper's adoring gaze and turned to face Thirza.

"Can you fix me, like you've fixed Piper?" she whispered, not trusting herself to say why she needed his touch, that could roll back ruin with his 'omkering van schade', to the moment before the havoc was wreaked.

Bram smiled. He hoped he could do just that. But now he knew for certain, forces were working against him. More distressing for him, against Thirza herself.

"I've fixed most of the hoops. They look a little drunken, but they'll serve again." He ran his hand along the net. He pulled from his pocket what he'd found clenched in Piper's teeth after the attack that left the plucky Kooikerhondje for dead.

He showed it to Thirza. She examined the scrap of cream coloured cloth.

"I recognise the stitching. It's a hem for a cuff. A man's shirt cuff. Do you need me to mend it?"

"I can mend my own garments, Thirza. But this isn't mine."

Thirza looked at the scuffle marks around the decoy area with new eyes. Canine paw-marks. Heavy bootprints. She tried to remember the grunts and crunches she'd heard from the hut when she was hiding there with Jem. The someone who'd followed her. She shuddered.

"Whoever came calling, damaged the decoy, hurt Piper, lost this."

They looked at each other, speaking what they knew, yet no murmur was exchanged.

"Can you stay? I've so much to tell you." Bram put the scrap of shirt back in his pocket. "The other night, when it was so dark here you couldn't see your hand in front of your face for the haze, I saw someone far off, following the fen-lights."

"Did you see this person's face? Were they following the phlogiston paths like you do?"

"Hush!" Bram stopped Thirza and turned to hold his ear edgeways to the breeze. He listened for the crackle of twigs, the alarm of the blackbird, but there was nothing stark in the smooth summer air.

"We must be more circumspect. I believe he came spying and, worse, gathering."

"A man? Gathering what? Rushes? Reeds?"

"You remember the night you were here when that storm was crackling round? You said once you saw a ball of lightning aboard 'Thistle', rolling up the mast?"

"Bram, you're frightening me. What riddle's this? Who's been here?"

Thirza remembered vividly seeing ball lightning as a toddling infant from her mother's lap on the keel. She'd watched the slow, incandescent ball bowling along the deck. She'd reached out a chubby hand towards it and Dinah had slapped it away with a terrified cry that had stayed with Thirza a lifetime.

The glowing ball had moved as if it was alive and had its own inner compass and intention. It bounded like a spinning orb of fire, from aft in the direction of the bows. Then it glided up the mast, along the yardarm high above Thirza's head, before exploding in a thousand wheeling sparks that made her chuckle and clap, though her mother had run down the ladder to where Jack was resting, snatching Thirza into her arms. Thirza felt her mother trembling though she couldn't understand what was said. Years after, her father would tell her and later her brothers, what a miracle that the ball lightning, so rarely seen, had spared the ship that day, not igniting her like a match, a floating inferno with them all trapped aboard.

"Ball lightning isn't so uncommon here," Bram explained. "It's a hazard to the unwary. You've seen the marsh gas, phlogiston, licking bright and cool, following you as if drawn by the dint your body makes in the still air? Some talk of fen-lights, Will-o'-the-wisp, ignis fatuus, foolish fire, so many names. As my ancestors harnessed this powerful little light, for purposes others might abuse, now our caution and secrecy are betrayed. The one I saw crouching and creeping was gathering phlogiston, and peat, and methane and the deadly nitrous deposits that sleep under our feet like dragons waiting to be unleashed."

"You know who came here."

"Of course I know. You know it too. I'm sure you guess what's happening at the windmill's not all it seems. It's what my own grandfather warned me about before he died. Everything he'd taught me would be swept away, he said, by those who plot evil, to dominate the marshes instead of guarding and celebrating their treasures."

"Why would anybody do that? Why would he?" Thirza couldn't say that name, but heard the urgency in Bram's voice. He felt the dread in hers, and wondered.

"Grandfather's father was watched one summer by that man who hung around, observing how he extracted and mixed these precious elements with natural alchemy, to transform the stilts to outrun invisible barriers, the decoy to cherish the birds and wild creatures that others killed by the thousand. That man asked so many questions my great grandfather grew suspicious about his motives. Triggering ball lightning's destructive potential seemed to fascinate him."

"The man you told me about."

"Pagnell Salkeld."

"I've seen his grave in the churchyard."

"There he lies, milk-innocent in his shroud. Grandfather Jan said Pagnell bequeathed what he'd learned to his family. I don't suppose they made much of the tales of phlogiston. I only knew of mistrust between our families that I inherited. They say now phlogiston is all a myth. Oxygen is what burns in air. But phlogiston is real, too. It burns up, igniting pockets of gas out here where nobody sees it now."

"Nobody but you."

"Those that see it sometimes wander from their chosen way and come to harm. I've heard tell of legends from

242

my land and others across Europe. People believe the lights are dead souls, the unbaptised, infants and self-murderers, beckoning them on, baptising them in death as they miss their footing and plunge into the hidden pools that are everywhere here. I try to guide travellers away from hazards and dispel myths."

"This phlogiston of yours..." Thirza began.

"Not mine. Nor his!" protested Bram.

"But you keep hinting this natural chemistry can be used for harm?"

"Is being used. Darnell's inherited Pagnell's obsession and he has the skill to use it monstrously."

Thirza thought of the diagrams and models and strange things she'd seen in the echoing chamber at Foljambe Hall, the wonders she'd glimpsed through the workshop door, the things she'd smelled and seen in the cap of the windmill.

"I fear there are terrible things afoot, lovely lass. Things foreseen by our ancestors. In the wrong hands, these explosive things could be fatal. Why the rumours of the Goatsucker to strike fear into people's hearts so they ask no questions?"

"To silence them. To stop their lips from telling all they see!" Thirza shouted the words, for she saw a glimpse of how her own lips had been stopped.

"There you are, delight of my heart!"

Thirza spun round. Behind a distant clump of willow, she saw Lucas standing, still a tiny figure from where she and Bram stood in the lee of the decoy. He was cupping his hands to holler to her rather than risk this impenetrable patch of swampy ground.

"Quick, go to him!" Bram dodged behind the nearest screen and pushed her gently away in Lucas's direction, hoping he hadn't been seen. When Thirza got within the distance for normal conversation, Lucas waved.

"The day's so fair, I've decided to go to Wickersley today instead. They said up at the mill you were out walking."

He offered her his arm, which she took without daring to glance back in Bram's direction, for fear of giving him away, or the position of the camouflaged, stricken decoy.

"This marsh is like a magnet to you, my sweet. But the foggy, foul air here does you no good. See how wan you are!"

He touched her cheek.

"When our new mill's open, not so long from now, there'll be roads criss-crossing this area, peat extraction on a scale never seen before, railway links here and here and over that way to York, Leeds, Hull, Lincoln, London, Edinburgh!"

Lucas pointed with his whip, stabbing in the direction of the different towns. Thirza could see those roads, the rails, cutting through the fragile marshes, ramming mercilessly through hidden nightjar nests, over warrens and burrows and Bram's precious wilderness world, the hiss of steam and the eye-watering smog of smoke pothering over it all.

"With you and I, in the centre, in our Alma Mill, like two love birds in an exotic nest," Lucas concluded with a sweep of his whip that made the peaty earth ripple under their feet.

"Or flies trapped in a spider's web!"

"Eh? You hilarious girl!" Lucas strolled on. Thirza tried to pretend she too had meant it as a joke. He helped her solicitously into his dog-cart, fitted up, Thirza suspected, by a design of Darnell's, with another stout unsprung cart attached on four sturdy wheels behind it. Thirza was relieved to hear the squire's breakneck swift phaeton was away for repairs.

"For transportation of the millstone," confided Lucas, "or a nice place to recline for a spot of canoodling on the return journey," he added with a wink, though when he saw Thirza's face, he reassured her, "My turn for a joke, Thirza, I am your perfect gentleman!"

Of that she was more thankful than he could know.

#

Bram petted Piper, then climbed into his punt with

the eager dog perched on the till in the stern.

"Delight of my heart, he called her!" Bram turned over Lucas's words to Thirza in his mind. He murmured his thoughts to the dog as he pushed off, as cheerful as the revelation of Thirza's intimate attachment to the squire would allow.

"There's much to do, if we're to keep our lovely lass safe and stop whatever's planned to poison this paradise." Bram sculled through pits and up and down dykes, avoiding the canal for as long as he had shelter on more hidden waterways.

"Delight of my heart, indeed she is," he sighed wistfully, as man and dog glided away beyond prying eyes.

25. GRINDSTONES AND GOATSUCKERS

The way to Wickersley took Thirza and Lucas through undulating countryside, underpinned north to south by Permian Magnesian Limestone, as the squire was at pains to point out to his captive audience of one. They travelled along tree-lined slopes, ancient ridges, slanting Pennine coal measures rippling over sandstone beds, in dramatic contrast to the flat expanses of the low-lying peat moors of the Humberhead Levels Thirza knew so well, founded on Triassic Mercia Mudstone, once the glacial Lake Humber.

Thirza begged Lucas to let her sit back to back with him, for the drive was over twenty miles. Looking back the way they'd come, she could rest her eyes if tiredness overwhelmed her, as it often did these past few weeks. She could spot if they were being followed and not be obliged to make constant smiling eye contact with her self-appointed beau and geology lecturer the whole of the way. Thirza noted the time by St Larry's clock as they passed at a brisk trot through Hatfield. It was just before eleven and they were soon passing through sleepy Hatfield Woodhouse with its two windmills, Ling's Mill and Hatfield Mill which Lucas pointed out with his whip.

"These old mills will soon be a thing of the benighted

past," he shouted back to her. "Soon there'll be new designs, engine-driven, gas-powered."

Thirza heard the boastful adjectives as she strained to hear the birds in the hedgerows that had sprung up by every wayside since the Enclosure Act parcelled out the farmland. She let the words and the birdsong blend into a lullaby, replying to Lucas only where it seemed polite, to keep herself from nodding off in the warm sunlight, the gentle breeze fanning her as they rushed along.

The busier highway around Doncaster turned the conversation to the River Don, where keels and sloops were ranged along the water's edge. Thirza was wide awake now. She leaned over to see the painted names and watch the familiar figures working on their moored boats, doing tasks she herself ached to be doing again.

"Might we stop here for a moment?" She felt Lucas lean back to catch her words, but the pace barely slowed.

"Still hankering after your old world? I suppose it's inevitable, with the stench of fish and the crude sailors shouting down there. But I'm going to go one better. I want to drive you past the new railway works. Eleven acres of land with workshops and machinery that will put Doncaster at the helm of history, the forefront of the future. Our future!"

Lucas sounded intoxicated with the enthusiasm of a young man whose head was crammed full of mechanical wizardry, from years of privilege, with funds for limitless tinkering, a devoted acolyte of engineers in every field, from Telford to Brunel, Bazalgette to Stevenson.

As the long profile of the Plant Works came into view alongside gleaming rows of rails, Lucas was almost bouncing with glee in his seat. Thirza clung on, as the rattle of the dogcart wheels was outpaced by the stream of admiring words from Lucas.

"Look at it all! Railways and speed and steam and thundering efficiency yoked to vision! We're being paid a visit here in the autumn by the great railway, canal and mill engineer, Sir William Cubitt!"

"He of the patent sails?" Thirza wondered why, if

railways were all the future was about, this Cubitt fellow still had his name associated with mill sails and her beloved canals? But before she could say as much to Lucas, he was already off again, cracking his whip and enthusing.

"Soon, they say, to travel past Doncaster's railway connections, end to end, its carriage works, its locomotive sheds, will take more than a day in a coach-and-four. Darnell and I have such plans to be a part of it and to better and best some of this current stuff. Darnell tells it better than I. But such wonders there'll be! We'll be flying overhead in carriages made of glass, streaming steam and sparks like..." Lucas paused to try and think of a suitable comparison, "...like unearthly things and whatnot! Darnell could tell you." He suddenly seemed to think better of it and fell silent for a moment. "Though, of course, our plans are a frightfully well-kept secret. Darnell is the genius, he ploughs his own furrow!"

Thirza knew better than to ask questions. What she'd seen so far, more by accident than design, didn't sound the open secret about which Lucas seemed so excited. She fingered the tiny clockwork bird in her pocket and noticed again how closely some of Darnell's designs seemed based on it. So much for ploughing his own furrow. She played with it in her hands as Lucas rattled on about the splendid intricacies of this design and that.

Having detoured into Doncaster to see the Plant Works, their route took them along the back roads, through Balby Carr, Warmsworth, then Thirza recognised Conisborough's wonderful ruined castle, standing out against the sky at the historic crossing of the River Don. 'Thistle' had so often glided beneath the castle, such a landmark in her world, it was a bittersweet joy to see it again. To Thirza, it seemed less imposing from the back of the dog-cart, than when it glowered down at her with its stone-rimmed eyes, set in its massive circular keep, like the helmet of a Norman giant ready to rush down from the Roman Ridge towards their little boat.

Lucas lashed his whip theatrically above the horses'

heads and they lurched south, away from the castle and the homely Don. Before long, they were climbing up through Micklebring, which Lucas pronounced several times to amuse her with its spiky Saxon sounds. While Lucas droned on about the name's possible origins in the Old English 'micel' meaning large and 'brinc', a form of 'burgh', a fortification on a hill, Thirza gasped at the views from that same large hillside to the west, north and east and was transfixed by the vistas all around. She wondered if the horses were tiring, as she was, as they made progress towards the upland plateau where Wickersley nestled, its ancient woodlands dropping away towards the lower slopes and its cottages of golden stone, glowing in the summer sunlight.

"I have a regular thirst on me," declared Lucas, "but first things first. The horses shall have a rub down over there at the inn, while I go and secure a capital grindstone from the quarry at the far end of the village. I don't see any milliners or such, but perhaps you can amuse yourself till I've done that spot of business?"

Thirza assured Lucas she'd need no entertaining. They arranged to meet by the little gazebo, where locals waited for the stagecoach outside the Needles Inn, as soon as Lucas finished running his hands over the newly quarried stones and, Thirza imagined, talking the quarrymen half to death. Perhaps in this weather they'd appreciate the diversion. Wickersley's reputation for millstones was second to none, Lucas had assured her. They transported their local product to Sheffield for the watermills there, where steel foundries blackened the air and led the world in the crafting of the sharpest blades.

To while away the time, Thirza set out to stroll the length of what she imagined was the main street, back towards the parish church of St Alban. She gazed at a pair of unusual bow-fronted cottages and puzzled how the occupants chose furniture that would bend to the shape of the room. Or did they design their own? It must be like living in a windmill, only a windmill cut in half.

Thirza passed the end of the little lane that led up to the church. The top of the church tower, according to what Lucas had told her on the way, till her head was spinning with heat and trivia, was the highest point between Bawtry and Sheffield. The parish would place a light there, St Nicholas' Lamp, to guide travellers and stop them missing their way in the darkness. Thirza dreamed of stagecoaches and travellers on the dry canals that were the highways, being seduced into straying from their route by strange lights. In her mind, she was back on the moors with Bram, watching the disorienting flicker of fen-lights that popped up unbidden and unpredictable, seeming to hover towards you or glide away at will. Only Bram seemed to know where to find these strange phenomena, to harness them with a touch or a breath, making what seemed shuddery and shifty into something fragile and breathtakingly beautiful.

Dreaming of this as she passed by the church, Thirza almost cannoned into a cart drawing out of a gateway from one of the many little farms dotted around the village. The farmer's lad laughed as Thirza apologised for getting in his way. She watched the cart wobble off, piled high with sheaves, laden with ripe wheat and barley as harvest time drew closer. Soon there'll be no time for dreaming, thought Thirza. When Harvest Festival comes around at the beginning of October, I'll have to give my answer to Lucas's proposal. Then my world will change in so many ways.

Lucas! Thirza realised she'd been meandering along, enjoying this delightful little place for longer than she'd intended. She turned and ran back towards the old coaching inn by the gazebo, but a sudden stitch in her side and an unfamiliar discomfort in her abdomen made her dizzy and short of breath. She leaned against the corner of the gazebo until she saw Lucas on the opposite side of the road, in the company of another young man. They emerged from where Wickersley Hall stood back behind a stone wall inscribed with its name.

"There you are, my dear Thirza!" The introductions floated over Thirza's head. She struggled with the heat as the chatter dragged on between the two old friends. Both seemed more interested in times they'd spent hunting together, than in her. They were comparing their dogs, their carriages, the price of stock at market and the starting prices of the horses they'd back or buy in the St. Leger, run in September on Doncaster's Town Moor.

"I'll bet my snake-eye ring and best gander on it!" Lucas's friend was saying, while Lucas didn't seem to notice how Thirza was swaying with exhaustion from the hot journey. Next he suggested a quick pint of ale at the Needles Inn. His affable friend concurred and an hour or more later, Thirza was still sitting on a bench under a tree in the shadiest spot she could find. Finally, unable to make her thimble-sized glass of lemonade last any longer, she saw Lucas emerging in a less-than-straight line of staggering steps in her direction.

"If I remember nicely, (hic) rightly," slurred Lucas, "the Needles hostelry is the best between Bawtry and Sheffield, bar none! Or is that the dashed church... top thing...on top... is the highest between here and Doomsday? One or t'other!"

The two old friends hugged and slapped backs and shook hands and hopelessly failed in an attempt at a manly clashing together of knuckles as they parted. Thirza thought Lucas was using his friend as a steadying post to lean on, for as long as it took the other to cross the road back to his home, while Lucas stood tipping his hat effusively to invisible passers-by and various nearby bushes.

Climbing back into the dog-cart, Thirza saw that with the extra bulk of the millstone they were towing, she'd be obliged to ride up front with Lucas to balance the weight more evenly. As they set off, she soon realised that riding beside him in his inebriated state, was not only more hazardous, but essential in helping avoid hazards like potholes, ditches and alarmed pedestrians. As they veered away from a cursing farm-hand, who'd narrowly avoided being mown down when their path unexpectedly converged with his as he carted manure in a hand-barrow, Lucas seemed more at pains to correct the fellow's grammar than to smooth the situation.

"Forgive me, Miss Hobblery," Lucas frowned at the unfamiliar sound of her name, but proceeded anyway, "but the thing is..."

Thirza never did find out what the thing was, but managed to grab the reins and keep them from toppling into a dyke on a deserted stretch of track between Kirk Sandall and Barnby Dun. The force of the emergency stop threw them both forward and, had it not been for the counterbalancing brake effect of their load, Thirza wondered if they might ever have arrived home unscathed.

As they resettled themselves, Lucas picked up something that had fallen at their feet during the jolting.

"Miss Hobble...obbery...Thirza, wherever did you get this model of the Alma Mill?"

Thirza stretched out her hand to take the little toy back but Lucas held it up out of her reach and tutted.

"Now, now! Finder's keepers. Where did you get it?" Lucas seemed slapped into sobriety by sight of the intricate machinery beneath the nightjar's camouflaging plumage. Thirza had wound a length of thread about the thing and tied it to one of several tiny clockwork levers that made it work, even without phlogiston.

"It's just a toy I inherited from my mother that I keep to remind me of her."

"Nice try!" Lucas shot her a strange look out of the corner of his eye, as if he was unable to judge whether she knew more than she was saying. A spy after all?

He detached the inner workings from the upper sheath of feathers that made the bird recognisable. He held the spinner that drove the wings, blades uppermost and pulled sharply on the thread, which promptly snapped.

"This is all snaggled! The mill works like clockwork when Darnell..." Lucas stopped, narrowing his eyes. Which part was a secret, if Thirza had this thing?

"Like this," said Thirza, taking it from him. She lifted the bird up higher, standing up in the stationary cart, feeling the wind lift her hair.

"I wound it the other way, you see, left-handed." She held the device in her right hand, gripping the gilded claw setting that seemed to clutch around empty air as if something was missing from its grasp. With her left hand she pulled the thread downwards with a smooth motion and let the little bird go kiting up into the air, steady as a gyroscope yet with such lift and thrust. Spiralling high above their heads like a disoriented skylark, it plummeted towards the earth again before slowing and lowering itself gracefully between two furrows in the field a few feet away.

For the first time that day, Thirza saw that Lucas was lost for words. A tipsy belch and an apology was all he could manage as he watched in utter amazement.

"It isn't supposed to do that!" he slurred. Thirza jumped down, retrieved the mechanical bird and came round to Lucas's side of the carriage.

"Why don't you let me drive? It's a straight run back home now. It'll save us any more close encounters with the scenery."

Lucas saw Thirza's tongue was firmly in her cheek. He could never fathom her out completely. Never the little woman but entirely womanly in his eyes, for all that. They swapped places for the last few miles of the journey. Lucas leaned closer to Thirza and offered her his whip to urge the tired pair of horses on.

"I don't need that," she assured him, without taking her eyes from the road, "there are other ways to move than by brutality and force, you know."

Lucas fell silent, fiddling with the stock of the whip and twisting the lash around the mechanical bird that Thirza had placed on the seat between them. He wound it clockwise and when the cogs connected and the concertina wings were taut, he launched it so it soared above the hedgerow.

"It still isn't supposed to be like that!" he seemed to be trying to convince himself.

"It's just a toy. My friend made it so it worked both ways, left and right. I don't know how. I can wind it left and it flies one way. You wound it with your right and it flies like that. It's designed to take fuel, too, so it can fly and not tire."

They saw the little bird flapping its wings with a pause this time, like a finch, then clapping its wings and thrusting its tail like the nightjar it was. Like a living thing, it flew until it lost impetus and direction, plummeting back towards the flat boggy stretch ahead of them. It levelled out and scuttled along by the side of the warp drain, moving its articulated feet for a few rapid steps, before it toppled over and grew still, lying there with its huge goatsucker eyes and whiskery mouth gaping like an avian frog.

Thirza slowed the horses to a walk and Lucas picked the bird up, untangling the driver thread from the feathers.

"It had a broken wing and wouldn't work for me until I was shown how to make it fly."

"It isn't for flying, though. The way it's fashioned," Lucas held it to try and explain what he meant, "Darnell told me this was for making the sails go more smoothly, even when there's little wind, or no wind at all to drive the mill. This is exactly like the finished machine he's working on. I've seen it, you see."

Thirza could see something was really troubling Lucas, something more than the hangover that would surely creep over him and hammer his head with a thousand splinters of sickness in the coming night.

"This was my mother's. Just a toy she left me, made by an old friend's family years and years ago. It's nothing to do with Darnell!" Thirza felt indignant at the very thought of Darnell using the bird in his design.

"But what goes here?" Lucas was asking the question, but didn't sound as though he expected Thirza to know the answer. He put his finger into the spherical empty space under the bird's belly where the claws were grasping at nothing.

"They aren't aligned as if on a perch, so what is it?"

"I don't understand." Thirza was so tired now, but something in Lucas's voice made her want to know why he was so alarmed to see the design of her mother's bird. She bit back the impulse to tell him the design was the same as the clockwork decoy ducks that Bram had inherited. What could Darnell be making up in the windmill? Then she remembered. She thought back before the joggle screen and the part of her life she wanted to forget.

"There was a big glass ball. Held by a hanging claw."

"Like this?" Lucas held her bird upside down so its feet seemed to snatch upwards at an invisible bubble of space.

"I suppose it was."

"Then...but no. All will be revealed at harvest. Your uncle's a genius. We lesser mortals can only watch and wonder. Always working to perfect his designs. Better millstones, more efficient sails, finer flour."

"Why the glass orb?"

"I only know it's essential, and terribly necessary, and secret! I leave all those fine details to Darnell. Ours not to reason why, ours but to do..."

Lucas's quotation from Tennyson trailed away. They were approaching the gateway to Foljambe Hall on the left with Carrdyke House on the right. Thirza spotted Darnell standing outside his front door. Wherever he was in the landscape now, she could never be unaware of him. He waved at them, an odd expression on his face that neither of them could interpret. Emma was fussing round him, grabbing at his arm and brushing at his collar with an enormous clothes brush that threatened to have his eye out, or her own.

"Tell me it wasn't the Ghost-sucker!" Emma appeared frantic.

"Goatsucker! Goatsucker!" Darnell's impatience with Emma contrasted with his ingratiating smile at Lucas and another look which Thirza felt, when she was strong enough to meet it, probed her every movement with an insolent intimacy.

"But, Darnell, dearest, the teeth marks! It has bitten you in the night! They say the Ghost-sucker has such talons and teeth like a demon!"

"Be quiet, woman!" Darnell exploded, without taking his eyes from Thirza. "I told you, it was nothing more than a stupid accident in my workshop. A coiled spring. A moment's inattention!"

He shook Emma off like a stallion shakes off flies with a flick of its tail. Darnell strode out of the porch, leaving Emma brushing empty air, while he approached the dog-cart with an approving nod.

"Perfect." Darnell ran his hand around the new millstone, then climbed onto it, hitching a ride back to the windmill, watching the couple as he rode behind them. Thirza pushed the clockwork goatsucker deep inside her pocket. To her surprise, Lucas didn't mention it to his cousin. His previous tipsy loquacity had given way to a thoughtful quietness. But under his breath, she could hear him finishing the quote as they stopped in the mill yard and as Darnell helped him unhitch the grindstone from the back of the cart.

"Ours but to do and die,
Into the Valley of Death,
Rode the six hundred."

Thirza went to lie down, dabbing her temples with rosewater she'd made herself from the dog roses in the hedgerow at the start of the summer. She didn't want Kezzie to fuss over her, so she went for a walk in the cool of the evening, out towards the reclaimed fields being harvested on the edge of the turbary, strips of varied colours and textures making a rainbow counterpane turned down to air under the sweltering summer sun.

Soon she became aware of a presence at her elbow. Goody Chester was walking alone, as she always seemed to walk, meeting villagers only when they most needed company, then melting away with a word of cryptic wisdom when they most needed solitude and discretion.

"I saw you three come home with the millstone round your neck," she said.

"It was just the two of us, Squire Charlesworth and I."

"The three of you, Thirza Holberry, mother and maiden, daughter of Dinah, granddaughter of Kezia, great grandchild of Kerenhappuch," repeated Goody, with emphasis. "Three."

"You mean Darnell?" Thirza saw Goody's expression, inscrutable at the best of times, change for a brief moment into a flash of loathing.

"Beware of him, young mother!"

"It's too late for that, Goody."

"I know it."

They went on in silence, past the churchyard as far as the pinfold, where the sunlight etched deep shadows and made patches of moss livid red on the stone wall. Thirza thought back to those first times she'd been there with Bram, the scarlet butchery someone had perpetrated there, blaming it all on Jem.

"Beware of him. He runs deep like a marsh pit, bottomless and unfathomed."

"Bram told me the pits aren't really bottomless, like they say, Goody. They're clear as crystal if you know how to see into them."

"That Dutchy knows more than he tells, child. Look to your uncle, the fragile hero."

"He seems so afraid of Darnell. Even now, with this millstone, Darnell had us go to fetch it because Jem couldn't do it. Now Darnell's getting a visiting millwright to prepare the stone because Jem will just ruin it."

Goody grabbed her arm and shook her head.

"He is dismantling him piece by piece. Delusion by delusion. Memory by memory. Till the nodding balance will tip."

Goody turned away before Thirza could ask anything more. As always with Goody, it was the spaces behind the things she said that seemed to open up like rooms down a dark corridor, just beyond knowing.

Thirza walked home as Mars burned red in the southern sky and Orion slanted towards the western horizon with his twinkling belt and sword pointing down towards the sails. How would she ever lie under her own sweet sails again? There was light coming from the crack above the lintel of the workshop, where Darnell was working to keep the wolf from all their doors. The sands of time were slipping through her fingers, as Harvest Festival drew closer, less than a month away. For Jem, for Bram, she couldn't let that happen. She would seize the moment. She'd discover why what Darnell had told Lucas they were building, and the truth of what he was up to, had somehow parted company in the hinterland of Darnell's duplicity and charm.

26. I AM THE GOATSUCKER

A shimmering heat haze flickered over the moor pools. It set the peat steaming, while the water was alive with smoky chocolate and caramel smudges. By the afternoon, the towering cumulus mountains of cloud above the Nab crackled with electricity. Thirza rubbed her eyes. That thundery headache was too stubborn to shift today. How she wished the storm would break.

Inside the mill, Darnell heard the first rumble of thunder and smiled. The day wasn't far away now when he would no longer be dependent on the vagaries of the weather to fuel his ambitions. He stroked the glass orb and in his mind's eye, saw the fire and discharging scribble of pure blue light in there, as the fork lightning grizzled over the sails.

"Have you seen to the new stone, Jem?" Thomas had held off from asking. These days, if you didn't ask directly, you'd never get one word volunteered. Not about business. Not about passing the time of day. Not about the preparations for extra trade at harvest. Not anything. Jem didn't answer immediately. Too long for Thomas.

"Darnell tells us Lucas and our Thirza brought it all the way from Wickersley last week. That should never have been needed, lad, if you'd taken care with the old runner stone. I haven't seen the new one, of course. That was your job! The surface of the old one was so cut about, damaged, cracked. In all my years I never knew it crack!"

"Thomas, my love, the lad's trying..." Kezzie used the same voice to Thomas she used to tell him when the cat had left mouse entrails on the hearthrug and he'd stepped in them without knowing. Thomas went on, hearing no murmur of response from Jem in the corner.

"Never mind that, Kez, it wasn't asking much of our Jem, was it? All organised for him. Squire and Thirza doing the carting, his long-suffering brother-in-law doing most of the paperwork and ordering, if I'm any judge. Darnell says you've had nothing to do but help him and the millwright heave the new stone into place. He's left you to the chipping out of the grooves with the bill."

"Thomas, leave him!" Kezzie looked from her husband's blind eyes to the unseeing eyes of her boy and longed to make peace between them as it used to be before Jem went away.

"All I asked was, how have you done? A yea or a nay? How hard is that, for pity's palaver?"

Thomas heard the chair scrape backwards like a scream. Still no words.

As the door slammed behind Jem, Thomas shouted after him, despair almost extinguishing his usual buoyant humour.

"Better to have a millstone tied round your neck than to be such a lazy lummock! That's what it says in my miller's bible!"

But Jem was already in the mill yard, where to his horror, an audience of farmers was gathered round something propped up by the pump. Someone was shouting over and over. Were they shouting at him?

"It was you all along! Murderer! Slaughterer! Ripper of cattle! Destroyer! It was you! You!"

Jem felt himself restrained from behind. He didn't resist. Someone else was screeching in his ear.

"Liar! Mester Salkeld warned us, but we tried to give you the benefit of the doubt!"

Darnell watched from the bin floor window, seeing but unseen. He'd been putting the final touches in place, ready to crank the cap around to point in the direction of Doncaster. He checked the compass in his palm, where it nestled in a compartment of his fob watch. As the volume outside rose, he coolly tapped the convex glass: south west, two hundred and twenty five degrees.

Thirza was at the other end of the village, gazing across the flats, plucking up her courage, trying to clear her head to use her wits. Today she had to choose her moment to do and dare instead of this endless waiting. This being waltzed here and there by the whims of others, manoeuvred into corners she didn't choose to be in. It had to end.

"We can fly, you and I, little bird," she touched the clockwork bird and promised herself it would begin today. She wondered when Bram would come back. He'd said he would let her know, but the days were slipping away with nothing resolved. It was never down to her, no matter how strong she was. It was up to her father to leave her here. Up to her brothers to choose a different life on the railways. Up to Lucas to propose and expect a convenient answer. Up to Darnell...

She heard her name being called from the other end of the Nab. She started to hurry in that direction. Again, someone else's choices. Here she was, heading towards their call instead of going to the moors where Bram must surely be back by now. Every other thing went out of her head when she saw it was her grandmother running and shouting her name.

"Come quick, lass, something awful. I don't know how it happened. He couldn't have done it. Who's done it?"

Thirza could hardly keep up with Kezzie, who'd found speed to run she hadn't used in all the time Thirza had lived with her.

"Grandma, wait! What's up?"

It was taking all Kezzie's breath now to hurry back towards the mill. In the end, Thirza gave up asking and strained her eyes to make out the crowd in the mill yard. It looked like the kind of mob Bram had faced down, who set out for the marshes, set on by lies against Jem, against them all. Fragments of dawning truth were swirling together, but the sense they made now made her feel sick as they reached home.

"No good Missus!" somebody shouted at Kezzie."We knew all along your lad was mad as a hare! Here's all the proof we need! God preserve us all!"

Thirza was close enough now to see what they were all pointing at. In the doorway, two burly men had Jem pinioned, though Thirza thought he looked so frail a breeze could blow him over. It was too late to stop her grandmother rushing towards Jem and being held back firmly by a forest of hands, a sea of angry faces closing around them.

She looked towards the pump, where the same millstone she and Lucas had fetched leaned upright, facing out with its surface ground down as flat as the day it was milled, without groove or runnel. Around the circumference, in wet letters that looked as if they were badged there in blood, the words of confession:

'I AM THE GOATSUCKER.'

#

For the attention of the Superintendent of the West Riding Pauper Lunatic Asylum, Stanley Royd, Wakefield in the County of York:

Sir,

I regret to have to inform you, further to our recent correspondence, that the mental state of my unfortunate brother-in-law, Jeremy Thomas Kitson, has deteriorated to the point that he is no longer safe to live in domestic surroundings.

He has of late become more agitated and disturbed of mind, deluded in his perceptions of reality, a danger to himself and to members of his doting family and the local community of which he has become a dysfunctional member, needing constant supervision and exhibiting behaviour which is wildly contrary to his own health and alarming to all who witness it.

I should be obliged if you could arrange to convey Mr Kitson to your establishment under strictest supervision. Might I respectfully suggest a strait-jacket and pacifying drugs may be required to assist you in his removal and conveyance thither?

Please advise me personally and solely of the date and time when this can be suitably and discreetly arranged, at your earliest convenience, to prevent further outrage and distress to other relatives.

I enclose a statement from Mr Kitson's physician, Dr Stenson Seagrave, authorising his committal to your care.

Yours in gratitude and concern,
-Darnell Salkeld, esq.

Darnell signed both letters with a flourish and wrote the address on the envelope in flowing italicised script. The doctor's letter and signature he made sure to write with his left hand, to disguise his own natural handwriting features, reducing each capital 'S' of the phantom physician's name to the kind of barely legible scribble he imagined all sawbones employed, to the confusion of their patients. It would be harder for any prying clerk at the asylum to look him up in any register that way. He'd never come unstuck before, for what he thought of as his creative counterfeiting.

Darnell saddled up his finest bay mare. He had best deliver the letter himself, to the main post office, for who was to be trusted? He'd another letter, too, in a different script altogether that he'd burned the midnight oil concocting, addressed again to Cubitt. No reply? He would make sure to deliver him the kind of blow he would never forget. There would certainly be no reply this time, but there would be reaction.

Too bad Cubitt's visit to the Plant coincided with the parish Harvest Festival service here. He couldn't change that, but so be it. Half Yorkshire would be shut for celebration, but he would blast it open. The festival would keep lesser souls out of his way so he could finally try out his perfect plan. Lucas might conceivably suggest going to moon after Cubitt, but what of it? Wasn't that the day when Lucas would demand his answer from the recalcitrant Thirza?

Darnell grew impatient. So many prattling pawns to work like clockwork mannequins for his purposes. They could squeak like mice in the sights of the mill cat, but they could not escape. He felt for the key to the workshop and remembered he'd left it in his jacket pocket hanging by the pump.

Perhaps not? Darnell felt in his waistcoat pocket and was reassured to feel both the letters there. He led the mare to the pump and felt in all his many pockets. The day was sweltering hot. He would leave his jacket in the mill after all. Everybody was about their menial harvest tasks. Nobody would have time to come interfering here today. Their heads were too full of the fall of Sevastopol to the allied troops to come bothering him. He snecked the workshop door and went in to make sure the sails were set in the St Andrew's cross. Though the villagers were staying away in their droves since the latest incident with the human goatsucker. Darnell chuckled to himself, spurred the mare and rode off to town.

The eyes watching him from the decoy saw him go at breakneck speed along the margin of the marsh. Bram knew there was no time to spare or waste. He transferred the key into his outer pocket so he wouldn't forget to leave it under the table when he left the mill a little later.

Thirza saw him striding across from the upper front window of the cottage where she was weaving corn dollies with Kezzie.

"Your dollies are all left-handed," Kezzie remarked.

"That's the way of their world, Grandma, as it's mine!" Thirza laughed, though her heart was skipping as she made the sign out of the window that they had arranged. All clear. All clear.

Bram saw her and signalled back. He met no-one as he slipped across the mill yard and into the workshop. He could see the indentations of the letters on the board where Darnell had just been writing. The practice copies of both letters were here too, screwed up carelessly, because Darnell had thought they would be under lock and key. Bram read quickly, without surprise or hesitation. He saw the fears of his ancestors coming true before his eyes.

Underneath the varied drafts of Darnell's correspondence, he spied a complicated diagram. He saw the wind-hover shafts and the clockwork, the waxed wings, the straps, the cogs and inter-meshing gears he had lived with all his life, held in his heart, now known and copied here in every detail but in so much bigger dimension, not a bird, but what? He read the words, written in gaudy Gothic script at the head of several sheets:

'The Phlogistox Flyer.'

But that was not all. No word of millstones, no word of 'Alma Mill' that Lucas hinted at constantly. No 'Alma Mill' that Thirza was to be mistress of after harvest was over. There were other words, other diagrams that made his soul shiver, even here in the stewing heat of the closed outbuilding with its constantly shuttered windows and insulated walls.

Bram replaced the papers carefully on the table. One sheet of Carrdyke House headed notepaper from the bottom of the pile floated away onto the floor. As he stooped to pick it up, Bram's eye swept down the letter to Sir William Cubitt, registering the depth of rage that snarled beneath each pen stroke. The majority of recent letters in the file were all addressed to this same man. Each meticulously penned epistle built on the grudges and perceived slights of the last. The nearer each letter was dated to today's date in September, the deeper the obsessive loops, serifs and crossbars dug into the hammered vellum paper, a building crescendo of murderous intent.

Bram checked behind him that Darnell hadn't set a trap for him and returned unannounced. But the dusty slow air, holding its heat, was undisturbed, and his nostrils filled with the heady scents of the fens, coming to him unbroken by human stirrings and delicious with ling and meadowsweet. Piper would bark from the scrape where he'd left the little chap quivering with alertness on guard, if anybody appeared on the horizon. Well, not just anybody. Only the one who had left him for dead that day.

Bram looked around at the flasks of coloured liquids, phials of powder suspended in liquescent brume and fissured blocks of minerals. Along one wall he saw bottles of every shade of brown: burnt umber, ochre, chestnut, russet, cinnamon and chocolate, the pigments of every type of peat he'd ever seen or crumbled in his hands.

Bram came to a cabinet locked with a key he'd not managed to take when carelessly left in an unguarded coat pocket. He'd watched for so many hours over the mill from the places only he knew. He'd seized that one opportunity of finding out the truth, reversing the ravage, that might never come again. He'd dashed to the pump when Darnell left his jacket there for the briefest instant to answer a call of nature, haring away again, leaving his stilts hidden for fear of drawing attention to himself.

He tried the glass door of the cabinet and felt around the hinges for a spare key, but his luck was out. What he could observe with his eyes told him all he needed to know, even without touching the contents. Perhaps it was nature's generous mercy that kept him from that touch. He could see the labels and substances exactly mirrored the ones his ancestors used to fuel the stilts, the triggers of lightning locked in the peat and only released by its sweet serendipity. Then there was a white powder, along with silvery stones. He read the label, distorted by the glass doors of the cabinet: 'Arsenic'. More labels: 'Suspension of Arsenic'. 'Cyanide'. 'Smallpox'. An eye bath filled with something that looked like acid, bubbling with dissolved solids.

Bram's eye began to travel more quickly around the tinctures, phials, labels, trying to spin them together to make sense of them. He needed to put a face and a formula to his growing sense of doom. He saw the components of the phlogiston, everything volatile and erratic that the marshes incubated in their mystical pools and peat deposits, gathered here in one place. Methane, corked and confined. 'Oxygen: pure' one label said. Nitrous substances, vaporous silicon, phosphorescent crystals that were like Bram's precious rainbows sealed in a cylinder, cold flames shedding an eerie lambent light in the confines of the room. As his mind raced to understand, he saw the words 'Phlogistox Flyer' again, this time on a small ticket inside the cabinet, and 'Ball Lightning Bomb' on another. Phlogiston plus toxin? Bomb? Bram backed away towards the door.

Checking he hadn't been seen by anyone but Thirza, he dropped the key to the workshop under the table for Darnell to discover on his return. He signalled to Thirza, watching from the upper window, absent-mindedly binding straw round her latest left-handed corn dolly, that it was safe to let her grandparents go out again without the need to keep them distracted. He set the seat of his staff to horizontal and pulled his stilts from their straps, triggered the jet of phlogiston to spark them into action and leapt away back to the decoy, by a route reminiscent of the way the skylark distracts potential predators from its nest.

27. LOCKED ON TARGET

Sir William Cubitt stepped out of the train carriage and was greeted by a reception committee on the platform.

"Welcome back to Doncaster, Sir William! How was your journey?"

Sir William was glad to see a modest number of strangers gathered to meet him. He'd been wondering, ever since it had been arranged, how this little northern junket would go. The main event was to take place tomorrow, Sunday. He'd been reassured his visit would be well attended by the great and the good of the town. He'd studied his brief, perusing papers on the table of the sunny railway carriage all the way from London, in between delicious snoozes. The idea was for him to share some encouragement with the management and to present an award of excellence to one of the most promising young engineers.

Cubitt's breath steamed in the crisp autumn air as he talked to the bosses and businessmen. He felt drowsy after his journey, so was relieved when they told him a landau drawn by an Irish cob was waiting to whisk him away to the Salutation Inn, a coaching inn on the Great North Road.

Alone in his room that Saturday evening, Cubitt sat in the window seat with a cup of cocoa, looking out onto South Parade, rubbing his eyes. They still felt bruised and gritty from sticking his head out of the carriage window on the moving train, to feel the velocity and rattling propulsion. He'd allowed himself to feel modest satisfaction, spotting the windmills dotted around the landscape, their sails known by his name and under his patent. At times, the world of civil engineering, the initial sketch turned into prototype, the prototype into functional masterpiece of steam and locomotion, still gave him that exhilarating tingle, like a little boy set free in a toy shop, even at the age of three score years and ten.

As sundown smudged into another burnt apricot twilight of autumn, Cubitt lit the oil lamp and pushed his portmanteau into the circle of light on the writing bureau. From a stiffened pocket in one of the compartments, he pulled out a sheaf of paperwork. He laid the text of his speech for the following day where he could read it without strain, with the certificate he was to present, which still required his signature.

After ten minutes spent in concentration on the tasks in hand, the letter he'd received just before his departure for Doncaster, resumed its uncomfortable role of gnawing like an ulcer in the pit of his stomach. Unable to ignore it, Cubitt sighed and drew the single sheet from its envelope out into the light and flattened out the letter. Its words were incised so deeply it was possible to feel them with eyes closed. Cubitt wished he could keep his eyes shut now rather than reread the accursed thing. But he found himself unable to resist checking yet again whether the threat behind the message was quite as vicious as he'd interpreted it at every previous perusal.

> *Sir,*
>> *I have waited for your reply in vain.*
>> *Therefore I will show you at first hand the feral ferocity I am now capable of unleashing on the world. Look to the skies. Look to yourself.*
>> *Yours in anticipation of fulmination,*
>> *a 'Friend of the Future.'*

#

The sheaves were all stacked from the harvesting by the first week in October, gathered into barns or in ricks under thatch in farmyards. Still there were stragglers who, prey to late storms or family crises, had yet to lay the scythe to the fields around the edges of the fen, marked out in an erratic patchwork of strips of gold and chestnut. Where the stubble was cropped short, rabbits and rats could no longer find a hiding place and scampered into new refuges along the dykes and drains.

Preparations for Harvest Festival at the church the following day were in full swing. A token sheaf, a turf of peat, a loaf of bread, a basket of eggs, a wreath of poppies and cornflowers were all now laid on the altar as an offering of the first fruits of the harvest of the land.

Lucas watched the servants from Foljambe Hall bringing the outlandishly opulent contributions from Lady Laura to add to the display in church. He could hear the shrill voice of Emma Salkeld from inside the church, where she was supervising the village women as they decorated the building.

"Not there! Over here! No, just here! The altar's crowded enough at that end with vegetable bric-a-brac. Spread that fan of her Ladyship's rhubarb out! Just so! Exquisite! Voilà! A mangold? Surely not! Under here where it will be less impertinently protuberant!"

Lucas smiled to himself. He checked the ring in his pocket that he'd shown to Thirza that day back in late spring when he'd proposed. He'd laid himself on love's altar, he thought, like a small but perfectly formed punnet of greengages. Tomorrow, Thirza would take him up, licking her lips at the prospect with a resounding 'yes' to make the celebration complete.

"Hours only, now!" he told himself. He'd gone to Kitson's Mill to pay court to Thirza several times over the past few weeks, determined she should have no excuse to forget her promise of an answer after the Harvest Festival. He'd also taken the opportunity to distribute more flyers from his private printing press illustrating the new mill.

"The outer elevation is a splendid foretaste of the banquet of delights within!" he'd said to anyone who would listen, building on the harvest theme. Even today, the eve of the unveiling, he was trying to keep his mind off what he'd seen of the inside, where Darnell was now in a frenzy of preparation for the demonstration of the new milling mechanism. The odd time Lucas had tried the mill door since the incident with the new millstone, he'd found it locked. Jem had been under supervision of his mother and father, on Darnell's instructions. The bewildered lad was actually keeping himself under voluntary house arrest, laid on his bed staring at the ceiling for days on end.

Since the unpleasantness with the millstone, when evidence of the Goatsucker's identity had been so shockingly demonstrated to all, the locals were taking their grain to other mills on the far side of the Nab, ones in Hatfield and Thorne and even further afield for those with the means to transport it. Jem Kitson's name was whispered, but not where his family could hear what was speculated about his state of mind or morality.

"They'll be back when they see what's afoot here on their doorstep!" Lucas told himself, for it seemed to him that nobody else cared a jot what he thought. This morning, after calling on Thomas and Kezzie and being told Thirza was out yet again, he tried the locked mill door, and seeing Darnell through an upper window, Lucas shouted up to him.

"Darnell, dear cuz, old chap, should I come up and see the final preparations you're making? Not that I should pretend to understand the finer points, you know, but to see the first fruits, as it were, of my investment?"

There came a pause, long enough to make Lucas wonder if he'd been heard, until Darnell appeared aloft on the reefing stage and the pause was further prolonged, making it plain he had indeed been heard, but that he was being wilfully ignored.

Lucas pressed ahead, laughing to cover his confusion at his cousin's unaccountable shutting him out of their affairs, now so close to completion.

"Well, well, tomorrow's the day, then, eh?" Lucas adopted his most jovial tone, rather deflated even as he spoke, by Darnell's turning his back on him.

"Our grand exhibition of this modern marvel of milling, as the yokels and locals stroll by after church."

Still nothing from Darnell above. Lucas laughed nervously, feeling in his inside pocket for his hunting flask. He realised he'd already transferred it to his Sunday suit, when he might have to steel his nerves for Thirza's emotional acceptance of his proposal, for further speeches and announcements about plans for their future and Alma Mill's.

"Then they'll be beating down the door to avail themselves of your prestigious new equipment, and work on the rest of the complex can begin 'ere the winter storms begin' as the old hymn has it!"

"Cousin, by your leave..." Darnell disappeared, leaving Lucas standing by the pump, looking up expectantly, awaiting the conclusion of the sentence. He waited in vain.

He stood listening to sounds he could no more interpret than if they were words spoken in an alien tongue. The sound of the rotation of the fantail wheel he recognised, but when he walked around the mill, squinting into the sun to see whether the cap was turning the sails into the wind, all he noticed was the widened gap between cap and buck, daylight between the moveable top and the brick bodywork of the tower. Yes, daylight, there in the space, but surely not? Something else that looked for all the world like sparks. But the sun was dazzling him. He must be mistaken. It would be foolish to make a fuss. Darnell knew what he was doing. Perhaps the whole edifice would grind itself together like an enormous flour dredger, crushing as it went. He would find out soon enough on the glorious morrow.

Lucas wished he could split himself in two, like the mill appeared to be about to do, by this new engineering innovation. Then he could be in church, with Thirza on his arm, lord of the manor, master of the new mill employing everybody from here to the coast, and simultaneously in Doncaster, hanging on the every word of that other paragon of engineering invention, Sir William Cubitt. Cubitt, who might soon be paying good money to hear Darnell lecturing crowds about his own inventions, with Lucas as his generous, if occasionally squiffy, benefactor. The thought alone made Lucas swell with pride.

#

Jack Holberry threw the hawser across and moored 'Thistle' for the final time in her old berth. He wouldn't let himself get sentimental. Dinah used to call him a sweet soft-hearted lummock. Perhaps he was. The money in his pocket from selling the clinker-built old lass would have to compensate him now for the loss of living afloat.

The price the younger man had paid him to purchase her, plus the extra money he paid to be shown how to manage at the tiller as a novice to the sailing of a keel, would have to pay the rent of Jack's new home down by the ferry in Mexbrough. When his screwmatics no longer let him haul boats along or afford the hay for the horse as a horse marine, that money would be all he'd have to leave to Thirza and the boys, apart from memories and good sense. It would all sort itself out, as Dinah used to tell him.

He ran his hands over the letters of her name, etched deep like intaglio on her tiller, painted red as sunset.

"'Thistle', my beauty. Sail well till the tide turns again."

#

Thirza looked out to the horizon. Locals said you could once see the top of Crowle church across the moors, but as the drying peat rose imperceptibly since the Great Drainage, now it was lost to sight. Was that why locals looked through Bram as if he, too, was invisible? They saw in him all the blame for his people making the salty tides seep up through the fertile soil, the drowning and the drying. It was in the way he looked at others, too, she knew. Why he kept himself apart and seemed to be of the fens, but never fully to belong. She felt the same.

She missed him like an ache in her soul, yet tomorrow she must answer Lucas, who'd helped her family, as Darnell had, when Jem had brought such disgrace and suffering by his savagery against innocent creatures. Even now her head told her the evidence was clear, but something in her gut and intuition told her there was more to this than it was easy to assume.

Between her and the line of the horizon, she could see a movement. She left Kezzie baking a harvest pie with Grace and walked out towards the rise and fall. Kezzie hardly questioned her comings and goings now, confident that in a little space, Thirza would be safely wed and their future secured by connection to the squire's family, security more than Kezzie could ever have dreamed.

When Thirza drew closer, she saw the motion was the top of a scuppit, the 'scoop-it' as Bram pronounced it, echoing some lowland dialect at odds with the Anglo-Saxon flat syllables heard all over the West Riding. Thirza skirted the moor pools by watching the lines in the peat, the direction of the ripples as Bram had taught her to keep herself safe. When she was within a few feet of him, she saw the top of Bram's hat as he stood in the bottom of the ditch he was cutting and cleaning out, or 'fieing' as he would say.

"The harvest rats are making work for me again!" Bram's gentle voice came to her from the bowels of the deep cut gash in the ground. "They've clean gnawed away the side of this ditch and the cattle have been wallowing. You always know where the greatest need is for repairs. It never ends, like the sun going down and coming up again. Each ditch calls to you its special wounds and weaknesses that you can set right before moving to the next."

"Like you do with the birds and the animals. You

listen for the greatest need and go there first."

Bram trod his way up the sides of the ditch.

"I'm finishing this job because I need to go to Doncaster. There's something I must do there."

"Someone else's greatest need?" Thirza looked at him and wished he would tell her everything as he used to, before all this complication began. "I wish I could come with you."

"You wish, lass, but you can't. You've other fish to fillet."

"I have to give him my answer tomorrow. I promised."

Thirza wanted him to ask what her answer would be, so she could surprise herself. She could say what she knew it would be unforgivable to say, to someone as patient and helpful as Lucas. If Bram had asked right then, she didn't know what she would say. But he didn't ask.

"What I saw in there," he began, "I have to stop it. I must do the right thing by someone who has no idea what's going to hit him. By the time Harvest Festival's done, it'll all be over and you'll be on your way to being a lady."

Thirza tried to say something, but she couldn't trust her voice.

"Though you've always been a lady, to me."

Piper was sniffing around the holes in the ditch, whimpering at the sound of rats beyond human hearing in the banks. He looked towards the village and gave a series of barks.

"Best you go back. Best you know no more."

Bram let himself imagine for a moment Thirza giving her answer to Lucas, Lucas giving his backing to Darnell. But if he could do this one thing, then it wouldn't matter and the worst of it would be thwarted. Yet Thirza would still be free to become Lady Charlesworth.

Thirza tried to see what Piper had seen, but she couldn't spot anybody between them and the line of houses leading along the road from the canal to the motionless mill.

"Hurry," said Bram, without looking at her. "Don't worry about anything."

As she turned to go, Thirza pulled out the clockwork

goatsucker from her pocket, that Bram had mended for her, somehow, at the decoy.

"I want you to have this," she said. "You made it fly when it had a broken wing. Keep it with your wind-up phlogiston decoy ducks. It must be so lonely here, away from its own. Let it fly with its friends. If you go away, perhaps it will help you remember me."

Thirza gathered up her skirts and ran, for she wouldn't let him see her tears again. She had to be strong to give Lucas the right answer, and not waver. For once, she couldn't be the headstrong lass who worked alongside Bram shoulder to shoulder. She was no longer destined to be the hardy keelgirl or the child of the margin between water and wilderness.

"You will always be a lady," whispered Bram. Piper's head cocked on one side, then the other, watching his master with curious concern.

"You and I, lad, we'll never forget her."

28. FAIR WARNING

Jeremy Kitson sat sleepless through the long October night, perched at the foot of his bed on his army chest, fingering the blade of his Cherry Picker razor, the one they all thought Darnell had locked away. He listened to his mother's regular breaths in the room across the landing, his father's snore, periodically cut short by a closing of the airways or a vivid dream. He listened to the creak of the mill sweeps straining to turn in the wind, fettered by the brake wheel into inaction. He heard the barn owl's nasal screech from the cock-loft, the hens stirring on their perches, dreaming of the fox. Jem watched the lucid nightmare behind his own eyelids: the ripple that ran through the ranks at the perverse order to charge, the plaintive parp of the bugle, Captain Nolan's vague gesture towards the invisible cannons, shot and shell thundering out of nowhere, shrieking through the air towards them, Matty catching his eye to remind him he wasn't alone, the thud of man and horse hitting the ground at gallop speed with screams beyond bearing, Samphire twisting under him, making not a sound as the lights went out.

#

Bram stroked the feathers of the automaton goatsucker, the tiny whiskers around its gaping frog-like beak, the cuckoo body and the flattened paddle of the tail, so perfectly aerodynamic to swoop and clap. He oiled the parts hidden under the plumage and lit the wound mechanism in its perfect circular cell, its wick soaked in phlogiston. As dawn broke to the east of his hut, he lifted up his little flock of wildfowl in the crook of his right arm, Thirza's goatsucker in his left hand and flung them all with a sweeping motion up into the lemon-gold sunrise, over the hoops of the decoy, making a perfect circle reflected in the water below, above the autumn mist that drifted across the Chase.

#

Thirza woke early, that Harvest Festival Sunday. She'd promised her grandparents she'd make sure Jem was settled before she came on to the service. She thought of Lucas sitting in his box pew, making a space for her at his side, perhaps laying his gloves there until she came, ensuring they would sit together as she whispered her answer in his ear. She thought of Bram, doing whatever it was today that was a greater need than sweeping her into his arms and taking her away from this life of dutiful death.

The service was timed to start an hour later than usual. She'd seen the parson pushing the reed marker into the sundial at the foot of the herringbone stonework on the church tower. Those who couldn't read would see when it was time to gather on this special day. She wondered who'd drilled that hole, hundreds of years ago, to harness the sun as a time-teller, when Bram's people and Darnell's had walked this way together, and her people lived out at sea, dreaming of days when they could bring their waterways snaking far inland, defying the drainage men with a forest of masts. Now she found herself moored to this anchoring place with ropes she couldn't snap and today would surely launch her into the future by a baptism of fire.

\#

Bram stilt-strode the back ways into Doncaster while most townspeople were still asleep or about their domestic tasks by the hearth, busy making the first fires of autumn. Soon the equinox would whisper that the sun was beginning to lose the battle against winter.

He noticed the suspicious looks from a servant already at work outside the Salutation Inn and darted forward to reassure her he meant no harm.

"They say Sir William Cubitt is staying here, miss."

"Was staying. Overnight. Up with the lark. Gone to the Plant. Bunch of toffs in toppers came to get him." The maid looked Bram up and down. "Who wants to know?"

Bram tipped his hat politely but hurried off without enlightening her. When he got to the Plant Works' entrance, he saw a group of men in their Sunday best. A grey-haired gentleman was looking with great interest at one of the locomotives being repaired in the nearest shed. Another man was enthusiastically showing him various features of the engine, while the others in the group leaned close, to catch any pearls of wisdom they could garner.

Bram waited. It was still early. Harvest Festival back at Turbary Nab wouldn't begin for a couple of hours. Perhaps he could catch Sir William's eye without making too much fuss. This might be his last chance.

His chance came more quickly than he expected. Sir William was telling his hosts he would have to slip back to the inn briefly before the presentation, as he'd forgotten some document or other he'd left in his portmanteau up in his room.

Like a shepherd and sheepdog separating a marked sheep from the rest of the flock, Bram and Piper got between Sir William and the railwaymen on his way back to his carriage.

"Sir, a word with you, if you will," Bram hoped he

wouldn't alarm the older gentleman by an unscheduled approach here in the street. But Sir William hardly reacted at all.

"Alright, sir," he muttered, "you'd better get in the carriage with me. We'll settle this once and for all."

On the brief ride back eastwards to the Salutation, sitting facing each other as Piper trotted alongside down almost deserted streets, Bram tried several times to apologise for his impertinence in taking up Sir William's time, but the engineer merely waved his hand to dismiss Bram's apologies.

"Don't agitate yourself, sir," he said, "wait until we have some privacy in my room. Calm, now!"

Bram was puzzled. He was rarely accused of being anything but calm, but he kept his counsel and hoped he could put his case clearly when they got there. As they drew up outside the main door of the Salutation, they passed the maid who had looked at Bram with such a frown not half an hour before.

"Please, sir," she shouted across to Sir William as he led Bram inside, "this fellow was looking for you here this morning."

Sir William smiled at her and said in a low tone, "Thank you, but now he has found me. There's half a crown if you will make sure nobody disturbs us until I come and fetch you."

Sir William indicated the stairwell and invited Bram to go up and wait for him on the landing. Then he stepped back outside, where Piper was attempting to make friends with the glowering maidservant, who was now emptying slops. Piper was finding these as intriguing with their complex messages to his nostrils, as anything he and his master had encountered on the way from the moors. The maid kept the dog away with the bristles of her besom, which he was too well-mannered to chew. Sir William offered her another shilling.

"If I'm not down again in a quarter of an hour, send for a constable, a watchman or your local magistrate. Do you mark me well, girl?"

The maid looked goggle-eyed at the old man, but took the money anyway. When Cubitt had followed Bram upstairs, she declared to Piper that she'd seen some rumbustious shenanigans at the inn in her time, but that this was a new scandal brewing, and no mistake.

Sir William closed the door firmly behind him and turned to face Bram without offering him a seat.

"Look here, my good fellow, what will it take for you to leave off pestering me with your interminable letters?"

Bram was momentarily lost for an answer. Fortunately, Sir William was in full flow.

"Forgive me for making no reply, but you have alarmed me, sir. Alarmed me! I cannot give you advice on your, your..." Cubitt pulled out one of a sheaf letters from the case on the desk and read out something written on it.

"...your 'Phlogistox Flying Bomb' as you call it. In the first instance, such a thing would be impossible. For the second, it would be highly dangerous, for the third, it would be against the laws of science and the laws of this land!"

Sir William dropped the letter as he sought the requisite number of fingers on which to count off these points of error. Bram could see the old man's immaculately manicured hands were shaking.

"Sir, please, you mistake me! It's not I who wrote you those letters!"

"Don't insult my intelligence, sir! Your last was full of threats, giving today's date. This, you wrote, is to be the day when I should look to my own safety and look to the skies! You rave at me as though you envy and hate me. Sir, what have I done to offend you?"

Sir William suddenly sat down, running his fingers through his white hair, his intelligent, steady gaze rooted pleadingly on Bram's face. Bram spread his hands out to try and show Cubitt he meant no harm. He condensed the explanation and warning he'd come all this way to give.

"Sir, you mistake me. I am not the man. The man who means you harm is..."

"Darnell Salkeld!" Sir William shouted the name, then immediately looked around at the closed door as if frightened of being heard. "Writing to me again and again. Obsessive, like a fanatic. This Salkeld knows all my innovations, all my achievements. He lists them, comments on their minor failings, then sends me his own plans for this 'Phlogistox Flyer' or 'Ball Lightning Flying Bomb' or goodness knows what other satanic aberration! I will not put my name again to something designed for improving the lot of mankind which then, like my treadmill, is used to punish and destroy! I write to discourage, yet the man redoubles his efforts to persuade me with his insane ramblings!"

Cubitt flourished the wad of letters, all in Darnell's hand, some disguised, some unmistakeable, under Bram's nose.

"I understand, Sir William, I know this man! But I am not he. My name's Bram Beharrell. I'm pinder, marshman, decoyman over on the moors near where this Salkeld lives with his family. They're honest folk, but he's used their old windmill to devise this instrument of destruction! I came today to warn you. I've seen the copies of these letters he's sent you and the plans he has to terrorise the region. His ancestor stole designs from my great grandfather, learned over long years living on the Yorkshire fens, the Humberhead Levels between here and the sea. Ways to use the hidden alchemy of the marshes, to harness fen-lights, phlogiston, ball lightning for natural power, for healing, for travelling at speed. So many things, but he has the knowledge now, developed for destruction, under the guise of progress in milling."

Sir William nodded, as though everything was becoming clear in his analytical mind. He drew a diagram from his bag.

"He sent me this latest diagram. A mill, you say? This looked like a mill, but it sounded to me like a mad scheme that could never work. A flying bomb? A dirigible thing that could be trained on a distant object, a target, and used to deliver destruction and death?"

Bram looked at the drawing, with Darnell's labels identifying every working part, similar to what he'd seen in the workshop, what Thirza had seen at the Hall. Cubitt spread it out on the table by the window and they both leaned over the sheet.

"These are the sails," Cubitt pointed to each part with a finger trembling less now he was fully convinced it wasn't Darnell who'd come to seek him. "Here the fantail, for balance and steerage, here the cap, with a point to penetrate and here..." he pointed at a large circle at the heart of the cap, with curlicues seeming to twist around it like bindweed, with scribbled lines and the letters 'AS' written in the midst of it.

"But 'as' what, exactly?" Cubitt scratched his head. They both heard a tapping at the window.

"As? As? What is this word here in the middle of the ball, this 'As'?" Cubitt chewed his index finger as he tried to puzzle it out.

"As indicated?" Bram was aware wasted moments were ticking by. The old man didn't seem to be treating the threat with the urgency he'd expected. Within the hour, the Harvest Festival would begin back on Turbary Nab. It'd already been rescheduled to allow the agricultural workers from more distant homesteads to get their families to the church. Time was running out like sand out of an hourglass.

"Hurry, sir! I believe this flying bomb of phlogiston and artificial lightning may be pointed your way as we speak!"

But Cubitt was problem-solving and absorbed in his own thoughts. The drumming at the window grew more insistent, though whatever was causing it was hidden from view by the curtains.

"Calm, sir," Cubitt said again, still poring over the schematic sketch of the windmill's converted apex. "If the flight of such a huge and weighty object were even possible, I should be fearful indeed, but no. Since Leonardo da Vinci's vision was committed to paper, nobody has ever yet achieved flight."

The beating at the window reached a crescendo. All at once one of the panes of glass shattered and both men looked up to see a gaggle of mechanical wildfowl flying through the window, while a smaller model, clapping and chirring onto the carpet at Cubitt's feet, was Thirza's little goatsucker Bram had thrown into the air nearly ten miles away.

This seemed to jerk Cubitt back from his contemplations. He looked in astonishment at the animated flock.

"But this isn't possible! Flight by clockwork? Powered by internal combustion? How? Animated avifauna? Sir, you have opened my eyes! If this 'Phlogistox Flyer' with the ball lightning bomb of poison at its pernicious heart, can navigate its course like your ornithological automata, then this blackguard Salkeld, I'll warrant, means to flatten me and all those in his way!"

Bram began picking up the scattered ducks and drakes and the nightjar, now lying upside down with its empty claws kicking towards the ceiling, gathering them under his coat into his hidden pockets.

"They're here only to warn you, sir, as I am! This is no idle threat of Salkeld's! Just as these simple birds can fly and navigate with accuracy over miles, so this windmill, now the 'Phlogistox Flyer' can surely do it!"

Sir William's eyes lit up as revelation dawned.

"As? AS! Arsenic! Cubitt, you dolt!" the old engineer snatched up the drawing in both hands, "The chemical symbol! My God, he means to spread death in a toxic explosion to wipe us all out! Today arsenic, tomorrow cyanide, smallpox, cholera, forgotten plagues preserved under the peat! His future plans encompass every vision of hell!"

They both looked at the symbol, joined with permanent pencil strokes to the scribbles of electrical discharge inside the central globe. At the same time, from the front of the building, they heard the maid shouting.

"He's up there, officer! Up in Sir William Cubitt's room at the front! Sir William said to get you if he didn't tell me different. Look at the hole in the window! Innkeeper will be hopping livid!"

Sir William opened the door and pointed the way down the servant's stairs at the back. He went as far as the top landing and shook Bram's hand.

"I believe you, Beharrell! Sincerely I do. Thank you! Your birds are something phenomenal indeed! Your perspicacity has proved a lifesaver to me this day! How can I ever repay you? I'll be back on the train and away from here before that madman can unleash his mayhem. Remarkable! Flying things! Well, look to yourself now. I'll put things right with the constables and the innkeeper, too."

Bram ran down through the back yard of the inn. The sound of heavy boots running and a whistle blown by someone out of breath was getting closer. Dashing up an alley, out of the corner of his eye, Bram saw a flash of an eager Kooikerhondje interposing his furry body between the end of the passage leading from the street and the yard from which Bram had escaped five seconds earlier. A brace of florid watchmen who rather fancied themselves, when called upon, as noble officers of the law, fell in a tangled heap on the cobbles, cursing and rubbing elbows and other painful body parts. This gave Bram just enough time to slide out both stilts from their straps and flick them into place so the telescopic parts meshed firmly as he vaulted onto the foot plates.

"Yackoop, lad!"

Man and dog were soon heading out of town and over the Don in the least likely direction they might be pursued by the clueless.

"Good morning, gentlemen! The shattered windowpane was an unfortunate accident I had with a spring-loaded bearing. I will make good the damage," Sir William was saying to the puzzled watchmen. "Meanwhile, would you be good enough to ascertain for me the time of the next stagecoach to London? I don't suppose we can hope that there are any trains on a Sunday, or indeed, that pigs might fly?"

29. BEWARE THE GOATSUCKER HARVEST

Goody Chester tilted back her head so her bonnet disappeared into the hood of her cloak. She stood by the gate of her cottage, gazing up at the strange birds flying south-westerly, high over her head towards Doncaster, whirring like metal toys as they flew, the Mallard with its metallic green face and white collar like a preacher, the smaller Teal with its emerald green mask, the Pochard with its chestnut cowl, the little Nightjar, still here though its flesh and blood cousins had already left on their journeys to their wintering grounds in Africa.

"Where are you now, Bram Beharrell, son of Isaac, grandson of Jan, great grandson of Gerrit Beharrell and Agnes Zeldenthuis? Beharrell, you exiled Huguenot boy! Zeldenthuis, you Dutch lad seldom-at-home!"

Goody cackled to herself, then glanced backwards at the mill tower and forwards to the tower of the church, acting as a magnet, drawing lines of country people in their Sunday weeds, traipsing across the flat panorama to celebrate the gifts of nature's harvest and beg heaven for another year of survival.

Goody watched Lucas arrive in his carriage, all aflutter with anticipation, shading his eyes and peering past

Goody's cottage to see if Thirza, his intended, was on her way to worship.

"She will never worship at your altar, little man!" said Goody under her breath. She caught sight of Emma, all flustered and flapping, without her man as so often she was these days, in the wake of Lady Laura's liveried carriage. Emma somehow contrived to step in a puddle and turn her ankle with a symphony of squeals, so that Lucas offered her his arm to tread the path together up through the churchyard, with Emma leaning heavily against him and gazing up into his eyes.

"You will get your wish granted, shallow sister, soon enough," whispered Goody.

"Not in church, yet, Goodwife?" Thomas and Kezzie drew level with the old woman, Kezzie leading her husband and providing a running commentary on who was standing where and what they were wearing. This alone gave Thomas the ability to demonstrate second sight in spotting Goody by her own gatepost.

"Why don't you come in with us?" suggested Kezzie. "We can have an arm each to guide this clodpole up the aisle!"

"My cup she runneth over!" groaned Thomas, letting himself be led onto the sunken path through the churchyard between raised banks on either side, the depth of burials down the centuries since the days of the Black Death.

"Young Thirza and your boy Jeremy not taking their pew-spaces early today?" Goody knew the facts, as always, but probed her old friends for an answer. Kezzie dropped her voice as they passed the vicar on the way in.

"I made Thirza promise to keep her eye on Jem so he doesn't get distressed and go making a Mister Punch pantomime of himself at the service or tonight at the supper. Darnell's busy over there as usual this morning, getting ready to show off his new plan for the mill. It's all so terribly cloak and dagger! Our Emma's lucky she has such a rock for a husband. We all are!"

"Indeed you're lucky to have a rock like me, my love,"

said Thomas dryly.

"You mistake me, as usual, Mr Kitson," whispered Kezzie, "I meant we are lucky our Emma is lucky. You, on the other hand, are like a lump of lardy-cake."

"God bless you, honey-tongued lass."

Kezzie poked him into respectful silence as the vicar came in, the organ wheezed an asthmatic first chord and the congregation struck up with 'Come, Ye Thankful People, Come' as the scents of fruit and flowers flooded ripe and rich through the nave.

#

The black coach drove away from Wakefield Asylum as soon as it was light enough to negotiate the roads all the way to the south of the county. When they stopped for a rest, having missed the way at a turning, the driver affected to look severe, as his youthful assistants tried to stuff a dead sheep carcass into the straitjacket they'd brought along in the back of the coach in case of a struggle. One worked its legs from behind and made its head wag in a macabre dance from side to side while the other, howling with laughter at first, began to gag at the stench of maggoty flesh coming from their woolly marionette.

"That's enough, now, lads," the driver snapped. "For pity's sake, learn some decency."

The ringleader of the prank pulled the straitjacket up and away from the sheep, letting the dead animal slump down again at the edge of the road where they'd found it.

"Come on," said the driver, "we've strict instructions to get to our business before noon."

#

Darnell took no notice now of the comings and goings of lesser mortals. Today was the day. He had to stay focused. First his letter to Wakefield would bear fruit. They'd told him the hour they aimed to arrive. He only listened now for the rattle of the wheels pulling into the mill yard. The professional physicians would do the rest, no questions asked.

Then it would all be about him. The taking aim to the hair's-breadth of a degree, the thrust to become airborne, the flight as the crow flies with minimal turbulence or friction. Then the payload that would make the world sit up and take notice of him. Only him. Lucas and his mill plans? They would keep. He would be marrying Thirza, so no more interference from either. Darnell listened for the wheels again. Nothing. Straining to hear, he caught the edge of the hymn-singing from the Harvest Festival. All the sheep and goats safely out of his way.

Darnell pushed on the fantail and was delighted to see the gap widen more than ever between the buck and the cap, crammed with the fine-tuned machinery of genius. His genius.

The sweeps lined up behind the mill cap as it turned to face Doncaster. Turned to face the place where, just beyond the horizon, his rival Cubitt and his sycophants and toadies strutted about in their little castle of dreams. But this was his castle now and his castle had no roots, it could soar across the landscape and touch down wherever he chose, bringing unknown destruction in its maw. He tapped the compass and swung his fob watch in time to the vibration beginning. Steady there. Steady as she goes.

Sir William Cubitt was due to begin his speechifying at eleven. It would, Darnell had calculated, take his 'Phlogistox Flyer' just less than half an hour to make the distance across the fields. He pulled out the glass slide that still separated the phlogiston from the other vital elements and the toxic white powder. It took a minute or two for the ball of blue lightning to reach its optimum size. Then he let the arsenic swirl around it inside its thick glass ball. Perfect.

Darnell closed his eyes for a moment, listening to the thrum of the burners and the clinking of the cogs and pistons, the crackle of the electric from the artificial lightning and the hiss and tick of the powder against the inside of the globe, like the wings of a giant moth before it's burnt beyond recognition in the flame of a gas mantle that is also broken by the impact. No time to lose now. The countdown was underway. Not even Darnell himself could reverse it now.

#

Thirza sat at the foot of Jem's bed. All she could think of was her appointment with destiny after church and the plain answer she must give to Lucas before nightfall. Like an auction by an inch of candle, when the final expiration of the flame is delayed by a stubborn knub of tallow, Thirza wished with all her heart something could delay that moment when she must promise her life away and cast off from the shores of possibility with Bram for ever.

"We could walk up as far as the pinfold, Jemmy, if you like," she suggested, "We could be back before the service ends."

Jem looked as if he was about to reply, gazing into her eyes as if searching for something. She wished he could find it again.

"It's no point you wasting this beautiful morning up here, Thirza." Darnell was standing in the bedroom doorway. Thirza saw Jem's whole body stiffen with terror and loathing. "You run along to the Harvest Festival. What's a bonnet for, if not to display? Your aunt and your grandparents will be waiting for you, and a certain eager squire to whom you've promised an answer today, if I recall rightly?"

The three of them went downstairs and out into the sunlight. Darnell stood with his hand on Jem's shoulder. Thirza thought it looked as though he was pressing so hard it was difficult for Uncle Jem to stand fully upright. To be here alone with Darnell, with only Jem for protection, was something she couldn't risk, for her sake or the baby's.

"I'll be back directly, Uncle Jem," something made her say it, for Jem looked as though every step she took away from the mill and towards the church, was a step across a crevasse where he could not follow. Thirza heard the sounds from above and was alarmed to see the sails turning in a way she'd never seen them turn before, a doleful hum accompanying the spinning, and a chatter of static like shingle pebbles being thrown about, in a wave turned completely to ice.

"Hurry," Darnell snapped, but followed it with the most charming smile. Thirza turned and walked as slowly as she could without stopping, away from the mill and her uncles. If only Bram was here. But he wasn't and she had to be strong.

When Thirza got as far away as the nearest cottages, Darnell put his arm around Jem's shoulders and walked him into the windmill, talking menacingly and low all the while. The words that pushed Jem over the precipice into madness were always on the same theme. Frankly, thought Darnell, I'm rapidly becoming bored, harping on the same old strings. Now there's nothing to lose.

"If you had ridden more boldly, I dare say Samphire would not have been so mangled by the first cannon, you know. But far be it from me to mention that again."

He wondered why Jem didn't seem to react as he always did.

"If you had pleased your sweet Susan more, you could have had this mill for her and your brood of brats. But she wrote you that sob-story letter, didn't she, not long after you rode away to war? Such a shame."

Jem seemed to crumple and bridle slightly at the words. Darnell was bored with holding back. He could hear the slight change in the pace of the sails and the fantail buzzed as it locked on target. He had calibrated the compass perfectly. Of course he had. He was Darnell Salkeld. Between each word, he listened for approaching wheels from Wakefield. It wouldn't be long now.

"Of course, you knew you couldn't compete with her new beau, didn't you? It was devastating to you to read her simpering apologies! 'My dear Jemmy, I am bereft to be obliged to write to you to tell you news that I know will perhaps break your tender heart. I have tried and tried to bear you not being here with me. The man I love is rich and clever and kind and oh so handsome, I sometimes think my poor heart will burst with joy at his loving me back.' Did you weep terribly, brother-in-law?"

Darnell paused for effect. Jem could barely form his words.

"How did you know what was in her letter to me?"

"How did I know? How did I guess?" Darnell threw his head back and mocked Jem's incredulous tone, "Her letter to me! Her letter to me! What a joke you are, Jeremy! She couldn't even be bothered to put pen to paper when I had her over the jog-scry, the evening after you left for your ship to Turkey! She was gasping for me, clawing at me to show her what a real man did, what a real man was!"

Darnell grabbed Jem's hand as he reached for the razor and held on to him, spitting the rest of the secrets he no longer had any need to keep to himself.

"It was me, brother-in-law, me. I wrote that letter. No more young master of the mill and his pretty bride-in-waiting. She had to leave in a certain condition. I covered up well for you, though I know a few in the village questioned your treatment of that sweet innocent thing. All the ladies love the jog-scry, you know. Your Susie. My Emma. A dozen empty-headed seamstresses and servant wenches. The virtuous Thirza."

Jem couldn't look at Darnell any more. The Cherry Picker razor felt as though it was burning a hole through to his heart from where it lay hidden in his pocket. As well to be hung for a sheep as a lamb. He was the original dog given a bad name, and by Darnell, every bad name under the sun.

"Give me the razor." Darnell's voice was full of the effortless menace of calm. Jem felt the grip tighten on his wrists. He let himself be disarmed as the slow drip of poison into his open wounds made him unable to move or think clearly any more.

Darnell took the razor and held it up to the light as if to admire it and stepped towards the grain hoist, while talking all the time. Punch-drunk with humiliation and grief,

Jem let him talk.

"That selfless act of yours in the hospital at Scutari. Giving your miracle cure panacea pill sent by that physician friend of a friend of a friend. What was his name again? Ah yes, the elusive Doctor Stenson Seagrave."

Jem heard the words and in his head, went somewhere deep and so dark that the truths would not penetrate to wound him any more.

"Who do you think sent you that magical pill to cure you? It was me. It. Was. Me. I wrote the letter, I sent you the pill. I thought that would be the end of you. Arsenic is so very effective and so very hard to detect. But poor milksop Jeremy loved his handsome Matty so much that he handed over his medicine and killed him stone dead. Did he die in agony? Of course he did!"

Jem saw Matt's face. Susan smiling at him. Thirza's sparky joy in life when she was a girl. Down the field of his vision, he saw red, scarlet runnels descending like coagulated tears of blood until he couldn't make out Darnell's leering face in front of him, fiddling with the grain hoist as if it mattered. As if anything mattered now.

"Oh, do I hear the stretcher and straitjacket coming?" Darnell made a theatrical show of cupping his ear towards the door. Jem couldn't tell whether this was truth or bluff, because now the mill herself was beginning to make the most extraordinary sound. The whole buck seemed to be rocking as the sweeps, driven by more than the languid autumn breeze, were generating a power on the point of being unleashed.

"Yes, I declare, I do. Too late for them to turn back. They're coming for you, the slavering mad miller of Kitson's Mill. The phantom Goatsucker who, they will say, eviscerated cattle, goats, poultry and even his own spavined old friend. Poor Nero!"

Jem didn't remember the impulse passing between his head and his limbs but in that instant he cannoned into Darnell, knocking him off his feet in mid flow. The razor skittered across the floor and both men reached for it, but now Jem had the advantage of surprise, for Darnell had seen only the irony of making his confessions to an innocent man, destined to spend the rest of his life confined, gagged and disbelieved. Jem closed his fingers round the handle and held it to Darnell's throat as he straddled him.

#

Reaching Goody's cottage, Thirza heard the noise from the mill change. As she looked over her shoulder, to her alarm she saw the cap was beginning to spin under its own momentum and where the gap was opening up between the cap and the dust floor, the bottom of the glass orb crammed with ball lightning and white powder was clearly visible, even from her position some distance away.

Thirza began to run, though she felt as though she was wading through treacle and every yard seemed like a mile. She was shouting the names of both her uncles before she arrived back in the mill yard. Were they in there? Where had they got to?

Thirza dashed to the mill door, expecting to find it locked as it usually was, since Darnell started making his improvements. But it opened smoothly as she pushed on the sneck and she stood panting on the lowest level. Above, high overhead, she could hear the unmistakeable sound of some object being dragged up on the sack hoist through the self-closing trap doors, that crashed and reverberated as they shut again via gravity, accompanied at each floor stage by a blood-curdling cry, as of a creature in torture.

Thirza began to climb the first ladder, then the next, up and up. The sounds from the hoist had stopped now but the mill continued to shake and rumble till she had to cling on to the ladder just to make progress. She called Jem's name and Darnell's but it was becoming more and more difficult to make her voice heard, out of breath as she was from the precipitous climb, above the menacing roar of the mechanism quaking the mill, till the whole body seemed to be rocking and groaning around her.

At last she reached the dust floor, and from the top rung of the ladder from the stone floor below, she looked up to try and make out what was happening through the pothering clouds of flour and the dust of centuries that filled the air and made her cough and choke. Fanning the whirling powder away from her face with a sack she found obscuring one of the windows, she looked up into the body of the cap above. The gap between the dust floor where she was standing and the cap itself was two feet wide or more. To her right, the sails were pivoting round and round with a snarling flap in a hurricane of their own making like a demonic eagle caught in a whirlwind. They were lifting the whole structure away from the ground, and inches from her face, the glass ball she and Bram had seen Lucas and Emma bring home from Hull, swung in its cradle of brass claws and leather straps. Inside it, an incandescent ball of fire, spitting out tendrils of lightning from an electric blue nucleus and a white powder that Thirza knew with dread was nothing like flour.

She had to do something to stop it exploding or that would be the end of the mill. Thirza pushed at the ball but it was red hot and she snatched back her fingers with a squeal of shock. The brake wheel handle was out of her reach as the whole of the cap tipped at an angle ever more acute to the ground, aiming itself over the fields to Doncaster.

"Jem! Jem! Are you up here?"

Through the swirling maelstrom of white and rainbow chemical smog, as the elements reacted to each other that Darnell had always kept in measured isolation, waiting for this moment, Thirza thought she saw Jem on the platform of the fantail, always just turning dizzily out of sight from the corner of her eye. She had the impression of him standing there, his razor in his hand, disappearing out into the open air.

"Help me turn it off!" Thirza screamed, as her line of vision travelled upwards again. Above the sack hoist, the windshaft and wallower now meshed with new cogs, gears and pistons, that looked to Thirza like a huge distorted version of her mother's little clockwork bird. Her gaze fell on something strung up on the sprattle beam, just feet from her face, as she climbed higher trying desperately to find something to jam the wheel or throw the ball bomb, with its toxic phlogiston payload, clear of the mill.

With a shock, she comprehended what had been dragged up on the hoist and strung up from the crossbeam. Darnell's dead eyes met hers, staring through the dust without blinking, his arms tied back to the beam, his feet still bound with the rope used to lift the farmers' corn sacks up to the top of the mill to begin the grinding.

Thirza couldn't tear her eyes away from his. She couldn't let him ruin Kitson's Windmill, the only thing her grandparents possessed.

"Jem! It's alright! Nobody can hurt us now!"

As the cap lifted clear of the brackets that were holding it down, it rose awkwardly under the unevenly distributed weight of its uninvited passengers. Thirza made one last effort to push the glass incendiary out of its mount. The upper attachments suddenly gave way and it rolled away from her hand with an ominous momentary silence, towards the green grass of the meadow behind the mill tower, beginning to fall in slow motion, diagonally towards the ground.

Thirza didn't remember the explosion, but she felt the top rung of the ladder, on which she was depending, give way completely as she began to climb down.

#

The rushes by the water
We gather every day.
All things bright and beautiful...

In the little church at the other end of the village, Lucas looked at Emma fondly as she dropped her hymn book. He didn't, at first, associate this with the faint impression he had of a low booming sound echoing across the marshes.

"What in the name of crikey was that?" hissed Thomas to Kezzie, his other senses more keen after the loss of sight. Kezzie shushed him fiercely, but with a sinking feeling in her heart. Surely Doomsday would have some trumpets as well, and Kezzie hadn't heard any?

The vicar realised it was in vain to continue with his homily as the last notes of the hymn faded away. Half his congregation had decamped to the porch to see what was the source of the unearthly explosive blast they'd heard, while the other half were gabbling wrecks in the pews, certain this must be the Last Trump, the Armageddon, the final great harvest come to rapture them into the skies.

"What is it?" Thomas tried to keep hold of Kezzie's sleeve as they stumbled out into the sunlight. He heard her gasp, the incredulous screams and shouts of the other parishioners around them. Then he felt Kezzie's sleeve pull away from him as she went running along the Nab towards the windmill. Someone was yelling.

"Mester Kitson, Mester Kitson! It's your windmill! It's all smoke and fire at the top, sails and everything!"

#

Steering the asylum wagon round the curved track from the canal, the driver had been hoping at least one of his assistants would have the wit to buckle the straitjacket securely, were it necessary to employ it.

He saw the windmill outbuildings on their left, and was slowing the horses to a walk in order to prepare for the removal. He glanced around, wondering where their charge might be being held. They'd been quite specific about timing, but Doctor Stenson Seagrave had been unavailable for further clarification, when the superintendent contacted him again for details of the afflicted man's condition. The driver leaned back as he drew level with the pump in the mill yard and caught sight of what looked like a young man, up on the platform of the fantail. The driver was about to shout to the figure for directions, when the whole top of the windmill was momentarily engulfed in shooting flames of an extraordinary and fearful nature, accompanied by a rumble that sent visible ripples through the quagmire of peat stretching to their right. One of the assistants was thrown to the floor but was soon back on his feet, pointing towards the top of the mill and yelling.

"There's somebody up there! Mind them sails don't scythe you! The whole top's going! It's going to fly off like a blooming scopadiddle!"

#

Bram had reached the outskirts of Rawcliffe. He hadn't stopped to rest since his escape from the watchmen in Doncaster and was making for the coast before he missed his chance to complete his business there.

"She'll be giving her hand to Lucas now, boy, and we must try to wish her well. Sir William will be half way to London, so Salkeld's evil plot will come to nothing."

Piper panted up at his master with total adoration. He felt the earth move under his paws and yelped loudly, feeling the air quiver in a way he didn't recognise.

Stepping off his stilts onto the soft peat deposits, Bram breathed in the saltier air coming from the North Sea. He was puzzled by the way the peat continued to ripple, imperceptible to anyone who wasn't used to the flow of the fen, even though he was standing still. He stroked Piper and was astounded to feel, more than see, he was trembling and whining softly with every breath.

"Come on, lad. There's people to see in the port, then ditches to clear and then to check all ravage is well reversed on the Nab. What ails you?"

But Piper was a dog and human words were beyond his power to master.

#

When Kezzie arrived at the mill, nobody could keep her away from the worst of the sights that met the eyes of all who approached the stricken building. Kezzie ran as if guided by unseen lights, round to the back of the mill where the fantail was still making its slow circles, dragging Darnell's 'Phlogistox Flyer' with it, facing it into the wind, then to the north, then towards the fen, then back towards the crowd gathered in disbelief. Kezzie reappeared from the back of the mill, following the fantail's every move with her rheumy eyes, as if she refused to let the sight out of her memory. There, from the high platform, tilted at a grotesque angle from the ground, that stayed perpendicular to the uprights like a geometrical rebuke, dangled the body of her beloved only son.

Nobody could pull Kezzie away or prevent her seeing the horror. She stood wringing her hands, moaning inconsolably.

"Surely never but maybe! Whatever will become of us now? Jem! My boy! Come to your dear old foolish mother!"

"Cut him down, for pity's sake!" Lucas said quietly to one of his tenants. "Where is Mr Salkeld?"

The question went unanswered. Lucas gave orders to the men to extinguish the few cold flames that still licked like will-o'-the-wisps along the frames of the sails, which were blackened with smoke and frayed into jagged holes by their unaccustomed adventure of learning to be wings.

When two field labourers, who'd followed Francis into the mill, came out carrying Thirza, it was Goody Chester who went inside with them as they brought her into Mill Cottage.

"That dress will be quite spoiled," Emma remarked to nobody in particular. She had an idea this comment was not quite what was required, but was truly shocked to see her poor niece as pale as death. Lucas looked at Emma, as if he'd just seen her for the first time, which pleased her.

When they brought out what was left of Darnell, wrapped in sheets of canvas to keep him whole, Emma was surprised to hear herself weeping, though she felt relieved he'd been wearing his best cravat that had retained its silk lustre through all the nonsense of the day.

30. SAILING HOME

For three weeks until Hallowtide, Thirza drifted in and out of nightmare oblivion. She became aware of images that came and went, figures that seemed to spend hours by her bed. Each shadow had its own special breathing, its own style of cough, its special presence. The days shortened and the nights bled together like indistinct stains on sailcloth. She remembered many impressions, but it was so hard to judge what was real and what imagination.

She heard the goatsucker's cry above the sails of the mill, Bram clapping his hands to bring them down to brush her forehead with their wings in the twilight. She saw Jem teaching her brothers to cartwheel, telling them to be careful to stop before they came to the canal at the end of the lane. She saw a little girl running across a meadow where curlew and lapwing talked in strange haunting voices that made the child laugh. She heard a voice soft like Bram's gathering cootlings into his arms and a little dog chased its tail. She smelled Dinah, her sweet scent of the sea as she held Thirza's hand and told her the names of the ships sailing through the clouds above them. She heard her father asking Goody if she thought the little baby would be at peace now.

"Father?" Thirza started to sit up, struggling to make sense of what she could see and hear, for the first time since the day of Harvest Festival. Goody was sitting by her bed, sewing running stitches around a sampler in which the central panel was a boat and a monochrome outline of a rainbow arched over its sails.

"Your father was here, but he's had to go and see to some customer."

"Coal, I suppose." Thirza murmured.

"Assume nothing, Thirza Holberry. How are you now after your long sleep?"

"I feel strange. But better, I think."

Through Goody's ever-cryptic utterances, her grandma's fussing, her granddad's jokes and snippets here and there, Thirza gradually pieced together what had happened. Or what people thought had happened. She realised, too, there were some things she had seen that day, things she knew, that they did not, things perhaps better unknown.

When she was well enough to stand, Thirza looked at herself in the long mirror that Emma had been given on her wedding day by some distant cousin in Goole, but which she'd left here in her old bedroom at Mill Cottage, as it had a "grandiose degree of hand-carving," according to Emma, "more à la mode in the days of Marie Antoinette, poor soul."

Thirza noticed she looked thinner in the face. She traced her finger over her flat stomach under her shift, as she prepared to put on her outdoor costume for the first time since the tragedy. She thought about Goody's words to her when nobody else was close.

"The little scrap of a treasure I put under the wall inside the churchyard gate where the path goes along to the canal. No matter the bairn didn't make it into this world. We all need a place, and a place to remember."

They'd said no more about it. But now Thirza knew what she needed to do. She persuaded Kezzie she was well enough to walk down to the end of the village, pacing her efforts so as not to overtire herself after the ordeal. In truth, she thought her grandma looked more affected by the events of harvest than she was.

Lucas was being such a support to her family. He'd been as astounded as the next person to discover the full extent of Darnell's deception. He'd taken it on himself to rebuild the windmill, to make all the promised improvements. He'd use designs by the tried and tested local millwrights as well as those with fresh ideas and expertise for expanding the mill site. He had plans to employ more villagers, to combine his interests in the mill with developing the peat lands he owned.

Lucas hadn't pressed Thirza for her answer.

"I know so much has happened. We're all wiser, now. I know you'll tell me when you are quite well," he said.

Thirza saw how Emma, now in her widow's weeds, seemed to hang on Lucas's every word. Her aunt would squeal with delight when Lucas talked to Thomas and Kezzie about his plans for the future, until she checked herself, realising that squeals and flutters might cause a "particular undertone" as she put it, with the gossiping neighbours, who had quite enough gossip already to last them till the turn of the twentieth century.

So it was, reluctant to make him wait any longer, Thirza gave Lucas her answer at last. He seemed chastened that the answer was "no" for a whole day. Then he and Emma came into the parlour one night, to break the news to the old miller and his wife, to Thirza and the servants, that he and Emma were to throw in their lot together, as Lord and Lady Charlesworth. Emma flashed the very ring on her finger that he'd shown to Thirza what seemed an eternity ago in a different world.

Kezzie and Thomas could stay at Mill Cottage as long as they lived and their doting surviving daughter and rich, if occasionally sozzled, son-in-law would make sure they never wanted for anything ever again.

Thirza was glad for them. After such dark days and tragic consequences of trusting somebody who could spin a web of lies out of the strands of other people's dreams, talents, joys and secrets, they deserved such hope of a settled future.

But somewhere in her soul, Thirza knew that was not for her, even when Lucas assured her that, in spite of her declining his offer of wedlock, she would always be welcome to make her home with them here on Turbary Nab.

So that morning in November, Thirza walked to the churchyard and was laying a posy of late flowers on the grave of Jem, in the section designated as unconsecrated ground and on the little unmarked mound under the wall close by. She felt glad these precious ones lay out of sight of Darnell's ancestral plot, in its pride of place by the church porch with carved angels pulling faces, as if they'd been turned to stone in the midst of a nightmare.

As she was kneeling by the wall, she felt a snuffling on the back of her hand as she brushed away the earth from the tended square of turf.

"Is a stranger still welcome here?"

Thirza turned around. Bram was smiling at her, his smile that always took her as she was. They hugged, and he could feel the sorrow still in her. He saw the graves over her shoulder and knew how fond she'd been of Jem, as they all had.

"At peace now, that brave man. Where nobody can taunt or trick or trouble him."

"Yes, Jem lies here and over here," Thirza swallowed what felt like a burning stone, "my child that never was meant to be."

"Your child?"

"Not yours, Bram. I'm sorry. Not yours." Thirza would have given anything on earth or in heaven not to have to tell him that. Bram heard the words and all the tears and wrongs behind them.

"I wish the decoy rainbow could put me together again, Bram. But I'm a big girl, now. A woman, I hope. I know this can't be fixed."

They stood together in silence for some time. Then it was Bram who spoke.

"I must go, Thirza. There are things I still have to do."

Thirza didn't answer at first, she couldn't. By the time

she found her voice, he had melted away into the mists that drifted from the moors as winter came on. She walked back to the windmill alone.

They told her Bram had called in while she was unconscious, more than once. He'd come in quietly, sat with her without speaking and left again without a word. Now he would never come here again. She felt utterly broken, but she must be brave. For everybody's sake, not least her own, she had to stay strong.

As they all sat at breakfast one day, Thomas was getting Thirza to read him the headlines from the newspaper, just as her father used to do.

"You know, our lass," he said, "since I stopped using that eyewash our Darnell used to make up special for me, I can make out those letters in the large print as clear as anything. Bright and clear as a roast chestnut on the brazier that comely lass with freckles sells down at Thorne Quay."

"That wouldn't be very bright, Tom," Kezzie sounded more up to his jokes than she'd been for a long while, "and how do you know she's got freckles?"

"Well, I didn't hear them! I tell you, since I've no eye bath swilkering my eye shut with all that white powdery stuff our Darnell used to stick in there, I can see properly again with this eye!"

Kezzie kissed Thomas on the head and they began to talk about the future for the first time Thirza could remember, since she came out of her trance of sickness.

"I should be thankful, I suppose, to be alive at all," she told herself. She congratulated her granddad on his miraculous restoration of sight and handed him the newspaper so he could practise his regained skill to his heart's content.

In her room, she read again her most recent letter from her father, that his new lady friend in Mexborough had helped him to write, full of news about Sam and Judd. Sam was loving his new life on the railway and Judd was going off with the fishing fleet into the North Sea, where the money was better than on the keels, "tho I reckon it's danger munny," Jack concluded. This made Thirza laugh.

The end of the letter had the opposite effect, so she slipped it back in its envelope without reading the rest. It was the part where Jack told her it was really final now. The keel was sold to some man to whom Jack had been teaching the basics of sailing.

Thirza shouted to her grandparents that she was just going for a little walk.

"Again?" deadpanned Thomas, "you'll wear your feet out, lass, doing that trick!"

Thirza walked out into the moody late autumn sunshine, that didn't seem able to decide if it was here to stay, or rather would turn to rain and sleet. She pulled her winter cape around her and felt for her mother's box and as she walked along, taking out the clockwork goatsucker that had somehow reappeared by her bedside while she was so ill. So Bram hadn't really wanted to keep it to remember her by after all.

#

Later, as Thirza walked along by the canal, she wondered how her father, so proud a keelman, such a fine master mariner, could have sold the keel to some hopeless, clueless landlubber who needed basic lessons before he could even sail her along a canal.

"Bet they'll be scraping her along the lock walls and using her as a houseboat. Stupid people! Bet they'll let their children throw stones at real keel people from the tops of bridges and repaint her with some stupid, stupid name that isn't hers."

Thirza was embarrassed she'd said the last bit out loud. She hadn't noticed there was a keel coming round the bend, the low sunshine off the fens shining like buttery gold through her sails, the mast wreathed in rainbows. The top gallant was unmistakeable, even as she rubbed her eyes. She was a clinker-built brig all done up with the pride of a heart that loved her. Through her tears she made out the name

'Thistle' on the bows and the tall figure at the tiller had a little Dutch spaniel with him on the deck at his feet.

"I met a lady along this stretch of the cut once. You look a lot like her. I've room on board for a permanent mate, as it happens!"

Thirza ran and vaulted from the bank onto the ship and flung her arms around Bram's neck.

"Your father wasn't certain, at first, that this landlubber could grasp the difference between the coamings and the coggy," he said, "but I'm getting there. In those months when the living's thin at the decoy, dykes and pinfold, 'Thistle' will hold you tight, as I will."

Thirza drew Dinah's box out of her pocket. Bram took the ring that never quite seemed to fit inside the puzzle part and slipped it onto Thirza's finger. She held the toy goatsucker in her left hand and flung it up towards the sky. It whirred for a moment, then began to clap and wheel above the sail, weaving a course through the shimmers of rainbow light that arched over them, full of healing and hope.

"There's more, wait," Thirza saw where Bram had made special slots along the sides of the mast for his stilts. He was cradling between his fingers a scintilla of that mystical light that flowed undimmed from his compassion across the face of the peatlands.

"Now your home, is my home, and my home is yours. No more outsiders!"

"Outsiders together!" Thirza watched as Bram spread his hands and let the lambent light spread softly around the tiller and the rudder. She felt the keel lifting with a motion like the flow of a waterfall through a thimble, as the whole ship began to set sail for the radiant clouds.

"Wait!" Thirza snuggled back into his arms as they stood as one body at the tiller, "Can we stay afloat, here on the water, not up in the air, just for now?"

Piper barked up at them, panting with joy as if the waterways were singing in his blood and breeding, too.

"Whatever's your heart's delight, my lady! Yackoop, boy!"

"Rise your tack, Mr Beharrell!"

So they followed the river of golden shimmering light that beckoned them onwards, across the perfect unbroken contours of the Levels, to the sunburst horizon beyond.

THE END

About the author

Joyce was born in 1961 in Yorkshire's Dearne Valley.
She grew up as a railway child, a dreamer, fascinated by the natural world. Once described as "having a pen where her mouth should be," she won a writing competition for which the prize was a tin of chocolate. This established writing in her mind as a delicious thing. Her enchantment with words and storytelling grew into a lifetime's passion. She can often be found wandering wide-eyed through greenery and graveyards digging up her ancestors' hidden histories, source of much inspiration in her fiction, including her historical fantasy novel "Goatsucker Harvest."

Joyce can be contacted on her blog:
jobiskaspinwheel.blogspot.co.uk
On Facebook:
www.facebook.com/joycebarrassauthor
Or on Twitter: @cardifolderol

Printed in Great Britain
by Amazon.co.uk, Ltd.,
Marston Gate.